THE GIRL . . . AND HER MEN . . .

DARLA DAWSON. The long-maned blonde actress turned legend. Betrayed wife was the most painful role she'd ever had to play . . .

MIKE BRADY. Darla's TV-star husband. He liked money, young starlets, success—and something heady to make him forget it all . . .

DANTE CORELLI. A shark in the underworld, he gave Darla the kind of loving she always needed . . .

TED WALTERS. The jaunty young sports star with a boyish grin and a devilish temper. He played tennis for high stakes—and Darla for pleasure . . .

A JOVE/HBJ BOOK

This is entirely a work of fiction, and all characters and events in this work are imaginary. No identification with actual persons or events is intended or should be inferred.

Copyright © 1978 by Leslie Deane

All rights reserved. No part of this publication may be reproduced or transmitted in any form or by any means, electronic or mechanical, including photocopy, recording, or any information storage and retrieval system, without permission in writing from the publisher.

Requests for permission to make copies of any part of the work should be mailed to: Permissions, Jove Publications, Inc., 757 Third Avenue, New York, NY 10017

Printed in the United States of America

Library of Congress Catalog Card Number: 78-019526

First Jove/HBJ edition published November 1978

Jove/HBJ books are published by Jove Publications, Inc. (Harcourt Brace Jovanovich) 757 Third Avenue, New York, NY 10017

Chapter 1

Darla Dawson kicked off the covers and stretched. She was slow coming out of sleep, and had to force herself to think what day it was. Wednesday. What did she have to do on Wednesday? Nothing? Something? Yes. There'd been a call from her agent yesterday about some casting thing on videotape for a commercial. She turned her head toward the windows that ran the length of the bedroom wall. The drapes were open, and California sunshine poured into the room. From beyond the closed door of Mike's bath at the far end of the bedroom she could hear the shower running and muffled rock music coming from the radio.

Darla stretched again and got out of bed. The wall opposite the windows was paneled with mirrors. She stood before them and studied her naked body objectively, as she did every morning. The proportions were good; she looked even taller than her actual five-eight. Belly flat, just a hint of hipbones showing. Breasts round and firm, no sign of sagging. But they could be just a little bigger, she thought. Legs slim, well-formed. She rose on her toes and turned sideways, flexing the muscles of her buttocks. Good. No sag there, either.

She stepped closer to the mirrors and studied her face. Skin clear, not a blemish anywhere. Eyes okay, their luminous violet-blue almost startling, even to her. But they were maybe just a shade dark underneath, and when the light came from a certain angle she could see a few lines under them also. Nothing a little makeup couldn't handle. She grimaced broadly and looked at her teeth. They really were incredible. Large, even, perfect, and snowy white.

She shook her head and the great mane of blonde hair swung to and fro. It looked even wilder and more tousled before she brushed it out each morning. Betty Frolich, her agent, wanted her to cut it. "Really, Darla," Betty had said just the other day. "Nobody wears hair like that now. It should be a lot shorter—at least up off your shoulders."

Well, maybe, Darla thought. But then again, having a mop of unusual hair is one thing I can do that makes me who I am, and different, and not just another Hollywood blonde. God knows there are enough of those in this town. In this racket you need a trademark, a gimmick. Still, I'm not exactly loaded with work. She went into her own bath and brushed her teeth.

When she came back into the bedroom, the door to Mike's bath was still closed. She stood before the mirrors again and began to do her regular routine of calisthenics. First she touched her toes, left hand to right toes, right hand to left toes, fifty times each. Then she lay on her back on the carpet and poked her lower torso up into the air and bicycled her legs as fast as she could, counting each revolution of her left foot.

When her count was in the seventies, Mike walked into the bedroom, the radio in his bath continuing to blare rock music. He paid no attention to her as he pulled open a dresser drawer and took out a shirt. Darla stopped bicycling and flopped her legs onto the carpet, watching him.

Mike was tall and heavily muscled. His naked body was that of the one-time jock who kept himself in excellent shape. His rugged face was youthful, and the broken nose enchanced its virile look. Without it his features would have been too fine. His thick hair was dark and curly.

Darla studied his back and shoulders, her eyes traveling down and resting on his thighs. Desire flooded into her. "Mike?"

"M-m-m?"

"What's the rush? You're not shooting, are you?"

He began buttoning the shirt. "Got a meeting with Hazelman. New ideas on the show."

Darla got to her feet and stepped close behind him. She leaned her head against his back and encircled his body with her arms. "Maybe you could be a little bit late," she said softly. She reached down and squeezed his penis.

Mike brushed her hand away almost roughly. "Hey, knock it off. I told you, I've got a meeting." He opened another drawer and took out a pair of shorts. They were French, little more than a pouch with a string. He stepped into them.

Darla choked back the quick rush of resentment. She crossed to her bathroom and stepped into the shower. The stream of hot water pounded on her back and shoulders and relaxed her a little. But the sense of bitterness mixed with her unfulfilled desire would not leave her.

Damn it, she thought. We haven't made love for days. When was it, Sunday? No, Saturday. And then he was so casual about it. Sort of like just going through the motions. Doing me a favor. Not like the old days at all, when he was so tender and affectionate. When he couldn't get enough of me.

And all those rumors I've been hearing. Nothing specific, just a lot of crap I could take either way. Well, sure, he's got girls. Let's face it. Am I that much of a fool? Everyplace he goes, they're all over him. Mike Brady, the big TV star. Shit.

She dried herself with a thick towel and pulled on a terrycloth robe. She promised herself she'd stay cool, not get into anything.

In the kitchen Mike sat at the breakfast table, drinking coffee and leafing through *Variety*. Maggie, the maid, flopped back and forth in a pair of pink mules, a flowered housecoat ballooning over her fat body, her black face shining.

Maggie smiled. "Mornin', Darla."

"Hi, Maggie." Darla sat down opposite Mike, who went on reading.

"What do you want to eat?" Maggie asked. "The usual sparrow food?"

"Right," Darla replied. "Maybe less one or two seeds. I gained a quarter of an ounce last week."

Maggie clucked disapproval as she went about preparing Darla's breakfast. "You think it's funny. Could be you'll get sick one of these days, starving yourself like this. Ain't good for you. And no matter what you think, it ain't no good for the way you look, either. No woman's going to look good without no meat on her."

"Maybe you're right," Darla said. "Maybe Mike would like me better if I was a little fuller. Would you, Mike?"

In answer, Mike merely grunted and turned the page.

Darla felt her resentment begin to rise again, but she was determined not to become angry, and anyway, she knew how to draw him out. "What's Hazelman have in mind?" she asked pleasantly.

Mike put down the copy of *Variety*. "I'm not sure, exactly." He lit a cigarette. "Selig has some ideas he's working on, and Dick wants to get my reactions. I feel there hasn't been enough fresh thinking lately. I've told them both they'd better come up with some new angles."

Darla nodded. Dick Hazelman was the producer of the detective series that starred Mike, and Harry Selig was the head writer. Darla knew that neither of them had much respect for Mike's opinion on creative matters, but with the show a hit they weren't about to make waves. If Mike had to feel that he was a creative force as well as the star, well, okay, fine. The last Nielsen showed a thirty-six share, and with ratings like that they could put up with his inflated impressions of his talent.

Maggie placed a small glass of freshly squeezed orange juice, a plate bearing one slice of dry whole wheat toast, and a cup of black coffee before Darla.

"What's the toast for?" Darla asked.

"'Cause you need it, that's what it's for." There was genuine concern in the black woman's voice.

Darla sighed. "Okay, so I'll get fat."

Maggie humphed and poured more coffee into Mike's cup, a small, triumphant smile playing at one corner of her mouth.

Darla turned her attention back to Mike. "How about the new writer, what's his name—Aaron, Aaronson?"

"Yeah, Aaronson," Mike replied. "He's doing okay, but this is conceptual. Only Hazelman and Selig work with me on the really big ideas, the broad premises."

Darla sipped some of the orange juice. "Are they shooting anything today?"

"Yes, but it's just pick-up stuff. Scenes that don't involve me." He snuffed out his cigarette and stood up. "See you later."

Darla looked up at him. "Mike?" Christ, she loathed herself for begging, but she couldn't help it.

"Huh? Oh, yeah." He bent and brushed his mouth lightly against her lips.

A moment later she heard the electric motor raise the garage door, and then Mike's Mercedes rolled down the driveway and the door closed again. Darla looked at the cup of coffee and pushed it away. Goddamn it, she thought. He never once asked if I was doing anything, or if anything was happening with me. And what if he had? What *is* doing? Nothing. A cattle call for some lousy commercial.

She got up from the table and walked back into the bedroom. She shut the door, dropped her robe to the floor, and lay down on the bed. I know what I need, she thought. I need a man. One who wants me the way Mike used to. I need a couple of days of real good sex to get me straightened out.

Without realizing what she was doing, she let her hand drift down her body to her mound, and her fingers began to brush gently against her pubic hair. An image of Mike came into her mind, his big, muscular body climbing on top of her, his mouth pressed against hers, his hands underneath her, holding her open as he took her with a raw, mindless vitality.

Oh, God, she said to herself. Stop it, stop it. You'll drive yourself crazy. She got up and went into her bath and brushed out her hair. She came out and dressed quickly in jeans and a blue cashmere sweater. As always, she wore no bra. She pulled her book out of her bag, checked the address of the casting service, yelled goodbye to Maggie, and left the house.

Chapter 2

Linda Ferter's casting service was on Gower Street in Hollywood. Darla drove her Mercedes—a five-year-old Model 250—east on Sunset, turned south into Gower, and then crept along until she found a parking space. The casting service occupied several rooms in a small stucco office building typical of the neighborhood. When Darla walked in, the reception room was already jammed with girls. She gave her name to the receptionist and squeezed into a seat on one of the benches that lined the walls.

There was a marked similarity among most of the girls in the room. They were tall, slim, young, and blonde. They wore jeans and carried zippered portfolios containing photographs of themselves. Darla knew many of them from the endless casting sessions that went on at the studios, the advertising agencies, and the casting companies like this one. She smiled and waved hello. There was a babble of animated chatter in the room.

"Hi, Darla." It was the girl sitting next to her.

"Oh, hi. Penny?"

"Right. Penny Lang," the girl said. She had a fresh, open face. The Iowa look, as Darla had once heard it described. "How goes?"

Darla shrugged. She never went in for the everything-is-just-wonderful crap that was the standard line of reply in the business. "The same. Running around like a nut on calls like these. How about you?"

"Pretty good lately," Penny said. "I did a Coke last week and I'm up for a McDonald's. The McDonald's would be great because I'd have lines."

Darla nodded. "Are you studying with anybody?"

"Oh, sure. I'm at Berensky's twice a week." Berensky's was an acting school run by a retired director who had worked in pictures for a long time and in the New York theater before that.

"How're you doing there?" Darla asked.

"Okay," Penny replied. "I never knew there was so much to learn. You know, not just how to handle dialogue, but moves and stuff. I did a 'Police Woman' a few weeks ago, and I think what I'd been getting at Berensky's helped me a lot."

"Uh-huh. I've heard quite a bit about him."

"He's really good, you know?" Penny said. "He's very patient, and he teaches you a lot of little tricks like voice projection and how to stay relaxed, things like that."

"How was the 'Police Woman'?" Darla asked.

"Oh, it was all right. I mean, the part was nothing much. I was a waitress in this cocktail lounge and a guy who hung around there got shot in a robbery someplace, and so Angie asked me some questions. I had two scenes."

"How'd you like her?"

"Angie? She's terrific. A real fine lady. Easy to work with and nice to everybody. You could see the crew was crazy about her. How about you, Darla? Are you still doing those Ranier eye makeup commercials?"

Darla shook her head. "No. That is, they're still on, but I haven't shot a new one for a year. I don't know what's going to happen with them."

"Mm-hm." Penny frowned understanding. "Residuals must be great, though, huh?"

"Sure." Darla smiled. "I hope they run forever."

"Yeah. You know, those are the best things for exposure, too. I mean, anything like cosmetics or hair products does a lot for you. Those big fat closeups."

Darla laughed. "You're right, except the Raniers are all *too* close. What they mostly show is eyes. They could be my eyes or anybody else's."

"Oh, yeah." Penny said. "I guess that's true. I never thought of that."

A door opened and a girl wearing thick horn-rimmed glasses poked her head into the room. "Betty Burnett," she called out. One of the models waved, hastily snuffed out the cigarette she'd been smoking, and followed the girl.

"God, they're going slow," Penny said. "At this rate we'll be here all day."

"What is this, do you know?" Darla asked.

"Yeah, it's a face soap. I don't know which one."

Darla glanced over at the receptionist's desk as another model arrived. She recognized the girl at once. Unlike the others in the room, this one was a redhead. She was strikingly beautiful, her face classic in the delicate structure of its proportions. Her name was Cathy Drake. Darla felt a twinge as she looked at her. This was one of the girls she'd heard whispers about. Cathy had had parts in a number of episodes of "The Savage City," the series in which Mike Brady starred. Darla looked away, and as she did she saw that Penny was staring at the girl. Penny's gaze turned back to fix on Darla, and Darla knew from her expression that Penny had heard the stories too.

Darla felt the twinge turn to nausea. So everybody knew. Mike Brady, famous stud. And his dumb little model wife who never quite made it, but just tagged along and looked pretty and did as she was told while Mike screwed his brains out all over town. And what did people think? That she was an idiot, to be pitied and held in contempt. Penny's reaction had spelled that out clearly enough. Oh, Jesus.

Darla forced herself to be calm and to keep her voice steady. "I hear they've started work on the new 'McShane' series at International."

"Oh? Is that the one with Dick Taggert?"

"Yes. It's supposed to be very good. They say NBC flipped over the pilot."

They chatted for a few more minutes and then Penny was called inside. After that, Darla buried her head in a magazine until her turn came and she followed the girl with the glasses into a room where Linda Ferter was sitting at a conference table with a young man Darla didn't know.

"Hi, Darla. Nice to see you again," Linda greeted her. "This is Art Blake from Maybell and Davis, the agency for Pearl Soap."

Darla turned on her most radiant smile and extended her hand to the young man, who took it languidly. He sat slouched in his chair, affecting a bored-with-it-all manner. He was casually dressed and wore his hair styled long over his ears. A thick mustache decorated his upper lip. The combination was as much a standard uniform among young men as the jeans were among the models.

"Sit down, Darla," Linda said. "We need a composite, if you have one."

Linda was thin-faced and intense and made no attempt to hide her plainness. Her dark hair was streaked with gray and pulled back into a bun. Her fingers drummed nervously on a stack of photographs and notes that lay on the table before her.

Darla unzipped her portfolio and produced a four-page brochure on which a variety of pictures were printed in black and white. The pictures showed Darla in several poses—wearing a raincoat, astride a horse, running in surf, embracing a man, and others. Her statistics, height, weight, bra, shoe, and glove size were listed on the back.

Linda glanced at the composite and handed it to the young man. "Got anything running in the soap area, Darla?" Linda was checking to learn whether there could be a conflict between a commercial in which Darla might be currently appearing and the Pearl Soap commercial she was now being interviewed for. A lot of models tried to cover up such information in order not to be put out of the running for a new commercial.

"No," Darla replied. "Unless you consider Ranier a problem."

Linda Fertig smiled. "That's what we like, an honest woman. I'm sure that's no conflict, is it, Art?"

"Eye makeup? No. No conflict," Blake answered. He looked at Darla's hair, and her eyes, and her mouth, and then his eyes slid down her sweater and fastened onto her breasts.

Darla felt like a piece of meat on display. She was here because she wanted and needed this work, not so much for the money as for the recognition, the step forward that any small victory in competition—if only for a commercial—would mean to her. That made her vulnerable to men like Blake, and it was obvious that he knew it. She hated being here, trying to project warmth and personality and sex appeal or whatever else this oaf might think attractive, but that was exactly what she had to do, and do convincingly, if she hoped to get the job.

"This commercial will involve lines on camera, Darla," Linda said. "I know you've done a number of those, haven't you?"

Darla nodded. "Yes. I've done several."

"Okay. We're going to have you read a script on tape. Just a rough."

They went into a small studio off the conference room. It contained a Sony videotape recording system and an operator, a few lights, and some straight-backed chairs. A cue card on which a script had been printed in crayon was taped to a stanchion just to the left of the camera. The camera operator told Darla to sit in the chair in front of the camera. He instructed her to state her name when he rolled the tape and then to read the script aloud.

Darla glanced quickly through the words on the cue card, and then the operator threw on the lights and started his camera. Darla spoke clearly, giving the copy as much brightness and animation as she could. She stumbled once, but kept going to the end. Blake and Linda sat on chairs behind the camera and watched.

"Should I do it again?" Darla asked when she had finished. "I got a little tangled up at one point."

"Not necessary," Blake said. "You did fine."

"It's just a rough, Darla," Linda added. "Just to get an idea. Oaky? We'll let you know."

Blake pulled Darla aside on her way out. "You know, I think you'd do all right with this."

Darla smiled up at him. "Great. I hope I get it."

"Actually," he said, "it's going to be a whole series of commercials built around one girl. A campaign."

"Really? A whole campaign?"

"That's right." His eyes traveled down her sweater again and then back up to meet hers. "Why don't we get together later on, to talk about it?"

Darla held her smile carefully in place. "I'm afraid I can't do that," she said pleasantly. "I really have a very busy schedule today."

Blake's voice was low and suggestive. "Doesn't have to be today," he said. "Could be tomorrow, or the next day."

Darla knew that Blake couldn't make a decision on which girl would get the Pearl Soap work, that his was only one word among many. Other people at the agency, and at the client company, would have a lot to say about the final choice. But he could help, and he could also hurt. Nevertheless, she was damned if she would get involved with this creep for a commercial, or even a whole series of commercials, which she doubted was actually in the offing. "Sorry," she said. "I have to go."

Outside, Darla got into her car and looked at her watch. Eleven-thirty. And she didn't have another thing to do for the rest of the day.

Chapter 3

"The Savage City" was produced at International Studios in Burbank. Mike Brady nodded to the guard at the gate house and slowly tooled his baby blue Mercedes 450 SL down the studio street to the parking space with his name on it. No matter how many times he had arrived here over the past two years, it was always a thrill to him. He was a big man, a star, deferred to by everyone from the studio management down to the lowliest grip, and he loved it. He always affected a casualness, an air of easy cool, but he was extremely aware of who he was, and that everyone here was aware of that as well. Not that any outward fuss was made over him; it was a tradition in Hollywood that studio people maintained a democratic first-name relationship with each other, no matter how exalted the status of a star or one of the executives might be. But Mike inwardly reveled in the sense of power he felt.

Harry Selig was already sitting in Dick Hazelman's office when Mike walked in. Harry was short and swarthy, and although he was only in his early thirties, most of his hair was gone. The few remaining wisps were combed over the center of his skull. Hazelman was about ten years older, but in much better shape. His sandy hair was streaked from the sun and his face was tanned. He looked like the tennis player he was. Both

17

men wore Levi's and sport shirts. They greeted Mike warmly.

"Have a seat, Mike," Hazelman invited. "We've got some really great stuff for you."

Mike took a chair and put his feet up on Hazelman's desk. The producer's secretary brought him a cup of coffee and he sipped at it while the two men began describing some of the new show ideas they had developed.

Selig did most of the talking. He described each concept at length, reading from a sheaf of notes and stabbing the air with a forefinger for emphasis.

Mike listened intently for a time and then raised his hand. "Listen," he said. "Most of this is just new situations, really. It's not anything different as far as my character is concerned, right?"

Selig and Hazelman exchanged glances. The premise of "The Savage City" was that Mike was a hard-nosed private detective. Basically, it was a cop show, but each script included action sequences and fight scenes that allowed Mike Brady to showcase his physical prowess and his fighting ability, the things that had brought him his first notoriety as an Olympic gold medalist in boxing. The show had a brutal realism, was produced on a fairly adult level, and its popularity depended on Mike's always coming out on top, no matter what the circumstances, no matter who the opposition. Fantasy played a large part in the show's success.

"I wouldn't say that at all," Selig said. "You see, these situations reveal new sides of you. In every instance, you're in totally new circumstances, handling different kinds of problems. So in that way you're giving the audience very different insights into your character."

"Harry's right," Hazelman added. "And these are all good action concepts. They move. Remember what Scott Fitzgerald said. Action *is* character." He looked pleased with himself.

Mike sat back in his chair. "Bullshit," he growled. "You tell me these ideas will show new sides of my character. Okay, then, how? And what new sides? Sure,

I want new angles. But they've got to be based on ideas that'll make the audience respond to me in a positive way."

"Hey, Mike, be reasonable," Hazelman said. "I think the way Harry and his guys have approached the problem has really hit it right on the button. You'd be doing things nobody has ever seen you do, and dramatically they're ideas that have real clout."

Selig nodded. "Take this story of your helping the kid who has a brain tumor. We've never done anything like this. It'll show that for all your tremendous strength and toughness, you're actually a very tender guy."

Mike grunted. "It's maudlin. Sounds like a fucking soap opera."

"I don't think so at all," Hazelman said. "It simply shows that fundamentally you have a hell of a lot of compassion that only a guy who is really strong and sure of himself could have."

"Umm. Maybe," Mike said.

"It'll work, believe me, Mike," Hazelman said. "It's a hell of a concept. It's the kind of thing that'll turn women on, too, because it's more than just muscle; it's sensitive, it's warm."

Mike nodded slowly. "Yeah. I can see that. Maybe you're right. Maybe that would be a new direction."

Hazelman slapped his desk with an open palm. "You're damn right it would. And so would every one of these stories. Each one says something new about you, and says it in a way the audience has to respond to deeply."

Harry wiped his face with his sleeve. "You know, Mike, I have a theory," he said. "It's that the people who're watching that show every Sunday night are in love with you. Not just the women, but the men, too. Not in a fag way, but because you're like the embodiment of the secret dream a man has about himself. He identifies because you're the ultimate of what he'd like to be."

Mike cocked his head thoughtfully. "You think so? Interesting idea."

"I think it is, too," Hazelman said. "And not so wild at all, when you stop to consider it."

"No, it's not," Mike said. "In fact, it's what the whole star thing is about and always has been. Every guy wanted to be Clark Gable and hump Claudette Colbert in the bus."

"Exactly," Selig said. "But there is a difference with you. That is, in this show, you display toughness and competence far beyond what a normal guy has and although the audience knows it's just a show, a part of each viewer feels emotionally that it's for real. They come to look at you as actually being that gutty, that much in control of any situation. That's why we agree with you that it's so important for us to show that you have depth of character as well. And these new concepts are designed to do just that."

"Mmm, yeah." Mike looked at the ceiling. "I see what you mean." He stood up and began to pace the office slowly. "But what about the athletic stuff I asked for? Where are some ideas along those lines?"

"We're working on them, too," Hazelman said. "But they may not be the best direction for us to be going in."

Mike stopped, looked at him, then resumed pacing. "Maybe. And maybe not. After all, the way the public first heard of me was as an athlete. They still think of me as a jock, and this country is sure as hell as sports-nutty as it ever was."

"That's true," Hazelman said. "And you're probably right. But what we have to do is to come up with something fresh. Something that would make the audience say, 'Hey! wow! Did you see what Mike Brady did there?' It's got to have the same kind of emotional wallop we want to have in all these other new ideas, you know?"

"Yeah. Well, okay." Mike said. "So come up with a new twist. But I think a story involving me and athletics could be powerful as hell."

"Sure, sure, Mike," Hazelman said. He stood up. "We just want to be confident that whatever we do, it's right for you. How about some more coffee?"

"No thanks," Mike said. He lit a cigarette. "Have you seen the dailies?"

"An hour ago." Hazelman smiled. "It'll be a great show."

"Really terrific," Selig added.

Hazelman walked around from behind his desk and flopped onto a leather sofa. "I think it'll be one of the best we've done."

Mike nodded. As far as Hazelman was concerned, every show was one of the best they'd done. "How does the girl look?"

"Sally Carpenter? Dynamite. She was a great suggestion, Mike." Hazelman grinned. "You really have taste."

"Britney finish up?" Mike asked casually. Rod Britney was the series director.

Hazelman shook his head. "They're still doing some pick-ups on stage nine. Why don't you have a look?"

"Maybe I will." Mike stepped toward the door.

"See you Sunday night?" Hazelman asked.

"Yeah, probably," Mike said. Sunday nights were a tradition at Hazelman's house in Holmby Hills for anybody connected with "The Savage City," as well as for any of the producer's friends who might care to drop in for tennis and the informal buffet supper. At eight o'clock they all watched the show.

"Try to make it," Hazelman said. "And bring beautiful Darla."

"Sure. See you guys later." Mike walked out of the office.

Harry Selig looked at Hazelman and exhaled slowly. "That pompous fuck."

Hazelman grinned. "Last Sunday night we picked up two share points."

"Wonderful. Sometimes I wish I'd become a plumber."

"It's not too late, Harry. It could still be arranged. Of course, you might have to change your lifestyle just a little."

Selig laughed. "You do have a point. He may be a shit, but at least he's our shit."

"Right on. And if he wants to think he's a fucking genius, we should all applaud. As a matter of fact, some of the things that come out of that cement head of his make a certain amount of sense."

Selig scratched his chin. "You're right, you know. He does have instincts that reveal a fairly high intelligence. He eats when he's hungry, and when he gets tired he falls down."

"No, I mean it. It's sure as hell true we have to keep showing new sides of him to the audience if we expect to hold them. Not just new situations, but new sides of his character. And as far as the athletic stuff is concerned, he's not so far off there, either."

"Oh, God, Dick, come off it. So we show that under all the muscle and brains he's warm and loving. Okay. That I'll buy. But showing him as a super-jock I think is bullshit."

"I'm not sure," Hazelman responded. "What he said about America and sports heroes is absolutely true. It couldn't hurt to have him in a story where you remind the audience what a great sports figure the real Mike Brady was. And you know, he really was a hell of a boxer."

"Big deal," Harry sneered.

"So maybe the way to do it would be to have him in something completely different, like tennis or swimming or golf. You know, not something as obvious as boxing, but another individual sport."

"Yeah, but what the hell is it? After we've had him toughing his way out of the most lethal and dangerous jams for two years, against almost impossible odds, who gives a shit about seeing him play a game, especially when nobody could possibly beat him without ruining his image?"

"But maybe that's just it," Hazelman said. "Maybe that's exactly the kind of thing the audience would love. You take for instance a situation where Mike comes up against a star in a given sport, somebody who thinks he's great stuff, and Mike makes an asshole of the guy. You don't think the audience would love that? You don't think they eat it up when some honcho gets knocked on his butt?"

"Well, maybe," Selig admitted. "Maybe there's something to that."

"Of course there is. There has to be a great emotional response to that kind of thing, and that's a big part of what this business is all about."

"Uh-huh." Selig began to warm to the idea. "I could see a tennis tournament. Wimbledon or Forest Hills, or maybe one of those World Tennis things in Vegas for all that dough and Mike knocks off one of those guys."

"Exactly," Hazelman said. "You take how everybody feels about Ted Walters. There is one of the top tennis players in the world, a nice, cleancut kid—the best to come out of Australia since Newcombe. And what does the public want to see? Why do they jam into the tournaments, and why do they watch him on the tube and give you the good ratings at a lousy time like Sunday afternoon in the summer? Because they want to see Ted Walters win? In a pig's ass they do."

"Yeah." Selig nodded. "They want to see him get beat."

"You're fucking right they want to see him get beat," Hazelman said triumphantly. "They want to see him get his brains kicked out. They don't give a shit about his being a great tennis player. They just think he's an arrogant young prick and they want to see him get his comeuppance. They don't care whether that French kid gives it to him or who else, they just want to have the pleasure of seeing Ted Walters lose."

"Mmm." Selig sat back in his chair. "Hey, you know? Maybe that's exactly what we do."

"What?"

"Walters. We get Walters himself to appear in the story."

Hazelman grinned. "Harry, you are a clever son of a bitch."

"That's what I keep telling you."

"If he'd do it."

"Why not?"

"Because Walters has a hell of an ego, too, you know. He might not love the idea of being made a fool of by a guy he could handle without even trying, and in front of a big audience."

"Yeah, but Walters loves money, and he's a ham."

"Sure, you're right. He'd go for the idea that it's only a television drama anyway. And he'd also jump at the chance to play a part in the series, even if he's only playing a tennis player."

"I'll have an outline worked up," Selig said.

"All right, good." Hazelman looked at his watch. "Got to go. I have a meeting at CBS."

Mike Brady stood just outside the setup on stage nine, watching Rod Britney direct the scene in which Sally Carpenter was being questioned by a CIA agent. When the take was finished, Mike caught her eye and smiled at her. She smiled back and he deliberately turned and walked to the far side of the stage, to his dressing room. He unlocked the door and stepped inside.

Ten minutes later there was a knock on the door. He opened it and Sally entered the room.

"Hello, Mike."

"Hi, baby." He closed the door behind her and locked it.

Her voice was low and husky. "I was hoping you'd come by."

He put his hands on her shoulders and looked into her face, a knowing smile playing at the corners of his mouth. "Wouldn't miss seeing you."

"I hope not. Have you thought about me?" She had slanting green eyes above high cheekbones and the combination made her look faintly catlike. Her full-lipped mouth was partly open.

"Of course I have." His gaze traveled down her body. She was wearing a light cotton dress, and apparently nothing else. He could see her nipples under the thin material, and the curve of her belly, the mold of her thighs. "You look delicious."

"Do I?"

"Yeah."

"That's good. Because that's the way I want to look for you."

He noted that tiny beads of moisture had begun to form on her upper lip. He pulled her close to him and slipped his hands down her back, aware of her firm, full breasts against his chest. He cupped her buttocks and she spread her legs a little and began to move her hips in a slow, erotic grind. "You know what that does? It gives me a hard-on."

"I know. I can feel it." Her breath was coming faster now. She put her arms around his neck and increased the pressure of her hips as she moved against him. "And I'm glad."

"Are you?"

She flicked her tongue across her lips. "Yes. Because I want to suck your cock so much I can already taste it."

Mike laughed, a low rumble in his throat. "So let's go." He pulled open his belt and kicked off his trousers and his shorts.

Sally sank to her knees, her eyes riveted on his penis. She held the shaft lightly in her fingers, watching the glans pulse as blood surged into it. "My God, it's enormous."

"Come on, let's have that good head."

She bent forward, closing her eyes, and took his cock as far into her mouth as she could. For a long time she held it there, her tongue working. Then she began to bob her head slowly.

There was a full-length mirror on the far wall. Mike looked at the image in it and grinned.

Chapter 4

Darla picked at her tuna salad for a few seconds and then put her fork down. She looked across the table at Betty Frolich. "Sometimes I just get so damn sick of it," she said. "All these go-see's and auditions and where am I? No further ahead than I was last year, or the year before that."

Betty smiled, her mouth full of cottage cheese. "You don't really think you're the first person in this business who felt that way, do you?" Betty was fat and dumpy, but she tried hard to carry off an air of chic.

"No, of course not," Darla answered. "I know that's the way most girls feel about it, no matter what they say. It's just that sometimes I feel as if I'm in a trap."

"You mean because of Mike?"

"Oh, I guess so. If only I were doing something else. You know, if I were a doctor, or a painter, or just about anything."

"Even an agent?"

"Darla laughed in spite of herself. "God, yes. Even an agent." She reached across and squeezed Betty's plump arm. "I really am grateful to you, Betty. I know how busy you are, and yet you always make time to listen to me bitch."

Betty smiled again. "Today you were lucky. Your call caught me just as I was going out the door. And I'm glad it did. It's good to have a chance to talk. In fact, I think we ought to have lunch more often." She looked at Darla thoughtfully. "You see, I really do understand how you feel. It's never easy when two people in the business are married. Their careers can't ever be on the same plane. One always has to be ahead of the other."

"Which is a polite way of saying that Mike is a smash and I'm a nothing."

"Not at all," Betty said patiently. After twenty years in the business, she was used to this, playing Mother Confessor to talent, shoring up their bruised egos, helping them to cope, offering a sympathetic ear to the endless stories of career disappointments and turbulent love affairs, the ambitions and fears and anxieties.

"But it's true," Darla said. "And it's at its worst when we're out somewhere socially. You know, at a party or something. Everybody crawls all over Mike and tells him how great they think he is, and there I am, little Miss Dum-dum."

"Oh come on, Darla. You really are overstating it."

"Am I?" Darla looked around the crowded room. They were in a sandwich shop on Wilshire Boulevard. "Sometimes I think I'd trade places with almost anybody."

"Wrong," Betty said. "You've got it backwards. The fact is, almost anybody would trade places with you. Sure, you have your problems with Mike. Any girl would have. You're married to a very exciting and dynamic man, and his career is zooming. He'd be a handful for you, no matter what your own situation might be. But look at it this way, Darla. You're one of the most beautiful women in Hollywood."

Darla opened her mouth to protest.

"No, I mean it," Betty went on. "You really are. Not just beautiful, but one of the most beautiful. It's only a question of time until you hit. But hit you will, sooner or later, and I know it just as surely as I'm sitting here."

Darla leaned forward, her eyes wide. "Betty, that's wonderful. But in my case, it's sooner or forget it. There won't be any later. I'm twenty-eight years old, and in this business that's practically over the hill."

"Okay, then we'll make it sooner. We got another

call for a commercial this morning, and this is one I think you'd be just right for."

Darla groaned. "Another cattle call? I feel as if I ought to be wearing a brand."

Betty shook her head. "This is different. You know Superfresh?"

"Mouthwash? Sure."

"Well, they're looking for a girl to represent them in advertising. Not just a model, but one girl who'd kind of be the Superfresh girl in everything. TV, magazines, everything."

"Sort of like Hutton with Revlon?"

"Even better. The girl who gets it would be their whole campaign."

"I think I've heard that before."

"This one's for real. What they want is to sell the stuff like a cosmetic. You know, 'Use Superfresh and it'll give you a beautiful smile while it freshens your breath.' So what they need is somebody with terrific teeth. And I can't imagine anybody in this town—no, in the world—who's got a better mouthful than you do."

"You mean you like me better smiling?"

Betty laughed. "I mean I love you any way. But your smile has great commercial value."

"Okay, so here I am, folks. The Teeth of the Year."

"That's my girl. The session is at Casting International at nine o'clock tomorrow morning. Go nail it down."

"Who's the agency?"

"Um, somebody in New York. I forget. Apparently they don't trust their West Coast office. They sent a vice-president out from New York."

"Uh-huh. Mister Horny visits California."

Betty shrugged. "Boys will be boys. But don't be so cynical. Not everybody is out to use you before they use you, as the saying goes."

"No. Just most everybody."

"Do I gather you got a little suggestion from the Pearl Soap guy?"

"Very subtle. I thought he was going to ask me to go down on him right then and there."

"Was he good looking?"

"God, Betty. What differences does it make? Yeah, I guess he was all right, if you like the type."

Betty sighed a mock sigh. "I really should have been an actress. They wouldn't even have to ask. *I'd* ask. I'd be doing more commercials than anybody in television."

"Betty, you're crazy." Darla laughed.

"I'd rather eat that than cottage cheese," Betty said. "And besides, it's even less fattening." She looked at her watch. "Hey, I have to go."

"Must be nice to be that busy," Darla said wistfully.

"Must be nice to have some free time this afternoon."

"Okay, you make your point."

"Well, of course. It's all in how you look at it. Why don't you go for a swim, or play some tennis?"

"I guess I will. Play tennis, that is." Darla paused. "That was Casting International for the Superfresh thing?"

"Right. Nine o'clock tomorrow morning. Now you run along and I'll get this." Betty picked up the check. "Ciao."

The Beverly Hills Racket Club was busy, as always. Darla changed into tennis shorts and a T-shirt and wandered out to look for one of the instructors. She had been playing since she was twelve, off and on, but she had never become very proficient. As she walked toward the courts someone said, "Hey, stranger."

Ted Walters had a wide grin on his boyish face. "How about we hit a few?"

Darla was genuinely glad to see him. "Ted! How are you?"

"Terrific. Just like I always am." His Australian accent gave his words a charming lilt.

"I thought you were in Italy or someplace."

"I was. And in Sweden and Germany with a couple of stops in between. I just came home to see you."

Darla laughed. "Okay, so here I am. Do you really want to play with me?"

"Of course I do," Ted said. "And anyhow, with the handicap, we're even."

"What handicap?"

"Well, I watch you bounce around in that T-shirt and it weakens me."

Darla flushed. "Boy, I walked into that one, didn't I?"

"I'm sorry," Ted said. He smiled. "You know I can't resist being a smartass. But I would like to play with you."

"Great, if you don't mind taking it easy."

"With you, I'd love it."

Darla was nervous for the first few moments on the court, but then she quickly forgot her self-consciousness as she concentrated on hitting the ball.

"We'll just volley," Ted had said. "That way I think maybe I can help your game a little."

Within a short time Darla found that she was really enjoying herself. She knew that Ted was deliberately placing the ball into position so that it would be as easy as possible for her to return it, but that didn't at all diminish her pleasure. If anything it enhanced it, especially since Ted kept up a running commentary on her game. It was easy to follow the instructions and comments he called out to her, and she felt her confidence building as she increased the force of her shots.

"Turn, Darla," Ted yelled. "Get into position. Don't hurry it. Wait for the ball. Get set and meet it. Good girl."

Darla marveled at the effortless grace with which Ted moved around the court. His slim body didn't appear at all muscular, but neither was there an ounce of fat anywhere. His movements were fluid and catlike, with hardly perceptible changes in speed, yet no matter where the ball went, he was there without ever seeming to try or to run hard.

They played for about forty-five minutes, and then when Darla missed a shot she waved her racket. "Hey, how about a breather?"

"Sure," Ted called. "You've about worn me out anyhow."

A patter of applause went up, and Darla was surprised to realize that a number of people had gathered on the sidelines to watch. Ted put his arm around her waist as they walked off the court. She felt marvelous.

Over iced tea at a table on the patio, Ted said, "You know, you really could be a very good player, if you wanted to be."

"Sure." Darla smiled. "As long as I had you to make me look good."

"No, I mean it. Know what your biggest problem is?"

"Yep. Weak forehand and no backhand."

"It's lack of confidence," he said. "You don't have enough of what I have too much of."

"Maybe we could split the difference."

Ted grinned. "I wish we could."

Darla looked at him. It really was amazing that this cocky kid who was years younger than she was had become one of the acknowledged best players in the world. He took on anybody—Australians, Europeans, Americans—anybody. And he beat them all. "Maybe if I was as good at anything as you are, I'd have that kind of confidence, too," she said.

Ted shook his head. "Not so. The way to get good at anything is to believe in yourself."

"Did you always feel that way?"

"Of course not. The old man helped me plenty."

"Your father?"

"Sure. He drilled it into me from day one. As soon as I could hold a racket, he not only told me I was going to be number one someday, he made me believe it."

"But didn't you ever have doubts?"

"Oh yeah, often. But then a funny thing happened. God, I was only about ten years old, and I was already in a lot of junior competition in Melbourne. All of a sudden, I found I'd get mad as hell if somebody beat me. Not just blind-dumb mad, but kind of insulted. You know, something inside me was saying, Hey, Walters. That bum can't beat you. You're better than he is. He can't do that to you. Pretty soon I was going into every match with that attitude."

Darla nodded. "And that's just how you feel today."

Ted grinned. "You've noticed, huh?"

"The whole world has noticed."

"You think that's bad?"

Darla shrugged. "I don't know, Ted. It certainly hasn't made everybody love you."

"No, but I'll tell you a secret. It's given me an edge beyond what my own self-confidence gives me."

"How?"

"By preconditioning my opponents. A guy comes onto the court with me, he's already half beaten, because he thinks I'm a wiseguy and he's too eager to knock me off."

"The crowd feels the same way, don't they?"

"You mean wanting to see me get beat?"

"Yes."

"Sure, they do. And you know what?"

"What?"

"Fuck 'em."

Darla threw her head back and laughed. There was something so incongruous about hearing this coming out of Ted Walters, with his long boy's haircut and his bright boy's face, that it was hilarious.

But he knew how to laugh at himself, too. He realized how comical he sounded. He laughed with her. "Anyhow," he said, "confidence is what you need more of, Darla. At least in tennis."

"And in everything else?" Darla asked.

Ted looked at her, a shrewd expression on his face. "In everything else you've got it made, right?"

"Not quite."

"But you're one of the top models in the business, aren't you?"

"Nowhere near it."

"Okay, but you will be."

"I hope so," Darla said. "Someday."

Ted sipped his iced tea. "What would you really like to do, Darla? I mean, what would you really like to do with your life?"

Darla looked into his eyes for a moment, and then she looked away. "Oh, I don't know."

Ted reached over and put his hand lightly on top of

hers. "Hey," he said softly. "It's okay. You can trust me."

"Can I?"

"You bet you can. I'm the head of your fan club."

Darla spoke slowly, hesitatingly. "Well, I'd really like to make it big. I'd like to be a real star. I know that sounds funny. I can't act and I can't sing—I can't do anything. All I am is reasonably pretty. But, oh, God, I would like to get somewhere, someday."

"Then you will," Ted said. "And the way to do it is to believe it. You believe it, and you'll make the rest of the world believe it, too."

Darla returned his steady gaze. "You've proven that, haven't you, Ted?"

"Sure I have. And you can, too."

Suddenly Darla realized that when Ted stopped clowning, when he was deadly serious, the boy somehow disappeared. In the boy's place there was a man, as tough and hard as he needed to be, and yet so gentle. She felt flustered. "Oh my, it's late. I really have to get going." She jumped to her feet. "Ted, thank you so much. For the tennis, and for—everything." Impulsively, she leaned over and kissed him quickly, full on the mouth. She picked up her racket and ran from the patio.

Chapter 5

Ben Thompkins awoke in the Beverly Hills Hotel with a pounding headache and a mouth so dry it hurt to open it.

His first thought was, How in hell am I ever going to get through this day?

He looked at his watch. God. Eight-thirty already. I'm due at that damned casting session in a half-hour. Never make it. He forced himself to sit up in bed and the pounding increased.

The room was a mess. There was an open bottle of Scotch on the desk, along with a couple of stale, half-full glasses, the ice long since melted. Articles of clothing were scattered around, some of them his, some of them female. A pair of women's slacks were lying on the floor, a bra nearby.

Ben looked at the form beside him in the bed. Long brown hair spilled out onto the pillow. What was her name? Helen? No. Holly, that was it. Holly something. Christ, what a night.

He got out of bed and went into the bathroom. His urine was dark yellow. No wonder, he thought. I must have drunk a gallon of booze. As he rinsed out his mouth, he looked at his face in the mirror and grinned wryly. Thirty-five? I look more like a hundred and thirty-five. What was the expression about eyes like that? Two pissholes in the snow. He stepped into the shower and let the hot spray pound his body as he lathered and relathered himself. After a few minutes he turned the handle from hot to cold and winced as the icy needles struck his skin. It was punishing, but when he stepped out he was already feeling a little better.

He had come out on American's Flight One the previous day and spent most of the afternoon at Casting International, looking through head sheets and composites. Whenever he was in California, Ben scrupulously avoided the agency's L.A. office, using it only as a facility for taking messages, or occasionally to provide a secretary when he needed some typing done. The office was only concerned with handling a few small local accounts anyway. It had almost nothing to do with the New York operation, whose staff held it in contempt, just as a large cosmopolitan family might regard a group of weak-minded cousins who lived in a rural area. Ben had known Peggy Benson, who ran Casting International, from the days when she was a casting director at J. Walter Thompson in New York. Peggy was highstrung, nervous, a one-time Broadway actress who had been living in California for about five years now.

"We've got some very good people coming in for you, Ben," Peggy had told him. They were sitting in her office, discussing the casting session she had scheduled for the next day.

"Good."

"Teeth are tough, you know."

"Yeah, I know."

"I mean, we can give you plenty of beautiful girls with a good smile, but finding one who has absolutely perfect teeth and who's distinctive at the same time is a tall order."

"Sure, love. That's why I came to a genius like you."

"Flattery will get you everywhere," Peggy replied. "But it's still a tough assignment."

"Yeah, I know. But the whole idea of this new campaign is that we're promising to give the consumer a beautiful smile as well as a fresh breath. So our gal has to have really great teeth."

"Sure, I understand that. But, the thing I don't get is

why the teeth have to be her own. No caps, you said."

"Right."

"But Ben, that's really kind of silly, don't you think? I mean, how's the audience ever going to know the difference? Even a top girl like Hutton has that filler she shoves between her front teeth before they put her on camera. God, I've seen her without it and you could stick your thumb in the gap."

"Uh-huh. But for Superfresh, no fake anything."

"Not even just a little fudging, here and there?"

Thompkins shook his head. "You just don't know the client. They don't even like us to retouch artwork."

"Square, huh?"

"No, just straight. They're a throwback to when a company made an honest product and sold it at an honest price. And that's the way they do everything."

"Oh, hey. I'm not knocking that. And I even buy their stuff. Been using Superfresh for years." Peggy smiled wistfully. "Not that it does me much good."

"How many girls do we have coming tomorrow?"

"About thirty, altogether." She indicated the pile of materials that lay on the table. "All the ones we have pictures on here, plus some others I called this morning."

"Okay," Ben nodded. "That ought to keep us busy."

"You want videotape on all of them?"

"No, maybe just the best ten or fifteen or so."

Peggy lit a cigarette. "You weren't having much luck in New York, I gather?"

"No. We must have called in every girl in town. They all have that gaunt, fashiony look. Somehow, the girls here look more natural." He smiled. "Even the blondes."

"Well, sure," Peggy said brightly. "Everything's better in California. That's why I'm out here."

"You like it, don't you?"

"Love it. God. I wouldn't go back to New York for anything in the world. All that cold and dirt."

"You don't care to be mugged and raped?"

Peggy grinned. "Of course I do. It's just nicer to be mugged and raped in the sunshine."

Late in the afternoon Ben had called his old friend Johnny Powers at NBC and asked him to have dinner. Johnny was delighted. They met at the Beverly Hills at seven and had several drinks in the Polo Lounge, reminiscing and entertaining each other with industry gossip. Johnny said he hoped Ben wouldn't mind, but he had lined up a couple of girls.

Ben didn't mind a bit. The four of them had dinner at Chasen's, along with more drinks and several bottles of wine. From there they went to a strip joint on Sunset Boulevard, and when that closed to a private club on Santa Monica that Johnny belonged to. Sometime after that they split up and Ben and Holly Whatsit went back to the Beverly Hills and drank more Scotch before they finally staggered into bed. Ben hardly remembered laying her.

In fact, he thought now as he brushed his teeth, it's a wonder I could get it up at all.

It was nine-thirty by the time Thompkins arrived at Casting International. Wearing sunglasses, he pushed through the crowded reception room and entered Peggy Benson's office.

"Hi. We were about to start without you," Peggy greeted him.

"You should have."

"Have a nice evening? Or shouldn't I ask?"

"It was fine. Made some popcorn and watched TV."

Peggy smiled. "I'll bet. Shall we begin the stampede?"

"You'd better get me some coffee first. I am in dire need."

"It's on its way."

Ben worked slowly and carefully. He made detailed notes on how each girl handled herself in conversation, how much poise she seemed to have, how well she moved. He probed about her acting experience as well as her career in commercials, and what her interests were. It was important to learn as much as possible, because the agency wanted a lot more than just a pretty face in a short-lived television commercial or in one magazine ad.

Some of the girls he rejected outright. Too old, he noted, or lousy hair, or bad smile, or face too round, or comes across as stupid, and so on.

But by noon, he felt pretty good about two or three of those he'd seen, and he began to relax. As vice-president in charge of commercial production for Baker & Barlowe, his job was to bring back to New York tapes of as many serious candidates as possible. After that the people at the agency would narrow down the choices, and then the agency's research department would conduct interviews with consumers to determine which girl, if any, would get this assignment. Finally, a recommendation would be made to the client and the ultimate decision would be reached.

If and when one of these models made it, Ben would be out here actually to begin shooting commercials, and the quality of his work would depend more on the looks and personality of the girl than on any other factor.

He was amused by the subtle invitations a couple of the girls made to him. Nothing really overt, but the expressions, the gestures, a few words, made it clear that if he would favor a girl, she would favor him. *Quid pro quo.* You give it to me, and I'll give it to you. He fantasized a little over one of them, a reddish-blonde with big tits who managed to turn every smile into a leer. Ben looked at her chest and she shifted slightly in her chair and drew back her shoulders to make her breasts more prominent. When he looked back into her eyes she smiled her drity smile and Ben thought for an instant about how interesting it would be to put that wide mouth to better use. But only for an instant. "Thanks a lot," he said. "Thanks for coming. You really look great. We'll let you know, okay?" Her expression went from why-don't-we to up-yours and she picked up her portfolio and left.

"How about it?" Peggy asked. "Want to break for lunch?"

Ben shrugged. "Might as well keep going. Anyhow,

some of those gals have been waiting all morning. Who's next?"

Peggy looked at her list and then picked up a composite. "This one you're going to like," she said. "Name's Darla Dawson. She has great teeth."

"Yeah." Ben lit a cigarette and yawned. When he looked up, Darla was standing there.

Ben was stunned. This girl didn't merely have a smile, she had a whole mouthful of dazzling white teeth that seemed to light up her face. Her hair, too, was unusual. It was thick and healthy looking and it curled and waved gently as it tumbled down over her shoulders. The color was just a shade lighter than honey.

She sat down, and as they began to talk, Ben couldn't stop looking at her teeth and her fantastic mass of hair. He knew at once that for most assignments the hair would be more of a handicap to her than a help. It would be too distinctive, would call too much attention to itself. But for this assignment, along with her incredible smile, Goddamn. "Is that for real?" he asked, indicating her hair.

"Yes." Darla smiled. "It's all mine."

"How about the color?"

"It's pretty close to natural. I have it touched up once in a while. Lightened, actually."

"And your teeth?"

"Also mine," Darla laughed.

"Any caps?"

"Not a one. In fact," she added, "I know this sounds strange, but I've only had two fillings in my whole life."

"Ever done anything on teeth? Mouthwash, toothpaste, anything?"

"No. Never."

"No TV, no print?"

"No, not a thing."

Ben sat back in his chair. He felt a rising sense of excitement as he looked at her. "Okay, Darla," he said. "Tell us all about yourself. What you've done in the business, and so on."

As Darla talked, Ben studied her face with the know-

39

ing objectivity of the professional. Good eyes, a pale violet-blue. Almost as unusual in their own way as her teeth and her hair. High cheekbones, fragile structure. Jaw somewhat squarish. Good. It would photograph well. Excellent mouth, wide, and lips just full enough. And the smile—Jesus, it was dazzling. He concentrated on what she was saying.

"I want to act," Darla said. "I hope to do more television. I've done some bit parts, but I expect to be getting more important ones. And eventually, movies."

Ben nodded. "You want to be a serious actress, hmm?"

"More than anything. And I'm going to do it. I really am."

As he listened to her, Ben realized that even the way she spoke was different, somehow. There was a childlike quality, an innocence mixed with determination, that he knew couldn't be put on unless this girl was already the most skilled actress he'd ever met. No, it was genuine. If he could ever get that to come across on camera . . .

"Okay, Darla," he said. "Go ahead into the studio. We'll tape a rough."

When she had left the room, Peggy turned to him. "You like, huh?"

"Yeah," Ben said casually. "I like. Maybe a little artificial, but not bad."

"Okay," Peggy said. "We've got plenty more girls to look at." She went into the studio.

Ben picked up Darla's composite and stared at the full-faced shot of the smiling girl on its cover. You never know, he thought. Maybe I'm wrong. Maybe the agency will hate her. Maybe they'll think she's too much, that her smile is too unbelievable. Maybe the client will hate her. Maybe we'll go through all our scientific research bullshit and the women will hate her. But maybe, just maybe, she could be the Goddamnedest discovery ever. As he went into the studio he was surprised that his headache had disappeared.

Chapter 6

Darla sat on the patio as Mike did laps in the pool. He swam with a strong, steady crawl, his stroke almost flawless. When his count reached thirty, he rolled over on his back and floated for a few minutes. It was a perfect day, no trace of smog for once, and the afternoon sun reflected brilliantly from the surface of the water.

"Lunch is ready," Darla called. Mike climbed out of the pool and she handed him a towel. She watched as he dried himself, reacting as she always did to the sight of the clearly defined muscles in his massive shoulders, his taut belly.

Maggie had set out chicken salad, sliced tomatoes, and iced tea on an umbrella-shaded table. As they ate, Darla asked who would be at Hazelman's that evening.

"The usual crowd," Mike replied. "People on the show, friends of theirs, whoever wanders in. You know."

"Mm. Sounds grand."

Mike looked at her. "We don't have to go, if it's that much of a drag for you." His tone was edged with sarcasm.

"It's not that, Mike. I know it's important to you, there are people you want to see and all that. It's just that we never seem to have any time together. It's really heaven to have a whole Sunday like this. I hate to leave to go anywhere."

"Uh-huh." He raised a forkful of salad to his mouth. "Won't be a late night. Anyhow, does you good to get out and talk to people."

"I talk to people all the time. You're the one I want to be with."

He put his fork down. "For Christ's sake, Darla. You will be with me. We're going together, and we're spending the whole day here, except for a couple of hours this evening. Now what is so terrible about that?"

"Nothing's terrible. It's not terrible at all. It's just that I like to have you to myself once in a while. Once in a great while, in fact."

"Yeah, well, try to see things my way, too." He went on eating.

"I do try to see things your way. It's the only way I see anything."

"What's that supposed to mean?"

"Nothing. It's just that I wish for once we'd do something or feel about something the way I want."

"All right. What exactly *do* you want?"

"I told you what I want," Darla said. "I want some time alone with my husband, instead of making what amounts to public appearances with him. That's not my idea of having a good time. And neither is watching every girl there try to move in on you."

"Ah, so that's it."

"That's part of it, sure it is." Despite herself, Darla felt her anger rise. "You think it's fun for me to go out someplace with you, when you're like a prize for every little snip with hot pants?"

"Oh shit, Darla." Mike's mouth curled disdainfully. "Stop acting like some hick kid from right off the prairie, will you?"

"Why should I?" Darla cried. "That's what I am. A hick kid. That's what I was when you married me, and that's what I am now." Tears welled up in her eyes. "But I love you, Mike. I love you and I want you for myself. Maybe I'm not as exciting to you as you want me to be, but I'm trying. I want to be everything for you."

"Jesus Christ." He threw his napkin down and got up

from the table. He walked over to a chaise, lay down, and buried his face in the *Los Angeles Sunday Times*.

Darla sat at the table for a long time, working steadily to get her emotions under control. You damned fool, she told herself. That is exactly the wrong way to behave. You couldn't turn him off better with a bucket of ice water.

She took a deep breath, and dried her eyes with her napkin. Where is all that confidence I was going to have from now on? Well, I will have it, if it kills me. I'm beautiful and I'm strong and I'm going to get exactly what I want. In my life. In my career. With Mike.

She stood up and walked over to where he lay reading. "Mike?"

"Hm?"

"Let's go and have a good time."

"Yeah," he mumbled. "Sure." He went on reading.

Dick Hazelman's house was a sprawling English Tudor, a mixture of half-timbers, stucco, and brick, set on two acres of rolling lawns and tall trees. When Mike pulled his Mercedes into the circular driveway, there were already a number of cars parked in front of the place.

"This is such a pretty house," Darla said as she got out of the car. "It always makes me feel as if I'm out in the country somewhere."

Mike shrugged. "Early Pretentious. Hazelman likes it because he has a secret yearning to be a British fag."

A maid led them through to the rear, where a large, informal living room opened onto a patio. Beyond the patio was a pool and a pool house, and beyond that were the tennis courts. People were scattered about, sitting at the bar or on the patio, watching a golf match on television, lying around the pool, playing tennis.

Hazelman bounced over to greet them. He was wearing shorts and a tennis sweater. "Hey, you guys—nice to see you." He kissed Darla on the cheek. "You look ravishing, honey, as always. Make yourselves at home. Drinks at the bar, or whatever. I'm just about to humiliate Barry Lieber on the tennis court."

Mike saw the producer of "Robbery Squad" talking with Bob Parsons of CBS and went over to join them.

"Darla," a voice called. It was Hazelman's wife, Brenda. "Come and sit with us. You know Ruth and Elise. We're engaging in our favorite sport—who's doing what to whom."

Darla said hello and sat down with the three women. She listened idly to their gossip.

"She met him in Mexico last year," Ruth Levy was saying, "when they were shooting *Sun Goddess* in Acapulco. He was on vacation with that wife of his, what's her name, Bernice, I think, and they were staying at Las Brisas and Bernice didn't know what was going on, she's loaded most of the time anyway. So pretty soon they were making it, and then they kept seeing each other when they got back to L.A., and now she says he's going to get a divorce and marry her."

"I think he's handsome," Elise Machlin said. "And from what I hear, hung like a horse."

"I don't care what he's hung like," Ruth replied. "With that kind of money he could have a mouse cock and he'd be one of the great lovers of history. You know his grandfather owned thousands of acres in the Valley."

As they talked, Darla noticed that several girls had joined the group on the far side of the pool where Mike was. She wasn't sure, but she thought she spotted Cathy Drake among them.

"You knew Bobbie Phillips, didn't you, Darla?" Brenda Hazelman asked.

"What? Oh, yes. Sure I did," Darla answered. "I had a bit part in one of "The Marauders" last year when she was the lead in the series."

"I can't believe she's dead," Elise said. "That bright, beautiful girl. So young, and so talented."

"There's still some talk it was an accident," Ruth said.

Brenda sniffed. "That was no accident. She took a whole bottle of barbiturates."

"I heard it was valium," Elise said. "And that she drank a lot of vodka on top of it."

"No, dear," Brenda shook her head. "Dave Samuels is Dick's lawyer, and he's working on settling the estate, which is still in a godawful mess. It was suicide, all right, and with sleeping pills."

"Did you have any feeling she'd do anything like that?" Ruth directed the question to Darla.

"No. Not really," Darla said. "From what I saw of her, Bobbie was always cheerful, an up person. I never had any idea what her problems were, or even that she had any."

"Mmm." Ruth looked disappointed. "She was living with Peter Barrett, wasn't she?"

"Yes," Darla said. "Or at least she was when I knew her."

"You know, I heard she was about to do a picture that Dan Isaacson was going to produce," Brenda said. "It was based on *Pandora's Box*, that novel by Thomas Chastain."

"Darla, didn't she start as a model, too?" Elise asked.

Darla nodded. "Yes. She was doing Old Wisconsin Beer commercials at first, and then something for a car. Ford, I think."

"Well, she didn't stay there long," Elise said. "She was no dope. As stunning as she was, she had brains and ability. Harry Daimler directed *The Long Walk*—you know that was her first big part in a picture—and he said she was one of the most gifted actresses he'd ever worked with. She wasn't just another pretty zero."

Darla looked at Elise. She guessed the other woman was in her middle forties, about the same age as Brenda and a little older than Ruth. All three women were attractive, in a way. They were slim and tan and it was obvious they worked hard to stay in shape. And it was also obvious that all three made the same mistake so many women do, exposing their faces to the sun for years, which produced the leathery condition that no amount of tanning oil or moisturizers could prevent. Darla wondered whether Elise was deliberately needling her, or whether her remarks were in fact devoid of malice. She decided that Elise probably liked the idea of being able to pigeonhole her as a beautiful nothing, that

45

it was a defense mechanism, a way in which an older or less appealing woman could assert herself, could feel superior to her. It's strange, she thought. Somehow I'm beginning to see things in a way I never have before.

Barry Lieber wiped his face with a towel. "Hazelman, you're a schmuck."

"That's what I like. A good loser."

"Beat me with a strong game and that I can take," Lieber said. "But give me all those junk shots, all that cheap little dribbly shit, and I have no respect for you."

"I don't want your respect," Hazelman said. "I want your money. So far, you owe me eighty bucks."

Lieber sighed. He was about forty pounds overweight, and perspiration kept popping out on his forehead and his cheeks. He took off his glasses and wiped them with a towel. "So at least you could buy me a drink. And anyhow, you said you wanted to talk."

They got Bloody Marys from the bar and sat down at a small table at one end of the patio.

Lieber gulped at his drink. "Okay, what's on your mind?"

Hazelman eyed him speculatively. "I need your help," he began. "No big deal, but it could be important, in the long run, for 'The Savage City.' "

Lieber arched his eyebrows. "You got a problem?"

The producer shook his head. "I want to prevent one."

"How?"

Hazelman leaned forward conspiratorially. "I'm going to be completely frank with you, Barry. You guys have a big stake in this series, just as I do. So I want to lay it out for you straight ahead."

A flicker of suspicion crossed Lieber's eyes. As one of UBS's top program executives, he oversaw a number of the network's properties, "The Savage City" among them, and reported directly to Peter Fried, UBS program boss. "What is it?"

"It's the ratings," Hazelman replied levelly. "I think the show is at a point where it has to be watched closely or it could start to fade."

Lieber's expression turned to incredulity. "Start to fade? What the fuck are you talking about? It just went from a thirty-six to a thirty-eight share." He snorted. "You know how many series would give their ass for those numbers?"

"Sure," Hazelman said. "The numbers are fine. For now."

Lieber lifted his glass, and as he noisily drained its contents, his eyes narrowed once more. He squinted at the producer, his sweating face reminding Hazelman of a crafty pig. It was obvious that he didn't believe what he had heard, that he regarded this as a ploy of some kind on Hazelman's part. He returned the glass to the table. "What do you want, Dick?"

"I told you," Hazelman answered calmly. "I need your help." He deliberately kept the fat man waiting, knowing that Lieber's imagination would blow the problem out of proportion.

"So ask. What is it?"

Hazelman toyed with his glass. He knew how to handle Lieber as well off the tennis court as on it. "You understand I wouldn't ask you to do anything like this except for our mutual interest in the series." Hazelman hesitated an instant longer. "It involves a girl," he said, finally. He coughed and squirmed a little in his chair, as if the prospect of discussing the subject was making him distinctly uncomfortable.

Lieber hunched over the table, his eyes narrowing again, this time to the point where they were mere slits deep within the folds of fat on his round face. "A girl," he said softly.

"Yeah."

"And Mike Brady." It was a statement, not a question.

Hazelman lowered his gaze and nodded reluctantly.

"So what is this horseshit about ratings?" Lieber growled. "Why didn't you come right out—oh, wait, I get it. If Brady's in some kind of a jam the ratings are going to be hurt, is that it? Well, let me remind you of something, my friend. There is a good tough morals clause in this guy's contract, and I want to tell you, it's got teeth in it. I don't know what kind of a mess the great stud has got himself into, but I'll tell you the network is very sensitive about any shenanigans involving talent right now. I mean, they always are, but right now it's especially bad, with all the publicity going around about that Polack director fucking the kid. You know they just might throw that putz out of the country? And who could blame them?" The fat face jiggled with indignation. "The son of a bitch! If Brady's got himself into anything like that, I'm letting you know early on there's no way I can help."

Hazelman raised his hand, a pained expression on his tanned face. "Hey, Barry—what are you talking about? Hang on a minute, will you? Did I say Mike was in any kind of trouble? All I'm asking right now is for you to listen to the problem. Why jump to all these conclusions?"

Lieber opened his mouth and closed it again.

"Okay?" Hazelman said. "May I at least tell you?"

"So tell me," Lieber grated. "I'm all ears."

Hazelman shook his head, the model of reason and restraint beset by impetuosity. "I will if you'll let me."

Lieber's voice rose again. "Who's stopping you, for Christ's sake?"

"All right," Hazelman said. "Just listen."

"Okay."

When Hazelman began, his tone was that of a missionary teaching an aborigine to count. "What I'm asking you to help with is to get a girl into the show."

It was apparent that this was the last thing Lieber had expected to hear. His thick-lipped mouth fell open. "Get a girl into the show?"

"Right."

Lieber leaned forward, his frown of puzzlement deepening as he considered this. "What do you need my help for? You're the producer. You want some cunt in the show, you put her in. What's the big deal?"

"I told you," Hazelman answered patiently. "There isn't any."

The crafty look returned to Lieber's bloated features. "Who is she?"

"I don't know yet." The producer's blue eyes were all innocence.

"Then why do you want her?"

"Because I think introducing a strong new female appeal in the show would hype viewer interest, especially among women."

Barry Lieber sat back in his chair and exhaled slowly, as if his head were a balloon that had sprung a slow leak. "How do you figure that?"

Hazelman smiled. He had completely disarmed the program executive, just as he had planned. "I've studied the ratings," he explained. "And what they're telling me is something I think we ought to be paying attention to."

Lieber shrugged. "A thirty-eight share?"

"Sure," Hazelman said. "Great. But some of the other things are not so great."

"Yeah?" Lieber was not nearly so interested, now that the conversation had taken this unexpected turn. "Like what?" He sounded almost bored.

"Like in absolute numbers, 'City' is in good shape. But the audience profile is becoming a little too heavy on men. I think the time is exactly right to introduce a strong new female character. Not just an in-and-out part, but a major new role in the show. That way we achieve two things." He held up a finger. "One, we immediately begin to attract more women viewers." He raised a second finger. "Two, we inject new interest into the show *before* it starts to slide."

"What makes you think it's going to slide?"

"Hazelman's law. What goes up must come down. You know very well that applies to this series as much as to any other. Sooner or later, it'll slack off."

Lieber nodded. "Okay, true enough. Either that, or one of the other networks will knock it off."

"Exactly. That's why I want to stay one step ahead."

"And the problem with that," Lieber said shrewdly, "is Mike Brady."

Hazelman smiled. "Barry, you are a very wise man. Which is why I knew that you, more than anybody else, would understand and want to help."

"Yeah," Lieber's tone conveyed a marked lack of enthusiasm. "And when Mike hears about this, he'll shit."

The producer shook his head. "No, he won't. Not if the idea comes from you."

Lieber sat bolt upright. "From me?"

"Sure. You know he respects your judgment even more than mine. Coming from you, he'll swallow the idea without a peep."

"You think so?"

"Sure." Hazelman lowered his voice. "And Barry, I don't have to point out that giving the show a boost could be quite a feather in your cap."

"That's not important to me. All I really care about is keeping the series up there."

"Of course, I know that. But it couldn't hurt for you to get the credit." Hazelman watched the program executive's face as Lieber ruminated. He knew that Brady would indeed accept the idea if it came from Lieber, because Mike would believe it was actually coming from Peter Fried, whose judgment Mike respected, and to whose absolute authority even he had to defer. Hazelman also knew that Lieber would not refuse an opportunity to look important and possibly also win plaudits. If it didn't work, Lieber could always blame the whole thing on the producer.

"Okay," Lieber said magnanimously. "I'll handle it."

Hazelman beamed. "Somehow, I knew you would." He swallowed the dregs of his Bloody Mary and rose from the table. "How about another set, Barry? You want to get even?"

The fat man got up. "You're damn right I do."

They headed back toward the courts.

Gary Zander took Darla's arm and guided her across the Hazelmans' patio toward the bar. "Baby, I have never seen anybody look so falling-down gorgeous. What we need to do is have a drink together, so I can whisper obscene propositions in your ear."

Darla smiled. "I can't be sure, but I'd say you've already had one or two, Gary."

"You'd be wrong, sweetheart. What I've had is more like one or two hundred."

He got them drinks, a double Scotch for himself, a glass of white wine for Darla, and took her over to a sofa. "Here's the deal," he said. "You're going to star in my next series, which I'm going to shoot in New York. I figure we'll be on location there for about six months."

Darla laughed. She liked Gary, for all his boozing and his half-serious overtures. He was about fifty, tall and graying, and the lines in his face made him look interesting. "Sounds exciting."

"What, the series, or shacking up with me in New York?"

"Both."

"Thatta girl. We'll stay at the Park Lane. That's the only new hotel in New York. Only good one, too. All the others are collapsing from old age."

"Okay. And we'll go to the theater every night. I want to see every play on Broadway."

"Fantastic. And I'll introduce you to all my favorite joints. You ever spent much time there?"

Darla shook her head. "I've only been in New York twice. Both times on publicity trips I made with Mike for 'The Savage City.'"

"Uh-huh. Well, when you see it with me you're going to love it."

"I'll bet I will. How's 'The Public Defenders' doing?"

"Very well, for the third year. We just may have another 'Gunsmoke.'"

"Wouldn't that be great?"

"Not really," Gary said. "I'm already getting bored with the damned thing. That's why I want to produce a new one, starring you. But first we have to establish a meaningful relationship. Meaning I get into your pants."

Darla laughed. "You haven't even told me the premise. How do you know I even want to be in the show?"

"Oh, you'll like it, all right." Gary swallowed some Scotch. "You think I'm kidding, but I'm not. I have a goddamn great idea, and I'm going to shoot a pilot. We'll talk about it."

Brenda Hazelman began urging her guests to get to the buffet table, rounding them up from outside, anxious that they have plenty of time to eat before eight o'clock, when "The Savage City" would come on. Darla got a plate and sat with Gary. They were joined by Patty Detweiler, who was in the network news department at ABC. While they ate they talked about the fight that was going on between the East and West Coast factions of the Television Academy of Arts and Sciences. A little before eight, Dick Hazelman switched on the big color console at one end of the living room, and everyone moved close to the set, many of the guests sitting on the floor.

As the show came on, Darla looked around the room, but she didn't see Mike. There was another set in the pool house, she knew, and some people were watching there. She looked out across the pool, but she couldn't see him in that group, either. The doors of the pool house were wide open. Even at that distance she could clearly make out just about everybody in the room, but Mike was nowhere in sight. A sense of uneasiness came over her.

The opening action of "The Savage City" crackled into the living room, and people leaned forward, watching it intently. The night skyline of a huge city appeared on the screen, the towering buildings ablaze with light. Over the roar of traffic a siren wailed and a black sedan screeched around a corner on two wheels, with a police cruiser in hot pursuit. The cruiser took the turn too sharply and flipped over on its side, skidding along the street with a hideous shriek of tearing metal. As the black car roared away, a tall, powerfully built man stepped off the sidewalk, a submachine gun in his fists, and stood resolutely in the path of the fleeing vehicle. No flicker of emotion showed on Mike Brady's tough, square-jawed face as the car bore down on him, its lights glaring, its oncoming rush as inevitable as death. At the last possible moment, Brady calmly raised the automatic weapon and blasted the sedan with a stream of slugs. The car burst into flames and then exploded, its twisted, burning hulk coming to rest only a few feet from where he stood. For a few seconds the camera held on Brady's handsome face, the light from the flames flickering on the high cheekbones, the cold blue eyes. The titles came on, and were followed by two thirty-second commercials.

Darla continued to look around the room until she was absolutely sure that Mike was neither there nor in the pool house. She got to her feet quietly and left the group crowded around the television set, walking over to where stairs led up to the wide center hall that ran to the front of the house.

Don't be silly, she said to herself. He's probably in the john, or maybe having a private talk with somebody somewhere. Yet she went on, slowly walking up the stairs as if she had no control over her body. There were several rooms on the first floor: a formal living room, a library, and a study. They were empty. She could hear a clattering from the kitchen as the help went on with their work.

On the second floor, a half-dozen doors led off the hallway. Darla opened one and found herself in an empty bedroom. She turned and was about to leave the room when she heard a slight noise from beyond a door. She opened it and saw that it led into a bathroom. There was another door at the far end of the bathroom and it was slightly ajar. Darla heard the noise again, a muffled groaning. She stepped close to the door and looked through the opening into the room beyond.

It was another bedroom. In it was a huge double bed. Cathy Drake lay on her back on the bed, her legs in the air. Mike was on top of her, the muscles of his buttocks slowly contracting as he thrust into her. Cathy's eyes were closed, and with each of Mike's movements the soft groaning Darla had heard came from the girl's half-open mouth.

Darla felt as if a fist had slammed into her stomach. Her head swam, and she put a hand against the wall to steady herself. For a long, agonizing moment, she couldn't look away from the sight in the bedroom. It was like being locked in a nightmare, unable to wake up. Finally, she turned and stumbled blindly back into the hall and down the stairs.

Gary Zander was coming out of the lavatory in the downstairs hallway when he saw Darla. "Hey, what's going on—"

Darla buried her face against his chest, choking on her sobs.

"Darla, honey. What is it?" He put his arms around her.

"Just take me home, just take me home, Gary. Please."

He opened his mouth and closed it again. He led Darla through the hallway and out the front door to where his car was parked.

Chapter 7

On a gray Monday morning in February, a dozen people sat in the screening room at Baker & Barlowe's offices on Madison Avenue, drinking coffee and talking mostly about how they had spent the weekend. All of them were part of the account group assigned to the Superfresh Mouthwash business.

David Archer was the senior man present. As vice-president and management supervisor on Superfresh, he was one of the most important men in the agency, outranked only by the two principals, Robin Baker and George Barlowe. Archer was tall and gray-templed, his manner usually polished and urbane. This morning he was impatient. He glanced at his watch. Nine-thirty. "Come on," he said aloud. "Let's get this show on the road."

Tippy Harkness was sitting next to him. She was a copywriter, a slim brunette in her early thirties who made a point of dressing severely and never wearing makeup. "What's your hurry, David? It's a shitty day outside, and it's warm in here. If we're lucky, this meeting will last until lunch."

"Very funny," he said. "You may not have anything to do, but I have."

"Then go ahead and do it. I'll send you a memo on what was decided."

"Sure, Tippy. That would be helpful."

55

"If you want to know the truth, it would be." She sniffed. "All these people wasting time on a subject they're really not qualified to talk about."

Archer was mildly annoyed. "What do you mean, not qualified? Why aren't they?"

"Look around you," Tippy answered. "What do you see? More than half the people in this room are men. How do you expect them to have any intelligent opinions on a woman telling another woman how to take care of her mouth?"

"I don't know," he said defensively. "It's a matter of judgment."

"Exactly. And their judgment on an issue like this is worthless. In fact, it can even screw you up, mislead you more than give you guidance."

"Okay, so what do you suggest?"

"That's obvious. All you males get out of here and let the women come to a rational decision as to whether any of Ben's little honeys are right for this. If he ever shows up, that is."

"This is just a preliminary screening," Archer said. "We want to see whether we've got any really good possibilities to show the client. We're not going to put anybody on the air in the next ten minutes. You'll get plenty of female opinion and reaction if and when we get to the research."

"And who conducts that?"

"Strauss, of course." David nodded in the direction of a rotund, bearded man who sat to one side, reading from a stack of reports on his lap. "Something wrong there, too?"

"Same problem," Tippy replied. "More men manipulating information on women."

Archer sighed. "I swear, Tippy. You are the most militant libber in the place. Maybe in New York. Does Bella know about you?"

"She should," Tippy said. "I contributed enough to her congressional campaign."

The door opened and Ben Thompkins and his assistant, Debby Whitworth, walked into the room. Debby had sandy hair and an open, snubnosed face. She never wore anything but jeans and faded chambray work shirts. The daughter of an insurance executive in Philadelphia, she had gone to Bryn Mawr, where she had become what she called radicalized. She had come to New York hoping to work in some area of television or motion picture production, but could find nothing but this agency job. She considered it something of a sellout to the establishment, but at least it involved television, if only in something as scabby as commercials.

Ben was carrying a videotape cassette. "Morning, everybody," he said pleasantly. "Sorry to keep you waiting, but we have some interesting things to look at."

Joe Fanelli, head of the agency's art department, was sitting in the front of the room. "Maybe Harry Reems's latest?"

Ben ignored him. He held up the cassettes. "There are a total of fourteen girls on this tape. They all have nice smiles, and they all have good acting ability. So don't worry if you like somebody but she doesn't do the smoothest job of delivering lines here. If she turns out to be the girl who's finally chosen, you can be sure she has the talent to give us what we want when it comes down to shooting the actual commercial."

As Ben spoke, Debby Whitworth took a sheaf of papers handed her by Phil Strauss and began passing them out to the people in the room.

Don Thayer, the agency's creative director, looked at the questionnaire Debby gave him and groaned. "Oh, come on, Ben. What is this bullshit? We're taking exams now?"

Thompkins smiled patiently. "Nope, just a couple of simple questions about how you react to the girls you're going to see." He knew that what Thayer was actually expressing was resentment that this grading technique reduced all votes to the same value. A highly political man, Thayer was sensitive to any real or implied threat to his status.

"Don's right," Tippy said. "This is silly. Why don't we just look at the tape and discuss what we've seen?"

Ben looked over at Strauss. "Phil?"

The research director got to his feet and peered at the

group over thick horn-rimmed glasses. With his tiny nose and close-cropped beard, and his shiny-pink bald head, he looked cherubic, like a young Santa Claus. He cleared his throat. "We certainly will discuss what we're going to see." He smiled. "Endlessly, I'm sure. But before we do, I wanted to have an unbiased first impression from each of you. If you'll look at those sheets, you'll note that what we're asking is very simple. Mostly the questions have to do with the personality of each of the girls you're going to see. That and whether you think she's believable. Then we want you to rate each girl for beauty, for attractiveness. Finally, an overall vote."

"That's insulting," Tippy said.

Strauss looked mildly surprised. "To whom?"

"To those women, of course," she replied. "Whoever they are. We're treating them like prize heifers."

David Archer held up his hand. "Hey, look. Let's cut out the bitching and get this done. I'm sure Phil has a very good reason for wanting to proceed this way."

As they settled down, Thompkins inserted the cassette into the playback machine mounted under the large television monitor at the front of the room. "All right, can everybody see this? We're going to stop after each girl so that you can write your answers to the questions on her. After that we can have a free-for-all. Okay?" He punched the play button and a handwritten slate loomed up on the television screen, followed by the first model.

It took nearly an hour to get through the tape. When it was over, Ben's secretary collected the questionnaires and handed them to Strauss, who glanced through them and then turned the stack face-down.

"Hey, Phil," Joe Fanelli called out. "What happens to us if we pick the right one? Do we get to keep her?"

Strauss chuckled. "No, but I'm sure Dave would approve your expense account if you'd care to take her to Big Sur or someplace for further photography testing. Wouldn't you, Dave?"

Archer nodded impatiently. "Yes, sure. Any time.

Now what about it, Phil? I've got another meeting to get to."

"Okay, everybody," Strauss said. "Let's talk about what we've seen. Does anybody have a point of view on the people we've just looked at?"

Don Thayer cleared his throat. "I'll say one thing. I think Ben Thompkins is to be congratulated for having put together one of the best groups of choices I've ever seen. I think they're all really terrific. With one or two possible exceptions, any one of these girls would do just great in the new campaign."

Ben smiled. "Thanks, Don. I appreciate that." And I really do, he thought. Even though it's an obvious invitation for some mutual ass-kissing. You support my casting work, I support your department's copy and creative ideas. Then when the new commercials are shot, at least we have some solidarity in the ranks before the account management guys and the client start pissing on the finished work.

"Well, I'm not so sure," Tippy Harkness said. "I think most of these girls are too flashy to be believable. I mean, nobody really looks like that. They're much too beautiful—you know, too Hollywood-gorgeous."

"I don't agree, Tippy," Fanelli said. "I thought quite a few of them came off very well. I'll grant you they're pretty, sure. But what do you want us to do—put on an ugly girl? Then the commercials would say, Hey gals! If you want to be like this poor schlump, be sure you use Superfresh Mouthwash."

"That's an exaggeration," Tippy shot back. "I'm not saying we should use somebody who's ugly. What I am saying is that she should be believable. She should be the kind of person whose attractiveness is at least attainable. If the women in the audience can't identify with her, then what good is it?"

Paul Scott, the account executive on Superfresh, spoke up. He was young and good-looking, his dark hair stylishly long over his ears. "I think Tippy has a good point. We want a lovely girl, but not so fantastic that she turns people off. The consumer should say,

Gee! I wish I looked like that, and maybe if I used Superfresh I would."

Ben Thompkins wondered idly if the rumor that Paul was having an affair with Tippy were true.

"Okay," Don Thayer said. "I certainly agree with that, Paul. But wouldn't what you're saying apply to a good many of the girls we just saw?"

"Jesus, no," Tippy said. " I think the average woman at home watching a commercial with one of those models in it would say, Oh, the hell with it. I could never look like that, and so I'll use Scope or some other stuff."

Ben glanced at Don Thayer. The creative director's face was perfectly calm, but Ben knew that he was undoubtedly thinking about how pleasant it would be to strangle Tippy. Don was probably also thinking about getting her canned or at least moving her off Superfresh. Christ, women in business could be a pain in the ass. Especially gung-ho libbers like Tippy.

Marcia Gelb giggled. The TV traffic girl on the account, she was as homely as any girl in the agency, and was perhaps the homeliest. A persistent nosher, she ate potato chips and Fritos and crackers at her desk all day long. Her buttocks were the biggest part of her, threatening to burst the slacks she invariably wore. Her face was acne-pitted, and among the ancient craters fresh new pustules were constantly erupting. Her dyed hair was a bad color job and hung around her fat face in blonde, lank strands. But curiously enough, Marcia was always cheerful, as if she had fully accepted her lot in life, and wasn't the least bothered by it. "I'll tell you what I think," she said. "I mean, let's face it, I don't pretend that I'm any beauty." She joined in the ripple of laughter that went around the room. "But if I see a commercial with a girl like one of those, and she tells me I'm going to look like her if I buy the product, boy, I'll buy it. I mean, what have I got to lose?"

The laughter was louder this time. Tippy looked at Marcia with contempt.

"How about some specifics?" Phil Strauss asked. "Anybody care to comment on any particular girl?"

"I thought number four was dynamite," Joe Fanelli said. "What a set of jugs."

Debby Whitworth tapped her foot. "We're not peddling brassieres, Joe," she said derisively.

"So I see," the art director answered, looking at her shirt. Debby flushed and turned away.

"I thought number seven, I think it was, had a great smile," Paul Scott said.

David Archer nodded. "So did I. In fact, I thought she was excellent all around. But especially her teeth. You sure those are her own, Ben?"

Thompkins smiled. "I made damn sure they were, Dave. They're all home-grown, right in the lady's head."

"She's the one that also had the beautiful hair, right?" Don Thayer asked.

"That's the one," Ben answered.

"I think I've seen her in some kind of cosmetic commercial," Thayer said. "What's the brand?"

"Ranier Eye Makeup," somebody said.

"Oh, stop," Tippy groaned. "You can't all really be serious."

"What's the problem?" Strauss asked.

"The problem is," Tippy said harshly, "that you're all wetting your pants over the most preposterous looking ninny in that whole bunch. Her smile is a joke. And no matter what you say, Ben, I'm not at all sure those teeth are her own. You can be fooled, you know. To me, they're the phoniest looking things I've ever seen."

"I take it you don't care for her?" Strauss asked innocently.

"I think she's ridiculous," Tippy said flatly. "If you want my opinion as to which, if any, of these creatures might come across as remotely believable, I'd say it's number twelve. I think her name was Harris."

Several loud protests went up.

"Come on, Tippy," Fanelli said. "That was the pale girl—kind of a strawberry blonde?"

"Right," Tippy said.

"Christ." He shook his head. "I would rate her a dead last. A real nothing."

Tippy's eyes flashed. "And just how much Superfresh do you buy a year?"

"None," Fanelli replied.

"Precisely the point," Tippy said. "Men use mouthwash, too, but women are the ones in the house who *buy* it. A man will use any brand he happens to find in the bathroom. Which is why we've got to have a spokesperson acceptable to women. What men think is unimportant."

"Maybe so," Fanelli said doubtfully. "But I'll tell you one thing. If I did buy mouthwash, that broad couldn't sell it to me. What a stiff."

"You see?" Tippy looked at David Archer. "You see how foolish all this crap is? We sit around all morning listening to a bunch of men blabbering away with all kinds of dumb opinions and not one of them has any notion of what would be effective in talking to women. It's like asking me what I use for jock itch."

"Okay, Tippy," Fanelli said. "What do you use?"

Tippy opened her mouth, her face darkening with anger. But before she could speak, Ben Thompkins looked over at Marcia Gelb. "What do you think, Marcia? Which one—or ones—did you like? Anybody special?"

Marcia giggled. "Sure, that's easy. I thought number seven was heavenly. That's the one with the hair and the teeth, right? Wow, would I like to look like her."

"Think she was believable?" Ben asked quietly.

Marcia composed her face as she thought about the question. "You know," she said finally, "she really was. She just seemed to me to be kind of, well, nice. Like she wasn't pushy or a snob or anything, but she was just nice. I mean, I kind of liked her as a person."

There was a moment of quiet, and then Philip Strauss stood up. "Okay, everybody. That's about all we have time for. Thank you very much for your help."

"Hey," Fanelli said. "No fair. That's a copout. How did the voting come out?"

Strauss smiled. "Well, I still have to study the questionnaires thoroughly, but at this point it looks pretty clear to me what your preferences are. With one exception, everybody in the room voted for number seven as first choice." He looked at his notes. "The blonde girl with the big smile, Darla Dawson."

A cheer went up in the room. Tippy's mouth set in a grim line as she gathered up her things to leave.

Ben pulled the cassette out of the machine and looked at it. "Round one," he said.

Chapter 8

Over the next week, Philip Strauss directed a series of four panel discussions at a research company's offices in a shopping mall in Huntington, Long Island. Following standard practice in this type of research, which was constantly being carried on for various advertisers, interviewers approached shoppers on the street and asked if they'd like to participate in a study on oral hygiene. The ladies who were willing were then taken to a comfortable room where they were served coffee and pastry. A discussion ensued, led by a female psychologist who got them to talk about their attitudes toward mouthwash and advertising. The ladies were then shown the same tape that had been exposed to the Superfresh account group at Baker & Barlowe's offices in New York. There were no men present at any of these sessions, but Strauss observed from behind a two-way mirror in an adjoining room. In every one of the sessions, the women overwhelmingly voted for Darla Dawson as the most attractive and convincing of any of the models on the tape.

"It's phenomenal," Phil said to David Archer when he reported on the project. "I've never seen anything like it." They were sitting in David's office. "It's one thing to have a lot of agreement that a girl is beautiful, but to have all these women feel that the same girl is entirely believable is nothing short of amazing. Usually there's a resentment, an edge of mistrust. In this case there's almost none of that."

Archer toyed with a pencil, tapping it on his desk. "You sure, Phil? I mean, are you really sure you can count on that reaction as the same one that they'd have to seeing her on the air?"

"Absolutely," Strauss said quietly. "And besides, isn't she the same girl that almost everybody at the agency rated number one? That ought to tell you something. *You* voted for her, didn't you, Dave?"

Archer nodded. "Yes, I did. But I'm a hell of a lot more interested in how consumers react to her. They're the ones who buy the product."

"All right," Strauss replied. "Our total sample was about eighty women. In each of the discussions the way they felt was the same. For some reason, they *trust* this girl. They believe she's telling the truth. Even though they're hearing more than a dozen other girls telling them the same story on the same tape. Imagine the impact she'd have if she were in a fully produced commercial."

"Okay," David said. "Maybe that would work against her. Maybe the simplicity of this presentation is where the strength of it lies."

Strauss shook his head. "Not a chance. It's the girl they're reacting to. I've been doing this stuff for years, and I've never seen a better empathy between an audience and an actress. I think that when Ben puts together the real thing and she's perfect in the way she's presented, her hair just right and a completely smooth delivery, she'll come across like crazy."

David gazed out the window briefly. It was sleeting, a cold gray shower of ice crystals that swirled among the buildings along Madison Avenue and ticked against the glass. "Okay, let's hope to God you're right. The next step is the client, and if they don't like her, you can take your research and burn it. And then we start all over again."

Strauss smiled. "You mean if *he* doesn't like her, don't you?"

"Yes. That's exactly what I mean."

The Superfresh Corporation's headquarters were on the east side of Park Avenue at Fifty-seventh Street. Three floors high up in the building housed the company's administrative, sales, marketing, and financial departments. Manufacturing took place at a plant in Pennsylvania, but the decisions were all made here.

The group from the agency arrived at a few minutes before ten o'clock and set up for their meeting in the conference room. The place was large and quiet, tastefully furnished in muted tones of beige and brown. A bank of windows looked out to the north, and from this height you could see all the way across Central Park and beyond.

Ben Thompkins sat comfortably at the long conference table and lit a cigarette. It always amused him to observe the tension that seized the group when the president of the Superfresh Company was to attend a meeting. David Archer fiddled with a stack of papers. Paul Scott chatted nervously with Phil Strauss. Tippy Harkness made notes on a yellow pad.

At exactly ten o'clock, Stanley Brinker, Superfresh's advertising manager, and Al Monahan, the marketing director, walked into the room. A minute later, John Rawlson entered and everyone sprang to his feet.

"Sit down, sit down," Rawlson growled. The Superfresh president was a tall, muscular man in his late sixties. His hair was white, above ruddy skin and piercing blue eyes. It was said that nothing went on in the entire Superfresh organization that he didn't know about, and Ben believed it. In this day of companies run by committees and faceless organization men, it was astonishing to find this reversion to the time when one man truly ran the show. And John Rawlson ran his show, from top to bottom. In all questions, ranging from trade discounts to union negotiations to the purchase of raw materials, Rawlson made the decisions. He listened to the advice of his people, to be sure. And he had a large, extremely competent staff. But no plan, no idea, was put into motion without his okay, and nearly all of the fundamental strategies affecting where the company was going and what its goals were, originated with him.

The meeting began with a recap by David Archer of the agency's efforts to find a girl who would be featured in the new campaign. Archer spoke quickly and crisply. He knew from bitter experience that John Rawlson had little patience for beating around the bush. He described the criteria for the girl and then turned the meeting over to Strauss.

As Phil began to speak, John Rawlson raised his hand. "Wait a minute. Who actually did the looking for this girl?" His gaze fixed on Ben. "Did you?"

"Yes, sir," Ben said.

"All right," Rawlson went on, "how many girls did you look at?"

"About sixty, altogether—roughly half of them here in New York, the rest in California."

"The ones you found in New York we saw a tape of earlier, right?" Rawlson asked.

"Right," Ben answered. "None of them were acceptable."

Rawlson grunted. "You're damn right they weren't. Looked like they came off an assembly line. All skinny, all phony, all lousy. Now let's cut out all this crap. You got anybody in this batch who's really worth a damn?"

David Archer cleared his throat. "Mister Rawlson, the research we were about—"

"Yeah, yeah," Rawlson hushed him. "We'll hear all about the research later." He went on with Ben, holding him with the clear blue eyes. "What I want to know is, have you got anybody now who is really outstanding?"

Ben nodded. "I believe we do."

"All right," Rawlson said. "So put her on the machine and let's have a look."

The room was silent as Ben inserted the cassette and ran the tape down to where Darla was. When it was set, he punched up the picture.

John Rawlson's face showed no flicker of emotion as he watched the test commercial. When it was over, he was silent for a moment.

"Run it again," he commanded.

Ben rewound the tape and repeated it.

Rawlson sat back in his chair. "Young man," he said to Ben, "who is this Darla Dawson?"

Ben gave him a thumbnail description of Darla's background and experience. The older man listened intently, nodding occasionally as Ben spoke.

When Ben had finished, Rawlson looked around at the others in the room. They stared back at him, their expressions rapt, intense.

"All right," he said at last. "You want to know what I think? I think that what we have here is a personality that could be worth millions of dollars to the Superfresh Corporation. Of all the girls I've ever seen try to do a commercial, I never saw one come off like that. By God, you *believe* her. And you know why? Because she's sincere. She means it. She's nothing like those fakes who come on like some kind of carnival shill. When that girl talks, you know it's coming right out of her heart. And her smile is tremendous. Any girl in the world would want to have a smile that looked like that."

Rawlson paused, and the others looked at him expectantly. "There's just one thing. You say she's got a lot of ambition and wants to become a successful actress. Okay, I respect that. But I'll tell you something. This campaign is going to help her just as much as she's going to help us. Maybe more so. We put her face in every living room in this country and people are going to know who she is damn soon. So what happens when she's a big star and thinks she's too important to do commercials?"

David Archer leaned forward in his chair. "We'll see that our contract protects us, Mister Rawlson."

The blue eyes swung to Archer. "You will, huh? Well, let me tell you something. Contracts can be broken by any lawyer who knows his business. And if you don't know that, then you don't know *your* business."

Archer's face reddened.

Stanley Brinker spoke up. "Perhaps we ought to rethink it, Mister Rawlson—at least look at the other girls on the tape."

"Good idea," Monahan chimed in. "We just might save ourselves a hell of a lot of grief by going with somebody who wouldn't be quite so, well, prominent. Somebody who'd be easier to control in the long run. What do you think, Mister Rawlson?"

Rawlson looked at the marketing man for a long moment, then turned to Ben Thompkins. "I want you to sign this girl and sign her fast. The sooner you get her on the air, the better."

David Archer smiled broadly. "Just as soon as we can, Mister Rawlson." He looked over at Thompkins. "How about it, Ben?"

"Sure." Ben nodded. "We'll set her today."

John Rawlson slapped the table with an open hand. "Okay." He stood up. "That it?"

"Yes, sir," Archer replied.

As Rawlson started to leave the room, he looked back at Strauss. "What did the research say?"

"That she's terrific," Phil answered.

"Good," Rawlson said. "That's what I told you." He walked out and the meeting was over.

At one o'clock New York time, Ben Thompkins telephoned Betty Frolich on the Coast. Betty was delighted to learn the good news that Darla had won the Superfresh competition, but she really couldn't say when Darla would be available for shooting. As a matter of fact, she explained, nobody knew where Darla was. Yes, of course she knew how important the Superfresh campaign was, and yes, certainly she understood that this could be the biggest break in Darla's career, but damn it, she didn't know where Darla had gone, and neither did anyone else. She had left town and hadn't told anyone where she was going. No, not anyone. Not even her husband.

Chapter 9

Darla and Ted Walters drove north along California's coast highway in Ted's Porsche Targa. The top was open and the wind whipped and tangled Darla's hair, but she didn't care. She felt exhilarated and strangely free. The terrible pain she had experienced when she saw Mike making love to Cathy Drake was still there, but it had receded to a kind of numb ache, and she was able to cope with it, to push it off into a corner of her thoughts, to dominate it with the sense of expectation and excitement she felt now.

There had been no confrontation when Mike had come home that Sunday night. Darla had simply avoided him. She didn't trust herself to tell him what she had seen, to pour out her emotions to him. She sensed that if she did, it would be all over between them, forever. And for all the agony and anguish she felt, Darla couldn't bring herself to take that irrevocable step.

For the next few days Mike was sullen, uncommunicative, saying even less to her than he usually did. Darla sensed that it was because he knew something was wrong, but wasn't sure what it was, wasn't sure that she had found him out, and didn't want to give her the chance to accuse him if she had.

On Friday she had met Ted at the Racket Club, and

he had guessed immediately that a crisis of some kind had developed between her and Mike.

"Want to talk about it, Darla?"

She shook her head. "There's nothing to say, Ted. It's just something I have to work out myself."

They were sitting on a bench under a grove of trees. Ted twirled his racket in his hands. His tone was nonchalant. "Okay, I understand. But if there's any way I can help, just let me know."

"I will, Ted," Darla said. "I'm going to go away for a few days, get out of Los Angeles. I think that's the best thing for me to do right now."

Ted turned to her with a grin. "Sensational. It just happens that I don't have a thing doing at the moment. We'll go together."

Darla was taken aback. She hadn't really thought through what she intended to do, or where she might go. She only knew that she had to get away from here, maybe for a long time, and if it came right down to it, maybe for good. She had to get her thoughts together, get her emotions under control. Then she could decide what she really wanted to do with her life, what she really wanted to do about Mike. But where she would go and how, she simply had not yet come to grips with.

"Well, how about it?" Ted asked. "Don't tell me you've already had a better offer?"

Darla laughed. Crazy, irrepressible Ted. "No, you've given me the only proposition so far today."

"Then let's go," he said. "I'm not scheduled to go into competition again for a couple of weeks. We'd have as much time as you like."

"I don't know, Ted," Darla replied. "I've—never done anything like that." But Mike certainly has, she thought, so why the hell shouldn't I? And if I am going to go away with somebody, if I am going to go off and try to get my head together, wouldn't Ted be the perfect man to go with? She looked at his clean-cut boyish features and a quick thrill of excitement rushed through her. Her needs as a woman were strong, and denying them for so long had made this surge of emotion all the more powerful. Here was Ted, with his understanding and his easy laugh, and his hard young athlete's body. "What would you do if I said yes?"

He grinned. "Handstands. Now I'll tell you what you do. Go home and put together the lightest bag you can pack. The less you bring the more fun it will be. For the next few days you're not going to do anything but have a hell of a good time. I'll see you back here in exactly one hour."

Darla was wide-eyed. "An hour? But I—"

"An hour," Ted said firmly. "Let's go."

And they went. As Darla looked down now at the breakers pounding against the rocks far below them, she realized that Ted had known exactly what he was doing. She hadn't had time to think about whether the trip was right or wrong or anything else, beyond her first instinctive reaction. It felt great, and it was exciting, and here she was.

The drive itself was beautiful. It was a hazy California day, sunlight bathing the mountains in a golden glow. Ted drove fast, his strong brown hands flicking the Porsche around the tight curves and switchbacks of the narrow, winding road with the sure reflexes that had brought him world fame.

When they were just south of Carmel, Ted pulled off onto a side road that snaked up to the peak of a mountain. There was a tiny inn up there, perched like an eagle ready for flight. The view was fantastic. It seemed to Darla that she could look all the way across the Pacific, the lowering sun sparkling on its distant reaches.

The owner of the place was an old friend of Ted's, a retired tennis player, named Joe Blakelee. He was tall and deeply tanned, and wore a luxuriant black mustache. He and his wife did almost all the work themselves. She was a long-legged, smiling, sandy-haired girl he had met at a tournament in Sweden.

"Hey, man," Joe called out.

"What do you say, Blakelee?" Ted replied. "Meet Darla. Joe and Carol."

They shook hands.

"Joe used to play tennis," Ted said. "Until he got so

old he couldn't even lift a racket. I carried him, the last couple of years he was on the tour."

"Bullshit," Blakelee responded amiably. "The only thing wrong with me is my legs slowed down a little. I could still whip your ass, hothead."

"I may give you a chance to try," Ted said, "if you're properly respectful. Now where are you going to put us? I hope you threw everybody else out when you heard we were coming. I don't like having to mingle with the public."

Blakelee smoothed his mustache. "We got three other couples. One retired and two honeymoons. The retired never heard of you and the others are too busy to care."

Their room was the only one on the top floor of the inn. There was a feather bed, a balcony that looked over the ocean, and a tub in the bathroom that was a good four feet wide.

"Like it?" Ted smiled.

"Love it." Darla threw her arms around him. "Oh Ted, you were right. I'm so glad we came."

He kissed her, lightly at first, and then hungrily. She felt herself responding in a way she had never experienced, even with Mike. It was as if a door had been opened and all her pent-up emotions set loose. Within seconds, she felt herself growing hot and wet. Ted pulled off her sweater and jeans and a moment later his smooth, firm body was entwined with hers in the soft depths of the feather bed.

Darla closed her eyes. She felt transported. It was like floating in ecstasy, and she was aware of nothing but Ted and their bodies and the pleasure they were sharing. She held him in her arms, thrilling to his strength, her exictement taking her higher and higher. They made love for a long time, and when they were finally spent, Darla felt more at peace than she had for as long as she could remember. She dozed, with Ted's arms around her.

Suddenly she felt his hand pulling hers, and she opened her eyes to see him standing beside the bed.

"Come on, girl." He grinned. "I want to see if you're waterproof."

They lay side by side in the huge tub. Ted had filled it with hot water and mountains of suds.

"God, this feels good," he said. "Almost as good as you, but more sanitary."

"Ted! That's a terrible thing to say." She pushed suds into his face.

"Trouble is, I'm frank. People can't stand my total honesty."

"Trouble is, you're an idiot."

"Okay, I'm an honest idiot." He sighed contentedly and wiped the soap off his face. "I hope you stay mad at your goddamn husband forever."

"Hmm. You'd get bored with me, after a while."

"Who would?" He groped for her, under the water.

"Ted!" Darla shrieked. "Stop. For heaven's sake, you're insatiable."

"You're damn right I am. That's one of the major built-in benefits you get with an athlete. I am in absolutely perfect shape, so I never go soft. I'm in the *Guinness Book of World Records* as the longest living perpetual hard-on."

"Don't get too smug," Darla said. "I just might wear you down."

Ted looked at her with mock severity. "What's that? A challenge? Do I actually hear a challenge?" He climbed out of the tub and scooped Darla up in his arms and carried her giggling and protesting back to the bed, where they made love again, dripping wet, their bodies slippery and cool against each other. Ted took her now with a quick fierceness that made this totally different from their earlier lovemaking. This time, when he again lay beside her, she felt completely drained and completely content.

It was late in the evening by the time they got down to dinner. The northern California night had turned typically chilly, and Joe Blakelee had built a great roaring fire of fragrant cedar logs. The other guests had long since left the dining room.

Ted and Darla ate steaks voraciously, along with huge bowls of salad and hot homemade sourdough bread with sweet creamery butter.

Joe brought them bottles of Cabernet Sauvignon. "From Napa," he explained. "Just north of San Francisco. Best damn wine country in America. And some of the best in the world. This is made from exactly the same kind of grapes they make all the fancy Bordeaux wines from in France. I think this is better. All most Americans buy is the label anyhow. If it says France on it, they think it's good, even if it tastes lousy."

"This is delicious, Joe," Darla said. The wine was full-bodied and mellow, and its big, hearty flavor was a perfect counterpoint to the steak. Carol had cooked the meat on a grill over the open fire, charring it on the outside, leaving the thick, tender meat dripping rare on the inside.

Ted nodded toward Joe. "He's done a lot of research on gin, too," he said, his mouth full of steak. "In England. Wherever he played, he got to be an expert on the local sauce. Couldn't play tennis worth a shit, but he sure learned a hell of a lot about booze."

"Up yours, buddy," Joe countered mildly. "At least I paid some attention to where I was and tried to learn something about the country. You never knew where you were playing because the boos were the same everywhere."

Ted scowled. "You trying to suggest I'm unpopular?"

"People just like to ride Ted because he's so sure of himself," Darla interjected defensively.

Carol had stood near the table, listening quietly. "That's true," she added now. She sat down with them. "They like to see a winner, but they want him always to be humble." Her voice was low, and her speech carried the lilting rhythms of her native Sweden.

"That's people anywhere," Ted said. "And in any walk of life. Not just tennis. I don't care who you are or what you do. You're supposed to make it, all right, but for Christ's sake, don't let anybody know you think you're good, or right away they get pissed off at you.

It's the same in anything. Business, politics, anything." He looked at Darla. "Show business, too. You know who's a good example of that? Sinatra. I was a guest last year at his place in Palm Springs. We got to talking about this. He got into hassle after hassle because he was always cocksure of himself and he always said exactly what he thought. So what happened? The press got on him, and the fans got on him, and in the end it didn't mean a goddamn thing because he was still the best singer ever, and a good actor, too."

Joe Blakelee thrust his arms out and sang in an exaggerated, off-key baritone, "I did it my way."

They laughed, and Carol said, "You do it your way, too, don't you, Ted?"

"Always." Ted grinned. "So let 'em boo. Only time they don't is when I play that crazy Crumanski. Then they boo Crummy because he's an even bigger shit than I am."

"You guys ought to tour together," Joe said. "Crummy and Crappy, the boys you love to hate."

"You wait and see, Darla," Ted said. "When you're a big star, you'll run into the same thing."

"No, I won't," Darla said quietly. "I mean, I believe in myself now, and I believe I'm going to make it. A few days ago I was ready to quit." She looked at the others, a little surprised at herself by what she was saying, and a little embarrassed, but she went on. "I know now I'm not going to quit, not ever. No matter what happens. But when I do make it," she smiled widely, "I'll still be the most amazed person in the world."

They stayed up talking until long after midnight. When the fire had died to a bed of coals and the last of the wine had been drunk, Ted took Darla's hand and they said good night to Joe and Carol and climbed up to bed.

There was no suggestion of further lovemaking. Ted kissed Darla once and they fell asleep in each other's arms.

During the night a shutter banged in the wind and Darla awoke briefly. For a moment she thought she was lying beside Mike and then she remembered. She felt a twinge of guilt, a sense of regret. And then she knew that for all the bitterness, she was still in love with her husband. She dropped into a deep, untroubled sleep.

Chapter 10

During the next few days, Darla discovered muscles she didn't know she had. From early in the morning until late each night, Ted kept her on the go constantly, playing tennis, hiking up and down the mountain, walking on the beach.

And in his lovemaking, she learned, he truly was insatiable. He never seemed to get tired. Nor did he ever seem to run out of new things for them to try, new ways for them to delight each other.

"You like grass?" he asked one night.

"Sure, it's okay." Darla had never really cared about smoking it very much, but if it would please Ted, she was willing to go along.

"Good. I got some great stuff a friend of mine brought me from Central America. So strong it'll blow your brain right out through your noseholes."

Darla made a face. "Ugh! That's supposed to be good?"

"And how." Ted laughed. "It's dynamite. Wait till you try it."

He rolled two joints and they sat naked and crosslegged on the floor of their room, facing each other. They were in semidarkness, the only light coming through the partially opened bathroom door. Ted struck a match, touched the flame to her joint, and Darla inhaled deeply. She felt the high start almost before he finished lighting his own.

"Wow," she said. "That stuff really is strong."

Ted blew out a thick stream of smoke. "I told you it was. Makes that Mexican crap seem like Winstons."

"It's fun." Darla giggled.

Ted had brought an open bottle of chilled white wine and two glasses upstairs with them after dinner. He poured some now. "Here. This will keep your mouth from drying out from the pot."

Darla pretended to sigh. "You're so romantic." She sipped the wine and dragged again on her joint.

"Of course. Any bum could give you champagne and caviar."

"I don't like caviar. Too salty."

"And champagne?"

"I'm not crazy about that either. Never could understand what all the fuss was about. It's not much different from any other white wine, except for the bubbles."

"You ever try anything else? Other than grass, I mean."

"Oh, coke a few times."

"Like it?"

She shook her head. "It scares me. I mean, I liked the high—it made me feel all warm and nice. It was a lot different from grass. But I'm afraid of it. I really don't want to have it again. I guess that sounds very provincial, but I don't care. I know people who use it all the time and I think they're nuts. But that's not my business. I'm sure that on the other hand they think I'm a silly little square." She inhaled again, deeply. "How about you?"

Ted shrugged. "I guess I've tried just about everything, one time or another. But I never touch anything now except grass. And no booze except wine or beer. I've seen too many guys get fucked up on drugs or alcohol or both. It's not worth it."

"I guess we're just a couple of clean-living boy scouts," Darla said.

"Speak for yourself." Ted grinned. "I never had a clean thought in my life."

"I believe you." Darla laughed. "You must be the world's horniest tennis player."

Ted frowned. "How dare you slander me, ma'am? I'll have you know I'm the world's horniest *anything*. Being a tennis player is just a sideline, when I have time."

"When *do* you have time?" Darla jibed.

"Not very often," he replied. He looked at her. "Christ, but you're beautiful, Darla. You know that? Here we are living in sin and I've never even told you that before. But you are. I love the way every part of you looks. Not just your face and that pretty smile, but I love your body, too." His voice became hoarse. "I love those sweet tits and your good legs, and that cute little round ass."

Darla felt herself stirring as he spoke. God, this was marvelous. She was high as hell and enjoying herself tremendously, and she could feel the wetness starting between her legs. She had come to know what that rasp in his tone meant.

Ted crushed his roach in an ashtray. "Put that out. You'll burn your fingers," he whispered.

Darla laughed softly and dropped the remnant of her joint.

Ted pushed her backwards gently and she lay on the carpet. He crouched over her and lifted one of her feet and began to suck her toes, at the same time stroking her leg behind the knee with his fingernails.

Darla shivered as the sensation traveled upward. It was delicious, but maddening—an erotic tickle that made her squirm with desire. She felt his mouth move to the inside of her calf and then to her thigh, his tongue flickering.

She moaned and twisted and buried her fingers in his hair, urging him upward. Then suddenly he was licking her vagina, and she cried out as he fluttered his tongue softly into the warm, wet lips and she came in a frenzy, kicking and squirming, holding his head, the incredible tingling sensation surging out to every part of her body.

His tongue didn't stop. She felt it darting and flickering and she couldn't get her breath. Ted's hands lightly stroked her belly and her thighs and his mouth pressed against her and again the hot rush of orgasm swept over her.

Darla lost herself in a half-dream of sexual ecstasy, floating suspended in a state of pure rapture, dizzy with the intoxicating mixture of marijuana and wine and the insistent, relentless caressing of his tongue.

Then it was over and she lay trembling and panting, exhausted.

She must have slept for a time. When she awoke she knew where she was, but she had no idea how long she had lain with Ted beside her. She opened her eyes. He was gone and she felt cold. She looked around. The bathroom door opened and he smiled down at her. He had dressed in jeans and a heavy sweater.

"Ted in heaven's name, what—?"

"The night's young." He grinned and pulled her to her feet. "We're going out."

"Out? You must be crazy." She felt rubber-legged, as if she would fall if she tried to walk.

"You heard me. I know a bar not far from here. Come on, get dressed."

A neon sign said "Mario's." Ted eased the Porsche into the crowded parking lot and guided Darla into the roadhouse. The place was jam-packed with people, all young, and the noise was earsplitting. There was a tiny bandstand, and a rock group crouched on it, trying to blow the walls out with an avalanche of amplified sound from two guitars, a bass, a Rhodes piano, and drums.

Ted and Darla struggled toward the bar, and a tall, dark-haired girl grinned and made room for them. Ted ordered mugs of ice cold beer. They had to speak directly into each other's ears to be heard over the roar.

"I'm having a hell of a good time," Darla said. The drive in the cold night air had revived her.

"You like it?"

"Sure, but not just here. I mean the whole trip. It's like being away from everything in my life—like having a secret time-out that doesn't count. It's given me a chance to think, away from all the things I haven't been able to be objective about."

"Everybody needs that once in a while," Ted said. "You have to just get the hell out and blow off some of your frustration and stop worrying about all the bullshit that seems so important and really isn't."

Darla nodded. The beer was cold and delicious and soothing in her dry throat. "I'm never going to forget this, Ted."

He looked at her. "Neither am I. But stop sounding as if it's over. We just may take up permanent residence."

"Do you think you'll ever really do that, anywhere?"

"Settle down? Oh, sure, someday. When I'm rich as hell and can't play any more. On or off the court." He smiled.

"You already are rich," Darla said.

"Not really. I've made over a million bucks in competition, but taxes ate up a lot of it. The really big loot is yet to come. I'm nowhere near my peak as a player, and I'm just getting started with the endorsements and all that stuff. Tennis has only recently opened up as a big-money game, you know. Back when guys like Kramer or Gonzalez were up there the dough was nothing. But it's getting now so it pays as well as golf."

"How are you going to keep any more of it?"

"I'm forming a corporation. Or my lawyers are. Ted Walters Enterprises. Then most of the money, like the royalties and all that, will come into the corporation and I'll only get hit with capital-gains tax instead of ordinary income. And I can write off all kinds of expenses against it, too. I don't really understand it, but I sure as hell understand that I'll be able to hang onto more of my hard-earned bread."

"I can't blame you for that. It doesn't seem fair that you can make all that money and then you can't keep it."

Ted swallowed some beer. "You know, you ought to look into that too, Darla. Get yourself set up now and you'll have less to worry about later on."

Darla smiled. "It'll be a long time before I have to think about those problems, Ted. You know how much money I made last year? Counting everything, the TV parts I had, the commercial residuals, the whole thing? Just over twenty thousand dollars."

"Okay, so what? You still want to be ready when you hit it big. And you know something? When it does come, it'll come fast. All of a sudden you'll be up to your ass in dollar bills."

Darla laughed. "Sounds wonderful."

"Sure, I can see *Variety* now. 'Darla Hot Shit at B.O.'"

"Ted, you really are crazy."

"You ever want to be on the stage?"

She shook her head. "That would be pushing my luck too far. Movies are my goal."

"Who's your favorite actress?"

"Oh, I guess I admire Katherine Hepburn as much as anybody."

"She's an old lady, isn't she?"

"Sure she is," Darla replied. "But she's been on top forever, and she's just as great as she ever was. She can do anything, any kind of part, and she always has that tremendous control."

"You know her?"

"I've met her. I wish I had the talent she has just in her little finger."

"What kind of stuff would you like to do?"

"Well, I'd like to have parts where I'd play a smart, tough-minded career woman. You know, the kind of thing Faye Dunaway is so great at."

"She is great, isn't she?"

"Terrific. Of all the actresses in pictures today, I think she's the best."

"How about TV? Admire anybody there?"

Darla thought about his question. "Not really. I mean, the ones who really made it on TV are okay, but they're limited. Look at Mary Tyler Moore, for instance. I think she's very skillful as a comedienne, and everybody loves her, and she's been in her own show for years now. And yet she never made it in movies because there's only so much she can do, and you see it all pretty fast, right there on TV."

They closed the bar, and Ted drove down to the beach. He took a blanket from the back seat of the Porsche and they wrapped themselves in it and huddled together, watching the phosphorescent breakers crash and tumble onto the sand. After the cacophony in the roadhouse, the sound of the surf seemed distant and muffled.

"You know something?" Ted said. "This has been good for me, too, Darla."

"Well of course," she answered, teasing him. "You have to have a girl every three hours or you get a headache, right?"

He shook his head. "No, I mean it. Sure, I'm on top of the world and it's all a big gag and all that. But I hardly ever let anybody get close to me. Not the way you have. You don't just make me feel happy. It's something much more than that. You're so straight, Darla. You never try to fool me or twist me around. You don't have a whole bunch of hidden motives, the way everybody else I know seems to have."

He raised her chin and kissed her very gently. "I guess I'm trying to say I love you."

Darla touched his face with her fingertips. "I understand, Ted. You're really very dear."

He was silent for a moment. "What are you going to do about Mike?"

Darla had sensed the question was coming. She took a deep breath. "I don't know. Not just yet. All I do know is that I'm not going to give up. It's a battle I have to fight and nobody can do it for me. But I won't quit."

"Will you let me help you?"

"How?"

"Just by being part of your life—by always being there when you need me."

Darla felt an aching, deep inside her. "Ted, of course I will. What you've given me—what this week has meant—it's as if you saved my life."

They lay back, curled together under the blanket. Darla could feel Ted's warm breath against her cheek, and she suddenly felt very tired.

When she opened her eyes the sky was gray, and the rocks along the beach glistened in the predawn light. Gulls wheeled overhead, their shrill cries answering one another.

Darla and Ted got to their feet and stretched. She was cold and stiff. She hugged herself and shivered as she looked out at the sea. The water seemed almost black.

It's a new day, she thought. And time I went back to reality.

Ted picked up the blanket and shook it. "You hungry?"

She nodded, still shivering.

"Come on, I'll race you."

They ran through the sand, back toward the car.

Chapter 11

Betty Frolich struggled through the front doors of the Holloway Thomas Agency, her arms loaded with books, envelopes and an overstuffed Gucci attaché case. She said hello to the receptionist and took the elevator to her second-floor office.

The place was pandemonium, as always. But it seemed even more so on a Monday morning. Two phones were ringing at once, and her desk was a mound of paper. She dumped the load in her arms onto the rest of the mess and flopped into her chair.

Esther, her secretary, set a cup of coffee before her. "How was the weekend?"

"Too short," Betty sighed. "Or maybe too long, I don't know. The air conditioning in the house wasn't working. Christ, if it isn't one thing it's another." She picked up a handful of telephone messages. "What's the order of battle?"

"Take your pick," Esther answered. "They're all in the usual panic." She was a heavy-breasted, slinky brunette who wore her pants so tight they looked as if they'd been painted on.

"Which one's the worst?"

"Well, Jack Vogel called from K&N. He says the Verve Detergent people are having a shit fit because Adele Bianca turned up in a pornographic movie. They want to know what you're doing about it."

86

"What *I'm* doing about it? What the hell has it got to do with me? I didn't put her in any pornography. The thing was shot before she started doing commercials and I never knew anything about it. And anyhow, there's no morals clause in her contract. I couldn't care less who she fucks—on camera or off."

Esther shrugged. "Okay, next problem. McCann wants Jack Reardon for the new Buick series."

"No good." Betty swallowed some of the coffee. "Ford wants him too, and that's what I want him to do. It's more money, and the whole campaign will be shot before the Rams go to training camp. What is it nowadays? All the car companies are queer for football players. What else?"

"Ben Thompkins. He's howling about where is Darla Dawson."

"When did he call?"

"First thing this morning, just like he calls first thing every morning."

Betty grunted. "She'll show up, sooner or later."

"And what if she doesn't?"

"If she doesn't, I'll sell him somebody else. If there's one thing we've got a supply of, it's blondes."

"If he calls back, will you talk to him?"

"I guess so. Say, get Clark Davies on the phone, will you, at Y&R? I've got an idea for that coffee thing. And speaking of coffee, I could use another cup."

For the next two hours, Betty was never off the telephone for longer than five minutes at a time. She held the phone in her left hand while with her right she made notes and signed letters and held the mail she was reading.

A little before one, she was talking with Brent Jacobs of Benton & Bowles when Esther gave her the three buzzes that signaled urgent. Betty got rid of Jacobs and punched the intercom button.

"Darla on five," Esther said.

Betty took a deep breath and exhaled slowly before she took the call. Her voice became pleasant, relaxed. "Darla, honey. Where've you been?"

"Hi, Betty. Just away. I went up north for a few days to kind of unravel a few things."

"Everything okay?"

"Oh, sure. Maggie says you've been calling?"

"Yes. Some good news. You got the Superfresh Mouthwash job."

Darla whooped with delight. "Hey, now—that is good news. That's really good news. When do they shoot?"

"Oh, I haven't worked out the final details yet. I'll get all that stuff from them later. I just wanted to let you know first."

"Gee, Betty. I'm really thrilled. That could be terrific."

"It will be, honey, it will be."

"How's the money?"

"I don't know yet." Betty lowered her voice. "But I think I can get twenty-five thousand. Maybe better. But don't you worry about it. That's my job. You just have a nice afternoon. And stay around, will you, in case I need to talk with you?" Betty hung up and scratched her chin thoughtfully for a moment. Then she told Esther to call Jacobs back.

"Don't you want me to call Ben Thompkins in New York, first?"

"No. Wait for him to call us."

At two, Betty went out for a quick lunch. She was back in thirty minutes, and as she walked in Esther said, "Ralph Beyer just called. They want Margot Simmons for the beer thing."

Betty smiled. "Get him back for me."

When Esther buzzed her that Beyer was on, Betty picked up her phone. "Hi, Ralph. How's it going?"

"Okay. Esther told you we want to set Margot for Krause?"

"Yes. I think she'll be just great."

"Yeah, well, the Krause people are enthusiastic about it too."

"Good. They should be. At a hundred thousand, they got themselves some bargain."

"Sure. We think it's a good deal."

"Good? It's sensational. A major film star who's never even been willing to consider commercials before, and for that money? You're just lucky her tax situation is what it is or you couldn't touch her for anything like that."

"Uh-huh. We're going to want some publicity shots. Signing the contract, stuff like that."

"Sure. No problem."

"Could she come to Milwaukee for it?"

"Oh, gee, Ralph. I can't promise anything. I think it may have to be here. You know, Margot's never been involved in advertising. I think if you want to do something, we could arrange a nice press party here. Say somewhere like the Beverly Hills or the Century Plaza. It'd be a lot more impressive to the client, too, you know? I mean, they *are* dealing with a star, and not just some little nothing."

"Yeah," Beyer said. "I suppose you're right. I'll call you back."

Betty worked steadily through the afternoon. Just before five, Beyer called back to say that a press party in L.A. for Margot Simmons and the Krause Beer people sounded fine. Betty said she'd try to get Margot to agree and would let him know in a day or two. In the meantime the lawyers would be drawing up the contract. Shooting dates would be worked out at some future time.

A half-hour later, Ben Thompkins called.

"Hi, there," Betty greeted him. "Working a little late, aren't you? Must be past eight o'clock in New York."

Ben's voice crackled with exasperation. "Betty, where the hell is Darla Dawson?"

"Now, sweetie, don't get excited."

"Don't give me that sweetie shit. What's going on?"

"Well, Ben—frankly, I hate to do this to you."

"Do what, for Christ's sake?"

"It's Darla. I know you people had your hearts set on her and all that, but well, you really never did make a firm offer, you know, and—"

"What the hell are you talking about, Betty? Of course we were firm. What are you telling me?"

"Well, what I'm telling you is that Darla's up for something else, and you never did get down to the money and whatever deal you had for Superfresh."

Ben exploded. "How the fuck could we get down to talking money when you couldn't even locate her? Or is that it? You were just keeping her out of sight while you were dicking around with this other whatever it is?"

"Ben, it wasn't like that at all. She was up on this other thing long before you ever had her in for Superfresh. But hey, wait a minute. Your Superfresh thing—it's mouthwash, right?"

"Yes, of course."

"Well maybe there's no conflict. The other product is a toothpaste. Could that be okay?"

Ben groaned. "A toothpaste? Oh, shit. I don't believe this. Of course it's not okay. A toothpaste is a straight-out conflict. Who is it?"

"You know I can't tell you that, Ben. But listen. Darla's great and all, but she doesn't have the only beautiful smile in California. Holloway Thomas has lots of sensational girls you've never even seen. Why don't I get some sample tapes together for you and send them out right away by the night pouch to our New York office. They'd get them over to you by noon tomorrow."

"Betty, is Darla signed for this other thing?"

"Well, no, not signed. But it's all set. They're talking about shooting right away."

"Then what the hell is the difference between their deal and ours?"

"I'm afraid I don't follow that. What do you mean, deal?"

"I mean if they haven't signed her and we haven't signed her, we're even, aren't we? We're both in the same boat."

"Oh, I see what you mean. Well, sure, that's technically true, but ethically, I don't see how I could go back to them now and turn them down."

"Ethically? Jesus Christ. What about ethically with me? I told you a week ago we wanted her."

"Yes, but you didn't say what the deal was or anything. I still don't know what you're talking about."

"We're talking about a guarantee of thirty thousand a year."

"How many commercials?"

"At least two. Plus print."

"Ben, I'm sorry. But you're not in the same ball park."

"How much more is the other offer?"

"Well, it's more. I can't tell you exactly. You know I can't."

"But is it a lot more? I mean, let's not waste each other's time. If it's way out of our reach—"

"Oh, it's not that much more."

"How much? Five thousand more?"

"Um. That's a pretty fair guess."

"So you're telling me it's in the neighborhood of thirty-five thousand?"

"I'm not telling you anything, Ben. Let's just say your guess is pretty close."

"All right. Okay." There was a long pause. "Suppose we made you a really good firm offer right now. Say we absolutely guaranteed you forty thousand a year."

"Same deal? Two commercials?"

"Plus print."

"How much print?"

"Couple of shooting sessions. But unlimited use in magazines."

"Well, that does sound attractive. But Ben, what could I say to these people? You and I are friends and all, but—"

"But nothing. Have we got a deal, Betty?"

"Oh, God. You're really putting me on a spot, you know."

"Have we got a deal?"

"Well, I guess so."

"I have your word?"

"You—have my word."

"Now, goddamn it, Betty. I want to be positive there won't be any more screwing around."

"Ben, I promise."

"All right, we're agreed. And it's exclusive on all oral hygiene and cosmetic products."

"Ben! Who said anything about cosmetics? I can't shut her off from that category. Not unless you want to pay an additional ten thousand for that kind of exclusivity. And anyhow, she still has something running for Ranier."

"Yeah. Well, you can forget about any additional ten thousand. My ass is stuck out a mile at forty. Exclusive on oral products, then."

"Okay. Exclusive on oral products."

"And an option to renew at the end of the year for an increase of, say, ten thousand."

"No way. All we'll agree to is negotiation."

"Mm. All right."

"And the residuals at SAG double-scale to apply against the minimum."

"Sure. No sweat."

"Now about the print. Let's say she does the photography sessions for three thousand dollars a day, also to apply against the guaranteed minimum."

"Agreed."

"Ben, honestly. You've done all this so fast you've made my head spin. What am I going to tell these other people?"

"That's your problem, Betty."

"Oh, I know it is. But I feel just terrible about it."

"Uh-huh."

"When do you want to shoot?"

"Right away. Within the next few days."

"Where?"

"There. L.A."

"Location or studio?"

"Studio. Probably Hank Duncan, if he's available."

"Oh, good. He does nice work."

"Now listen, Betty. I'll be out there in a couple of days, but as far as I'm concerned, we positively have a deal. I still have to get some okays here, but I'm sure I can. Now, is that it?"

"Ben, dear. Of course. I've given you my word."

"All right, all right. I'll have a letter of agreement with me, spelling all this out."

"Fine. Our lawyers will look it over and I'm sure there won't be any problem."

"Okay. If it turns out there are any questions still hanging here, I'll call you tomorrow. Otherwise I'll see you before the end of the week."

"Wonderful, Ben."

He hung up. Betty put the phone down and sat back in her chair.

Esther buzzed. "Want me to try Margot Simmons now?"

"Yeah." Betty kicked off her shoes and was massaging her feet when Esther buzzed that Margot was on.

"Margot," Betty said brightly, "how are you, love?"

"Hell, I don't know. You tell me."

"How does a hundred thousand a year guarantee for the Krause Beer commercials sound?"

"Betty! No shit? A hundred thousand guaranteed?"

"You're all set, honey. It's definite. And I've talked them into a big whoopee press party here in L.A. when you sign the contract and all."

"Oh, wow. You have no idea what this means to me."

"I think I do," Betty said softly.

"God, this will take care of school bills, and get the IRS off my back, and God knows what all. Do you know that schmuck Michael is six months behind in alimony payments?"

"That's terrible."

"I'll say it is. But Betty, you are fantastic."

"I thought this might brighten your day."

"Brighten it? Christ, I thought I was ready for the old lady's home."

"Never say die, love."

"Betty?"

"Yes?"

"Thank you."

"Don't mention it. Talk to you as soon as I know more about the party and all."

When Betty hung up, Esther walked in. "She happy?"

"Delirious," Betty replied.

"How about Darla? Did you set her?"

"Uh-huh."

"How much?"

"Forty thousand."

"Hey, that's some deal."

"Yeah."

"While you were on with Thompkins, Vogel called again from K&N. The Verve people are going to sue."

"So? Let 'em sue. They can sue K&N. I should give a shit." Betty stood up.

"You leaving?" Esther asked.

Betty stretched. Her dress was rumpled, and there were dark crescents under each armpit. "I sure as hell am. I need a bath and a martini."

"Vogel said he'd call again. What should I tell him?"

Betty picked up her attaché case and headed for the door. "That I went to Chicago."

Chapter 12

Darla hung up the phone and danced around the living room and into the kitchen.

Maggie looked at her in astonishment. "Whatever happened to you?"

"Everything." Darla laughed. "Everything." She clapped her hands.

"You look like a little girl on Christmas morning."

"Sure. That's what I feel like. Maybe even a big girl on Christmas morning."

"You inherit a fortune?"

"Nope. I'm going to make one."

"How? You going to tell me what's going on?"

"Of course I am. Pour us some coffee and I'll tell you about it."

They sat at the kitchen table and Darla related to Maggie the details of the casting session for the Superfresh assignment, and then told her about Betty's call.

"How much you going to make?" Maggie asked.

"I don't know—a lot. Betty thinks she can get me as much as twenty-five thousand dollars."

Maggie arched her eyebrows. "Say now, that *is* a lot."

"It sure is," Darla said. "Mike won't think it's any big deal, and compared to what he makes, it isn't. But for me it is, and the exposure'll be great."

"The what?"

"The exposure. I'll be seen a lot," Darla explained. "And I'll be seen in the kind of commercials that'll get me noticed."

Maggie looked puzzled. "Why do you need commercials to get noticed? You're always going off to these casting things, ain't you? Don't the producers and those people see you then?"

"Oh yeah, but this is different. If I look good in these commercials, people will start to talk about me, and that's worth everything. Don't ask me why. It's just the way it works. I could go to a hundred casting sessions and I'd be just another face. But let them see me in the right kind of things on TV, and right away I start to be something special. Then they begin asking for me."

Maggie poured more coffee for them. "Then this really is a big thing for you, and not just for the money."

"I'll say it is." Darla hugged herself. "What a break." She thought about Betty's call again, relishing it. Her mind kept turning to telling Mike the news, wondering what he'd think about it.

Maggie sensed what she was thinking. "Mister Mike's going to be happy for you."

"Mm. I think he will. Maggie?"

"Yeah?"

"What—what happened while I was gone? Did he ask about me? You know, ask if I'd called?"

Maggie sipped her coffee. "He asked. Sure he did."

Something in Maggie's tone told Darla that the answer was merely perfunctory. "What did he say?"

Maggie put her cup down. "Now honey, I don't feel I should get into anything between you and your husband. It ain't my place, ain't my business."

Darla felt an uneasiness, a growing sense of anxiety. "Maggie?"

"Yeah?"

"I want to know."

The black woman sighed heavily. "All right. But for heaven's sake, you got to understand I ain't getting into no argument between you two. I ain't looking to be part of no trouble."

"Maggie, I know that. I just want to know what happened while I was away."

"He wasn't here," Maggie said. "He asked about you the first night when he came home, and I told him you went off for a few days to kind of think things over, just like you told me to say, and he, well, he kind of got mad and slammed around some. Then he took off. The only times I seen him since then is when he come in to get some fresh clothes and stuff like that."

"Did he—did he ask then, about me?"

Maggie shook her head. "No, honey. He didn't say nothing."

Darla felt her exhilaration turn to lead, a cold lump in her belly.

Maggie got up from the table. "I got some cleaning to do. Thanks for telling me all your nice news."

Darla nodded silently. Maggie left the room, and in a minute Darla heard the vacuum cleaner whirring in another part of the house. She poured herself another cup of coffee.

Shit. Here she was, right back where she'd started. Okay, so what did she expect him to do—sit home and suck his thumb? At least she didn't have to speculate any more about whether he was screwing around. She'd seen it for herself. So there wasn't much doubt about what he'd been doing while she was gone. He was shacked up with some sexpot someplace. And what had she been doing? Exactly the same thing, right? So what did she have to bitch about?

And yet, if Mike had been straight with her, if he hadn't treated her like a little fool, somebody who meant no more to him than a built-in convenience that he didn't ever have to think about or be nice to or worry over, then none of this would have happened. After all, she was human, she had feelings. How much was she supposed to take? And why wasn't she enough for Mike anyway? God knows she had turned Ted Walters on. In fact, she'd even surprised herself by the intensity of her feelings at times during the days they'd spent together. In some ways, she'd felt passion that was even stronger than she'd ever known with Mike. God, some of it had been wild. Wild and wonderful.

All right, now what? Were things suddenly so much different between Mike and herself? Of course not. The only differences were that now she knew for sure what she'd only speculated about earlier, and that now she had gotten even, after a fashion. She had taken revenge. But there was something else, too. In a crazy kind of way, having an affair with Ted had restored her self-respect. Instead of making her think less of herself, she felt more confident, more sure of her own identity. Instead of guilt, she felt pride. How could that be? It didn't make sense. It was completely opposed to the way she'd always thought about things. But it was exactly how she felt. An extremely attractive, highly desirable man had found her not only adequate, but so fulfilling that he'd fallen in love with her. And the knowledge made her feel marvelous.

Wouldn't that shake Mike up, if he knew? Well, he *wouldn't* know. *She* knew, and that was what counted. What's more, the fact that she knew about Mike's infidelity while he didn't know about hers gave her an advantage. In that respect she was more in control of the situation than he was. She knew the score, and he didn't. In fact, he didn't even know that *she* knew.

So what would she do about it? She'd fight like hell to keep him, that's what. And to turn their relationship into a real husband-and-wife partnership of the kind she deeply wanted. In just these few short days, two things had happened that had bolstered her ego enormously. One was the affair with Ted, and the other was the glorious news that she'd won the Superfresh assignment.

Well damn it, *she* had done those things. None of it was a fluke, it had all happened because she really *was* somebody special. She really *was* able to stand up for herself and win. And she could win with Mike, too. It wouldn't be easy, but she could do it.

Darla put her empty coffee cup into the sink. She suddenly felt elated again. She knew what to do, how to fight her battle. If she was going to win Mike, then she had to make her own moves, starting right now. She called out to Maggie.

The black woman poked her head into the kitchen. "You yelling to me?"

Darla smiled. "Yes, I was. How long has it been since you saw your sister?"

Maggie's expression was one of mild perplexity. "My sister? I don't know. Couple months, I guess. Why?"

"She lives in Long Beach, doesn't she?"

"Uh-huh. But why you asking?"

Darla's smile widened. "Because I think it would be nice if you paid her a visit, that's why. You could take the rest of the day off and go down and see her. Be back tomorrow morning, say."

Maggie's shining face broke into a broad grin. "Well, sure. Now I get it. You don't have to hit me over the head. You figure on a romantic evening, right? Just the two of you."

"That's exactly what I'm figuring on," Darla said. She was delighted with her plan. "Now you go ahead. Don't worry about anything that needs doing. Just go."

Maggie was out of the house in less than thirty minutes, carrying an overnight bag. She waved to Darla as she backed her Ford out of the driveway.

Darla sat down again at the kitchen table and made a list of things she needed. Then she telephoned Mike's answering service and left a message that she had returned and was expecting Mike for dinner at seven.

She drove down into Beverly Hills and stopped at a supermarket, a florist's, and a liquor store.

It was late afternoon by the time she got back home, and she whirled around the kitchen in a frenzy.

By six-thirty she had everything ready. One of Mike's very favorite dinners. Fresh asparagus vinaigrette, cracked crab with mustard sauce, a mushroom salad. And a bottle of Pinot Chardonnay. She set the table carefully. Pale peach-colored linen, her best Meissen china; tall candles in sterling candelabra; a centerpiece of double camellias, their blossoms almost startlingly white against the deep green leaves, their delicate fragrance filling the dining room.

She took a bath, rather than her customary shower. After brushing her teeth and combing out her hair, she looked over the bottles of perfume on the tray on the vanity and chose the bottle of Joy that Mike had given her for Christmas. She put just a touch behind her ears, at her throat, between her breasts, behind her knees. God, she thought, I'm as excited as I was when I was in high school, getting ready for a big date.

It wasn't necessary for her to debate with herself what to wear. She knew exactly the effect she wanted to create. She got out white silk lounging pajamas, as light and thin as gauze. She put them on, along with a pair of white ballet slippers. She wore no jewelry of any kind.

When she finished dressing, Darla stood in front of the mirrors in the bedroom. She had left the top three buttons of her shirt undone, and she noted with satisfaction that she could see shadows through the silk, created by her nipples and the patch between her legs. Her tan skin and masses of blonde hair created an extremely dramatic contrast against the silk. She smiled happily.

After one more check of the dining room, Darla went into the study and turned on the evening news. The room was on the side of the house beside the driveway, so she would hear Mike's car as he drove in. When the news ended at seven-thirty with no sign of him, she wasn't at all concerned. He was often late, and she had been careful to prepare a dinner that wouldn't spoil, one that could be made ready to serve within a few minutes' time. She curled up on the leather loveseat and watched with casual interest as "Hollywood Squares" came on.

After "Hollywood Squares," Darla watched Merv Griffin, whose guests were Buddy Hackett and some Latin singer she'd never heard of. With still no sign of Mike, she flipped back and forth between a pair of atrociously stupid situation comedies, until at nine "Hawaii Five-O" came on.

Darla was forever amazed at how permissive TV was getting. When she was a kid it was unheard of to see anything sexier on television than a kiss, or to find a show involving anything very daring in the way of subject matter. Today, in contrast, the networks seemed to be standing on their heads to portray themes and premises that were as outrageous as possible. When it came right down to it, sex was the most fascinating of all human activity.

And speaking of that, where the hell was Mike? She went into the kitchen and poured herself a Fresca over ice. At ten o'clock she watched a documentary about microbe research on Channel 28. It was the kind of subject matter that would help to keep her mind off her husband.

The eleven o'clock news came on with nothing more than a rehash of what she had seen at seven. Darla was about to turn the set off when she was startled to see Cathy Drake's face leering at her. It was a commercial for a new lipstick, and the sight of Cathy in a tight close-up, holding the lipstick's red tip against her moist, half-opened mouth sent pangs through Darla.

She was worried now. She walked into the living room and paced back and forth, wondering what Mike was doing and where he was. She couldn't get the picture of Cathy Drake's lips out of her mind.

Darla snapped her fingers. Maybe Mike hadn't gotten her message. She dialed his answering service again. Yes, he'd called in earlier in the evening and yes, he had been given her message. She put the phone down, feeling a little numb.

Back in the study an old movie had come on. Darla stared at it uncomprehendingly. Despite her anxieties, she dozed. She awoke with a start, feeling cramped and uncomfortable. The television set was still on. She looked over at the clock on the desk. A little past two. As she got up to turn off the TV, she heard a door close.

Mike was standing in the living room. Darla knew the instant she looked at him that he'd been drinking heavily. His face was flushed, and his body weaved almost imperceptibly as he stared at her.

"Mike," Darla said. She took a step toward him and stopped, suddenly no longer feeling so sure of herself.

His voice was a snarl. "Where the fuck have you been?"

Darla felt her mouth go dry. "I—was away. I left word with Maggie."

"I don't give a shit what word you left. I want to know where you were."

The room was very still. Darla could hear the sound of their breathing. "I was up north," she said. "I went away to do some thinking. I wanted to sort some things out for myself."

"What things?"

"Just—things. Some of my own problems." She was deliberately keeping her answers vague, and that, she knew, could send him into an even greater rage.

"Problems? What problems, for Christ's sake? You don't have any problems. I take care of things in this house. If something's on your mind, goddamn it, you come to me."

Darla was stunned. The sheer gall of this, after what she had seen that Sunday night at Hazelman's, was almost overwhelming. Her anger rose. "Come to *you*? What for, a pat on the head? Do you think I'm so stupid that I'm simply going to let you run my life the way you think it ought to be run? Do you really think I need this—a husband who's so damned involved with himself that he can't imagine I might have feelings and needs of my own?" As the words tumbled out, Darla's pent-up emotions broke loose, and her anger turned to fury. "You—you *bastard*."

Mike's jaw dropped. His right hand shot out and grabbed Darla's shirt-front and with his left he gave her a hard, open-handed slap across the face.

The blow sent Darla reeling back against the wall. Her thin silk shirt came away in his hand. She stood glaring at him, panting, her naked breasts heaving. The right side of her face was already swelling and she could taste blood in her mouth. She leaped at him, her arms flailing, a high-pitched scream rising in her throat.

Mike grabbed for Darla's hands, but before he could seize them she raked his face with her nails, leaving bloody streaks down one cheek. He pinned her arms to her sides and held her against his chest. "You little bitch." She tried to knee his groin, but he held her tight.

To her astonishment, Darla realized suddenly that he had become sexually aroused. She could feel his hard penis pressing against her. Fighting for breath, she stared at him, her violet-blue eyes blazing.

Mike carried Darla into the bedroom and threw her onto the bed. He pulled his clothes off and then with one violent motion, he tore the white silk pants from her body.

She kicked at him, but he straddled her, holding her down. Then he gripped her thighs in his powerful hands, forcing them apart.

Darla looked up at him, her breath coming in short, hot gasps. He seemed enormous, crouching over her. Involuntarily, her eyes went down his body. His cock was huge.

"Goddamn you," Mike hissed. He rammed into her, and Darla nearly fainted from the shock, the pain and the ecstasy that mingled together like some wild, uncontrollable force. He rode up on her, his hands beneath her, holding her open as he thrust into her.

Darla came, overcome by a rush of pure, animal passion. Then Mike's body convulsed and a groan rose from within his chest and she took his climax.

Mike rolled over and was asleep almost immediately. For a long time, Darla lay quietly in the dark, listening to him breathe, her eyes wide open.

She was exhausted and bruised and the side of her face stung. She thought about what had happened and a small smile turned the corners of her mouth. Somehow, she knew, she had won a victory.

Chapter 13

The call at Videocam Studios was for eight o'clock. The girl at the desk directed Darla to Studio Three, where she found the crew already at work, setting up lights and moving live potted trees and plants toward a platform that rose about a foot above the stage floor. Somebody yelled her name and she turned to see Hank Duncan striding toward her, a huge grin under his bushy mustache.

"Hey, babe!" He held her in a bear hug and kissed her. "You look sensational."

Darla laughed and wriggled free. "That tickles."

"It's supposed to," Hank said. "What the hell do you think I grew it for? Actually it's even more effective as a pussy bumper."

"I haven't seen you in over a year," Darla said. "We did that commercial for the exercise machine, do you remember?"

"Remember? Christ, how could I forget? What a ball-breaker that was. And then I hear the thing ran maybe twice and that was it."

"That's my life," Darla said.

"Not this time, honey. This time we're going to make *Love Story* in one thirty-second spot. You won't believe how great you're going to look. The agency and the client got here yesterday for preproduction and I'll say it right now, this one'll be a fucking smash."

"You really think so?"

"Absolutely. It's all you. Here, look at the board." He called to the script girl, who brought him a storyboard of the commercial. The drawings on it described the action in eight frames with the copy typed underneath each frame. He handed the board to Darla.

She studied the drawings and read through the copy. She looked up in surprise. "It's all in closeup."

"What do you think I'm telling you? The whole thing is one big luscious head shot. Just you with the product. And see, with the package on the whole time, I don't have to cut away from you for a shot of it. And look at the copy. Only fifty words or so." He pointed to the frames. "There's time for a big smile here, and one here at the end. And for this bit where you kind of flip your hair."

"That's terrific."

"And how it is. Usually they want to stuff the history of the company into the damned thing, but with this the pace will be nice and easy. You'll be fantastic."

"I hope so."

"Leave it to me, babe. I guarantee you America will cream when you pop into the living room."

Darla laughed. "That's an interesting picture."

"I'm telling you, it's guaranteed."

"Who's doing hair and makeup?"

"The best. We got Bobby Benbo on hair and Lee Merriwell for makeup."

Darla nodded. "That's fine. Are they here?"

"Here and waiting for you. Want some coffee first?"

"No thanks, I've had some."

Duncan pointed out Darla's dressing room to her and began a conference with the cameraman.

Benbo and Merriwell were sprawled in canvas chairs, half asleep, when Darla walked into her dressing room. They greeted her with yawns and struggled to their feet.

"Sorry to wake you up," Darla smiled.

Bobby shook his head. He had long, silky dark hair and delicate features. "God, I hate these early morning calls. It takes me forever to get going."

"Just be grateful we're not on location," Lee said.

"That's even worse. I did a 'Little House on the Prairie' last week and we were out stumbling around at six every morning." He was taller than the hairdresser and his features were coarser, but there was no mistaking his manner.

"Somehow the locations don't bother me as much," Bobby rejoined. "I guess it's the fresh air." He looked at Darla appraisingly. "How are you feeling?"

"Wonderful. I'm really in very good shape."

"You look great." He touched her hair. "Maybe just a bit dry. A conditioner will fix that."

Several bottles of Superfresh Mouthwash were sitting on the vanity counter. Darla picked one up and looked at the label. "This really is good stuff, you know. I've been using it for years. Seems funny to me now to think that I'll be doing commercials for it."

Lee held his fingers under Darla's chin and studied her face. "A little color," he said. "And maybe just a touch of work under the eyes." He smiled. "Really, Darla, for a nineteen-year-old you're holding up very well."

"Don't I wish," Darla said. She pulled her tee shirt over her head and tossed it aside. She felt no more self-conscious with these two than she would have in a dressing room filled with women. But for that matter, she never thought of them in terms of their sex. She merely accepted them for what they were, without thinking about it at all, pretty much as women always accepted homosexuals when they worked together. In fact, if she *had* thought about it, she would have realized that she preferred them to female makeup and hairdressing personnel. They were highly skilled, they had superb taste, and they were never the least bit bitchy.

Darla pinned a towel around her chest and sat down. Bobby washed her hair and treated it with a conditioner. Then he combed setting lotion through it, put it up in rollers, and moved a dryer into place.

At that point Lee Merriwell took over. He applied a base, and then used brushes to bring her color from its uniform tan to an effect that was more toward ivory, with just a hint of pink in the cheeks. He accented her eyebrows and brushed blue shadow onto the lids. After that he spent a long time under the eyes, getting rid of the tiny, almost invisible lines there. Then he cemented black lashes into place. Finally he worked on her lips, achieving an effect that looked moist and natural, as if she were wearing no lipstick, and yet with a smooth, sexy texture.

There was a knock on the door, and a girl with long, sandy hair thrust her head into the dressing room. "Hi, Darla," she said. "I'm Debby Whitworth from the agency. I'm Ben Thompkins's assistant. I need to get an affidavit from you."

Darla introduced Becky to Bobby and Lee, and signed three sets of affidavits testifying to the fact that she used Superfresh Mouthwash.

Debby then had Benbo sign as a witness. "It's a nuisance, I know," she apologized. "But you wouldn't believe what we have to go through nowadays. The networks are all scared shitless that the FTC might blow the whistle on somebody for a phony commercial."

Darla nodded. "I know. Didn't somebody put marbles in soup or something?"

"Yeah, big deal," Debby said. "They wanted to push the vegetables up to the surface so that they'd show on camera. But I could tell you dozens of stories like that."

"We've all worked on little bends in the rules," Merriwell said. "Personally, I think it's all a lot of hysterical nonsense. Sure, it's wrong to try to trick the audience into buying a fake, I'll grant you. But just getting an effect to make the product look good—I don't see anything wrong with that."

"Depends on what you do," Benbo said. "The toy people used to be the real charlatans. They'd show some piece of plastic junk doing things it could never do in a million years and the kids would see the commercial and scream for the toy, and then on Christmas morning, zilch. Nothing."

"But that's okay, that's different," Merriwell replied.

Darla was puzzled. "Why do you think that's okay?"

"It's educational," the makeup man explained. "The

children were being prepared for a lifetime of getting screwed."

They all laughed, and Darla made a face. "That's awful."

Thirty minutes later Bobby combed Darla's hair out. She was startled when she looked into the bank of mirrors and saw the transformation that had taken place. "Hey—you guys are magicians."

Benbo and Merriwell beamed. "You mean artists," Merriwell said.

The hairdresser tucked in a stray hair here and there and then sprayed Darla's head. He held up his hands. "Cinderella is ready for the ball."

Ben Thompkins was talking with Duncan and the lighting man when Darla walked out on to the set. He made a big fuss over her, remarking on how marvelous she looked, introducing her to Stanley Brinker, the Superfresh advertising manager, and to Tippy Harkness of the agency's copy department. Darla thought Tippy seemed a little cool, but she shrugged it off.

At Hank's instruction, Darla stepped up onto the platform and faced the camera. A narrow table had been built to chest height for her to lean on. A bottle of Superfresh was standing on the table. For the next half hour, Ben Thompkins, Duncan, the cameraman, and the lighting man worked on achieving an effect that would satisfy all of them.

"Something isn't right," Thompkins said. "You're getting some kind of funny bounce off her cheekbones."

The lighting man was an old hand. "I'll get rid of it," he said. "Trouble is, I got to have some fill or I'll get shadows on her forehead."

Hank squinted at Darla's face. "It has to come from underneath. The whole trick is to get the light coming from down there without anybody being aware of it. Makes her look ten years younger."

"Great," Darla said. "Turn 'em on."

Joe Malzone, the cameraman, moved back from the viewfinder and shook his head. "She's starting to look pretty good, but it's leaving the product in shadow. You'll never read the label, the way you got it now."

"You're going to have to hit the package separately," Hank said to the lighting man. "But soft. Use something small, or we'll get kicks off it."

"Let me have a look," Thompkins said. He climbed up onto the camera rig and leaned over the cameraman to peer into the viewfinder. He studied the image in the glass. "Hank, I think the greenery is too close. The color contrast with her hair is terrific, but I can see the leaves on the plants too clearly, and it looks phony."

"No sweat," the director replied. He instructed a prop man to move the potted plants and trees back a short distance, until they were just at the rear edge of the camera's depth-of-field.

"That's got it," Thompkins called.

When they were finally in agreement, Duncan explained to Darla how he wanted her to deliver the copy, and the points at which she was to smile, to move her hair, to pick up the product. It was past eleven before they were ready for the first take.

A teleprompter was mounted just above the camera lens. It rolled the copy into place silently, and its proximity to the lens made it impossible to tell from the finished tape that Darla had been reading her lines. Duncan called for a slate and Darla took a deep breath as the bell clanged and the red light on top of the camera went on, signifying that tape was running.

"Okay, honey," Duncan said quietly.

Darla looked at the copy on the teleprompter. "Hi. I'm Darla Dawson. A nice smile and a fresh breath can be big assets. You can have both when you use Superfresh Mouthwash." She paused for a broad smile. "I know, because I use Superfresh, and I love it. Superfresh makes me—my—oh, shit."

The crew laughed, and Ben Thompkins called out, "Hey, that's great copy, Darla."

Duncan smiled. "Okay, settle down, everybody. That was going fine, Darla. Slate, please. Take two."

After the fourth complete take they crowded around a portable monitor that stood on the stage floor and watched the playbacks. Each of the takes contained a number of flaws. Looking at them, Darla felt embarrassment and frustration. Christ, she thought, I look like a puppet. Stiff and wooden. And I sound so damned dumb.

Ben Thompkins put his arm around her. "Coming along, Darla. Few bumps and hitches here and there, but you'll get it. You look fabulous."

"Most important thing is to relax," Duncan said. "You've got plenty of time for a nice, easy delivery. These are running twenty-four, twenty-five. When you slow it down you'll do even better. But right now, let's break for lunch." Darla was surprised to see that the clock on the wall said twelve-thirty.

The studio had ordered in box lunches. Darla sat in a canvas chair and chatted with Ben Thompkins, Stanley Brinker and Tippy Harkness while she nibbled on a hard-boiled egg.

"Just imagine if they had to shoot features this way," Brinker was saying as he chewed his sandwich. "It would take five years to finish one. And the budgets. It boggles the mind. This day will run us about twenty thousand dollars for thirty seconds of finished commercial. Try translating that into a two-hour picture."

"And this is just one setup," Thompkins added. "With virtually no editing involved. Could have cost a lot more if it involved other scenes."

"What's the most expensive commercial you ever worked on, Ben?" Tippy asked.

Thompkins scratched his jaw. "Gee, I don't know. I guess the one we did for Hasenko last year." Hasenko was another B & B client, a Japanese watch manufacturer. "That ran just under a hundred thousand."

Brinker winced. "Why so much?"

"Oh Christ," Ben said. "It was one of those torture-test things. We dropped a watch from a helicopter in the path of a parade going up Fifth Avenue. The idea was that a marching band and a dancing bear and God knows what-all went tromping over the watch and look, everybody! The damned thing still runs."

"How long did it take to shoot?" Darla asked.

"We got it done in one day," Ben said. "But God, what a day."

"Darla, how long does it take to shoot a television show?" Stanley Brinker asked. "You know, an hour of some adventure series like 'The Savage City'?"

"Depends on how complicated the premise is," Darla answered. "But usually a week or so."

"Must be interesting," Tippy said innocently, "being married to a star."

"It is." Darla smiled. She wondered why Tippy had her claws out.

"Nice, too," Brinker said. "Both of you in the same business and all."

"Sure," Tippy added in a friendly tone. "Gives you something to talk about."

Ben smiled. "Don't pay any attention to Tippy. She thinks all ladies should wear overalls and work with pickaxes."

Oh, Darla thought. That explains it a little. Maybe she's a dyke, too.

"Okay, everybody," Duncan called. "We promised the client we'd finish by the weekend."

"Don't say that, even kidding," Brinker said.

The afternoon ran to thirty-two takes. There was a fluff, or Darla held the bottle wrong, or some hair was out of place, or she spoke her lines too quickly or too slowly, or there was a shine on her nose, or the sound man picked up studio noise, or Ben didn't like her delivery, or something. It was hard work, and nerve-wracking.

I will do it, Darla thought. And I will do it perfectly. As much as I feel like screaming and running out of here, I will do it.

At around four o'clock, Betty Frolich dropped in to see how it was going. She gave Darla the thumbs-up sign. Darla was beginning to feel very tired. Her legs ached, and the towel around her chest was wet. The heat from the lights was terrific. Lee Merriwell had to keep blotting the sweat from her face and repairing her makeup.

Shortly before six they all stood around the monitor once again, and Hank said very softly, "That, ladies and gentlemen, is one beautiful take."

Stanley Brinker nodded. There was excitement in his voice. "I like it."

"Like it?" Ben said. "Hell, I love it. It's fabulous. And man, does she grab you. What a reading."

"Run it again," Duncan said.

Darla tried to wipe all the previous takes out of her mind and to look at this one as objectively as possible. The commercial ran through again and she was amazed to see that it was not only technically flawless, but that her delivery had a quality of genuine sincerity.

"Perfect," Ben Thompkins said. "I'm telling you, it's absolutely perfect!" He was elated.

They played it back three more times, and after the last run even Tippy Harkness agreed that it was a beautiful job. There was an air of jubilation in the studio.

Hank Duncan held his hands over his head and yelled, "Thank you, everybody. That's a wrap."

Darla slumped in her chair in her dressing room and listened, exhausted but happy, as Betty raved about the commercial.

"I can't wait for this thing to start running," Betty said. "You look absolutely stunning. And your delivery comes across like crazy. Darla, I told you you'd be fantastic in this. It's really exactly right for you. Your hair, the smile—it's glorious."

Darla smiled. "Makes up, a little, for all the ones I didn't get."

"Of course it does," Betty said. "And not just a little. It makes up for everything."

"Whoever got the Pearl Soap job?" Darla asked. "Do you know?"

"Oh, gee," Betty said. "I did hear. Who was it, now? Um. Oh, I know. Cathy Drake."

Darla nodded. There goes some of the air out of my balloon, she thought. She no longer felt happy, only tired.

"Come on," Lee said. "Let's get that makeup off."

Chapter 14

The stuntman had played tackle with the Denver Broncos before two bad knees retired him from the NFL. He was a hair over six-feet-five and had stayed close to his playing weight of two-sixty. He came at Mike Brady with an iron bar, slashing viciously at Mike's head.

The bar missed by an inch as Mike ducked and rammed his left fist into the big man's belly and then landed a right on his jaw. The force of the second blow sent the man crashing through the window and out into the street, where he landed in a heap.

"Cut!" Rod Britney, the director, walked over to Mike. "Looked good. We'll print that." He turned back to the cameramen. "Okay for you, Charley? All right, everybody. Back in an hour."

"I'm still not happy with it," Mike said.

Britney shrugged. "We'll make another one after lunch, if you feel that strongly about it. Personally, I'm satisfied, and we're running a little behind."

"I don't give a shit," Mike said. "Go complain to Hazelman."

The director looked at Mike coolly. "Do me a favor, will you? I don't know what your bitch is with Hazelman, but keep me out of it."

Of course he did know. Everyone on the International lot knew that Brady was enraged because a female lead would be introduced into "The Savage City," and with

113

Hazelman's approval. The concept was that the girl would have the same kind of toughness that Mike possessed and would be more or less his female counterpart. Hers would not be a co-starring role, but almost. Brady had been infuriated by the idea from the moment Barry Lieber had brought it up, and the mere thought of it now was enough to send him into orbit. For days he had been angry and irritable, seizing upon any excuse to lash out at those around him. At this studio, as at all others, nothing was of greater interest than gossip involving a star, and Mike Brady was a constant subject of conversation. The topic of Mike's resistance to the idea of a girl lead in the series was currently the hot one, and Britney wanted to stay as far away from it as possible. He had a show to get out, a schedule to keep. If Brady wanted to be pissed off at the producer, fine. Let him be. But let him also not screw up Britney's work. "See you at two," he said. He picked up a clipboard and studied the scenes he had blocked for the afternoon's shooting.

As Mike walked off the set, the A.D. ran up to him. "Hey, Mike, Dick Hazelman said to remind you you're having lunch with him. He says he has someone he wants you to meet."

Mike nodded tersely. He went into his dressing room and washed his hands, leaving the makeup on his face.

Lunch with Hazelman, hm? The son of a bitch. This would be as good a time as any to tell the producer he could stick the whole idea of a female lead up his ass. Mike wasn't buying that bullshit about helping the show for one minute. And what really rankled, what really had him pissed, was his conviction that Hazelman had known about this and had even approved it, without ever saying a word to him.

And where the hell was his legal protection? Arnold Gross, his dumb schmuck of a lawyer, had had the gall to tell him that contractually he had no recourse. He had gone directly to Gross's office as soon as he'd had his first blowup with Hazelman on the subject.

"There's nothing in your contract about any female lead in the program," Gross had said. His slim, refined features and Harvard manners seemed slightly out of place in his lavish suite on Santa Monica Boulevard.

Mike glared at him. "Then why isn't there? You wrote the fucking thing, didn't you?"

"I did indeed," Gross answered. "Together with David Samuels. And as far as your interests are concerned, it's a good contract. But at the time it was written, who could have foreseen that anything like this would ever come up?"

"You could have, that's who," Mike snapped. "What the hell do I pay you for?"

Gross remained unruffled. "Now look, Mike. I'm a lawyer, not a fortuneteller. This agreement has you protected seven ways from Sunday. The idea of building an important female character into the series just happens to be one of those things—a totally unpredictable turn of events."

Mike snorted. "There must be something in that paper you could interpret as being violated."

"There may be," Gross replied. "I'll certainly see if it would be possible to come up with something. But there's one issue I would like to raise, if you think you might maintain some degree of calm while we discuss it."

"Yeah? What's that?"

"Well, frankly, I think Hazelman just may have a point. It's entirely possible that he's not trying to deceive you at all, but that this new character could stimulate a great amount of viewer interest, especially among women."

"Holy Christ," Brady growled. "Is Hazelman paying you too?"

"I'll ignore that, Mike," Gross said quietly. "What we're trying to have here is a rational discussion. At least, that's what I'm trying to have."

Mike waved a hand in disgust. "All right, all right. Go on with what you want to say."

"The point I'm exploring," Gross said, "is that in order to interfere with the introduction of this character, we would have to show that putting her on the air would do you harm. From a legal standpoint, that would be the only effective position we could take. And I have to tell you that under any circumstances, our chances of getting an injunction against her appearance would be pretty slim. But be that as it may, let's look at this from Hazelman's perspective. It really wouldn't make much sense for him to sanction something that would injure his own property. In many respects, he'd have as much to lose as you would. True?"

"Well, maybe," Mike conceded. "And maybe not, too."

"Oh, I think he would," the lawyer said. "Now, on the other hand, let's say that the theory is correct that the introduction of this new character would heighten audience interest in your series. Let's say that it did just that, and as a result, your show got a nice boost in the ratings and that they held at the higher level. Wouldn't that be a positive effect for both you and everyone connected with 'The Savage City'?"

Mike shrugged. "For God's sake, Arnold. The ratings aren't the only thing in the world I'm worried about."

The lawyer studied his client's face. "Then just what is it, Mike? What else concerns you?"

"Well, what the hell." Mike pointed a finger at the window. "There are a lot of people out there who are loyal to me. The show has built a damned good following, and of course I'm the drawing card. Sure, I'll grant you the stories are interesting, and that's part of what attracts people to watch it. Hell, I work on the creative concepts all the time, just to be sure that the quality stays up. But my character is the main reason the show's a success. What those people turn on to is not so much 'The Savage City'—it's Mike Brady."

The lawyer's face remained expressionless, but his eyes registered a flicker of understanding. "So you think this new female character might in some way damage your image?"

Mike brought his fist down on Gross's desk. "Exactly. How the hell do you think it would look to the world to have some cunt running around doing the same kind of stunts that I've made famous?"

Gross nodded slowly. "Or that have made you famous?"

"Either way." Mike shrugged impatiently. "The fact is that it would take all the balls out of the things I do, the things people watch the show for."

"Yes, I see." The lawyer looked out the window for a moment before his gaze returned to his client. "I realize how you feel, Mike. I really do. After all, your reputation is an extremely valuable commodity. But I must tell you that I think you may be overreacting to all this, just a bit. My advice to you would be to take it easy, cool off a little. Give yourself time to think about it as objectively as you can. Then let's get together and talk about it again."

Mike stood up. "Jesus Christ, Arnold. I have thought about it, plenty. And all you can tell me to do is stay cool?"

Gross smiled. "Well, at least give *me* time to think about it, will you? I want to study the contract further. I'll call you as soon as I have a clear view of what our course of action should be."

That had been a week ago, and Mike hadn't heard a goddamned word from Gross since. Well, fuck Hazelman. He'd make the son of a bitch wish he'd never had anything to do with this crazy idea. He strode into the commissary building and entered the private dining room.

Hazelman was sitting at the table when Mike walked in. He jumped to his feet. "Hi, Mike. Great to see you!"

Mike opened his mouth to snarl at the producer, and then closed it. He was surprised to see someone else sitting at the table, a girl he didn't know.

"I'd like you to meet Andrea Derringer," Hazelman said. The girl smiled and held out her hand.

Mike took it and stared at her. Even in this town, she was something special. Her eyes were large, and a kind of smoky gray color. The smile revealed even, very white teeth in a wide, full-lipped mouth. Her hair was chestnut, thick and curling just to her shoulders. There was an animal vitality about her that Mike sensed strongly.

"Sit down, Mike, sit down," Hazelman said. "Andrea here is the girl we've just signed for a part in the series. I thought it would be great if you two could meet."

Mike was stunned. This was the last thing in the world he had expected today.

"Actually, this lunch was Barry Lieber's idea," Hazelman went on. "But I was all for it. I invited Andrea over so we could have a private, informal chat. You know, no big deal, just give you a chance to tell her some of your own thoughts, maybe some advice on how her character ought to be developed." He turned to the girl. "You see, Mike isn't just an actor. He's actually the creative force behind his series. Most of the really important ideas come from him. Right, Mike?"

The question caught Mike off guard, still amazed at finding himself in this situation. "Yes, sure," he mumbled. "That is, I usually set the main directions we're going in."

"Wonderful," Andrea said. "I'd very much appreciate any suggestions you could give me." Her voice was low-pitched, rich in timbre. "I've watched your show so often I feel as if I know you. And if you'll forgive me, I'm just a little bit starstruck. I'm a real fan."

"Uh-huh, good. I'm glad you've enjoyed it." Mike noted that she was long-limbed, and very well built. Probably quite tall, standing up. "What have you been doing?"

"Oh, I'm new to California. Most of my work has been on and off Broadway and in summer stock. The only television I've done has been occasional parts in soap operas. But my agent knew Barry and got him to watch me in 'The New Day,' and Barry liked it and brought me out for an audition. And here I am."

Mike nodded. "So I see." The more he looked at her, the more he listened to her speak, the more impressed he was. His emotions had become a mixture of diminishing anger with Hazelman and growing admiration for this girl.

A waiter brought a tray of dishes into the dining room and began to serve them.

"Knowing you were shooting and wouldn't have much time, Mike, I took the liberty of ordering for us," Hazelman explained. "I hope everybody likes veal piccata, or I'm in trouble."

"Yeah, it's fine," Mike said absently. He continued to stare at Andrea.

"I don't know whether you caught the last episode of 'The Savage City,'" Hazelman said to her, "but that was entirely Mike's concept."

"Of course I did," she answered. She looked at Mike in open admiration. "That was all about the dope-smuggling operation. I thought it was brilliant. I had no idea it was your story as well. It's very rare, you know, to find a highly skilled actor who can conceptualize on that level."

Mike smiled. "We have a damned good team of writers. Actually, I simply head them in what I see as potentially a good direction, or else keep them from getting off the track."

"Don't let him kid you," Hazelman said. "The truth is that he has an almost uncanny knack for knowing what audiences want, and what turns them on. If he weren't so valuable as an actor, he'd make a hell of a program executive for a network."

As Hazelman prattled on about Mike's creative capabilities, Andrea listened with rapt attention, glancing over at Mike and smiling occasionally as she ate. Finally she put her fork down and said, "May I tell you something, Mike? Very seriously?" Her face wore a determined expression.

"Sure. What is it?"

"Well, I shouldn't admit this in front of Dick, but I'm very nervous about starting to shoot next week. In fact, I'm scared to death. Oh, I don't mean just about taking on this role, although I certainly understand very well the kind of pressure that's on me there, and what kind of an opportunity the show represents to me. But what really worries me more than anything else is the possibility that I may botch the character. I know that prob-

119

ably sounds silly to you, but it has me terribly concerned."

Mike found himself surprised by her candor. The day was turning out to be full of unexpected twists, he thought wryly. "Are you uncomfortable with the script?"

Andrea shook her head. "No, the script's fine. It's just that, well, I don't want the way I interpret the character to come off as too—masculine. Do you know what I mean?"

Mike thought about it. "Yeah, I think I do."

"I don't mean that she'd be dykey," Andrea said. "It's more a matter of her being too strong to have appeal as a woman. It just might be too much, might turn off the guys in the audience. What do you think?" There was genuine concern in her tone.

Mike chewed his veal slowly, mulling over the question. "I think it's entirely a matter of how you handle it. If you play the character with too much confidence, make her cocky and overbearing, you're probably going to get just the effect you don't want. On the other hand, if you keep her sort of humble, and even sweet, it could work fine for you."

Andrea nodded enthusiastically. "I get it. In other words, play her as being modest."

"Exactly," Mike said. "You could get a beautiful set of contrasts going there. The woman could be tough and intelligent—and yet she'd be sweet and feminine and even a little shy."

"Oh, Mike." Andrea's eyes were wide. "That's absolutely brilliant. I can see that totally. What you're suggesting would take what could be a flaw in the character and give it real strength."

"If you play it right, it could," Mike said.

"What did I tell you?" Hazelman beamed.

Andrea continued to look at Mike, excitement lighting her face. "You know, that could even make the detective work all the more dramatic."

"Of course," Mike said. "That's what I meant by the opportunity to make the most of the contrasts. Tough but sexy. And I don't think you'd have any trouble being sexy."

She broke into a wide grin, obviously pleased. "That's some compliment, coming from you. Especially because I'll confess to having felt a little jealous, sometimes, of all those marvelous girls you've always had in your show. Even though I'd never even met you."

"Andrea isn't kidding about being a fan," Hazelman said. "She's seen just about every episode of 'City.' "

"I don't thing there's one I've missed," she agreed.

They talked about various plot ideas for a few minutes, and then Hazelman said, "Hey, Mike. I hate to break this up, but it's after two." He smiled. "And nobody knows better than I do that time is money."

Mike shook hands with Andrea again. Her grip was warm and firm. "Good luck," he said.

She squeezed his hand. The gray eyes were inviting, her interest in him obvious. "Thanks, Mike. I hope somehow you'll know how much this has meant to me."

When Mike returned to the set, Britney scowled and made an exaggerated gesture of looking at his watch.

"Sorry, Rod," Mike said. "But listen, the fight shot is okay with me. If you're happy with it, let's keep the one we've got."

"Sure, I think it's fine." Britney's expression suggested that he was wondering how Hazelman had managed to defuse Brady. He picked up his clipboard and walked over to confer with the cameraman.

Chapter 15

Four people sat in the living room of Ted Walter's suite in the Sahara Hotel: Stan Lockridge, president of the UBS television network's sports department; Jack Mansfield, Ted's manager; Poppy Higgins, the girl Ted had brought to Las Vegas for the weekend; and Ted.

"What if the word gets out that you're paying him?" Mansfield addressed the question to Lockridge.

The television executive shrugged. "I don't think it will. And if it does, it just makes him look bad, not you or the network." He ran pudgy fingers through his curly, reddish-brown hair in a nervous gesture.

Mansfield frowned. He was heavyset, graying, a onetime ranked player. "How do you figure? The way I see it, a news story could slant it so that we all come out like assholes. The public thinks it's seeing a hundred-thousand-dollar, winner-take-all match. How are they going to feel if they find out it's rigged for Dumas to get fifty grand even if he loses?"

"So he lost his nerve," Lockridge said. "If he had any balls he would have stuck to the original deal anyway. Trouble is," he glanced at Ted, "he knows he can't win."

Ted wore slacks and an open-necked shirt, as usual. His bare feet were resting on the cool marble surface of the coffee table. "And that's why he *won't* win," he said. "Dumb fucking frog. What an attitude to take into a match."

"I don't see what's wrong with what he wants," Poppy said. Her strawberry-blonde hair was piled up on top of her head. She wore shorts and a halter that barely contained her full breasts. "Why should he play a big match on TV when if he loses, he doesn't get anything?"

Ted ignored her.

"I think you'd do better to make an announcement about it before the match," Mansfield said to Lockridge. "Instead of waiting for somebody to blow the whistle on you."

"Can't do that," Lockridge replied. "If it came out now it would call too much attention to it, make it look as if there might be something phony about the buildup, maybe even make people think the match was fixed. And on top of everything else, it could give the ratings a kick in the ass. Believe me, *that* I don't need."

"So what happens if it comes out later?" Mansfield asked.

Lockridge curled his lip derisively. "Later who gives a damn? I simply say we were forced into it by Dumas and it blows over. By then the match is old news anyhow and the public is interested in something else. Better it gets left alone."

Mansfield got up from his chair and stepped over to where liquor and mixers were set up on a sideboard. He poured tonic over ice and dropped a slice of lime into the glass. "Anybody want anything? Stan? Another drink?"

"No thanks," Lockridge said. "I'm fine."

"How do you think we'll do today for an audience?" Mansfield asked.

"Pretty good," Lockridge answered. "They got some snow in the East, so a lot of people will be spending Sunday afternoon at home."

The telephone rang, and Ted started involuntarily.

"I'll get it," Mansfield said. He answered it and looked over at Lockridge. "It's for you."

As the UBS Sports president got up to take the call, Ted reflected on how every time the phone rang these days, he thought it might be Darla. She had said she'd telephone, if she got a chance. Briefly, he thought about calling her, but dismissed the idea as being too chancy. Goddamn it, he thought, how did I go and get myself so flipped out? And if I had to flip, why the hell did she have to be married?

Lockridge finished his conversation and hung up. He returned to where the others were sitting. "I'm going to get on down there," he said. "Some things I want to go over with the crew."

"Okay, Stan," Mansfield said. "Let's talk some more later about Crumanski as the match after this one."

The television executive nodded. "Sure. If the ratings do what I think they'll do today, no reason we can't set that one for a lot more dough. As far as I'm concerned, the sky's the limit. And for that matter, the bigger the stakes, the bigger the audience." He waved a hand. "Good luck, Ted. See you all later."

Ted yawned and stretched. "Guess it's about that time." He got to his feet and walked into the bedroom. Poppy trailed along behind him. He put on a pair of loafers and then opened a dresser drawer and took out a shirt and fresh socks and jockey shorts to wear after the match. He dropped them into a lightweight leather bag, along with a portable electric hairdryer and a kit containing a toothbrush, toothpaste, and a can of antiperspirant. All the rest of his gear Mansfield took care of; it would be waiting for him in the locker room at the tennis club. He zipped up the bag.

"Ted?" Poppy's tone was plaintive.

"Yeah?"

"Was I—okay for you? You know."

"Sure, babe. You were great."

"No, I mean it. Really, Ted. You know I'm crazy about you. I'd do anything for you. But this weekend you were kind of, well, different. As if you weren't really interested."

"Yeah? Well, don't let it bother you. I got a lot of things on my mind. You were terrific."

Poppy moved close to him. "I know I'm not your steady girl or anything. And that's okay. I understand. It's just that when we are together, I want it to be good."

Ted looked at her. It was true. He hadn't been very interested. Just as he hadn't been interested when he'd slept with Patty Woolcut a few nights ago. All he could think of was Darla. Christ, it was driving him nuts. He'd thought that a weekend with a well-built, sexy broad like Poppy who really loved to ball would straighten him out, make him forget Darla. Instead, he'd thought about her constantly.

He put his arm around Poppy and patted her round, firm buttocks. "Don't worry about it, honey. You're the best." He kissed her lightly.

"If I didn't know you better," Poppy said, "I'd say you were in love."

Ted grinned. "Holy shit, don't I have enough trouble as it is?" He patted her again. "Hey, what do you say we have a little party after the reception tonight?"

Poppy smiled. "I'd love it."

The locker room of the Las Vegas Tennis Club was full of people when Ted arrived: sportswriters, club officials, members of the UBS crew, others Ted couldn't identify. He waved to Claude Dumas, who was sitting on a bench talking to a sports writer from the *Los Angeles Times*. The French star raised a hand in acknowledgement of Ted's wave, but his expression didn't change.

Fuck you too, Ted thought. He dressed quickly and brushed off questions from a couple of reporters. One of them he knew fairly well: Dave Crampton from *Sports Illustrated*.

"What's the matter, Ted, you uptight?" Crampton asked.

Ted smiled. "You know me better than that, Dave."

"Dumas says he's been studying your game, says he's spotted several weaknesses."

"Good. Should make the match more interesting."

"Are you that confident?"

"I'm always confident, going in. I think attitude is an extremely important part of the game." Ted's tone was serious, but he knew he was merely parrying Crampton's questions. He had learned the hard way to avoid saying anything a reporter could bend too far. As it was, he knew that writers would distort anything he said as much as possible. Simply being a well-mannered, polite young athlete was not the role they wanted to see him in. Dull people made dull copy, whereas the Ted Walters who was arrogant and snotty, who threw tantrums and insulted opponents, officials, and spectators—that was the man reporters loved.

Crampton knew this very well. He also knew his business. "If Dumas does beat you, do you think he should get the number-one ranking?

Ted snorted. "One match doesn't mean that much. He'd have to prove that he's a consistently better player than I am."

"Then you don't think this match is so important?"

Ted felt his anger rise, but he held himself in check. "I'm not saying any such thing. This is an extremely important match, between two of the top guys in tennis. Dumas would love to have my spot in the rankings and I don't blame him."

"But he shouldn't get it, even if he beats you today?"

Despite himself, Ted grimaced. "He's not going to beat me today. I'm going out there and whip his ass. There, goddamn it, is that what you were looking for?"

Crampton grinned. "It'll do. How do you feel about the winner meeting Crumanski in another—"

"I think I've shown I can handle Crumanski, too," Ted said. "Now if you'll excuse me, I'm going to play some tennis." He brushed by the reporter and walked out into the brilliant desert sunlight.

The stands were packed. Like that of most tennis clubs, the capacity here was limited, accommodating no more than a few thousand fans. But the home audience would be something else. UBS was anticipating around an eight rating, which would mean more than twelve million people. No wonder Lockridge was so willing to set purses in the hundreds of thousands of dollars, Ted thought. Why not? No skin off his ass, or the network's. The more audience, the more money commercial time would cost the advertisers. And if this match did as well as expected, Mansfield could really hit UBS for the next one. Compared to that, this hundred grand would be birdshit.

There was a wave of applause as the crowd spotted Ted. He grinned up at them, recognizing many friends and celebrities in the stands. Charlton Heston was there, and Andy Williams, both big tennis buffs. Ted waved to Jackie Smith, who was sitting at one end of the stadium, close to the rail, where the television cameras would be sure to pick her up often. She smiled and returned his wave. God, she was a beautiful girl.

He crossed to where Mansfield was sitting with Ted's equipment. As he did he glanced up again, and found that he was looking directly into Frank DiNero's face. The swarthy gambler was wearing dark glasses, but Ted knew that DiNero was staring at him. A flashy blonde showgirl was sitting on either side of him. DiNero nodded slightly, and Ted looked away.

Ted picked up a racket and inspected it, thinking as he did so of the conversation he'd had with DiNero on Friday night. He and Poppy Higgins and several other people had gone to the Flamingo to catch Cher's act. Later, they had been invited to a party at another table and DiNero had been with this group. Looking back, Ted realized the meeting had not been as casual as it might have seemed.

Ted found himself sitting next to DiNero. The gambler was wearing the ubiquitous dark glasses. With his slim mustache and thickly waving hair, he had a rather theatrical look. Ted wondered if he wore the glasses to bed.

"How you feeling?" DiNero asked pleasantly.

"Never better," Ted said. He had met the man on a couple of other occasions here in Vegas. As far as Ted was concerned, DiNero was just one more of the vast crowd of operators who were part of the scene. He'd heard the guy was mob-connected, but in this town, who wasn't?

"I'm looking forward to the match on Sunday," DiNero said. "Wouldn't miss it for the world."

"Good," Ted answered. "Seems to have stirred up a lot of attention."

DiNero smiled. "I'll say it has. You never would have thought it, would you, a few years ago? All of a sudden, boom. Terrific interest in the sport. You know, I'd say you probably had more to do with that than anybody, Ted."

"Oh, I don't know," Ted replied. "Guys like Rod Laver and Newcombe did an awful lot to get people involved."

"Sure, but you were the first young guy since Gonzalez to really turn people on. That makes a big difference, you know, your being such a kid and so good. You're more of a hero to the public than the Americans or any of those European guys."

Ted laughed. "A hero? Me? More like somebody they'd like to hit with a rock."

DiNero dismissed this with a flicking gesture of his hand. "Nah, not really. So you pop off once in a while. That just makes you human, like everybody else. And the betting has been terrific, which is another way to tell when an event has really grabbed everybody."

Ted nodded.

"The Greek has you at seven to five," DiNero said.

Ted looked at him. "That's not too much of an edge, I'd say." He was deliberately noncommittal. Was this guy going to pump him for inside betting information?

As if reading Ted's thought, DiNero smiled. "I already got money going on you, Ted," he said. "As far as I'm concerned, you're the best. When I bet on tennis, I bet on Ted Walters."

"Uh-huh." Ted was wary. He wondered where the conversation was leading.

"The papers say if you win Sunday it brings you to over three hundred thousand for the year, so far."

"Yeah, something like that."

"That makes two big winners," DiNero remarked. "You and the tax collector."

"Right," Ted said. "Me and my partner."

"Doesn't always have to be like that," DiNero said.

"Oh? How do you figure?"

A Scotch-on-the-rocks sat untouched on the table before DiNero. He raised the drink now to his lips and sipped it before answering. "You could have money deposited for you where no one would never know a thing about it."

Something told Ted that this would be a good point to cut off the discussion and get out of there, but his curiosity held him.

"Yeah? Where would that be? I thought the government had a pretty good fix on you, no matter where you were."

"I'm not talking about reported income," DiNero replied. "I'm talking about money deposited where nobody has any word on it at all. In a country like Liechtenstein, say."

"And how does it get there?" Ted asked. He knew he was getting in deeper, but he was fascinated. And what the hell, he told himself, it was only a conversation.

"It gets there when certain people put it there," DiNero said. "Let's say there's a big match, even a lot bigger than the one on Sunday. Let's say it has the fans all over the country even more worked up than they are now. And let's say the way that match comes out might be kind of a surprise, to a lot of people. For instance, the favorite might lose. Okay, and then some money gets deposited in that account in Liechtenstein." He sipped again briefly at his Scotch. "The money I'm talking about could be big. Over a million. It goes into an account with just a number on it. No name. And no record of it anywhere. But the account would belong to Ted Walters."

Ted took a deep breath and exhaled slowly. He looked around at the others at the table. Poppy was chattering animatedly with another girl, and the rest were all involved in conversations of their own.

"Maybe you ought to think about it," DiNero said.

129

"I already have thought about it," Ted said. "It sounds like a good thing for me to stay away from." He reached for Poppy's arm.

DiNero's face remained expressionless. "Maybe. If you don't like money. But if you do, there never could be an easier way to pick up a nice chunk of it, with nobody ever being the wiser. No trace, no record, nothing. Just you and more than a million bucks." He smiled. "Have a nice evening, Ted. If there's anything you ever need, just say the word."

Despite himself, Ted had thought about DiNero's offer several times over the weekend. Over a million in cash. That was nothing to just shrug off. And yet, Christ, what a crazy idea.

Ted stretched and swung his arms in circles over his head. He would serve first. He felt the way he always did just before a match started—like a coiled spring. He tossed the ball up and down lightly a few times, looking down the court at Dumas.

The Frenchman's face wore an expression of grim determination. All right, you asshole, Ted thought. I am going to run you right straight into the ground.

Chapter 16

Ted won the first game handily. He was a little on the cautious side, and very precise. After that he relaxed and played in his usual style, stepping into every shot and hitting the ball with all the force he could muster in his hard, lithe body. He concentrated on placing his shots, sending boomers down the line and into the corners with great accuracy, despite the velocity he was able to achieve. With each swing, an audible grunt expressed his exertion. He made no attempt at a change of pace, no effort to cross up Dumas with drop shots or top-spinning stuff. He merely played the kind of tennis he personally enjoyed most, slamming the ball as hard as he possibly could hit it, daring Dumas to stay with him in the blazing rallies.

The crowd loved it. The wiseguys and hecklers in the stands threw out the usual remarks, and to their delight, Ted answered them. He didn't lose his temper, and he kept his voice low enough so that the television microphones couldn't pick up his sallies. But when he missed a shot or lost a point, he exchanged a word or two with the sharpshooters in the audience.

"Hey, Walters, you blew it," a fat, redfaced man in a Hawaiian shirt called out when Ted double-faulted at service.

"Come on down and hit it for me, lard-ass," Ted responded.

131

A little later he overpowered what should have been an easy lob shot and it went out by a yard.

A big blonde in a low-cut sundress leaned forward. "Can't argue about that one," she taunted.

"I'd argue with you any time, baby," he answered with a grin, and the crowd applauded.

The set ended with Ted winning it, six to four. He could have made it more decisive if he'd been willing to play with more finesse, instead of simply pounding the French player into submission. But he wanted to play it his way, not merely to win, but to dominate the other man with his wide-open, cannoneering style.

Stan Lockridge watched the match on the monitors in the UBS mobile unit parked just outside the Las Vegas Tennis Club. Fred Berg, the show's producer, stood with him behind the director and the technicians who were crouched over the console.

"Fucking guy is unreal," Berg remarked.

Lockridge shifted his feet. "Yeah. He is that."

"Wonder if anybody could beat him."

"Oh sure," Lockridge said. "This guy Dumas could, on the right day. He has, a couple of times."

"No, I mean in a real showdown. If in one match there was an honest-to-God championship at stake. And a much bigger pile of dough." Like most of the top UBS sports personnel, Berg was a former jock himself, a onetime Bowdoin hockey player.

"Hell, no," Lockridge said. "Unless Walters had ptomaine poisoning and a broken leg. And even then he'd find a way to pull it out. There is nobody who hates to lose worse than that guy. Only reason he ever does is because he's also a stubborn bastard. Look at him now. Banging away like a madman, no matter what the situation."

"The Frenchman is okay, though, you know?" Berg said. "He really hangs in there."

Lockridge nodded. "It's the one way you can stay on the court with Walters. You just have to keep coming back to him."

In the second set, Dumas caught Ted several times with shots that just made it over the net, and with a couple of unexpectedly hard, perfectly placed service aces. Playing a deftly mixed, unpredictable game, he took the set five to seven.

Ted mopped his face with a towel and looked around the stands. He was in his element now. He felt strong and sure of himself, confident that he would handle Dumas in the third and decisive set. His shirt was completely soaked, and he thought he could feel the beginnings of a blister on his right heel.

"Flatten out your backhand," Mansfield said. "You're lifting it a little and it's losing some speed. That's why he's able to get to it."

Ted nodded. He swished water around his mouth and spat it out.

As he moved into position for the beginning of the third set, Ted put his hands on his hips and grinned broadly at Claude Dumas. The gesture was unmistakable and the crowd began to hoot. Ted could see Dumas react and he threw his head back and laughed. The French player's mouth was set in a grim line and his sweating face was flushed with anger.

The strategy worked. Several times during the set, Ted made derisive moves in Dumas's direction, and on each occasion the other man grew visibly more angry. He began to play Ted's game, hitting the ball as hard as possible in every exchange, growing careless and impatient. At one point on a questionable shot the linesman's call went against Dumas and Ted laughed and gave him the choke sign, fingers around the throat. Dumas spat out something in French and pounded his racket on the surface of the court. Ted imitated his actions and raised his voice in a falsetto parody of Dumas's French curses. Dumas then threw his racket down and shook his fist. He resumed the match only after the umpire had warned both men.

After that, Ted simply enjoyed himself and ran the match out, winning the set six to three. Dumas refused to shake hands and stomped off the court.

Inside the UBS mobile unit Stan Lockridge lit a cigarette. "Now who would you say won that match?"

Berg shook his head. "I'll tell you who lost it. Dumas just came apart and handed it to him."

"It's all part of the game," Lockridge said. "Walters psyched him right out of his shoes."

The producer smiled. "Maybe Dumas knew what he was doing when he insisted we'd have to pay him fifty thousand if he lost."

"Wrong," Lockridge said. "Walters knew what *he* was doing. Whether the Frenchman realized it or not, he went in thinking like a loser. But Walters went in like he always does. Ready to piss in the devil's eye if he had to. A winner all the way, bless his heart."

Berg looked at his boss questioningly.

"This will just pump up the audience for the next one," Lockridge explained. "The more people get furious at Ted Walters, the more I love him."

UBS gave a reception that evening at the Sands. There was a rock group and a lavish buffet, and the place was thronged with well-wishers who heaped praise on Ted Walters. He reveled in it, delighted with the match he'd played, feeling full of himself.

By that time Claude Dumas had long since cooled off, and could even smile sheepishly as Ted kidded him about the afternoon's play.

"You son of a bitch," Dumas said. His accent made the epithet sound comical. He was taller than Ted, handsome with his slim features and brown eyes. He wore his thick brown hair down to his shoulders.

"Don't get mad." Ted grinned. "Get even."

"I will," Dumas replied. "Sooner or later I am going to beat the living shit out of you."

"Terrific," Ted said. "Only make it later. Much later. Hey, try some of this shrimp. Fucking stuff is dynamite." He stuffed food into his mouth. As always, he was ravenous after a match.

Poppy Higgins linked her arm with Dumas's. "You were wonderful, Claude. Really. For a while there I thought you were going to win it." She pressed her full breasts against him.

134

"Hey, Claude," Ted said. "What are you doing later on tonight? You free?"

"I guess so. What do you want to do?"

"Maybe a little private party." Ted winked. "Okay?"

Poppy rubbed her breasts against Dumas's arm again. "I'll find a friend to bring along for you, Claude. Somebody real nice."

The Frenchman looked at her and grinned. "Sounds like fun."

During the next three hours Ted Walters shook hands with a U.S. senator, the governor of Nevada, an assortment of actors and actresses, motion picture and television executives, journalists, gamblers, showgirls, and sundry other admirers.

At a little after ten o'clock he gave Dumas the high sign and he and Claude and Poppy and the girl Poppy had invited to join them slipped out of the hotel and into a cab. The other girl's name was Candy. She was a tall, willowy brunette.

As soon as they reached Ted's suite in the Sahara, Poppy put the chain into place on the living room door. She turned on the stereo to a band pounding out acid rock. "First thing everybody has to do is get comfortable," she yelled. She pulled off her blouse and threw it high into the air. "Come on, Candy, you too."

Candy unbuttoned her top. Her breasts were not as large as Poppy's, but they were very firm. She smiled at Claude, who took her in his arms and bent over and began to suck one of her nipples. "Gee, this is a thrill for me." She beamed. "I'm a real tennis fan."

"Beautiful," Ted roared. "Claude is a real tit fan." He doubled over, laughing.

Poppy brought out a plastic envelope filled with carefully rolled cigarettes. She lit one and passed some around to the others. In a few minutes the room was filled with the heavy, slightly acrid reek of marijuana smoke.

"How about something to drink?" Claude asked. "You got any wine?"

"Sure we have," Poppy replied. She opened a wood-grained cabinet that contained a refrigerator and brought out a bottle of white wine. "What's anybody else want?" she called. "We got beer, brandy, champagne—anything."

"Oooh," Candy said. "Champagne. I love it."

Ted took a bottle of Piper Heidsieck from Poppy. "Permit me." He shook the bottle vigorously.

"Hey, don't do that!" Claude shouted. "Crazy bastard!"

Ted wrestled the cork out of the bottle. There was a loud pop as it came free, and a geyser of foam shot up, spraying Claude and Candy.

Ted held his thumb over the opening, squirting champagne in a fine mist.

"Be careful!" Candy shrieked. "You'll waste it!"

"Never," Ted yelled. "Waste not, want not." He gave the bottle another shake and put his free arm around Candy, holding her tight. He thrust the bottle under her skirt and released a jet of the wine upward. "There we go, madam—Doctor Walters's Super Douche. Guaranteed to make your pussy kissing sweet!"

Candy wriggled and went into a paroxysm of giggles. "Now look what you've done—I'm soaked."

Ted laughed. "Terrific. You know what they say. The wetter the better." He handed Candy the half-empty bottle of champagne. "Have a drink, honey."

Candy tilted the bottle upward and took several long swallows.

The stereo was now slamming out a slow disco beat. Poppy had begun to dance to the rhythm, moving her pelvis in and out in a series of suggestive bumps while she inhaled deeply on a joint. Ted moved over and began to dance with her.

"Hey, no fair," Poppy complained. "You're not in costume." She unbuttoned Ted's shirt and pulled it off as he continued to move in time with the music.

Ted grinned. "Don't stop."

Poppy smiled back at him. "I don't intend to." She unbuckled his belt and slowly unzipped his fly. She slid his pants down his undulating hips and Ted stepped out of them without missing a beat. Poppy repeated the process with his shorts.

Still dancing, Ted kicked off one loafer, then the other. The second flew across the room and sent a lamp crashing to the floor. "Bullseye!" he yelled.

Poppy laughed. "You win the golden goose." She poked an extended middle finger between his cheeks.

Ted turned and saw that Claude Dumas had taken off Candy's champagne-drenched skirt and pants and had pushed her down onto a sofa. He was kneeling in front of her, kissing her and fondling her breasts.

The sight of Candy's long, supple body turned Ted on. He stepped over to them and while Dumas continued to kiss the girl, Ted spread her legs and slid into her. "You don't mind, do you, pal?" he asked Dumas.

Candy groaned and began to move her hips in phase with Ted's slow gyrations.

"Hey, wait for me," Poppy pouted. "I don't want to be left out!" Squirming to get into position, she sat on the floor between the French player and the sofa and began to suck him.

Dumas pulled away from Candy, a stupefied look on his face. A low animal sound came up out of his chest. Poppy held the base of his penis in one hand as she continued to work on him. Dumas groaned and shuddered as he came.

Ted laughed. "That's the trouble with French athletes. All speed and no endurance."

The party lasted until early morning. Sometime after his fourth joint and his fifth or sixth glass of wine, Ted's consciousness of what was happening became a blur. He was aware only of a seemingly endless pattern of bodies uniting in outlandish combinations, of blasting rock music, and of laughing so hard his stomach muscles ached. The pot and the wine carried him higher and higher, until he felt detached from the scene, and even from his own body, as if he were sailing somewhere above them all, looking down on their hysterical revels and experiencing only a quiet amusement at the sight.

At around six o'clock, Ted staggered to his feet, vaguely aware that he had been asleep for a while. The stereo was still blaring. He turned it off and made his way into the bathroom and urinated. His heart was beating rapidly and he felt as if the top of his head was about to come off. He picked up the phone that hung on the wall beside the toilet and asked for room service.

Fifteen minutes later, Ted answered the knock on the door. He still felt terrible, but better than he had earlier. He stood naked and groggy while the waiter wheeled a table into the room.

"Where should I put it, sir?" the man asked.

"Right there is fine," Ted said. He picked his pants up off the floor and rooted around in them.

The waiter looked around at the carnage in the living room. Empty bottles and beer cans littered the floor. Here and there roaches had been ground out on the carpet, leaving a trail of marijuana crumbs and burns. Several chairs and lamps were overturned.

In one corner Claude Dumas and Candy lay curled up together, asleep. The French tennis star was lying on his back. His mouth was open, and he was snoring. Candy's head was nestled against his shoulder, one of her arms thrown across his chest.

Poppy was sprawled out on the sofa. She was also snoring, and from her slack mouth a thin chain of saliva ran down her chin.

Ted found a twenty-dollar bill and handed it to the waiter.

The man thanked Ted and gazed down at Poppy's lush body. His face remained blank, expressionless. "Have a nice day, sir." He bowed and left the room.

Ted forced scrambled eggs into his mouth. His head still hurt like hell. Through the window he could see the first rays of the sun streaking the desert sky. A picture of Darla's face came into his mind, and he felt the familiar sensation in his chest as he envisioned her as she had looked that last morning they were together, on the beach near Carmel. His gaze swept over the wreckage in the room, and his mouth curled in a faint smile. It didn't work, he thought. But I sure gave it some try.

Chapter 17

The man from A. C. Nielsen Company stood at the front of the Superfresh conference room and waited patiently for his audience to quiet down. Like all Nielsen representatives, he was well-dressed, poised, and articulate. His name was Harold Lake and he had been a member of the company nine years.

Lake was with the marketing division of Nielsen, which measured the retail sales of various products by conducting audits in a total of eighteen hundred stores across the United States. That is, Nielsen field personnel literally went into those stores on a regular basis and counted the pieces of a given brand that stood on the stores' shelves. They then counted the number of pieces in the storage rooms, and checked both figures against the stores' order books. The resultant information enabled Nielsen analysts to tell a manufacturer who engaged the research firm's services at what rate the manufacturer's products were selling to consumers, and how their sales measured up against those of the competition.

Unlike the more glamorous division of Nielsen that measured television audiences and published ratings on them, the marketing division was virtually unknown to the general public. But its work was vital to the planning and sales operations of some of the largest corporations in the world. The Superfresh Company paid

Nielsen one hundred and fifty thousand dollars annually for sales information on its mouthwash.

Lake smiled. "Gentlemen, I have our bimonthly report to make to you today, and I'm happy to tell you the news is good." He looked down the table at the expectant faces. Only John Rawlson seemed impassive. The others, Superfresh staff members and people from the advertising agency, leaned forward in their chairs, waiting for the figures he was about to present.

Lake turned on the overhead projector and placed a sheet on the machine's pickup table. As the chart flashed onto the screen, a murmur went around the room.

"As you can see," Lake said, "the Superfresh performance continues to be nothing less than remarkable. At the present time, we're pegging the mouthwash category, all brands, at three hundred million dollars a year in retail sales. Since our last report, the Superfresh brand has picked up another three full share points which brings it up to a twenty-one percent share of the category. Therefore, we find your brand presently selling at the rate of sixty-three million dollars a year."

There was another ripple of low-pitched talk around the room. The atmosphere had become charged with excitement.

Lake continued his report, illustrating the various aspects of the Superfresh sales situation with additional projected charts. "You'll note that the Superfresh brand is growing five times as fast as the category. That means, of course, that most of your sales increases are coming at the direct expense of other mouthwash manufacturers. In other words, you are clearly taking business away from them. People are switching from their brands to yours. And when you consider that the category includes brands like Listerine and Scope, we must conclude that your growth record is especially outstanding."

Lake was interrupted several times by questions and remarks from Bill Morgan, vice-president of sales for Superfresh. A bluff extrovert who had spent all his business life as a salesman, Morgan was also a shrewd analyst. He carried with him an almost encyclopedic knowledge of the health and beauty aids business, the category of goods including mouthwashes, shampoos, toothpastes, and various other products men and women used to help them look or feel or smell better.

Morgan shook his head. "I've never seen anything quite like it. Maybe that phony quiz show—what was it—'The Sixty-Four Thousand Dollar Question'? But this is different. The only thing we changed was the advertising, back eight months ago."

Stanley Brinker turned to him. "What do you mean, 'the only thing,' Bill?" The advertising manager smiled. "What we did was to put into action the most effective new campaign in the entire business. And what Harold is showing us is how well it's working."

Lake nodded assent. "It's clearly indicated that the advertising has been the key factor in helping the product to take off. Prior to the introduction of your new campaign, the brand was on a sales plateau, and had more or less shown only slight growth over the previous year."

The meeting went on for another half-hour, while Morgan mulled over details of sales performance in various markets, and others among the group asked the Nielsen man further questions. At the conclusion of the discussion, Lake thanked them all for their attention, packed up his material, and left the room.

When Lake had gone, Brinker looked at the others around the conference table. "I think the agency is to be congratulated for having done a hell of a fine job."

He was answered by expressions of agreement.

"It was a team effort," David Archer said modestly. He had been around the agency business long enough to know better than to take too large a share of the credit, no matter how importantly the advertising might have contributed to Superfresh's present success.

Bill Morgan shifted in his chair. "Now the question is, where do we go from here?"

Al Monahan, the Superfresh marketing director, leaned forward. His bald head contributed to, rather than detracted from, his air of vigor and purpose. He extended a long index finger and touched its tip to the table. "Right now is the time to pour it on. I think you people at the agency should study these new Nielsen figures and come back to us as soon as possible with a recommendation for increased spending. We also ought to be looking at new creative ideas."

"Absolutely," Brinker said. "The fact is that we have got ourselves a cannon, and this is when we should fire it off."

David Archer cleared his throat. "We're already at work on new creative material, which we're scheduled to have ready to show you at the beginning of next week." He looked at Paul Scott, the B & B account executive on Superfresh. "Paul, perhaps you'd like to describe the direction we're taking for the new concept."

Scott swept thick, dark hair back from his forehead. He was obviously proud of his deep voice. "What we're working on is an exciting new idea. It would feature Darla Dawson in a variety of settings. She'd be shown running on the beach, or riding a horse, diving into a pool—doing all the things that an active young woman does these days. We're also going to show her in some romantic situations, such as on the deck of a sailboat with a handsome guy. Naturally, in each instance, her attractiveness is the result of using Superfresh."

"Sounds interesting," Bill Morgan remarked.

"And expensive," Brinker added. He looked at Paul Scott. "Do you have any idea what it would cost to produce commercials of that type? The stuff would be all location, wouldn't it?"

Scott leaned forward. "Yes, it would. And you're right that this kind of production doesn't come cheap. What exactly the new commercials would cost we can't say at this point, but they'd be in the vicinity of forty thousand apiece."

"Okay," Brinker said. "What about print?"

"We'll also have layouts for new ads featuring Darla, and a magazine schedule to present," Scott replied.

"What are the books we're in now?" Morgan asked.

Archer snapped open his attaché case and withdrew a media schedule. He read from it. *"Cosmo, McCall's,*

Good House, Mademoiselle, Redbook, the Journal. All four-color pages."

"That needs some rethinking too," Brinker said. "We ought to expand the list to include more younger books like *Glamour* and *Seventeen*. Christ, you wouldn't believe the mail we're getting. It's coming in by the sackful, and most of it from kids."

"That figures," Monahan said. "The younger girls are especially turned on by Darla. And that's good, because TGI research data shows they're an increasingly important factor in this market."

Morgan held up a hand. "Let's not get carried away," he warned. "Younger women, sure. Kids, no. You can get your tit in a wringer when you put too much effort into teenagers; they're too fickle. That's why there are so many short-lived brands. A product will take off like a rocket and then fizzle. Why? Because kids were buying it, until something else caught their eye. Kids will listen to whoever talked to them last. Any kind of a nutty idea can catch hold, and for awhile, it's hot. Hell, I remember Stripe Toothpaste, and all those chlorophyll brands that were supposed to cure bad breath from the inside out, chemically. What nonsense. The trouble is, most of those things are nothing but fads. Junk products, and junk business."

Al Monahan pursed his lips. "Okay, Bill. You're right. But I'm not suggesting we position Superfresh strictly against kids. I agree with you that would be suicide. All I'm saying is that we shouldn't neglect the younger end of the market, which I think we have to some extent, up until now."

He tapped his index finger on the table. "I won't hold you to this, Dave, but just off the top of your head, what would you estimate these Nielsen figures suggest we could set as a new budget level?"

Archer shifted in his chair. "I wouldn't want to say, without a careful study of the numbers, Al."

The marketing director raised his eyebrows. "Not even a guess? All I'm looking for is some guidelines." He swung his gaze over to Paul Scott. "How about you, Paul? Could you give us some idea?"

The younger man hesitated for an instant. He reached into his case and produced a pocket calculator, which he placed on the table before him. "This would be strictly ballpark, of course."

Monahan nodded. "Understood."

Scott punched at the buttons on the calculator. He looked up. "Assuming we would continue to spend at the same advertising to sales ratio, I would say that we should be moving up to a budget of ten million dollars a year."

David Archer felt sweat trickle from his armpits and run down his sides. Son of a bitch. Scott had popped off without having had a discussion on brand strategy back at the agency, and he had also made Archer look bad. So what's new? he thought. Scott would love to have my job. He's just lining up his guns.

Monahan leaned forward. "Ten million, hm? Good. I would say that would give us some clout."

Throughout the discussion, Archer noticed, John Rawlson had remained silent, as he often did. The old man's face was immobile, the cold blue eyes unreadable.

"Okay," Monahan said. "You'll be getting back to us at the beginning of the week. I guess that about concludes the discussion for today. Unless you have anything to add, Mister Rawlson?"

Everyone in the room looked at the president of the company. He returned their stares, his level gaze moving slowly across their faces. "Yeah, I have a couple of things to say."

Okay, Archer thought, here it comes. Now we'll find out what the state of the world really is.

"Some of what you say makes sense," John Rawlson said. "And some of it doesn't. Let's start with the budget. A little while ago, we heard this fellow from Neilsen tell us we have a little over twenty percent of the mouthwash market in the United States. Why shouldn't we have thirty percent? Or forty? Or more? We make the best product in the field, so why not?"

Monahan had reddened slightly as John Rawlson was speaking. "We were only trying to be prudent in our planning, Mr. Rawlson. We can't expect to hold this trend forever, and after all, we're talking about spending a lot of money here."

The blue eyes fixed on Monahan. "Of course we are. It takes money to make money, doesn't it? That's why I want to see a plan that's going to get us *where we want to go*. How much should we spend to get there? Twelve million? Fifteen? Whatever it should be, that's what you recommend. Not what you consider safe. I'm not interested in your protecting yourselves, I'm interested in performance."

Monahan looked at the table. "Yes, sir."

"This new creative material you say you're working on," Rawlson said to Paul Scott. "The television sounds like quite a departure from what we've been doing."

"It is," Scott responded. "We're going to show you some really exciting new ideas."

"I think that's stupid," Rawlson said.

Scott's jaw dropped.

"We've been running the present commercial for eight months," Rawlson went on, "and we've just reviewed the sales response. It's excellent. I believe you also Burke-tested that commercial before we used it. True?"

"That's correct," Archer said.

"And the score?" Rawlson asked.

"It got a forty-eight," Archer replied, "and very good recall on sales points." He had a feeling the old man knew the test score as well as he did. Burke was the largest television commercial testing company in its field. Most of the major TV advertisers used its services, which involved random telephone calls to homes in several cities the day after a new commercial was first put on the air. The greater the number of people who recalled seeing the commercial, the higher the score.

"A forty-eight," Rawlson reflected. "That's not a bad score, is it?"

"It's phenomenal," Archer acknowledged.

Rawlson looked at Paul Scott. "So you want to throw the commercial out and do something entirely different."

The account executive flushed. "Our creative people felt it might be time for a change of pace," he said lamely. "People could be, uh, getting a little tired of seeing the same thing."

"Let's understand something," John Rawlson said. He paused for emphasis. "I am certainly not against good ideas. Good ideas make money. Good ideas built this business. And good ideas will make it keep right on growing. So when you've got a good idea, you get down on your knees and you water it, and you give it sunlight, and you protect it with everything you've got. Because ideas are not hard to come by, but *good* ideas are priceless. Darla Dawson in that commercial is a *good idea*. It's already made millions for us, and that's indisputable. Now. You want to top it? Great. You've got a better idea? Wonderful. I'm all for it. But what you do is, you test this new idea, and you prove to me that it's better. Then we use it. Until then, we use the commercial we've got. Because the advertising campaign we're all bragging about is *that commercial*. Print? Sure. You want to use some younger magazines? Fine. But you know what the magazine ads do? They simply remind women of the commercial. That's their value. Because today, we live in a television world. Television is where women see and hear Darla Dawson tell them in her own voice why they should try Superfresh Mouthwash. Television is where they see her smile and flip her hair while she *convinces* them that Superfresh is a better product. Television is not just a printed page. Television is where she somes to life."

The room was quiet again for a few moments. "There is one other thing," John Rawlson said, "that every one of you should get into your heads and keep there." He paused again. "And that is that all the best advertising in the world can do is to get women to try Superfresh once. After that, it's up to the product. If women don't like it, it doesn't matter what Darla Dawson says. And if they do, they're going to keep on buying it. The reason we've got this success going on is because women discover that what they hear in the commercial is the truth. Superfresh is a good product, and it does good things for their smile and their breath. Morgan is right when he says we don't make junk, and we don't create fads. What we do is, we make the best mouthwash money can buy. And when it comes right down to it, that's what it's all about. Our future, in the long run, is inside that bottle."

David Archer watched the old man get to his feet. Rawlson's back was ramrod-straight. "Gentlemen," he said, "I will see you later." He walked out of the room.

An embarrassed silence ensued. Paul Scott stared at the conference table, his ears red. Monahan shuffled papers in an attempt to hide his chagrin at having been humiliated in front of the agency, while Brinker looked at the marketing director with satisfaction, enjoying his associate's discomfort.

If there was one thing that Archer knew enough to steer clear of, it was client politics. In a carefully neutral voice he said, "Gentlemen, I think the meeting is over."

Chapter 18

"A poster?" Darla said into the phone in surprise. "What does anybody want to put me in a poster for?" She was standing on the patio beside the pool, dripping wet. Maggie had called her from a late afternoon swim to take Betty's call.

"Because you're beautiful," Betty answered. "That's why."

"Oh, come on, Betty," Darla said. "I don't want to do anything like that. Those things are kind of, well, dirty, aren't they?"

A hint of exasperation crept into the agent's voice. "Darla, let me explain a few facts of life. With a good company, a poster is not dirty. It might be a little sexy, but that's exactly the image you want to project, right?"

"Well, yes. Sure," Darla said. "But I'm not going to do one of those things like you see on the wall of a gas station. You know, with the boobs hanging out. I mean, it's not like a *Playboy* kind of thing, is it?"

"Darla, listen to me. I assure you this would be a perfectly acceptable kind of picture. No bare boobs, no bare anything. It would simply be fresh and modern and you'd look absolutely terrific. It would be done with a top photographer, and you'd have the right to okay the shot before it was released."

Darla hesitated. "Gee, Betty. I just don't know. Who buys those things?"

"Kids buy them. By the hundreds of thousands. By the millions. Didn't you ever have posters of Elvis or Jimmy Dean or somebody like that when you were a kid?"

"Oh sure, I suppose so."

"Well, this is the same thing. Do you know who's in the top-selling poster right now?"

"I haven't the faintest idea."

"It's the Fonz, that's who. His poster has already sold over a million copies. Now, you wouldn't call him dirty, would you?"

"Mm. It depends on your point of view."

"Darla, look. It's one day's work, it's a clean deal, and you stand to make a lot of money. Now what could be wrong with that?"

"Nothing, I guess. If it's everything you say it is."

"It is, or I wouldn't even propose it to you."

"What do you call a lot of money?"

"It works on a royalty basis," Betty explained. "For every poster they sell, you get ten cents. And that happens to be a very good percentage. A hell of a lot of posters are only a nickel deal. You'd be getting twice that."

Darla laughed. "So intead of a nickel deal, I'd be a dime deal? God, how I've come up in the world."

"Don't sneeze at this, Darla. I got you a guaranteed advance of twenty thousand dollars."

Darla paused. "Twenty thousand dollars?"

"I thought that might change your tune. That's twenty thousand up front. It's the least you'd make for one day's work, and I feel confident you'd make a lot more than that."

"Gee, that's not too bad, is it?"

"It's terrific," Betty answered with conviction. "They ought to sell at least a half a million of them, maybe a lot more. But let's be conservative. For every hundred thousand they sell over the first two hundred thousand, you collect another ten thousand bucks. So let's say they only sell a total of four hundred thousand. That's forty thousand dollars for the day's shoot. Have you ever heard of a model getting that kind of dough? Any one of those Ford broads would pee in her drawers if she got an offer like that."

"Well, it does sound pretty interesting."

"Of course it does. All I'm trying to get you to see is that posters can be big money. And not only that, but good money. Every place that poster is on display, it's an ad for you."

"Who are these people?" Darla asked.

"The company is called Star Graphics. They're in Pittsburgh."

"Pittsburgh?

"Darla, there is nothing wrong with Pittsburgh. It's where their printing plant is. But relax. You don't have to go there. The shot would be made out here. And as I said, with a top photographer. Somebody like Peter Samerjan, or that—what's his name—Charrington."

"How did they hear about me?"

"The way everybody's hearing about you. They saw you in the Superfresh commercial, and people are talking about you. You're getting to be a hot property. Which reminds me. I've had another call on the 'Billy and Sue' show. They want to know about the guest shot."

"Oh, I don't know about that, Betty. I mean, I don't sing or dance or anything."

"Doesn't mean a thing. They'll work you into comedy routines."

"Uh-huh. I suppose that could be pretty good for me."

"And how it would."

"Okay, we'll go ahead with that, then."

"Of course. Now what about the poster?"

"Yeah, I guess that's okay. What you said about it being a kind of an ad for me makes sense, and the money sounds attractive."

"Thatta girl. I'll get a contract over to you and we'll set the photographer and a date. The president of Star Graphics is named Corelli. Dante Corelli. He's a nice man. He'll supervise the shooting personally, so you'll be treated right, and the shot will be just what you want it to be. Okay? Gotta run."

The wind had come up. When Darla put the phone down she noticed that she had goose bumps on her arms. She pulled on a robe and went into the house.

Sid Brock had operated his own photography studio for ten years. He had started as an assistant to Dan O'Hara, who had shot the famous calendar photograph of Marilyn Monroe stretched out naked against a background of red satin. When Brock struck out on his own, he used the Monroe calendar as an example of his work, presenting himself as the unsung talent whom O'Hara had exploited. The truth was that O'Hara was one of the best photographers in Hollywood or anywhere else, while Brock's success over the years that followed owed principally to his willingness to lie, cheat, and steal other people's work. He was available to shoot absolutely anything for a buck. He did fashion and food work for agencies, regularly bribing art directors for assignments, and also picked up jobs from magazines like *Hustler* and *Gent,* which he called cunt work. When things were slow, he shot straight-out pornography, employing teenaged drifters and aspiring models as his subjects.

Brock's studio was in a red brick building on Yucca Street. When Darla arrived, a receptionist led her into Brock's office. The room was ultramodern, furnished with squashy leather chairs and zebraskin rugs. Brock's desk was an expanse of black glass on chrome legs. He was on the phone when she walked in, and he let Darla stand there while he leisurely finished his conversation.

Darla noticed that the walls of the office were decorated with enlargements of photographs Brock had shot for what the trade called skin books. They were all in color, and all showed nude young women. The poses were different, but in every shot the girl's legs were spread, and the lips of her vagina were open and wet and prominently featured. In some of the pictures the girl's fingers were touching her clitoris, as if she were masturbating. In these shots the model's eyes were half-closed and her mouth was open in an expression of ecstasy.

151

"I get thirty grand for a fuck book," Brock said into the phone. "That's for an average of fifty shots in color, and say half a dozen or so models, boys and girls or all one or the other if it's gay. I can give you niggers, too, if you want." He paused. "No, no animals. It gets too messy. We had a pony in here one time, and it shit all over the place." He paused again. "Well, yeah, a dog would be all right, if it's trained and it's just going to lick her snatch."

Darla felt the hair prickle on the back of her neck. Was this for real? Was she really hearing what this man was saying into that telephone? She had never heard of Sid Brock, but Betty had assured her that if Star Graphics was using him, he had to be top-notch. And yet—

"All right, sweetheart," Brock continued. "Give me a couple of days notice so I can line up the kids. And come to the shoot; it's a blast. You can ball the chicks after, if you want. Ciao." He put the phone on its cradle and stood up to face Darla, a broad smile on his face. The top of his head was bald, and the hair on the sides hung down in thick, greasy fringes. "Hiya, babe. You're Darla, right? For the poster shoot."

Darla stared at him, speechless. There had to be some mistake.

"Sit down, sit down," Brock said. His shirt was of the embroidered Mexican type, open down to his belt buckle. He scratched among the hairs on his chest as he moved to a liquor cabinet that hung from the wall. "You want a drink? Go ahead, sit down."

Against her judgment, Darla sank into a chair. "No thank you. I don't care for anything to drink." Maybe she was in the wrong place. "Are you Sid Brock?"

"Yeah, sure." He poured Chivas Regal into a squat glass and dropped an ice cube in on top. "And you're here for the Star Graphics job, right? Terrific. I wanted you to be here before the client so we could get acquainted, you know?"

Darla nodded dumbly.

"Cheers," Brock said. He swallowed some of the Scotch. "Hey, you want anything else? Grass, hash? Or I got coke, if you want it."

"No, nothing," Darla replied. She noticed that her voice had grown weak.

Brock leaned against the desk, his eyes wandering down Darla's body and back up to her face again. "You ever done a poster before?"

She shook her head.

"Nice piece of luck for you. It could make you a pisspot full of dough." He leered at her. "This guy Corelli's a friend of yours probably, huh?"

"No. I've never met him."

Brock's eyebrows rose. "No shit? And he's giving you a poster deal? He must have a hard-on for you, then. Say, haven't I seen you someplace? You on TV?"

Darla nodded.

"In a commercial, right? For mouthwash? Sure, I seen those spots. You look dynamite. No wonder Corelli's after your ass." He grinned and swallowed more of the Scotch.

I have got to get out of here, Darla thought. Contract or no contract, I have to get out of this crazy place. Betty must have lost her mind entirely.

Brock was studying her body again. "Let me tell you a couple things about posters," he said, "The whole trick is, you want it dirty, but not so dirty it won't get displayed in novelty store windows, you know? No bare tits, no cunt showing. But it's got to *say* dirty. So you do other things. Your face, for instance, could look like you're getting it. Or you put your hand under your tit, cupping it. Or you open your mouth a little with your tongue showing, so it looks like you're going to give head, you know?"

Darla felt hypnotized, as if she were gazing at a cobra.

"Believe me," Brock went on, "I know what I'm talking about. I bet I shot more cooz than any guy in the business." He waved an arm toward the photographs that adorned the walls. "You see how this stuff is lit? So you can really see everything? I was the first one who ever did that." There was genuine pride in his tone. "You take a book like *Playboy,* all you see is hair, you know? But with my stuff, I put a key light on her box so you're looking right into it. Makes a hell of an effect, don't it? Now everybody imitates it."

In spite of herself, Darla looked at the pictures as Brock pointed to them. Her stomach turned over.

The leer returned to the photographer's face. "Hey, you got a good body, from what I can see. Of course, I could tell better with your clothes off." The leer widened. "But even in them pants it looks okay. If you want, I could set you up in a layout for one of the skin books. Maybe even a centerfold. It'd be tremendous publicity for you."

This is it, Darla thought. I am going to run like hell out that door. She stood up.

Brock misunderstood her action. He reached out and grabbed one of her hands. Stepping closer, he encircled her body with his other arm. "You're okay, Darla," he breathed. "I really dig you." His hand slipped down her back and squeezed her ass.

Darla clenched her free hand into a fist. She wondered wildly whether it would be better to punch him or to knee him in the groin.

The telephone rang.

"Shit," Brock said. He let go of Darla and walked around behind the desk and picked up the phone, "Yeah? Oh, hiya, Sam. Uh-huh. The stuff's in the lab now. I haven't seen the blowups yet, but the contacts looked great. Broad's got a set of tits on her you wouldn't believe." He looked around. The door of his office was open. "Wait a minute, Sam." He held the phone against his belly. "Hey, babe—hold it!" he shouted.

But Darla had gone.

Chapter 19

Scandia was busy, as usual. The lunchtime crowd was bronzed and casual-chic. Betty permitted the maitre d' to fuss over her. "How nice to see you, Miss Frolich. You're looking wonderful!"

Betty was not deceived. She was five pounds heavier than she had been a week ago, when she had promised herself she'd be more faithful to her diet. The trouble was, the greater the pressures on her, the more she ate. It had been that way since she was a child. Now, as an adult, she did exactly the same thing. When a deal fell through, or one of her pet plans backfired, or one of the talent she represented got into a mess or blamed her for a failure, she noshed and stuffed and noshed some more. This week had been a bitch, and she had hardly stopped eating except to sleep. The Halston suit she wore today had cost her nine hundred dollars, but on her bloated body it looked frumpy. Nevertheless, she didn't blame the maitre d'. He was only doing his job.

"Miss Simmons is already here," he said. "I put her at a lovely table by the window. It's such a nice clear day for a change, I thought you would enjoy the view." He led her through the bright, sunny restaurant to where Margot was sitting.

"Betty, darling." Margot flashed her famous smile. "I'm so glad you could make it. I know how busy you are, but I just had to talk to you. I'm bursting with good news, and I wanted to share it."

Betty kissed the actress's cheek and dropped heavily into the chair the maitre d' held for her. "You look marvelous, Margot." And that's the truth, she thought. She doesn't look a day over forty, even in this bright light. Betty ordered a Beefeater martini, straight up.

Margot offered her guest a cigarette and then lit it and her own with a gold lighter.

"That's pretty," Betty remarked.

"Isn't it." Margot held the lighter up for Betty to admire. It was a Dunhill. The monogram MS was set in sapphires on its side. "From you know who."

"Then I should get ten percent of it," Betty grinned.

Margot laughed. "It's true. In all fairness, you should."

"I take it things are going fairly well on that front?"

"Things are going like gangbusters, on every front."

Betty's martini arrived. Margot was drinking a white wine spritzer. They touched glasses and Betty took a long swallow, grateful for the effect as the cold gin burned and then soothed as it coursed down into her stomach. "I'm glad, Margot. You deserve it."

"Well, I don't know about that," Margot replied, "but it's amazing how my life has turned around, all thanks to you." She was wearing a mauve Mollie Parnis dress, the color contrasting handsomely with her gently waving auburn hair.

"Don't kid yourself," Betty said. "All I did was to give you an opportunity. You're the one who made the most of it." The martini was making her feel generous and expansive.

Margot sipped from her glass. "That's nice of you, Betty. And of course it's true. But it's also true that I was right flat on my ass when you got me the Krause Beer deal. If it hadn't been for that, God knows where I'd be today. I don't even want to think about it."

"Then don't," Betty said. "Just tell me all your good news. I could stand to hear some."

"Well, first off, a piece of irony. Michael, the prick, has joined AA, and hasn't had a drink for months. His old law firm has taken him back, and he actually seems to be on his feet. God, when I look back at what I went through with that man. And when I married him I thought I was being so clever to get the hell away from actors and to tie up with a good, solid square from a rich, old-line Pasadena family. Salt of the earth, right? Jesus, did he ever fool me. He got loaded at our wedding reception, and he never drew a sober breath from that minute on."

"What's he doing about alimony?" Betty asked.

"That's the irony. Now that I don't need it, he's paying again. Can you believe it?"

"Put it in the bank against a rainy day."

"That's not a bad idea either," Margot said.

Betty swallowed more of her martini. "What about the boys?"

Margot had two sons from her first marriage, to Robert Stuart. Michael Cook had been her second husband. "They're wonderful," she smiled. "Tim is a junior at Yale, you know. He came out for Easter and brought this adorable girl with him. She's a freshman. They've been living together since January. My God, when I think back to Raleigh, North Carolina, when I was a kid. My father would have had a convulsion if he'd ever caught me living with some boy. And then he would have dragged me home by the ear."

"Times have changed," Betty said. Her own father would have done worse than that. A picture of him standing over her with arm upraised, his heavy leather belt poised to swing down and cut into her flesh, came into her mind. He had beaten her for the slightest infraction of his petty rules. If he had ever caught her so much as kissing a boy, he would have killed her, she reflected. Not that many boys had wanted to kiss Betty Frolich when she was young. Or when she was grown up either, for that matter.

"Billy's doing fine too," Margot went on. "Although he's nothing like his brother. No student, that is. He's at Berkshire, just getting by. What he thinks about mostly is his guitar. He and some of his friends have formed a group, and they're threatening to go on the road this summer. Not much danger of that, though. Tim's heard them and he says they're terrible, thank God."

They finished their drinks and ordered two more.

"I have a hell of a lot to do this afternoon," Betty said. "But you know what? Fuck it. This is the first time I've been able to relax this week."

"Good, I'm glad you're enjoying yourself. It always does you good to get your mind off your problems for a little while, anyway."

"I certainly agree," Betty said. "And it's so nice to hear how well you're doing. Now what about the knight in shining armor?"

"I've been saving that for last. But of course anything I tell you about it has to be strictly confidential."

"Margot, are you kidding?" Betty was wide-eyed. "You're an item, honey. You're in the columns, haven't you seen them? What's to keep confidential?"

"Plenty. It's one thing for us to be seen together, or even for the papers to pick it up. I know that's happened before in Donald Krause's life, and often. The thing is, this time he means it."

"What about his wife?"

"That's just it. She's one of those society types back in Milwaukee, riding to hounds and all that shit. I saw a picture of her once, in *Town and Country*. She's spent so much time around horses she looks like one. Anyway, I think Don's little flings are something she chooses not to know about."

"How do you know that?"

"From hearing talk about him from the people at the agency, and then from others in his company, before I met him. Everybody loves to gossip about the guy at the top, you know. Whether he's the head of a studio or the president of a brewery, he's number one in their world, and that makes him an object of fascination."

Betty sipped her drink. She was feeling more comfortable than she had in days. "So what's different about this time?"

"What's different this time is that he wants to marry me."

Betty smiled. "It seems to me I've heard that song before."

"Oh hell, so have I. More times than I can count. Everybody I know has been in that kind of situation at one time or another. Or at least, something like it. They've either been the wife or the girlfriend."

"Or both," Betty said dryly.

"What makes this one for real is that Don and I have a timetable," Margot said. "It's all going to take place this year."

"Oh-ho," Betty said. "The plot thickens. So what happens when?"

"What happens is that his lawyers are putting together a hell of a settlement. She gets the place in Milwaukee and a large pile of money. Plus another little bauble that'll bend her mind. Remember I said she's a horse nut. Well, there is this breeding farm in Kentucky she's done business with. Seems it produces marvelous hunters, I think they're called."

"Have I guessed what's coming?" Betty asked.

Margot smiled. "Probably. Everyone has a price, right? So shrewd Donald is going to buy his loving wife that entire breeding farm, and that is how he's going to get her to become his loving ex-wife."

"Brilliant," Betty said. "Where there's a will there's a way."

"Where there's love there's a way," Margot amended. "And Donald loves me, bless him. The plan then calls for us to be married in New York, and from there we fly to Rome."

"Will you be staying there long?" Rome was the city Betty considered the most beautiful in the world. The idea of Margot honeymooning there made her wistful.

"No, we're going to be moving around some. We plan to visit a few favorite places. Ones we both like but have never been to together. The Greek islands, for instance, and then we'll get over to Spain and spend a few weeks in Marbella. After that we'll be dividing our time between New York, Milwaukee, and here."

"Won't it be rough to deal with Milwaukee as the

new Mrs. Donald Krause? Old friends have a way of making that kind of thing pretty uncomfortable, you know."

Margot flicked a long, elegantly manicured hand. "I couldn't care less. And besides, Don never gave a damn about his wife's horse crowd. There's no reason for us to have anything to do with them. We'll have our own friends and we'll be on the move a lot anyway."

"Sounds wonderful," Betty said. "Every bit of it. I have only one regret."

"What's that?"

"I'll be losing a valuable talent."

"Oh, no, you won't," Margot said.

Betty's wide face registered surprise. "What? Don't tell me you're going to go on doing beer commercials after you're married?"

"Of course not. Somebody new will be doing them. And you know who'll decide who it's going to be? I will, that's who. Naturally, I'll see to it that the new somebody is represented by none other than my old friend and former agent, Betty Frolich."

Betty laughed. "Margot, you're terrific."

"You didn't think I'd let you down, did you? After what you did for me?" Margot shook her head. "There I was, over the hill, I thought. Hadn't had even a sniff at a picture for so long I couldn't remember, and up to my ass in debt. Do you have any idea how I felt when I'd see myself on the late show in a movie I'd made twenty years ago?"

"I think so."

"Christ, what an experience. I'd be sitting there alone in the living room at one o'clock in the morning, watching this girl who was all young and pretty and dewy-eyed. Talk about seeing ghosts. Then I'd go look in the mirror, and there was reality, staring back at me." Margot shuddered. "That's when I'd get out the vodka and have a good cry."

Betty nodded in sympathy. "Sounds awful."

"It *was* awful. You know how many pictures I did as romantic female lead? Twenty-six, and a lot of them made money. Sure, I spread my legs in more than one producer's office, but hell, who didn't? You needed a lot more than talent to get anywhere in this goddamn business. But the thing was, I didn't just screw my way up there. I really did have talent, and a lot of it. So you know what happened when I couldn't cut it any more as a sweet young thing? I started getting offered shit parts. Not just character roles, but shit. Where I'd be a clapped-out hooker, or a drunk, or a blowsy old bum. And you know why? Because those fucking vultures knew it would be a kick to an audience to see me and say, *Hey! That's Margot Simmons. Doesn't she look terrible?* Because there's a sadistic side to audiences, and don't you ever forget it. Like in the French Revolution when the dear ladies brought their knitting to the executions. As much as they love to see you climb up there, it's almost as much of a thrill for them to see you get your head cut off, too."

"I know," Betty said. "I know."

"So I wouldn't take the shit parts, and pretty soon what they offered me was *no* parts. And that, I discovered, was even worse."

"I'm sure it was." Betty sipped her martini.

Margot brightened. "And then, all of a sudden, right out of the blue, pow! Captain Betty and the U.S. Cavalry to the rescue. And now look at what's happening. No indeed, dear. I won't forget."

"All's well that ends well."

"What's ending? You haven't heard the rest of my scheme."

"There's more?"

"Yes, but let's order first," Margot suggested. "I'm starved."

"So am I," Betty said. "As usual."

After a brief discussion they ordered broiled filet of sole and watercress salad, on the theory that this would be the least fattening lunch they could eat.

"Some wine?" Margot asked.

"God, no, I'm loaded now."

"So as I was about to say, the new Mrs. Krause is going to get very involved with the doings of the Krause Company."

"How's your new husband going to like that?"

"He's all for it. Thinks it's a great idea. And I have lots of plans. New advertising, for instance. And a new agency."

Betty raised her eyebrows. "A new agency? What's wrong with Beyer and Shaw? I thought they were doing such a good job. I know sales are up, and after all, they're the ones who made those commercials with you."

"Exactly," Margot said. "And the last thing I want is an agency that looks at me as the broad who used to be in the TV spots."

"Oh, I see," Betty said, understanding. She felt admiration for Margot's matter-of-fact ruthlessness. "And I guess you're right. Tough on Beyer and Shaw, though."

"It's a tough world."

Betty nodded. "It sure is. And you can only be in one of two categories. The screwers, or the screwees."

Their food arrived, and as they ate, Margot told Betty her ideas about how the Krause advertising could be improved, and other observations she had made of the company. Betty was amazed at how much Margot had already learned about the internal structure of the Krause organization and its operations.

When they had finished, the captain reappeared at their table, rubbing his hands. "Now I must tempt you with a little treat." He smiled, then signaled, and a waiter pushed a towering dessert wagon over to their table. The wagon was heaped with elaborate confections: a chocolate mousse, Bavarian cream cake, Napoleons, eclairs. "What shall it be, ladies?"

"Nothing for me, thanks," Margot said. "But you go ahead, Betty."

"Not on your life," Betty said with determination. "As of today, I am turning over a new leaf. A new me is going to emerge."

The captain's face expressed disappointment. "Nothing? Not even a tiny tart, or a soupçon of pudding, perhaps?"

"Just coffee," Betty said. By God, Margot's reserve

was inspiring. What it took was to set a goal and stick to it.

A second waiter approached. "Miss Frolich? Telephone for you, please."

Betty excused herself and followed the man to a booth in the foyer.

It was Esther. "Hey, sorry to bother you, but you better call Darla Dawson, and fast."

Betty's senses snapped to alert. "What's up?"

"I don't know. She phoned in here a minute ago, and I never heard her that mad before. Geez, was she pissed. Screaming and yelling. She almost took my head off."

"For Christ's sake, Esther. What I want to know is, what's wrong?"

"She wouldn't tell me. But I looked on my calendar, and today's the day she was supposed to do that poster shoot. You know, for Star Graphics?"

"Oh Jesus," Betty said. "Something must have gotten screwed up."

"You're telling me?" Esther said.

"Okay, where was she?"

"Home, I guess. Before I could ask, she just slammed the phone down in my ear."

Betty hung up and fumbled for a coin. Damn it, she couldn't even have a nice relaxing lunch for a change, without a problem coming up. Lately, she reflected, Darla had been showing unmistakable signs of growing headstrong. What the hell could have happened now?

Maggie's pleasant tone answered the ring. "The Brady residence."

"Maggie, it's Betty Frolich. Darla there?"

Darla came on an instant later, her voice rising to a shriek. "Betty! You lied to me. You told me one thing, and it turned out to be nothing like that at all! What the hell do you think I am? Do you really believe I'm so hard up for work I have to go running around doing things like that?"

"Like what, Darla? What happened?"

"That—that *pig*. He wanted me to do pornography!"

"Who did? Dante Corelli?"

"No, the photographer," Darla howled. "That Sid Brock! He was absolutely the most disgusting man I ever met in my life. Wanted to get me to do sex pictures. His place was full of them!"

"But that's impossible. What about Corelli? He wouldn't want you to do anything like that."

"The hell he wouldn't! He picked this Brock, didn't he?"

"Well, yes, but Corelli is no pornographer. What did he say?"

"Say? He didn't say anything. He wasn't even there. But this Brock creature—Betty, if you think you're going to get me to do that kind of stuff, I'm going to find a new agent. I have never—"

Beads of sweat appeared on Betty's forehead. She could feel them. "Darla! Listen to me. I know you're upset, and I don't blame you. But there must be some kind of mistake. I've spoken with Corelli, and he's nothing like that."

"How do I know what he's like?" Darla asked. "How do I know what to believe?"

"Will you please do this? Will you please sit down and get control of yourself and give me a chance to find out what happened? Nobody wants you to do pornography—"

"They don't, huh? Well, that Brock certainly didn't get the message, then."

"Darla, please. I'm not in my office now. Wait till I can get back there and look into this. Do you hear me?"

"Sure, I hear you, all right. The question is whether I believe you!"

"Darla, I'll call you later this afternoon. Try to calm down and let me find out what went wrong. Will you please do that?"

"Oh—I guess so. But I'm telling you, Betty, you'd better come up with some damn good answers." She hung up.

Betty found another coin and dialed her office. "Esther, listen. See if you can reach Dante Corelli. I think he's staying at the Century Plaza."

"He just called you." Esther said. "Just this minute. And guess what? He's pissed, too."

"Oh, God."

"He said he got to the studio and Darla was gone. Said the photographer told him she just took off. Corelli says he has a contract and you better get this straightened out fast."

Shit, Betty thought. What a beautiful day this is turning out to be.

"You coming back to the office?" Esther asked.

"Yeah." Betty pulled a handkerchief out of the pocket of her pants suit and wiped her forehead. "I'll be back there just as soon as I can."

"Everything okay?" Margot smiled as Betty returned to the table.

"Oh, sure." Betty mopped her face again. "Just a few of the usual problems." She raised her hand and a waiter scurried over.

"Yes, Miss Frolich?"

"I've changed my mind. I want a slice of that Bavarian Cream Cake."

"Of course. Right away."

"And waiter?"

"Yes, Miss Frolich?"

"Make it a big one."

Chapter 20

The day after the debacle at Sid Brock's studio, Darla came home to find three dozen yellow roses in a vase in the living room. Maggie handed her an envelope. It contained a sheet of notepaper bearing the crest of the Century Plaza Hotel.

> Dear Ms. Dawson,
>
> Please excuse my monumental stupidity. I didn't know that photographer any better than you did. He had been chosen by an art director who is no longer with my company, as of today. That's a poor excuse, I know, but it's what happened. Nevertheless, the responsibility is entirely mine. If you can find it in your heart to forgive me, I would be happy to assign any photographer you wish to do this work. You would honor Star Graphics by appearing in a poster for us. I am convinced that one day you will be a great star.
>
> Sincerely,
> Dante Corelli.

Darla dropped the note onto the coffee table.

"Betty Frolich phoned," Maggie said. "Wants you to call her."

"Mmm." Darla went into the kitchen and took a celery stalk out of the refrigerator. Celery was one of the few snacks she permitted herself. It contained no carbohydrates, and it was something to chew on. She walked back into the living room.

"She said it was important," Maggie said.

"Uh-huh." Darla flopped into a chair and draped a leg over one of its arms.

Maggie shook her head. "I swear, I don't know what's got into you sometimes lately. Seems like your head is somewhere else."

Darla shrugged. "I've just gotten tired of people pushing me around. From now on I'm going to do what I want to do, the way I want to do it." She crunched on the celery.

A knowing expression came over Maggie's face. "Them roses got something to do with that mess yesterday?"

"Yes. The head of the poster company claims it was all a big mistake."

"Well, could be," Maggie said. "Least he's trying to say he's sorry."

"Yeah. Maybe he is, and maybe he isn't. One thing I'm learning is that everybody is at their nicest when they want something from you."

"Ain't nothing surprising about that."

"I suppose." Darla finished the celery and crossed over to a telephone.

Betty's tone was warm and cheerful. "Darla! I've been trying to reach you. I finally got this thing all sorted out—you know, about Star Graphics and the photographer—and it was all just a misunderstanding. Nothing to get upset about, really."

Darla was cool, reserved. "Oh, is that so? Well, that's nice to hear." What the hell did Betty take her for, anyway?

"Yes, I talked with Corelli several times about it, and he found out that this dumb art director had just gone ahead and booked that awful photographer without clearing it properly, and when he found out the truth about it, Corelli was just as mad as you were. So he fired the guy, and now he's willing to do just anything to get back in your good graces."

"Uh-huh." Darla wondered if the roses had been Corelli's idea or Betty's.

"Well, really, Darla," Betty went on, "as long as it was just a mistake, I think we ought to give him another chance."

"Betty, I'm not so sure I want to do that poster now."

There was a pause, and when Betty spoke again, Darla was aware that a note of urgency had crept into the agent's tone. "But I'm afraid we made a commitment, Darla. You signed a contract, and Corelli came out here just to get this photograph taken. I know you're angry about what happened yesterday and all, but I think it would be in everybody's best interest if we could forget it and start over again. It was just one of those things. You know, just a royal screw-up."

"I'll say it was." For the first time since she had started in the business, Darla was experiencing a sense of power—the feeling that she was calling the shots. For once, she was aware that somebody really wanted her a lot, and she hadn't had to go through any auditioning or anything else to get there. She was also still smarting from her encounter with Sid Brock. So it was all a big terrible mistake? So this poster company was so awfully sorry? And they'd do anything now to please her? Well, maybe. And maybe Betty could sweat a little, too. Maybe one of the things people would learn was not to take Darla Dawson for granted. The little dope who ran around hoping somebody would throw her a crumb was gone for good. An idea was beginning to form in her mind.

"Why don't I call Corelli," Betty said, "and see if we can't set up a new date? Would that be okay?"

Darla's tone was neutral. "Set up a new date for what?"

"A new date for the photography. You know, to make the shot. With another photographer, of course."

Darla noted with satisfaction that Betty sounded a little more anxious. "What photographer are we talking about?"

"Well, I don't know—whoever they come up with. But naturally, this time it would be somebody you approve," Betty added hastily. "May I do that?"

"No," Darla said slowly, "I don't think so. But I'll tell you what. Who is the most expensive photographer in Los Angeles?"

Betty hesitated. "I don't know offhand. But right now the hottest one is probably Raymond Sand."

"All right," Darla interrupted. "Here's what I want. Sand is the one who'll take this picture, and he gets his top fee, whatever that is. But before the picture is taken, I want a conference with him, and with this Corelli. You should be there too. The shot is to be planned when we meet, and what Sand shoots is what I agree to, and nothing else. And then, of course, it's not to be released until I okay it."

There was a long pause before Betty answered. "Getting agreement on all of that might be a little difficult, Darla."

"But that's what I have you for, Betty."

"Well, sure, but—"

"That's the way I want it," Darla said. "And I think Mr. Corelli can agree to doing it that way in writing. When you've got his written agreement, call me and we'll see about a date."

Raymond Sand's studio was on La Cienega. The foyer was decorated with framed magazine covers Sand had shot. There were dozens of them: *Cosmopolitan*, *McCall's*, *Mademoiselle*, *Glamour*, *Seventeen*, *People*, *Vogue*, and *Ladies' Home Journal* were all represented. The room had white walls and a white carpet, and was furnished with white furniture.

Betty Frolich and Dante Corelli were waiting in Sand's office when Darla arrived. Corelli was not at all what Darla had expected. He was above average height, trim and athletic-looking, his smile friendly and pleasant on his tanned face. A few streaks of gray showed in his thick black hair. He wore a lightweight suit of European cut. Sand was also a surprise. He appeared to be not yet thirty, with long, dark-blond hair, wearing jeans and sandals. With his credits and reputation, Darla had thought he'd be older. Sand was relaxed and easygoing, almost to the point of seeming bored.

Betty made the introductions.

"Darla, once again, I am terribly sorry about that mixup," Corelli said. "But I'm delighted that we could get together. Picking Ray here to do the work was a terrific choice. I hear he's the best there is."

Darla was all business. "Okay, fine. I'm glad we got it straightened out, too. Now let's talk about this shot."

"Before we do that," Sand said, "why don't we have some coffee?"

"I thought you'd never ask." Corelli smiled.

Sand touched a buzzer and an assistant came in with a tray bearing a pot, cups, and cream and sugar.

When everyone had settled down, Corelli said, "May I start the discussion? Darla, obviously what we want to do most of all is capture your personality. The spirit of this poster ought to be young, casual, and happy. You ought to look as though you're just having the time of your life."

"You're thinking mostly about a head shot?" Sand asked.

"More or less," Corelli said.

Darla looked at the others. "Why not full figure?"

"It would reduce the size of your face too much," Corelli explained. "The poster will be thirty inches long. If you were standing in it, that would mean your head would occupy only a relatively small part of the finished shot."

"I think Dante has a point," Betty said. "After all, the way people have gotten to know you is the television commercials, and the way you're shown there is always in tight closeups."

Darla realized that they were all waiting for her reaction; for her approval of the layout concept. That had never happened before. It was flattering and exciting. She was enjoying herself. "I see what you mean about not wanting my head to be too small, but at the same time, I don't want just a big face. I think we ought to see more of me, if we're going to get the effect of personality you're all talking about."

Sand sipped his coffee and put his cup down on the table. "Darla's right. The shot ought to have some character of its own. You don't want a picture that only duplicates what people are seeing on TV." The photographer had long, expressive hands. He gestured with them as he spoke. "You take any really great shot, especially of famous people. There's always an element that either says something about that person's character or has some little surprise in it. Look at the portrait of Churchill that Karsch shot, for instance. Or the one Avedon did of Audrey Hepburn. You don't just see a picture of somebody; instead, the picture is telling you a story about that person."

"That's true," Corelli said. "And yet your magazine covers don't do that. They're usually just closeups of faces."

"There's a reason for that, too," Sand answered. "The main purpose of a magazine cover shot is to get newsstand sales. It's going to sit there on a rack alongside a dozen or so other magazines, and the customer spends only a second or two looking at them. You have to catch the eye in that tiny bit of time or you lose the sale. A poster, on the other hand, is meant for display. The customers buy it to put up on a wall. They want something that's going to be interesting to look at for as long as it's up there."

Corelli nodded his understanding. "Fair enough. You're right about a poster having to be interesting as well as beautiful. At the same time, though, it shouldn't be too complicated. We've made that mistake with other things we've produced—like some of the so-called psychedelic designs we've done featuring rock groups, for instance—and they failed."

"Okay," Darla said. "If it's not going to be a tight closeup and it's not going to be full figure, it has to be somewhere in between, right? Kneeling or sitting or something like that."

"Or at the wheel of a convertible," Betty added.

"There are nighttime effects we could get, too," Sands said. "If we want to go that route."

Darla saw that they were looking to her again for agreement on direction. "I don't think nighttime," she said. "I want it to be outdoorsy. But not location either."

"Why don't we start putting a few things down, so we can look at them?" Sands suggested.

They went into the studio, where Sand's two assistants were waiting. Lee Merriwell and Bobby Benbo were there also. They greeted Darla warmly and thanked her for having requested them for the assignment. While the others waited, Sand occupied himself with directing his assistants to set the lights for the effect he wanted, and Lee and Bobby worked on Darla's hair and makeup in a dressing room.

"Hey, that Superfresh job turned out well for you, Darla," Lee remarked.

Darla smiled. "It sure did."

"Everybody talks about it," Bobby said. "And I see it a lot when I watch TV. You really look fabulous, and you know, I feel so proud when I see you I want to cheer."

"That's exactly how I feel, too," Lee said. "I think, wow—there's our girl. It gives me goosebumps."

When Darla emerged from the dressing room, Sand had set up his camera for a limbo shot. This effect was achieved by shooting the subject against a background of seamless paper unrolled down across the floor from brackets suspended eight feet up the wall. No line of demarcation showed between the background and the floor. The end result was a photograph that looked as if it had been shot in limbo—no wall and no floor.

Sand was using a tripod-mounted Hasselblad with a Polaroid film magazine. This enabled him to see the results of a test shot immediately and to make corrections. Later, when he was making actual takes, the Polaroid magazine would be replaced with one containing high-speed Ektachrome color film. Like virtually all photographers, he preferred to work to music. A record player pounded rock from the Rolling Stones into the big, high-ceilinged room as he prepared to shoot.

Darla was wearing pants and a pale lavender silk blouse. Sand staged her in a variety of poses, and after he made each shot, Darla, Corelli, and Betty crowded around him to look at the black-and-white Polaroid print. All of them made comments and suggestions, but in the end they left the decision on each shot, as well as what they would try next, up to Darla. It was stimulating, and it was fun. And to her surprise and pleasure, Darla found that what she had to say made eminent good sense, and they accepted her ideas without question.

As the work went on, Darla found that she was developing a strong rapport with Dante Corelli. He defferred to her opinions on the photographs, but he treated her as an equal. The discussions they had were spirited, and there was mutual respect for each other's point of view. In a relatively short time, the four of them had assumed a different relationship. Betty had almost withdrawn from making any important contributions, or even being very much involved, except to remark on what she liked. Sand was the medium through which the creative ideas were expressed on film, and Darla and Dante Corelli were deciding what directions to take, with the final creative judgments being made by Darla. By noon, Sand had shot about two dozen Polaroids. One of his assistants tacked the shots up on a bulletin board.

Corelli was enthusiastic. "I think a lot of these are excellent. Darla, look at this one. Or this one, where your head is turned a little. Really terrific."

"I agree," Sand said. "Any one of these would be very good. Especially the last few we made."

"Mmm," Darla mused. "I'm not so sure."

Betty peered at the prints. "They're beautiful, Darla. Really. Just imagine how the finished shots will look in color. I know it's hard for you to be objective, but honestly, I think they're just fine."

Darla was still not convinced. She continued to study

the pictures, and as she did, she remembered something Sid Brock had said to her. As horrible as he had been, a couple of his remarks had had the unmistakable ring of truth. She turned to Sand. "Do you have any wardrobe here?"

The photographer nodded. "Yeah, sure. A roomful. What are you, about an eight?" He called to one of his assistants. "Sammy, show Darla what we've got."

Corelli looked confused. "Hey, what's wrong with what you're wearing?" he looked at Darla's pale lavender silk blouse. "I think that looks delicious; it matches your eyes." He looked at her and smiled.

Corelli's meaning was not lost on Darla, who returned his smile warmly. "Thanks," she said, "but I have an idea. Bear with me."

In the wardrobe room Darla rummaged through the dresses until she found what she wanted. It was a sleeveless white evening dress of soft, clinging silk jersey. She took off her clothes and slipped into it. When she walked back into the studio the others turned to her and were suddenly silent.

Sand spoke first. "Dynamite," he said softly.

This time Corelli did more than glance. His gaze moved slowly down Darla's body, feasting. When he looked back to her face, his dark eyes were bright with excitement.

Only Betty was unsure. "Darla—really? I mean, you look great, but that's awfully sexy."

"I'd say fantastic," Corelli said.

"Amen," Sand added.

"Do you really like it?" Darla asked. She addressed the question to Corelli, her face wreathed in a little-girl smile. She clasped her hands in front of her, forcing her breasts together in the low vee of the neckline.

"Beautiful," Corelli said. "Just beautiful." He suddenly put his hands into his pockets and turned away, and Darla realized with a jolt that he had been beginning to get an erection and was hiding it. She was delighted. She felt strong and very feminine, and aware that she was a little aroused herself. She stepped in front of the camera and sank to her knees.

"Hey," Sand exclaimed. "That's something. That's really something." He squinted into the viewfinder of the Hasselblad.

Darla threw her head back and smiled.

"Jee-zus!" Sand exclaimed. He looked up. "Gimme a little more fill on this side," he ordered, and an assistant moved the lights closer.

Darla noted with satisfaction that the photographer was showing more interest than he had all morning. She turned her smile on full force, giving it all she had.

Sand's eyes were riveted to the viewfinder. "Sammy," he yelled, "let's have Ektachrome, fast! The hell with the Polaroid." He snatched the magazine from the back of the camera.

When the Hasselblad was ready, Sand began shooting rapidly, one frame after another. The camera was synchronized to the strobe lights, so that each time he pressed the trigger, Darla was momentarily flooded in brilliant light.

The photographer worked quickly, pouring out a running line of chatter to Darla. "That's it, honey, smile. Let's have it. Even bigger this time. Way to go, babe. Again. Yeah. Fantastic!"

Sand was shooting as fast as he could operate the Hasselblad, pressing the trigger, cranking the film advance, shooting, cranking again. His rhythm, Darla realized, was in sync with the Stones' beat, and the affect was somehow surrealistic and wild. Sand went through ten magazines of twelve exposures each, the huge lights popping as the music reverberated through the studio. Darla varied her expression, but kept the broad smile in place, holding her shoulders forward so that her breasts pressed more closely together. She could feel sweat running down her cleavage and dampening her lower body, and she knew she was becoming more and more excited. At one point she sneaked a glance at Corelli and this time there was no mistaking his reaction.

Sand suddenly jumped to his feet and stepped back from the camera, a broad grin on his face. "Yeah!" he yelled. "That's got it. Terrific!"

Darla stood up and they crowded around her, exul-

175

tant. Bobby and Lee had also been watching and were smiling broadly.

"Goddamn, Darla," Sand beamed. "These are going to be absolutely fantastic shots. You were unreal!"

"How did you know?" Corelli asked, admiration evident in his tone. "How did you know just what look to go for?"

Darla laughed. She wiped perspiration from her face with a towel Betty handed her. "I just knew, is all," she replied. "You could call it instinct, but it's clear to me that a good poster has to have some, you know, punch. It has to be sexy, but not in a way anybody could call pornographic. It has to be okay to hang in any novelty or stationery store window, but it still has to have what it takes to turn you on when you look at it."

Corelli nodded. "You're exactly right," he said. "In fact, I couldn't have put it better myself. Where'd you learn so much about the poster business?"

Darla gave him her little-girl smile. "Dante, you'd be amazed at what I know."

"I'll bet I would," he said softly.

Darla became aware that Betty had remained silent. She looked over and saw that the agent was staring at her, an expression of awe on her round face. Take a good look, Darla said to herself. Take a good look at the new Darla Dawson.

"We'll have this stuff late this afternoon," Sand said. His manner was buoyant, happy, in marked contrast to the offhanded attitude he had affected all during the earlier part of the session. He knew before seeing the transparencies that what he had shot would be unusually good, even outstanding. The conviction was instinctive, and yet he was as certain as if he'd already inspected the finished work.

"So fast?" Corelli asked.

"Sure," Sand answered. "I have my own lab right here. It'll be ready in a few hours."

"Okay if I come back to see it then? Say around five or so?"

"Of course," Sand said. "You're paying the bills."

Corelli clapped his hands. "Darla, the least I can do

to say thanks is to give you a nice lunch. How about it?"

"Wonderful," Darla replied. "I'm starved."

"I'll run along then," Betty said. "Got lots to do." She turned to Corelli. "Dante, it's been a great pleasure."

Corelli took her hand. "Can't tell you how much I appreciate all you've done," he said. "You really straightened out a hell of a mess, all concocted by me."

"Nonsense," Betty said. "It was just one of those things. Nothing but a big misunderstanding, and what's important is that it turned out fine. I'm convinced we're going to have a great poster."

"*You* are—hey, I can already see it. It's going to be fabulous." He shook his head in wonder. "Fabulous." He looked at Darla. "The lady's not only beautiful, but creative. What a talent."

Chapter 21

The lobby of the Century Plaza was thronged with guests, as usual. Built in 1966, the hotel was modern and chic, considered by some to be the *ne plus ultra* of Los Angeles inns. Nevertheless, its clientele tended to be comprised largely of business executives and professionals rather than show business people. To the latter, the only place to stay was—and always had been—the Beverly Hills. Darla considered the Century Plaza interesting, however, and even stimulating, with its expanses of marble and terra cotta, and its rather splashy elegance. As she walked through the lobby, her arm loosely linked with Corelli's, she was keenly aware of the stir she was causing. Men and women looked, and then stared, the women seeming to scrutinize her even more closely than the men, studying her clothes, her hair, her sandals, while the men concentrated their attention mostly on her face and her breasts. As always, she wore no bra, and the effect in the thin silk blouse was, she knew, mildly sensational. She was also aware of the contrast between her radiant blondeness and Corelli's darkly masculine, well-tailored good looks. The attention made her feel wonderful. It was a lot like making a stage entrance.

Corelli was enjoying it too. He guided her into the Grenada dining room, where the beaming maitre d' showed them to the best table in the place.

They ordered tiny bay shrimps, shipped in fresh that same morning from San Francisco, and asparagus Hollandaise.

"How about some wine?" Corelli asked.

"Are we celebrating?"

"Hell, yes. I feel so good I could climb up on this table and dance."

"They might think it was a little gauche," Darla said. "But as they say around here, if it feels good, do it."

Corelli laughed. "Okay, you called my bluff. But let's have some wine anyway." He called for a wine list and chose a Batard-Montrachet. The sommelier returned in a moment with a bottle and proffered the label for Corelli's inspection. He studied it carefully and nodded approval. "I suppose you consider this traitorous," he said to Darla.

She was puzzled. "What?"

"Ordering French wine in California. To a lot of people out here that's a great show of bad manners."

"Doesn't bother me," Darla said. "But I have some friends it might upset a little."

Corelli tasted the wine. "Just right," he said to the steward.

They ate with enthusiasm, savoring the excellent food, complemented perfectly by the chilled Montrachet, with its great round flavor.

"California wine is really very good," Corelli remarked. "But there is nothing in the world like a white Burgundy." He held up his glass and looked at the pale golden liquid. "Beautiful."

Darla glanced at him thoughtfully. "You really surprised me, Dante."

"How so?"

"Oh, I guess after the experience with that horrible photographer, I didn't know what to expect. I thought you'd have warts and horns and a hairy nose."

"Was it that bad?"

"It was awful. You talked to him, didn't you?"

"Sure. But he didn't treat me the way I imagine he did you."

"God." Darla laughed. "I hope not. That would make him even weirder."

As they ate, Corelli responded to Darla's questions by telling her something about his background and his business. He had been born into a poor Italian immigrant family in Scranton, Pennsylvania, the third son, the fourth of seven children, of a steelworker who had never learned more than a hundred words of English. At times there had been barely enough food to go around, and he had never owned a new suit of clothes until he had attended college.

"Then how did you go?" Darla asked. "To college, I mean."

"Football. I went to Penn State on a scholarship, and what the scholarship didn't pay for, the alums did. By the time I was a senior I had a closetful of clothes and a new car. I thought it would last forever. And that I'd be the greatest back in the NFL."

"But it didn't turn out that way," Darla said. "What happened?"

"Oh, I was drafted by the Steelers, and then in the first scrimmage in training camp, bang. Tore all the ligaments in my left knee." He grinned at her. "You know the value the pros put on a halfback who can't cut? A big fat zero."

"So how'd you get into the poster business?"

"A Penn State fan in Pittsburgh gave me a job in his printing plant as a salesman."

"And you worked your way up?"

"Sort of." Corelli grinned. "I married his daughter."

Darla laughed. "Oh, my. I never would have guessed. You don't seem like the type."

He laughed with her at himself, and Darla liked him for it. "It wasn't really as easy as all that," he said. "My father-in-law was a boozer who liked to play the horses. If there's a worse combination than that, I don't know what it is. He died of a heart attack a few years ago, and I woke up with a bankrupt company and a stack of bills. I had a Cadillac and a big mortgage on a house I couldn't afford, and that was about the extent of my assets."

This was interesting. Darla was always fascinated by people who had fought adversity and won. "What then?"

"We went into Chapter Eleven. Know what that is?"

She shook her head.

"It's the bankruptcy law that lets you defer payment of your debts while you reorganize your company and try to get on your feet. So that got the creditors off my back for a while, anyhow. And afterward, I took a gamble. A big one, as a matter of fact."

"How?"

"Well, I looked around and tried to figure out what you could do to make money in the printing business. A lot of money. Before he died, all the old man had ever done was to take on the standard kind of jobs. Brochures, handbills, labels for a canned dogfood company, that was what most of our business was like. Big orders, sometimes, but it was always a rat race, competing with every other printer on the basis of price, or money under the table, or setting up a buyer with a girl, the usual crap. But then I heard about the volume that could be done with posters, especially star posters, and I thought, what the hell. We've got these big five-color lithography presses, we could do that work as well as anybody. So I went to a company out here in L.A. that was very big in posters, and told them that I wanted to sell out. I told them about our shop, which was called Thomas Bacelli, Incorporated, after my father-in-law, who naturally had named it after himself. I was very humble, hat in hand, and they got interested right away, because they saw it as a way to pick up a pretty good facility cheap. They could even use our losses to help reduce their taxes. I played dumb, pretending I didn't know any of this. All I wanted, I said, was to be sure they knew their business, and that I'd be selling to somebody reputable and with a good future. Well, if you want to learn somebody's secrets, just give them a chance to brag. Hey, how about another bottle of wine?"

Darla was wide-eyed. "Another one? Dante, I'm half-high now."

He laughed. "Is that all? Hell, Darla, you don't expect me to leave you in that condition, do you?" He signaled to the sommelier and ordered another bottle of Montrachet. When their glasses were filled, Darla pressed him to continue.

"The president of their company was a schmuck. Once he got it into his head that the way he could screw me was to convince me how much he knew about the poster business and how successful he was, he told me everything. Some things two or three times. He showed me contracts he'd written with talent that shafted them—"

"How?"

"Easy. He paid them a big chunk up front, or at least what would seem to them like a chunk, but then as the volumes increased, the royalty percentages went down. Actually, it should be the other way around, like it is in the book business, for instance. The more posters sold, the more the talent makes. Or should."

A light went on in Darla's head. A red light. "Then how come you're paying me a straight ten percent?"

"Because that's the agreement I worked out with Betty Frolich," he replied. "But don't misunderstand, it's a good deal."

"But it could have been better, couldn't it?"

"Sure, it could. Hey listen, don't let what I'm telling you make trouble between you and your agent. That's the last thing I want to do."

"Okay," Darla said. "I won't. I'll chalk it up to education. My education."

"That's smart," Dante said. He looked at her. "Know something, Darla? You're not dumb, not by a long shot. You certainly showed that this morning. The thing is, nobody on this earth—nobody—is going to look out for you the way you can look out for yourself."

Darla nodded. How many times had she seen that fact demonstrated? For a long while she had suspected that despite Betty's friendly, supportive manner, the agent actually had no more respect for her, and cared no more about her as a person, than did most of the other people with whom she came in contact. All any of them really wanted was to use her. Betty was no different from anyone else who saw a way to exploit her; she was only more skilled in how she went about it. But after all, that was Betty's business, wasn't it? "What else did you learn?" she asked.

"Oh, how he stuck it to retailers when he had a hot property. If a poster suddenly took off, he'd cheat on the quality of the stock, start filling orders printed on lighter, cheaper paper. While he charged them the same price, of course. If there was enough demand for the poster the retailers wouldn't complain, even though they knew they were getting stung."

"Sounds awful," Darla said.

Corelli smiled. "Sounds like business."

"Is it all like that?"

"No, of course not. There are plenty of honest people around. It's just that you always have to be on your toes, looking out for the sharpshooters and the ripoff artists."

"Was there more?"

"Oh, sure. He even screwed the other stockholders in his own company."

"How?"

"By skimming."

"Skimming? What's that?" The wine was making Darla feel a lovely lassitude, but her mind was entirely alert. She was enjoying herself, and her instincts told her that what she was learning was valuable, that someday she'd be able to use this knowledge in her own behalf.

"It's taking money off the top of a business's income," Corelli explained. "Writing off phony expenses and so on, so that the money is tax-free. In his eagerness to convince me what a genius he was, Mr. Schmuck even showed me his books, and I knew right away what he'd been doing. He didn't know I knew, but I did. My dear departed father-in-law had been doing the same thing, on a lesser scale. The only difference was, he shoveled it right straight into the track, which is a very effective way to piss away money fast."

"So of course you didn't sell your company."

"No. After a week of being wooed, while I learned

everything I could, I went home to Pittsburgh, knowing there were only two things I needed."

"Which were?"

"Money and a star."

"Obviously you got both. How?"

Corelli refilled their glasses. "I probably shouldn't tell you all this stuff, Darla, but I'm having a hell of a good time." He put his hand on her thigh.

"Don't do that," Darla said.

Corelli's dark eyes shone. "Why not?" His voice was soft, but in its timbre was an eloquent hoarseness.

"Because," Darla replied, looking directly at him, "it makes me excited."

Corelli opened his mouth and closed it. "Do you know something, Darla, what you do to me? I could come, right now. Just sitting here."

Darla smiled. "Don't do that, either. Tell me some more."

He put his hand back on the table and took a deep breath, as if to get his emotions back under control. Darla wondered if he had an erection again and decided that he most certainly had. She realized that she also was responding to the feeling of mutual attractiveness and intimacy between them, and that she had become quite lubricious.

"So I got the money and the star," he said finally.

"Come on," Darla said. "Don't tease me. How did you do it?"

Corelli swallowed a little of his wine. "I went to see some people in Pittsburgh. Some people who have a lot of money and a lot of power."

"Who?"

"The organization," he said shortly.

Darla didn't understand. "What organization?"

Corelli gave no answer, but merely looked calmly at his wine glass.

Darla got it, then, and the realization of what he was telling her produced an icy thrill. It was like looking at a deadly spider. The thing was repulsive and dangerous, but you couldn't take your eyes away. "Weren't you— taking an awful chance?"

"Sure, I was. I told you I took a big gamble, didn't I?" His smile assumed an ironic twist. "You couldn't find a much bigger one than that. Lose, and you wake up dead."

"But, Dante," Darla said. "wasn't that worse in some ways than selling out to those other people? I mean, I've heard that getting mixed up with the—well, it's the Mafia, isn't it?"

He nodded. "You hear it called that."

And isn't it true that once they get hold of you, they never let go? You know, kind of own you?"

Corelli shrugged.

"But isn't it?" Darla pressed. "I remember I was at a party one night and Francis Ford Coppola was there. We were talking about *The Godfather,* and of course he directed both of them, and he said that just about all of it was true. Either it happened just as he showed it, or it was very close, or else he put several things together to make one scene, you know?"

"Uh-huh." Corelli looked at her thoughtfully. "Darla, let's just say that it isn't quite the way you think it is. It isn't quite the way Mister Coppola thinks, either. I made a deal. I got the help I needed. As soon as I had the money, getting the talent to work for me was a snap. I changed the name of our company to Star Graphics, and I signed Joni Bickford, you know, the folk singer. That was our first poster, and it hit. And so did our second, and our third. People found they could trust me—that unlike Mr. Schmuck, I wasn't out to screw them. In a very short time I was able to pay back the money I borrowed, and we were off and running. Okay, so I also paid heavy interest. Usurious rates, I admit. But what the hell, I could never have gotten it anywhere else. You know what it all amounts to? Business. And on a pretty high level, at that. I wasn't some bum who owned a shoeshine parlor and who went to a loan shark for money."

As he spoke, Darla understood instinctively the complexity of what he was expressing, and why it seemed somewhat contradictory. On one hand, he was ashamed of having become involved with the mob, and on the other hand, he was proud of it.

"If you had to draw up a balance sheet," he continued, "you'd see that it's still in my favor. Sure, it's dangerous, doing business with them. If you don't come through on your end, that is. But if you do, it's okay. You have no idea what it means, to be connected. Christ, if you knew what went on in Pittsburgh. Or anywhere else, for that matter. Yeah, the Mellons and the Carnegies and all those old Wasp families are powerful as hell. But where do you think they got started? When I was at Penn State I took courses in sociology and American history, and when I read stuff like *The Robber Barons* I learned that people like the Rockefellers weren't a goddamn bit different in the beginning from a lot of guys who run the organization today. They just got going sooner."

Darla grasped it clearly then, and she was sure she was right. Corelli was a man, and a courageous, toughminded one at that. He was also Italian, and his mixed pride in his origins was the basis of his ambivalent feelings about his business connections. Men are men, she thought. And some more so than others. Whatever anyone else might think of Dante Corelli, Darla liked him very much. In fact, she found him extremely attractive. She looked at his strong hands and his square jaw and his full-lipped mouth and felt herself stir again.

As if she had spoken her thoughts aloud, Corelli squeezed her hand as he looked into her eyes. "Let's go," he said, the quality of his voice expressing urgency now, as well as desire.

His suite faced south on the eighteenth floor, the living room commanding a stunning view of Los Angeles, stretching away for miles, its farthest reaches lost in a faintly yellow haze of smog. Corelli led her directly through the living room into the bedroom, making no pretense that he had any other idea in mind.

He put his arms around her, and crushed his mouth against hers, and Darla responded warmly, holding nothing back. She could feel his male hardness against her belly and her knees began to tremble. One of Dante's hands slid down her back and pushed her more tightly against him. He pressed a finger between her buttocks and held her there, caught between the two hard members of his body. She moved her pelvis in a slow rotation and sucked his tongue.

"Jesus Christ, Darla." His breath was coming in hot gasps. "I've got to have you, right now." His fingers went to her blouse and fumbled with the buttons. When he got it off, he said softly, "Baby, baby, you are so beautiful." He bent down, and cupping her breast in his hand, licked the nipple, teasing it with his tongue. Darla could feel a hot, slippery wetness between her thighs as he undid her pants and pulled them off. He pushed her down onto the vast double bed and all but ripped his clothes off in his haste to undress.

Darla lay on the bed, watching him. Corelli was not quite as big as Mike, but he was heavily muscled, and obviously in excellent condition. His skin was dark, almost an olive tan, and covered with short, curly black hairs. A maze of scars crisscrossed his left knee. When he pulled off his shorts, Darla gasped at the sight of his penis. She had never seen one that large. He stood over her for an instant, looking down at her as she stared at it. "Come down here," Darla whispered. "Come down here."

Corelli lowered himself to the bed, but as he attempted to lie atop her, Darla moved aside. "No," she commanded. "Lie still. Don't move. Just lie there."

He did as she ordered, rolling over onto his back, and for a long moment Darla simply lay propped on one elbow, her face inches away from his huge cock, staring at it, her lips parted, her breath rasping.

"Come on, Darla," he pleaded. "Come on, honey. I can't hold it. I swear to you I'm going to come."

"Don't you dare."

Corelli groaned.

Darla reached out and brushed the hair on his thighs with her fingertips and then slowly bent her head forward until her lips touched his scrotum. Her tongue flickered, licking him as lightly as if it were the wing of a butterfly, and the groan in Corelli's throat became a low, strangled cry.

"Oh, my God," he moaned. "I can't stand it."

"Yes, you can," Darla whispered. Very slowly, she moved her darting tongue upward. Then, quickly, she knelt beside him, and leaning forward, took him as far into her mouth as she could. Her free hand went to her mound, and she began to stroke herself gently.

Corelli suddenly went rigid, his muscles tensing. Darla felt him begin to tremble, then he shuddered, and moments later his powerful body bucked and convulsed under her, and then she was coming too, the tremulous agony of orgasm flowing through her in an exquisite current.

Corelli became totally limp. Darla remained still, crouching over him, the only sounds in the room their deep breathing. She felt more powerful than she ever had in her life, in control not only of herself but of this man, this tough, aggressive male who had bet his career and his future and even his life on his ability to win. She had made love to him more than he to her, and the sense of freedom and independence she was experiencing now was exhilarating.

What a marvelous day, she thought. She had come into her own not merely as a photographer's model, or as the principal in a television commercial who was merely mouthing a copywriter's words, but for the first time as a creative force on her own terms. Sure, she thought with a tiny smile, much of her thinking about how to make the morning's shoot a success was what she had gleaned from Sid Brock, but so what? It had been she who had had the boldness and the intelligence to understand that she could use what she had learned, and wasn't that an important part of anyone's life? To succeed you had to seize upon opportunities and ideas and experiences and put them to work for you. The bad, the useless, the mediocre you threw out. But the good you grabbed and used and when you did it became your own.

Darla looked at Corelli's face. His eyes were closed, his lips slightly parted as he breathed deeply in a slow, regular rhythm. Even in repose, his face was strong and handsome. She wondered if he was asleep. Her gaze traveled along his body, studying it. His shoulders were very broad, and although he was completely relaxed, his pectoral muscles still bulged. His hips were narrow, the belly as flat as a boy's. His thighs were heavy but firm, his calves full, undoubtedly developed, she conjectured, by the football he had played as a youth. She glanced at his left knee again, and at the pale, faded scar tissue. Fate, she thought. If some mountainous member of the Pittsburgh Steelers football team hadn't crashed into that knee years ago, mangling it, then Dante Corelli would never have gone to work for a printing company, and would never have gotten into the poster business. Then would she have made this poster? She decided that she would have. If not with Corelli, then with someone else. That was fate, too. She was going to succeed, and mightily. And she was as certain of that now as she was that the sun would rise each day.

But it was nice that she had made the shot with Corelli. Her eyes moved to his limp penis. God, she thought, in awe, what an unbelievable thing. Even flaccid, it was gigantic, dozing there half-curled against his thigh like some thick worm. Well now, Darla thought mischievously, won't it be fun to wake it up.

She began by licking him again. First the heavy pectoral muscles, occasionally interrupting the flicking of her tongue with tiny bites on his nipples, all the while stroking him with her hands, beginning with her fingertips and then following that lightly with her nails. Next his belly, the thick mat of hair tickling her nose, but exciting her too. She kept it up, exploring his body with her tongue and her teeth and her fingers, letting her breasts brush against his skin as she knelt over him. He was awake now, she knew instinctively.

Darla lifted her head and looked at Corelli's face, a small grin playing on her lips. He was staring at her, desire again lighting his eyes. "Do you know what I'm going to do now, Dante?" her voice was low, teasing. "I'm going to fuck you."

Corelli uttered no reply. His cock responded more eloquently than any words he could have articulated. Darla gave a little cry of delight and when Corelli was fully erect, she climbed up on top of him and guided him into her.

She had never felt anything like it. Receiving him, she was stretched and distended almost to the point of pain. But it was not pain. It was ecstacy. Sitting there, looking down at him, she again experienced a great surge of emotion within herself, a sweeping sensation of power. She threw her head back and groaned as she felt her juices pour down onto him. When the orgasm had passed she was hotter and wetter than ever. She bent forward and Corelli reached up with his strong brown hands and fondled her breasts, his thumbs brushing the nipples.

Darla rode him, rocking back and forth, varying her rhythm now and then with a twist of her pelvis or with a hard thrust. Corelli's body moved with hers, his eyes and his hands part of his love response. At last his mouth opened in an access of passion, his lips drawing back from the strong teeth, incredibly white against his dark face, and Darla quickened her pace until he cried out.

Later she lay beside him, totally drained. This time they both dozed, Corelli still on his back, Darla snuggled up against his warm body, one leg thrown across his thigh. When she awoke he was up on one elbow, squinting at his watch.

"Christ," he said. "Would you believe it's six o'clock?"

"Mm-m-m," Darla responded sleepily. "If you say so."

"I've got to get going. I told Sand I'd be back to see those transparencies."

"Just like all men. You never think of anything but business."

Corelli chuckled. "Sometimes I think of other things. This afternoon, for instance." He leaned over and kissed her mouth lightly. "Know something, Darla? I love you."

She opened her mouth to protest, but he gently laid

his finger across her lips. "No," he went on, "I mean it. Not the way you think—not like some moonstruck kid who falls in love with the first pretty girl he goes to bed with. But as a, well, as a friend. I honestly believe in you. And I admire you. And as sure as we're here together, I know you're as straight as they come. Now do you know what I mean?"

Darla nodded silently. She did know. She understood. And she suddenly realized she felt the same way about him.

"You're married, aren't you?" Corelli asked. "To an actor, didn't Betty tell me?"

Involuntarily, Darla smiled. Corelli knew only that she was married to "an actor," and not that she was the wife of the famed Mike Brady. Somehow, that pleased her very much. She realized then that this was still another dimension of the experience of emerging as her own person, of assuming her own identity. "Yes," she replied. "I'm married."

"You happy with him?"

"Happy enough. Some problems, of course."

"Sure." The dark eyes registered awareness. "I just want you to know something. If ever you need help, help with anything from somebody you can depend on absolutely, you call me. You know what I'm saying?"

"Yes, Dante. I do know." And she did. Intuition told her that this was fate, too. She didn't know how or why or under what circumstances she would need Dante Corelli, but something told her that someday she would.

"I'm not trying to complicate your life, or to get between you and your husband." He grinned suddenly. "Not that you invited me to."

She returned his smile.

"But if the time ever comes when you need me, you call me. Got it?"

"Got it."

He climbed out of bed and stretched. "Who knows," he said. "Never can tell when you might have use for the biggest prick in Pittsburgh." He turned and walked into the bathroom.

Darla laughed, watching him. You may be right, Dante, she thought. Righter than you think. She rolled over and looked out the window. Night was descending upon Los Angeles.

Chapter 22

Ben Thompkins sat at the conference table listening quietly as Phillip Strauss read his report in a flat monotone. Ben shook his head in disbelief. This was incredible. Was he really hearing Strauss correctly? He looked around the room. David Archer, Paul Scott, Don Thayer, and Tippy Harkness were all giving the Baker & Barlowe research director their full attention as he spoke. Only Tippy did not look troubled by what Strauss was saying. On the contrary, a small smile played at her lips.

When Strauss had finished reading, he dropped the report onto the polished wood surface of the table and glanced up at the others. "So there you are," he said matter-of-factly. "It appears that we have a problem. People have become so infatuated with the presenter that they don't pay attention to what she's presenting. They see Darla Dawson, and all they think about is her hair and her teeth and her eyes. But they don't think about what she's telling them concerning Superfresh."

"That's no problem at all," Tippy said sweetly. "We just get rid of the little twitch."

David Archer cleared his throat. "I don't know. Doesn't seem to me to be quite that serious. Not necessarily." He sounded cautious.

"Serious enough," Don Thayer said. "The last thing we want is trouble with this campaign. I don't have to remind you that Superfresh is this agency's biggest account."

"All the more reason to consider what Tippy's suggesting," Paul Scott said. He glanced over at her for approval. "We probably ought to replace Darla Dawson."

Tippy smiled at him. "Of course," she said to all of them. "It's exactly the thing to do, and just as soon as possible. She's run her course, and that's it. So we dump her, and get somebody else. And this time we get somebody who's going to last awhile and not burn out." She looked at the men who sat around the table, their faces glum. "I told you, if you'll recall, that you were making a mistake with this Darla. Maybe next time you'll listen to me." The expression of triumph was unmistakable on her pug-nosed face.

Thompkins could stand this no longer. He leaned forward and placed his hands palms-down on the table. "Bullshit," he said loudly.

The others looked at him, startled.

"Let's take a little stock here," the producer said. "We've got the hottest property in the history of commercials, for Christ's sake, and the minute we run into one small problem, everybody is ready to go along with getting rid of her. You know what I think? I think you're out of your fucking minds."

David Archer, ever the diplomat, held up his hand. "Easy, Ben. I know how you feel, but let's try to keep control of our emotions."

"Yes," Tippy said. "Let's be objective, for once."

She's actually enjoying this, Ben realized. She's having a good time. What an honest-to-God, first-class bitch. "Listen, Tippy—"

Strauss interrupted. "May I?" He smiled.

"May you what?" Tippy snapped. "Is that research accurate, or isn't it? She fell on her ass, right?"

Strauss's eyes were bright in his cherubic, bearded face. "I wouldn't put it quite as elegantly as that, Tippy." He nodded. "Yes, the research is accurate, but I think that some interpretation is in order."

"Then let's have it, for the love of God," Thompkins

growled, "before we throw the baby out with the bath water."

"Sure." Strauss sat back in his chair and formed a temple with his pudgy fingers.

"What's happening is that the retention of sales points in the commercial is low. The audience simply does not remember what Darla is telling them about a sweeter breath, whiter teeth, and so on."

"That's no surprise," Tippy said. "The thing is, Darla comes across like a Barbi Doll, and nobody believes her."

"Oh, I think they believe her, all right," Strauss said mildly. "In my opinion they just don't seem to find the promises in the commercial all that important. They don't care that much about Superfresh."

Don Thayer's face registered exasperation. As creative director of the agency, his job was on the line when it came to matters concerning Superfresh. "Hey, listen, Phil. Let's cut out the doubletalk. We have a brand that people like. Your product testing showed that." He added sarcastically, "Or was that phony, too?"

Strauss refused to become ruffled. "Not at all. It's an excellent mouthwash. People who try it like it very much."

"Okay," Thayer went on. "So why don't they remember the commercial?"

"Maybe it's the copy," Ben Thompkins said, looking directly at Tippy. "Personally, I think it sucks."

The copywriter's mouth became a thin white line, but she said nothing. She pulled a More cigarette out of the pack on the table before her and lit it, puffing furiously.

Strauss smiled benignly. "It always amazes me to observe how little patience people have for listening. I don't believe any of you really listened to what I said."

"Oh shit," Thayer snapped. "Knock off the Doctor Freud act. What the hell *did* you say?"

Strauss deliberately wiped the lenses of his glasses with a handkerchief before answering. He inspected his work and, satisfied, set the thick horn-rims back into position on his nose. "What I said was that people remember Darla Dawson, and they remember Superfresh, but not much else." He pointed to the sheaf of papers that lay on the conference table. "That, in a nutshell, is what this report is all about. And you know, it's natural enough, when you think about it, because Ben's right. She really is a remarkable personality in commercials. Her impact is tremendous. But she's so overwhelming that people don't retain much when she starts talking. They simply refuse to absorb the information we want them to about Superfresh."

"Okay then," Tippy said. She stubbed out her cigarette in an ashtray with a vicious jab. "So whether she's overwhelming or underwhelming, she's not doing the job. And maybe you don't give a shit about how effective these commercials are, Phil, but I certainly do." She swung her gaze over to David Archer. "I say get her the hell out of them before she helps us blow the account."

Despite himself, Thompkins admired Tippy's skill at infighting. In one shot, he thought, she's managed to cast doubt on Strauss's loyalty and to set Archer trembling. If you ever want to get an account man's ulcer fired up, just tell him the agency might lose the business he works on.

But Strauss still wouldn't bite. "You're mistaken, Tippy," he said pleasantly. "I care a great deal about the Superfresh commercials. And all the other advertising that Baker & Barlowe produces, for that matter. In fact, an important part of my job is to keep you creative people from making costly mistakes."

Touché, Ben thought. Stick it to her, Phil.

Don Thayer leaned forward, his face tense. "Okay, then, what are you suggesting?"

"I'm not suggesting anything," Strauss replied. "That's your responsibility, not mine. I've reported to you as accurately as I'm able that we have a problem, and I've tried to explain why we do. How we solve it is in your province."

Tippy snorted. "You want a creative solution, Don? I've already given it to you. Step one—replace Darla."

"We can't do that," David Archer said.

"Why the hell not?" Thayer countered. "She's the problem. So the way to lick it is to get another girl."

Archer shook his head. "No."

"What do you mean, no?" Thayer said, annoyance edging his tone. "What are you afraid of?"

Paul Scott is not about to let that opportunity go by, Ben reflected.

Ben was right. The young account executive's handsome face expressed innocent puzzlement. "Yeah, what is it, Dave? Are you afraid of telling Rawlson about this?"

"I'm not afraid of anything," Archer said impatiently. "The research has done what it's supposed to do. It's shown us a weakness in what has been a remarkably effective advertising campaign. And what we need now is a damn good creative response to repair the weakness." He looked at Tippy. "But I certainly agree with Ben that the answer is not to throw out Darla Dawson. Good God, do you realize what that girl has been worth to the company? And for that matter, to us?"

"Oh Christ, come off it," Tippy said. "If it hadn't been her it would have been another of those little hookers Ben had on videotape. What the hell is magic about Darla Dawson? Whatever she is, the Superfresh commercials made her. So now let's make somebody else."

"Dave, is it that you're worried about John Rawlson's reaction?" Scott asked. His tone was solicitous.

The son of a bitch won't let go, Ben thought. When you've got 'em by the balls, squeeze. Wouldn't Scott love to have Robin Baker, chairman of the agency, get the notion in his head that his vice-president on Superfresh was becoming fearful of maintaining an honest relationship with the client? That, to Scott's way of thinking, would be the shortest route to a corner office. Cut Archer's throat, and presto! Paul Scott, boy V.P. The prick.

"Of course I'm worried about John Rawlson's reaction," Archer replied. "Because it's stupid to tell a client a problem without proposing a course of remedial action at the same time. Especially this client. You know John Rawlson has no patience with people who run around yelling that the sky is falling. One thing you have to learn, Paul, is that solving problems is the main responsibility of anybody in account management."

Scott flushed and Thompkins grinned. So old Archer hasn't forgotten how to fight back. What was it agency people called a junior account executive? Ah, yes—a mouse in training to become a rat.

"Do you have a solution that makes sense?" Archer pressed Scott.

The younger man shifted in his chair. "I think what Tippy's saying is right," he replied. "Even if Darla Dawson is a big success, she is one because of the Superfresh commercials. So why couldn't we do the same thing with another girl?"

"Let's be practical, Paul," Archer said. "It's true that John Rawlson would never permit us to simply discard Darla." He looked at Tippy. "He understands her value, even if no one else does."

"I'm not so sure of that," Scott said. "If he felt that she was doing more to hurt the effectiveness of the advertising than helping it, he'd drop her in a minute."

"You're damned right he would," Tippy said. "He's a businessman, first and foremost."

"True enough," Archer said.

"So why are we asking for trouble?" Tippy went on. "Darla doesn't get the copy across, and she's already turning into a pain in the ass in other ways, too."

"What ways?" Ben asked.

Tippy shrugged. "Oh, you know. She's getting harder to work with, and she's got that porn poster now. Wait till John Rawlson sees that."

David Archer smiled. "Personally, I think he'll love it. She looks terrific."

"She does, huh? Well, not to me. And I'm telling you that sooner or later, this one's going to blow up in our faces. Just read the papers and you'll see all the sleeping around she and that husband of hers have been doing."

"You mean those cheap scandal sheets?" Archer

said. "I wouldn't pay too much attention to anything in them."

Ben snorted. "Let's get back to the subject. Can we please try to make a little sense out of all this? What Phil has told us is that we have a problem. And the reason we have it is that we also have a very powerful personality doing these commercials. But the idea that we ought to dump her is absolutely crazy." He looked at Archer. "What about sales? They're still going up, aren't they?"

The account supervisor nodded. "Yes. The brand has had excellent gains."

"Then for the love of God," Ben said, "let's work on new commercials that'll register the sales points more effectively. But whatever we do, let's not get rid of the girl everybody else in the business would love to have."

"Ben's right," Archer said. He stood up. "And now I suggest we get to work. Don, I'd like to see new storyboards just as soon as you and Tippy and the others can work out some ideas. Call me when you have something to discuss."

As the group filed out of the room, Archer motioned to Ben to stay behind. When the two men were alone, Archer smiled. "Don't let 'em wear you down."

Ben shook his head. "The longer I'm in this business, the nuttier it seems to get. Here we are talking about losing a talent who's better than any I ever worked with, all because of one lousy little research report that you could read two or three different ways."

"It isn't just that," Archer said.

"What else then? Don't tell me Tippy's getting to you, too? What's eating her is jealousy. She can't stand Darla because Darla is everything Tippy hates in a woman."

"Yeah. But nevertheless, Ben, I want you to do something."

"What's that?"

"I want you to start putting together a file of possible replacements."

Ben's mouth opened.

"That's right. Don't let anybody know you're doing

199

it, but do it. Sooner or later we're going to need it, believe me. Okay, Ben?"

Thompkins nodded.

"Good," Archer said. He gave the producer a friendly pat on the back. "I knew you'd understand."

"Yeah," Ben said. "I understand."

Chapter 23

Dick Hazelman wound the silver BMW coupe along the twists and turns of Benedict Canyon, climbing higher and higher through the drought-parched hills. Although he was on his way to get laid, Hazelman never stopped thinking business for a moment. Selig's late with a script and two outlines, he reflected. Got to get on his ass. Machelburg is interested in the "Super Spy" property for ABC. Should meet with him to discuss it. Maybe lunch Thursday. And Barry Lieber is making noises like he's a genius—thinks he created "The Savage City" all by his little pointy-headed self. The nerve of the son of a bitch. The show's a hit, so right away Lieber gets conveniently forgetful. Well, fuck him. Executive producers are a dime a dozen. Hazelman decided he ought to start maneuvering with Peter Fried to slide Lieber's replacement into position.

Just below Mulholland Drive he turned east on Sierra Drive, and fifty yards along the narrow street he headed into a driveway that led to a low, rambling ranch-style house. One of the doors of the two-car garage was open. Hazelman pulled the BMW directly into the garage, and after climbing out, closed the garage door. No sense advertising with a car as conspicuous as his. The other half of the garage was occupied by a yellow Corvette. Hazelman stepped around it and walked through an inside door into the kitchen of the house.

Margarita, the Mexican maid, was loading the dishwasher. She offered no sign of recognition as Hazelman entered, and in fact did not even look up as he passed. He walked into the living room and out onto the patio at the rear of the house.

In the center of the patio was a kidney-shaped pool. The area was completely surrounded by an ivy-covered wall to which bougainvillea bushes also clung, their leafy vines heavy with purple blossoms. Beside the pool, on a white chaise, Andrea Derringer lay on her back, her eyes closed against the strong early afternoon sun. Except for a gold belly chain, she was nude.

Hazelman stood still for a moment, taking in her deeply tanned body. Even now, as he felt the first stirring of desire, his thoughts were at least partly business-oriented. It was true, he ruminated, what some of the network guys said about Andrea's body. Good, but the boobs could be better. But the rest of her—Jesus. Tight skin, flat gut, and the best legs he'd ever seen. He studied the triangle of brown hair between her thighs and felt himself growing harder. It was kind of fun, standing here without her knowing it, watching her like a kid enjoying a peep job. He laughed to himself. If I really were a kid, he thought, and I was looking at this, I'd jerk off. But seeing I'm not, what I'm going to do will be a whole lot better.

Andrea's voice was low-pitched and lazy. "Afternoon, Dick."

Shit. She'd known he was there all along. It was typical of Andrea. Everytime you thought you were putting something over on her, she let you know you weren't. On those occasions, the bitch made him uncomfortable. Dumb girls were better. They kept their place and were content to simply do as they were told. "Hiya, Andrea."

She rolled over on her side and looked at him, shielding her eyes with her hand.

"I was admiring your tan," Hazelman said.

Andrea smiled. "Is that all? I'm disappointed."

"Don't be," he said. "I was also looking at your cunt."

"And?"

Christ, didn't anything faze her? "And it was giving me a hard-on."

"That's nice."

"I knew you'd be pleased," he said dryly. "How about coming inside? I don't have a hell of a lot of time."

She climbed off the chaise and stretched languidly. "Delighted."

Standing, her body was even more impressive. She was a little over six feet tall, and beautifully proportioned, despite the opinion of Hazelman's network acquaintances. She stepped past him. "I'll go first," she said. "That way you'll get a chance to stare at my ass."

Goddamn it, Hazelman thought. No matter how you play it, she always makes you feel like a dummy—like she's in charge of you, somehow. Instead of the other way around.

He followed her into the house, observing as he did that he was again carrying out her orders, staring at her ass. It was round and full, unusual in a tall, slim girl, and the sway of her hips as she walked ahead of him was mesmerizing.

When they reached the bedroom Andrea drew back the spread and lay down, her body now appearing much darker against the snowy sheets. Hazelman quickly pulled off his clothes and draped them over a chair.

Her lovemaking was anything but perfunctory. As soon as Hazelman joined her on the bed, Andrea began to work him over, touching him, fondling him, nipping him, her own passions obviously rising as she moved about his body. When he entered her, Andrea was wet, and she climaxed almost immediately.

The impact was not lost on Hazelman; obviously she thought of him exactly as he did of her—as a sex object, there in bed for the simple purpose of satisfying her lust, to be used and enjoyed. It was a little unnerving, if not humiliating, to him. He had never had that kind of relationship with a woman before. But then he had never known a woman like Andrea Derringer. On one hand it was extremely satisfying, because of her skill and sophistication in sexual technique, but on the other hand she made him feel barely adequate. It was a mystery to him and half the time he didn't know what the hell to make of her. But invariably when he was away from her and he thought about her he would find himself eager for another visit.

Just before Hazelman reached orgasm, Andrea employed one of her little tricks—this one a favorite of his. She placed the middle finger of her right hand into her mouth and withdrew it, glistening with saliva. As Hazelman's pace quickened, Andrea jammed the long wet finger into his anus and fluttered it.

"Jesus Christ," Hazelman cried. He threw his head back and his feet twitched involuntarily as he came. Completely spent, he lay sprawled on Andrea's body like a great rag doll, his breath whistling through his open mouth.

After a few moments she slapped him lightly across his buttocks. "Roll off, Richard. You're heavy."

"You didn't think so a minute ago," he mumbled. He flopped onto his back and lay beside her, still breathing hard.

"I did, but I didn't feel like discussing it at the time." She reached for the cigarettes and matches that lay on the bedside table and lit one. "When I was in boarding school we used to say that a gentleman was one who rested half his weight on his elbows."

"You must have had a very genteel upbringing."

"Oh, I did. The very best of everything. I probably wouldn't even have laid you in those days. It's only since I've grown older that I've become more democratic."

Now what the hell did she mean by that? Was she anti-Semitic too, this meshugah yenta? Probably. Unable to think of a suitable reply, he simply cleared his throat, in what he hoped would sound like a meaningful tone.

"I never liked Jews," Andrea said.

"I believe you." The cunt was a mind reader.

"We were always taught that they were not only avaricious, but also not very refined."

Enough, already. "Your reviews look good," he said, as much to change the subject as anything else.

"Uh-huh. Better than Mike's."

She didn't miss a trick. "That must make you pretty happy, even if it doesn't thrill him."

"He has other things to be proud of. His cock, for instance. It's quite a bit bigger than yours."

"Thanks a lot."

"You're welcome."

To his surprise, Hazelman was experiencing sharp pangs of jealousy. "You don't have to fuck him, you know. The idea in the beginning was just to build up his ego, so he wouldn't raise so much hell about your series."

"I don't have to fuck anybody, Richard," Andrea said, exhaling a stream of blue cigarette smoke, "including you. I just do it for fun. And whatever else you might say about him, Mike Brady is some stud."

"That's nice."

"It's even better than that. It's divine."

"So why not save it all for him?" Hazelman said petulantly.

"Is that what you want, Richard?" Her voice teased him.

He snorted. "Shit no, it's not, and you know it. But I have feelings too. And what the hell, if it weren't for me, there wouldn't be any series for you."

"Correction, Richard." An almost imperceptible edge appeared in her voice. "If it weren't for you, there wouldn't be any 'Savage City' for me. But there would be a series. If not this series, another series."

Um. She was right about that, too. There was no way Andrea Derringer would fail to be successful in this town. Hollywood was made for her, and vice versa. But at least she could be a little more appreciative. "At least you could be a little more appreciative," he said.

"I am appreciative." Her hand went to his cock, her fingers stroking it lightly. "Would you like another demonstration of my undying gratitude?"

Hazelman sighed regretfully. "I sure as hell would, but I don't have time." He reached for his trousers.

"That's the trouble with you, Richard," Andrea said. "You never stop thinking about business. Not even to enjoy a superb piece of ass like me."

"Not true," Hazelman replied. "I enjoyed that very much."

"Then what's your rush?" Andrea grasped his penis and began to move her hand up and down.

His voice became hesitant. "I have a meeting."

"Wonderful," Andrea said softly. Her stroking quickened and Hazelman's penis grew larger in her hand. "I'm sure you'll enjoy that more than you would my giving you a super-fabulous blow job."

"I would?" Hazelman's voice was weak. "I mean, no I wouldn't. But I have to go."

"Wouldn't you rather come?"

"Jesus, Andrea."

"And besides, I want to talk to you about a new contract."

His tone became firmer. "New contract? Are you out of your mind? Your contract is only five months old. You've got seven months to go, and then the options are in my favor."

"That's why I need a new contract now," Andrea said. "After all, the show has done a turnaround, thanks to me, which proves I'm worth a great deal more than the paltry salary you're paying me now." She tightened her grip.

Hazelman groaned. "Eight thousand an episode for a relative unknown is damn good."

"The last Nielsen gave us a forty-one share," Andrea said. "And the audience demographics skew upscale in both education and income. With those numbers, eight thousand a show is dogshit."

Hazelman had begun to breathe hard. He stared down his body as if hypnotized, watching as Andrea accelerated her stroking. "I . . . think it's . . . fair."

Andrea lowered her head and drew her tongue slowly across the head of his cock. "But you'll at least discuss it with my agent, won't you, Richard?"

His voice was a barely discernible gurgle in his throat. "I . . . I . . . yeah. I will."

"That's good, Richard," Andrea purred. She smiled. "You're a good boy." Her lips parted, and she moved her mouth slowly downward.

"Oh, Christ," Hazelman moaned. "Holy Christ." For once, all thoughts of business vanished from his mind.

Chapter 24

Zander-Cohen's offices were on South Beverly Drive in Beverly Hills. They were furnished in standard California-plush, or what those in the television industry thought represented good taste. The walls were paneled, the furniture was contemporary, the tropical plants were huge and thickly green, the carpet was deep, and the receptionist was stunning. She was also, Darla noted with amusement as she walked in, carefully imitating the Darla Dawson hairdo, her dyed blonde tresses tumbling to her shoulders in long, streaky waves.

The girl looked up and did a take. "Miss Dawson? Darla Dawson?" Her tone was almost reverent.

Darla smiled. "Yes. I have an appointment with Gary Zander."

The receptionist nodded. "Gee, this is a pleasure. I think you're so beautiful." She pressed a button on the intercom on her desk.

"Thank you," Darla said. It was amazing. In this town, and in this business especially, you'd think people would get used to having celebrities around. Instead, it was the direct opposite. There were no fans like show business fans.

"You may go right in," the girl said.

Gary Zander rose from his desk and stepped around from behind it to greet Darla. "Hey, baby, you're looking dynamite, as usual." He put his arms around her and kissed her. He waved a hand. "You know my partner, Art Cohen?"

Darla said hello to the other man, who sat sprawled in a deep armchair. He was in his middle forties, bald, thin, ascetic looking. Both men wore casual clothing: slacks and open-necked sports shirts.

Cohen did not bother to rise. "Hiya, Darla."

Betty Frolich was seated on a sofa, a cup of coffee in her pudgy hand. "Morning, dear." Betty was wearing a pale gray pants suit and two thin gold chains around her neck. She looked frumpy, as usual.

"Sit down, baby, sit down," Gary said to Darla. "You want some coffee? Tea? Anything?"

Darla declined the producer's offer and sank into one of the deep chairs. She noticed that Art Cohen was staring unabashedly at her body, examining it with the experienced eye of a diamond merchant looking for flaws in a stone.

Gary returned to his seat behind his desk. He opened an ebony box, and chose a long, thick cigar. "You mind if I smoke, Darla?"

She shook her head. "Go right ahead. I like the smell of cigar smoke."

Zander smiled. "Good. Then you'll love this." He decapitated the end of the cigar with a heavy gold clipper. "Havana," he said proudly. "I have 'em sent to me from Canada. It's illegal, you know, to buy Cuban cigars in this country." He lit the cigar with a gold desk lighter that matched the clipper. "Can you imagine that, for Christ's sake? All on account of that asshole with the beard and his Russian friends." He puffed thick clouds of fragrant smoke into the room. "Darla, what I wanted to talk about this morning is a series idea. You remember one night at Dick Hazelman's I told you I had a great premise I thought would be right for you?"

Darla nodded calmly. She remembered that night, all right, but not for the reason Zander thought. The picture of Mike making love to Cathy Drake reformed in her mind, as it had so many times since, and she felt the inevitable pain in her chest. But Zander apparently was oblivious of her true reaction, even though it had been he who drove her home that night, as tears coursed down her face. The producer remembered only that he had mentioned to her that he had a brilliant idea. More showbiz, Darla thought.

"Okay," Zander continued. "So the time, I would say, is now ripe." He grinned at Cohen before looking back at Darla. "In fact, we should have signed you then, when we could have got you a lot cheaper."

"That's the story of my life," Cohen said dourly.

"Hey, be realistic, you guys," Betty said. "You're catching Darla now at an absolutely perfect time. Just when she's really starting to take off. You'll be cashing in on what's going to be the hottest personality in television."

Cohen stared at Darla's breasts. She was wearing no bra, as usual, under her customary thin silk blouse, this one a pale shade of orange that contrasted beautifully with her tan skin. Cohen licked his thin lips reflexively.

"Anyhow," Zander went on, "what we've got here is a hell of an idea. Something absolutely different than anything else on the box. Not just now, but ever. I'll tell you, if you want my honest opinion, I think what we're doing here this morning is making history. You think I'm exaggerating?" He dragged on the cigar and swept the room with his hard gaze. "Okay, I'm on record right now. This one's going to be the top-rated show on TV." He paused dramatically.

Betty looked faintly amused. "That's very exciting, Gary. It really is. But what the hell is the premise?"

Zander waved the cigar. "It's an adventure show, kind of. There are these two girls, see? And they—"

"Whoa!" Betty interrupted. "What two girls? Who said anything about *two* girls? I thought this show was going to star Darla."

The producer scowled. "Hold your water, will you, Betty? It *is* going to star Darla. The other broad will be just, you know, a foil. She'll play off Darla, who's a blonde. The other one will be dark. We don't even know who she'll be yet, for Christ's sake."

"Then why do you need her?" Betty asked.

Zander looked at the agent as if she had begun to

decompose. "Are you going to let me tell you the fucking premise or not?"

"Let him go on, Betty," Darla said. "I really would like to know what this is all about."

Cohen sniffed, his eyes now fixed on Darla's belly. "Yeah, let him talk. I haven't got all morning."

The room grew quiet, and Zander resumed his description of the proposed new show. "The girls are like secret agents, and Darla is their leader. They get into all kinds of wild situations, every one of them real tense and hairy, real heart-stopping suspense. You know, one time they bust up a gang of international jewel thieves, another time they knock over a bigtime vice ring, and like that."

"Is it sexy?" Betty asked.

"Is it sexy?" Zander's tone was heavy with sarcasm. "Now what the hell do you think, Betty? Of course it's sexy. I told you it was going to be the top-rated show on TV, didn't I? Didn't I practically guarantee that was going to happen? So how the hell could it *not* be sexy? Do you think I don't know what makes ratings? Sex and violence. The same things that packed 'em into the Globe Theatre when Shakespeare was doing the scripts, the same things the ancient Greeks got their rocks off on. So what are you asking—if I'm an *amateur*? This show will be so sexy the Catholic Church in its entirety will be up in arms. The bishop will shit in his cossack, or his cassock, or whatever they call that thing. Would that be sexy enough for you?"

"Okay," Betty said. "I was just asking."

"And I'm just telling," Zander said. "If you'll let me."

"Sure," the agent replied. "I'm all ears."

"Anyhow," Zander continued, "the production values will be fantastic. We're going to spend a fucking fortune on this, and the shows will look it!"

"Have any of the networks heard the idea?" Betty asked.

Zander looked pained. "UBS has expressed very sincere interest. In fact, it's as good as sold. Unless NBC grabs it first."

Betty nodded, her eyes bright. "Have you offered it to all of them?"

"Naturally," The producer said. "And they all like it. But it looks to me like UBS will move pretty quickly. Pete Fried is a sharp boy."

"The best," Cohen chimed in. He was squinting at Darla's crotch. "Guy's a genius in picking hits, moving properties around. He's brought UBS from schlunk losers to number one. Nobody would ever believed it could be done. But that momser did it." He shook his head, keeping his eyes carefully focused. "A genius."

"How much of it will be shot on location?" Betty asked.

"Practically all of it, Mrs. District Attorney," Zander replied. "I told you, we're going first-class. It'll look like a feature picture all the way. And not just the pilot either. Every episode. There'll be a lot of helicopter stuff and cars like Ferraris and Maseratis. And every time the girls have to go somewhere long distance we'll have 'em fly in their own Learjet, you know?"

"Where will the locations be, besides here?"

"Hawaii, Mexico, New York, Europe. Anyplace. The moon, for Christ's sake."

Betty pursed her lips and looked at the ceiling. "Sounds good," she said finally. "If you do everything you say. Sounds really good."

"What do you mean *if*, Betty? My word is my reputation, you think I don't know that?"

"Of course you do, Gary." The agent looked at him and smiled. "I'm just making sure of these things in order to protect Darla."

"Yeah." The cigar had gone out. Zander reignited it with the gold lighter. "I know," he said, puffing. He looked at Darla. "How about it, babe? What do you think?"

Darla shrugged, her face wearing its most innocent expression. "I don't know, Gary. To me it sounds wonderful. It's a modern idea, and I've never heard one like it. It would be a great showcase for me. I got all excited just hearing about it."

Art Cohen grinned wolfishly. The idea of Darla becoming excited obviously appealed to him. "You want to hear some more?"

"What would you say was the chief motivation of my character?" Darla asked.

After thirty years in Hollywood, Zander knew something about handling actresses. "That's a good question," he replied. "And a very intelligent one." He stroked his chin. "But I'm afraid I don't have a simple answer for you. It's kind of complicated, you know?" He looked at Darla, his expression apologetic, begging her understanding. "But I'll try. Okay?"

Darla nodded.

"I would say," Gary said, "that you are a woman who is really in charge of her own destiny. Strong, tough, but obviously very feminine and beautiful. More than a match for any man, even though a lot of guys don't realize it until it's too late. I mean, they make the mistake of taking you for granted, you know? They think, what the hell, anybody who looks that great couldn't be very strong or smart, but by the time they wake up that you're both—zap. You've handled them. At the same time, the other girl in the show obviously has great respect for you because you're the leader, right?"

"Yes," Darla said. "I see."

"I could read you an outline of one of the scripts," Zander suggested.

"No, I think I understand the premise well enough," Darla replied. "Betty? Is there anything else I should ask?"

The agent smiled at her. Ever since the Sid Brock-Dante Corelli-Raymond Sand affair, Betty had been much more solicitous, even deferential, in her dealings with Darla. "I'll handle it from here, dear," she said.

"All right, fine," Darla replied. Her voice hardened a fraction. The change in her tone was so slight it would go unnoticed by the men, but Betty would get the message. "Let's just be sure I have the right to okay the scripts."

Gary Zander opened his mouth, but before he could speak, Betty said, "Of course, Darla. Understood." She looked at Zander. Something in her expression told him to shut his mouth, and he did, slowly.

Darla got to her feet and tucked her blouse into her pants. Art Cohen leaned forward.

"Catch you later, honey," Betty said. "You going to be home?"

"Yes, around four." Darla waved to the two men. "Thank you both," she said.

Art Cohen raised his hand in farewell and alternated his gaze between Darla's chest and her buttocks, which he hadn't been able to examine while she had been seated.

Gary Zander came out from behind his desk again and hugged Darla and kissed her. "You're a star, baby. Practically already you're a smash."

When Darla had left, Betty sat back in the deep cushions of the sofa. "Okay, the moment of truth."

Zander looked at her for a few seconds, then returned to his seat behind his desk and for the third time lit his cigar, which was now little more than a stub. "How much time you got, Betty?" he asked.

The agent was surprised. "Not too long, I guess. But enough. Why?"

Zander studied the smouldering end of his cigar before returning his gaze to Betty. "I think there's a way we can cut this short."

Suspicion narrowed her eyes. "How?"

"By getting right to the bottom line. I'm going to tell you what that is, and what it is finally, without any fucking around, and later if you want to tell Darla we fought for hours and you finally won because you broke my arm, that's just fine with me."

Betty's expression turned to one of outright distrust. "What's the number, Gary?"

Zander dropped his cigar butt into the heavy crystal ashtray on his desk. The finality of the gesture was unmistakable. "The number, which does not change, no matter what bullshit you go through after I tell you, is five thousand per episode."

Betty's mouth dropped open. "Five—thousand— per—episode? Are you out of your tiny fucking mind?"

Zander glanced at Art Cohen, an expression of boredom on his face. "What are you going to do?" He shook his head. "With some people it's like that Doctor what-the-hell-is-his-name and his dog. Pablum? Pabloff?" He directed his gaze to Betty. "So you have to go through with it, huh?"

Betty stood up. "I'm not going to go through anything. That's not an offer—it's a goddamn insult."

"You're right about one thing," Zander said. "It's not an offer. It's my final word. You walk out that door and some other blonde cunt goes into that show. And she won't be anybody you handle, either."

Betty sat down. "Couldn't we at least—"

"We couldn't at least do anything," Zander said. "This is the big one for Darla—the break of her career. And you know it. What's she done, up to now? Some television commercials and a couple of bits in other series, and a few walk-ons in shit movies and that's it, right?"

"Balls," Betty shot back. "She's had some damn good parts in TV, and not just little ones, and in *Casey's Dream* she practically ran away with the picture."

"Her tits are too small," Cohen said.

Betty ignored him. "And those television commerials are only the talk of the business," she said to Zander. "She's getting a flood of mail, and whoever heard of that from commercials? The Superfresh people are swamped with letters. They've never had anything like it."

Cohen yawned.

"Five thousand," Zander said quietly.

"Jesus Christ," Betty said. "For how many originals—twenty-six? That's a hundred thirty thousand for the year. She gets almost that much for her commercials now from Superfresh."

"Five thousand," Zander said.

Betty's shoulders slumped.

"And you can forget about script approval," Zander added.

She looked at him. "Could we at least put in a 'reasonable right of review'?"

Zander nodded. Such a clause was merely a sop to actors' egos, and had no real teeth. "Yeah, sure."

Betty got to her feet again, more slowly this time. She put her hands on her hips. "One thing I insist on. If it's five thousand, I want favored nations." This was a contractual provision which guaranteed the star of a vehicle that no other performer in the production would be paid at a higher rate.

Zander looked at his partner. "You got a lunch date?"

Cohen shook his head.

"Then let's go over to the Derby for a Cobb's salad."

"You on a diet?" Cohen asked.

Zander nodded. "Yeah. For a week now." He patted his belly. "Lost four pounds. Not bad, huh?"

Exasperation curled Betty's upper lip. "I said I want a favored nations clause in the contract."

Zander's expression of boredom grew more pronounced as he redirected his gaze to her. "And I said you get five thousand an episode. Period."

Betty's voice rose. "Then you're going to pay the other girl more money?"

"Not if we can help it," Cohen said darkly.

Zander's tone suddenly became almost kindly. "Look, Betty. I told you, we don't know yet who the other broad is going to be. Frankly, and this is off the record, I'll deny it if you quote me, we may have to pay her more than five. Why? Because we gotta have at least one real actress. Somebody who not only has experience, but a reputation. Couple of the networks guys are already into that. You know, the show sounds great, but who are these girls and what have they done? That's the kind of thing they're asking. So maybe we have to pay somebody else a little more, but it's worth it, you know? Kind of like an insurance policy."

Betty frowned resignedly. "Sure. I understand. Maybe you'd have to go as much as ten a show for somebody with a track record."

Zander smiled warmly. "Right, you got it." He looked over at his partner and nodded.

"Then goddamn it," Betty snarled, "you can pay

Darla the same thing. What the hell is a lousy five grand more a week if the show is going to have this great big budget you're bragging about?"

Art Cohen picked his nose as he stared at her. "It's five grand more a week," he said. "That's what it is."

"Betty," Zander said. "I told you. We don't have all morning to fuck around. Do you want this deal or don't you?"

"You're telling me," Betty said, her round face expressing incredulity, as if she were hearing all this for the first time, "you want the most beautiful girl in this business to work for less than somebody else and you don't even know who this somebody else is?"

Gary Zander slowly got to his feet. He placed his fists knuckles-down on his desk and leaned toward the agent. "I said—for the last time—do you want this deal, or don't you?"

"I want it," Betty said, and the meeting was over.

At two o'clock that same afternoon, Cathy Drake and her agent, Bob Mitchell, came into Zander-Cohen's offices. Even in this mecca of the world's most beautiful women, Cathy was remarkable, so perfect were her delicate, classical features. Framed softly by gently waving, dark red hair, her face looked as if it might have been carved by Michelangelo from a piece of flawless, peach-colored Etruscan marble.

Mitchell sprawled on the sofa as Cathy sat gracefully on a chair before Zander's desk. Her body was encased in soft, smoothly fitting gray slacks and a white cashmere sweater. Her breasts were a shade fuller than Darla's, but stood just as firmly, also unfettered by a bra. For a moment the only sound in the room was Art Cohen's slightly adenoidal breathing.

Gary Zander smiled warmly at Cathy as he prepared to light a fresh cigar, snipping its end with the clipper. "I always said you were the best-looking girl in the business."

She returned the smile with a polite one of her own. "Always, Gary? I've only been in it for five years."

Zander laughed. "Okay, you got me. For the past

five years, I always said you were the best-looking girl in the business."

"Thank you," Cathy said. "Bob tells me you have a property you think I might be suited for."

Zander ignited the gold lighter and puffed on his cigar. "I'll say we do." He returned the lighter to his desk. "What we've got is so good," he paused dramatically, "that I'm telling you right now it's going to be the top-rated show on TV."

"Wonderful," Cathy said coolly. "I hope I'm right for it."

"Right for it? You'll be sensational," Zander replied. "In fact, the whole damn show is built around you."

"What's the premise?" Mitchell asked.

Zander blew out a cloud of smoke. "It's an adventure show, kind of. It stars Cathy, but there's another girl in it, too."

"She's just a foil," Cohen said, gazing steadily at Cathy's sweater.

"Right." Zander nodded. "She'll just be there for Cathy to play off, you know?" He went on to describe the kind of situations on which the series would be based, emphasizing the high dramatic standards they would maintain.

"It can't miss," he concluded. "Absolutely can't miss. I'm telling you right now, what we've got is going to be the biggest hit of the fall season. The number one show on TV."

"Sounds exciting," Cathy said. Her voice was low-pitched and pleasantly modulated.

"It's going to be dynamite," Zander said.

Bob Mitchell had listened quietly. One of the new breed in Hollywood, he looked more like an actor than an agent. His face was square-jawed and boyishly handsome under his long, wavy brown hair. He wore tight black velvet jeans, gleaming black boots, and an open-necked Sulka sport shirt of subtly printed gray-blue silk. A gold Roman coin hung from a thin chain around his neck. He had been born Ignatz Mizinski in Brooklyn, New York, but the name Bob Mitchell, he had decided upon his arrival in California, was better suited to the image he wished to project. "What about the production values?" he asked. His voice was soft and gentle, almost effeminate, another affectation currently in vogue.

Zander looked at the agent with undisguised distaste. Over the past three decades he had met and done business with what he had thought was every conceivable type, but straights who tried to act like fags? Mitchell, he knew, was married to Betsy Bernard, who played Jungle Jill in the ABC series for young kids. So why the limp-wrist act?

"What do you think I've been telling you?" he asked. "The production values will be sensational. We're going to spend a fucking fortune on this show."

Mitchell glanced at Cathy. "If the money and all is right, I think this could be a good vehicle for you."

"I think so too," Cathy said. She looked at Zander. "You say there'll be another girl?"

"Like I told you, she'll just be a foil," Zander said. "Just a character for you to play off. She won't even be an established actress. We want it clear right from the start that you're the star of the show."

"How about the director," Cathy asked. "You said he'd be somebody really good?"

"We're thinking about Jack Eastman or Sal Caretta."

Both were award-winning directors, noted for their work in serious drama. "Good," Cathy said. "And the writers?"

"They'll be first-rate," Zander replied. "The head guy is George Louda, and he's already signed."

That was impressive. Louda had written novels and screenplays as well as television scripts. His best credit was "New York, N.Y.," the crime drama that had been a top-rated show on CBS for three years. A smile spread slowly across Cathy's face. "Sounds as if you're really serious."

"Serious?" There was a note of incredulity in Zander's tone. "I keep telling you, we're going after the top rating in TV. It's as simple as that. What we want is number one."

They chatted for a few more minutes and then Cathy left the office. Zander told Mitchell their budget called for five thousand per episode for Cathy.

"That's pretty low," the agent responded.

"Not for somebody who's never been a series principal before, it's not," Zander said. He puffed on the cigar. "And you know goddamn well what this is going to do for this kid's career."

Mitchell nodded slowly. "Who's the other girl?"

"We don't know yet," Zander replied. "Naturally, we wanted to set Cathy first."

"Yeah." The agent regarded the rug for a time. He looked up. "Favored nations?"

Zander waved the cigar. "Can't promise that," he said. "But figure it out. If we're building the show around Cathy, then what the hell. We wouldn't have the budget to go any higher for the other girl."

"Then why not put it in the contract?" Mitchell asked.

"Because we just can't get pinned down like that," Zander replied. "There'll be enough bullshit we'll have to put up with later on with two broads in the same show without making things any more complicated than they have to be in the beginning."

"Okay," Mitchell said. "Five thousand per episode. Agreed."

Zander rose from the desk and stepped around it to give the youthful agent a friendly hug. "Smart, Bob. Real smart. We'll get an agreement over to you in the morning." He hugged the agent again and ushered him to the door.

"One thing," Mitchell said.

The smile disappeared from Zander's face. Once again, he was on the alert. "Yeah? What is it?"

"What's the title?" the agent asked. "Of the series?"

Zander relaxed, and the smile returned to his tanned face. "The title is a fucking beauty. Are you ready for this?"

"Go ahead," Mitchell said. "Thrill me."

"We're gonna call it," Zander said, dropping his voice to a hushed, intimate level, " 'The Witches.' " He slapped Mitchell on the back and grinned broadly. "Is that a title? Is that hot shit?"

Mitchell's mouth pursing into a prissy line. "It's a title, all right." He waved his hand languidly. "See you both later. Ciao."

When they were alone, Zander flopped into one of the easy chairs. "What a fucking day."

Art Cohen rose from his seat and stretched. "I'd call it a pretty good day. We got both broads and we're right on budget."

"Both witches," Zander said. "And you know, I have a feeling that title is going to be a lot more appropriate than we think." He dropped his cigar stub onto the mound of debris in the crystal ashtray.

Cohen scratched his nose. "Personally, I think Cathy Drake's got the best tits."

Chapter 25

Darla studied her image in the dressing room mirror. Bobby and Lee had done their usual work—she looked sensational. Nevertheless, she was nervous. She turned to Betty. "Well?"

"Terrific, Darla. Absolutely terrific."

"I'd better be."

"Hey, what are you worried about? You'll make that Drake broad seem like a hag."

"Will I?"

"Of course you will. And besides, you're the blonde, right? Who do you think the audience's eyes will automatically go to? You'll steal every scene."

"I can't steal her closeups," Darla said.

"Well, no. But on balance you're going to run away with the show."

"Why did it have to be her? Of all the girls in this damn business, why did I have to wind up doing a series with Cathy Drake? I still can't believe it."

Betty sighed. "Darla, this is the break of your life. Never mind who it's with. For you, this is the big one."

"I suppose so."

"And anyway, you shouldn't let a few silly rumors bother you. In this town, everybody gossips about everybody. When I heard that crap about Mike and Cathy I just ignored it. And that's what you have to do, too. Tell yourself it's bullshit, and forget about it."

"Sure," Darla said. "It's bullshit."

"That's all it ever was," Betty said. "Nothing but talk."

There was a knock on the door, and the A.D. called that they were ready to shoot the scene.

Darla took a deep breath and walked out onto the set.

Cathy Drake was already there, and she looked stunning. Darla took in her co-star's hair and makeup at a glance, noting the flawless skin and the perfect features, not missing the curve of her breasts in the light blouse she was wearing. Cathy was talking with Sal Caretta, the director. She waved and smiled when she saw Darla approach. "Hi, Darla. Good to see you."

Darla returned the smile warmly. "Good to see you, too, Cathy." She shook the other girl's hand. "Hi, Sal. This is a big day."

The director grinned. He was slim and dark, with a cap of curly black hair and a short goatee. "Welcome to slavery. From here on, it's nothing but ass-busting work."

"Suits me," Darla replied. "I've been looking forward to it."

"Me too," Cathy said.

Caretta glanced at his script for a moment. He folded it and stuffed it into the back pocket of his jeans. "Okay. You know your lines? Good. Let's walk through this."

The set represented the living room of a diplomat's house in Washington. "You two come through the French doors there," Caretta explained. "You're cautious, because you don't know what to expect. Darla, you spot the body, lying over here by the sofa. You recognize the man as a suspected foreign agent you were trailing earlier. You see at a glance that he's dead, but you don't dare call out to Cathy, because you don't know who else might be in the house. Camera comes in on you while you take this in, and meantime Cathy starts rummaging around on the desk there, oblivious to what you've found. Your face has to tell us about the mixture of reactions you have to what you see. Okay?

Let's run it down." He looked around. "Body!" he yelled. "Where's the body?"

An actor scurried onto the set and took his position on the floor. Caretta ran through the scene until he was satisfied, working with Darla until her moves and her expression were what he wanted, and then he called for a take.

Darla experienced a tiny thrill as she heard the slap of the sync board and the director's command for action. She moved through the doors and walked stealthily across the living room, her body slightly crouched, her hands extended as if ready to ward off a blow. When she reached the body on the floor she bent over it, conscious of the camera silently dollying in on her. Concentrating hard, she widened her eyes exactly as she had done in the run-through, opening her mouth slightly, registering a mixture of shock and horror and apprehension. She crouched lower.

There was a crash, and Darla jumped a foot.

"Cut!" Caretta yelled. "What the hell was that?"

"I'm sorry," Cathy said. "God, that was clumsy of me." She stood looking down at the shattered remains of a vase.

"Okay," Caretta said. "Let's get that cleaned up and we'll make another one."

Darla went back to her place and waited, trying to regain her concentration. She was aware that she suddenly felt tense. She blew the next take, and the next, and it took two more to get one Caretta would accept.

The next shot called for both girls to kneel beside the body, Cathy holding a telephone she had brought from the desk. Cathy was to make a call to a police inspector the girls were working with, and to whisper that they had found the agent dead. They rehearsed it, and when the camera was rolling, Cathy delivered her lines.

As Cathy spoke into the telephone, Darla slowly extended the fingers of one hand so that the tips gently touched the dead agent's cheek.

Cathy's eyes flashed downward, and then up to Darla's face, narrowing as she finished her speech.

"Cut," Caretta called. "And print. Okay girls, take five."

Darla smiled. "Nice take, Cathy."

Cathy did not answer. She walked off the set, and went to the coffee table.

Betty was standing nearby, watching. "Beautiful," she said, as Darla walked over to where she stood. "I knew you wouldn't have a bit of trouble, just as soon as you started working together."

"Uh-huh."

"I've got to get over to my office," the agent said. "I'll try to stop in this afternoon. But really, Darla. I'm glad to see you're off to such a good beginning."

"It's the beginning, all right." Darla looked across the set to where Cathy stood drinking coffee and chatting with the actor who was playing the dead foreign agent. "The beginning of the cold war."

Chapter 26

The early-evening traffic on Sunset Boulevard was heavy in both directions. Mike Brady drove west in the slow-moving mass of cars until he reached the tall white apartment house. He swung the Mercedes into the driveway and down into the basement garage. One good thing about this chick, he thought to himself as he got out of the car, she's convenient. He walked up the stairs into the lobby and waved to the security guard. He stepped into the elevator and pushed the button for the fifteenth floor.

Cathy Drake opened the door and Mike brushed past her into the apartment. "Hey," she said. "Don't I even get a kiss?" She was wearing only a bath towel.

"Sure." He reached over and jerked the towel away from her.

"Mike!"

He laughed, and bending over, kissed her breast. "Evening, ma'am, how you been?"

Cathy shook her head, feigning consternation. "You are the rudest man alive."

"And the best hung." He pinched her buttock and dropped into a deep chair. "Get me a drink, will you? Chivas."

Cathy hesitated. "Wait till I get dressed."

"Don't you dare. I like you just the way you are."

She looked at him and a smile turned one corner of

her mouth. She walked over to the bar and poured drinks for both of them.

"Lots of ice," Mike called, studying her legs.

"I know."

He glanced around the living room. The place was extremely modern, with thick white rugs on a black-lacquered floor, the furniture mostly black and white with occasional touches of red. The drapes were open, and through the expanse of glass on the south wall he could see for miles, all the way to the lights of downtown Los Angeles. "Going to be a nice night," he said. "No smog, for a change."

Cathy returned with their drinks. Mike took one from her and pulled her down onto his lap.

"So let's spend it together," she said.

He swallowed some of the Scotch. "Can't. Be grateful for small favors."

Cathy pursed her lips in a pout. "Dinner, anyway?"

"Not even that. I have to go to a party."

"With Darla, I suppose."

"Yeah, with Darla."

The pout deepened. "So you'd rather be with her than with me."

"That's not it at all. This is a thing I have to go to. Business. Some people'll be there I want to talk to."

"Why don't you ever schedule things like that for dinner, and then take me with you?"

"Because I don't like to mix business and pleasure unless I have to."

"And with me you don't have to?"

"Right. With you I don't have to, and with you I don't want to. You're too good a piece of ass to waste sitting around a dinner table, jawing about business."

"You put it so sweetly."

"Oh, I put it sweetly all right. I put it right in your pussy." He laughed, and with his free hand reached between her legs and stroked her.

"Sometimes I think you just use me."

"Sometimes? Every chance I get." He drank more of the Scotch.

"I just wish that once in a while we could do something nice together."

"You don't think what we do together is nice?"

"Oh, Mike. Be serious, will you? I mean, you could take me somewhere for the weekend, or something. You know, we could go to Palm Springs, or maybe up to San Francisco. Something nice like that."

"How about something nice like this instead?" He brushed her mound again with his fingertips.

"I mean it."

"So do I. Can't you feel it?"

"Who else is going to be there tonight?"

"Lot of people. Some of the network characters, and a guy who wants me to do a TV movie."

"Hey, very good. You going to do it?"

He shrugged. "Depends on the money. But probably. I have to keep moving my image around. Don't want to get locked in."

"What's the role?"

"Business tycoon who finds out his wife's been screwing around, so he decides to kill her. But what he doesn't know is, she's plotting to have him knocked off, too."

"Better not let Darla see it."

"Why not?"

"She might get ideas."

"Not a chance. Number one, she wouldn't want to, and number two, she wouldn't dare if she did."

"Would you say you had a fairly big ego?"

"Almost as big as my schlong, sweetie." He drained his glass. "How's your drink?"

"It's okay. I still have some."

"I want a new one." He stood up, holding her in one arm, and set her on her feet. "And just to show you how polite I can be, I'll make it myself."

He walked over to the bar, with Cathy trailing behind him, and poured himself another Scotch.

"Mike?"

"Yeah?" He drank some of the whiskey.

"Why don't you just forget about that damn old party and stay here with me?"

"I told you, it's business. And besides, you have to get up too early. I don't like to be disturbed."

"Darla has to get up early, doesn't she?"

"That's different. I have her trained. Don't even hear her leave."

"Doesn't seem fair that we have that crazy early call every morning. Damn limousine gets here at five-thirty."

"Yeah."

"So how come you can sleep in? You're working, too."

He grinned. "Two reasons. One, makeup's easier for me. I don't have to get a permanent wave in my cooz, the way you do. And, too, I'm a star, while you two dingalings are struggling to make it, as we say."

"There's that ego again."

"Uh-huh."

"I have an ego too, you know."

"Yeah."

She stepped close to him and brushed her fingers lightly against his fly. "And there are lots of things I can do better than Darla. Acting is only one of them."

"I believe it."

"Well, isn't it true?" Her fingers continued to stroke him.

"What, that you're better in the sack than Darla?"

"Mm-hmm."

"Different, anyhow."

"Is that all?"

"It's part of it. You know what they say. Fucking your own wife is like striking out the pitcher."

"Oh, Mike." Her fingers tightened around him. "I want you to think I'm something special."

"I do think so." He put his glass down on the bar. "I think you're very special."

"That's good." She put her arms around his neck and pressed her body against him. Mike kissed her open mouth, slipping his tongue in and out slowly, in the rhythm of coitus.

"Mike," Cathy breathed. "I want you. I really want you."

"Yeah." He turned her around and pressed himself against her buttocks. He cupped her breast in one hand, his thumb caressing the nipple, and put his other hand between her legs. Cathy rolled her head back, and he kissed her shoulder and then her neck. It was exciting to him to control her like this, to dominate her completely, handling her as if she had been created solely for his enjoyment.

Cathy groaned and moved her hips. She reached back and gripped him. "You're nice and hard."

He moved a finger in and out of her. "And you're nice and juicy." He brought the hand that had been caressing her breast back to his belt buckle and opened it. He undid his pants and kicked them off.

"Mike," Cathy pleaded. "Mike, please. Now."

That was exciting too, hearing her beg. "Take your time, lovey. We'll get there." He took his cock in his hand and stroked her with it slowly, sensuously, sliding it up and down in the crevice between her buttocks.

She squirmed in his grip. "Give it to me."

Holding his arm around her, his finger still slipping in and out, Mike pushed her to the end of a sofa and bent her over it. Then he put both hands on her hips and slid into her from behind.

Cathy moaned and shook her head from side to side, her eyes closed.

His voice was hoarse. "Play with yourself," he demanded.

Obediently, Cathy put one hand on her mound and began to move her fingers.

"That's it," he whispered. He pushed in and out of her slowly, continuing to hold her by the hips. He wanted to prolong this, to experience this sense of power as long as he could. He stared down at her buttocks, watching as he withdrew almost completely and then again buried himself inside her. "Christ, that's good. Love your beautiful ass, honey. Love it."

Cathy moaned again, her fingers working, her hips grinding. She began to tremble. "Oh Mike, I'm coming."

"Ah, Jesus." He quickened his pace, then suddenly

tightened his grip on her hips and plunged into her as far as he could. He held himself there, muscles straining, teeth clenched, for a long moment. Then he withdrew, and pushed her away from him.

Cathy flopped over onto the sofa and lay sprawled out, breathing heavily, her face flushed.

For the next minute or two Mike stood where he was, his chest heaving. The room suddenly seemed very quiet. He glanced out the window, noting that it had grown darker outside, and that it had indeed turned out to be a clear night. As his pulse returned to normal, he smiled to himself. He felt relaxed now, and loose, ready for the evening ahead. There was nothing in the world like a quick piece to settle a man down. He stepped to the bar, picked up his glass, and drained the rest of the Scotch in it in one long swallow. As Cathy watched, he retrieved his pants and pulled them on. "Got to get going," he said.

Cathy continued to watch him. "I don't like this, Mike."

He glanced at her, amused. "You didn't seem to mind it a minute ago."

"I mean it. I don't like being treated like this."

"Yeah." He fastened his belt buckle. "But that's the way it is."

"It makes me feel dirty."

He grinned. "Me too." There was a bowl of fruit on a table. Mike stepped over to it and picked up an apple. He bit into it. "It also makes me goddamn hungry."

Cathy got up from the sofa and walked over to where he stood, her eyes flashing. "You think you can come in here anytime and use me. Like I was just some whore."

Mike chewed on the apple. "You're not just some whore to me. You're a real special whore."

Cathy bared her teeth and swung her hand at his head.

Mike caught her wrist and backhanded her hard across the mouth.

She landed on the rug, her face registering shock. "You son of a bitch."

"Yeah." He tossed the apple core aside and started

231

toward the door, but she got to her feet and ran at him. Mike caught her with one arm, pinning her hands to her side. She tried unsuccessfully to knee his groin. He pinched one of her nipples with his free hand.

"Ow. Goddamn you, that *hurts*." She twisted her head toward him, struggling to bite his neck.

Mike reached back to the bowl of fruit and picked up a banana. "Here," he said. He jammed the banana between her teeth. "I want to remember you with something long and thick in your mouth." He shoved her, and Cathy reeled across the room and fell backwards onto the floor.

Cathy pulled the banana out of her mouth and lay on the rug, choking and sobbing, as Mike went out the door.

He took the elevator to the lobby, nodded to the security guard, and walked down the stairs into the garage. As he guided the Mercedes out into the Sunset Boulevard traffic he wondered idly whether seeing her again would be worth the trouble.

Chapter 27

Art Cohen was annoyed. He had just paid the first service bill on the car, and now look. The traffic light changed from red to green, he put his foot down on the accelerator, and the thing schlumped along like a piece of second-hand junk. He had half a mind to write General Motors a letter and let them know how pissed off he was. A new Cadillac, for Christ's sake, and it was already giving him fits. For two cents he would trade it in on something else. But what? A Continental? Not enough prestige. A Mercedes? Never. The day he spent ten cents on a German car, hell would freeze over. He pulled into the parking lot behind his company's office building and steered the car into his space.

The blonde receptionist smiled as he walked in. She was a pretty girl with good tits, and he had fully intended to screw around with her a little, when he had time. But now with "The Witches" in production he couldn't help it; whenever he looked at her all he could think of was Darla Dawson. She had her hair done the same way, and she even had a big toothy smile. Jesus. If there was one thing he didn't need to be reminded of, it was Darla. Or that other shiksa either, for that matter. The pair of them were nothing but trouble.

Cohen walked into his office and sat down behind his desk. The papers were laid out there for him, the way

233

he liked to have them. The trades were on top, first the *Daily Variety* and then the *Hollywood Reporter,* and underneath, the *Los Angeles Times*. He glanced at the headlines as his secretary brought him coffee and a Danish.

The news wasn't much. *Jaws* was breaking box-office records, and *King Kong* was a stiff. The dollar was sinking in value in the world money markets, and Saudi Arabia's trade surplus was growing at one hundred fifty million dollars a day. Those fucking Arabs. The thought of them made Cohen's blood boil. He ate the Danish and drank his coffee as he studied the previous day's stock prices. When he had finished the coffee he pulled the entertainment section out of the *Times* and headed for the men's room.

As he passed through the outer office the phone rang, and his secretary answered the call and looked over at him. She punched the hold button. "Betty Frolich," she said. "On one."

Cohen kept on walking. "I'm in a meeting."

"She said to tell you it's important."

Jesus Christ. A man couldn't even take his morning shit. "All right," he growled. "I'll talk to her."

He went back into his office and sat down. He picked up the phone. "Hello?"

"Art?"

God, the broad's voice pierced his ear like a knife. "Yeah. Good morning, Betty."

"Good morning, hell. I'm not going to waste words with you, Art. What is this bullshit about Cathy Drake wants to horn in on Darla's van?"

"What Darla's van?" Cohen sputtered. "Who said Darla had a van?"

"You did!"

"Oh, Jesus, Betty." The machine, called a van in the industry, was actually a motor home, highly coveted by star performers as a portable dressing room when a company went on location. Cohen sighed. "What I said was, we got a van for the girls. Nobody said it was Darla's van."

234

Betty's tone expressed heavy sarcasm. "Oh? Didn't they? Well, I'm telling you right now, Art Cohen, you can stick your penny-pinching cheapo schemes up your ass. Darla is the star of this series, and she expects to be treated like it."

Budgets and cost control were special areas of expertise presided over by Cohen, as were logistics and accounting. Managing money—and where possible, saving it—was as aesthetically satisfying to him as were the creating of good teleplays to his partner. To Zander, the goals were critical acclaim, big audiences, homage from the network, and confirmation of his threatrical skills by A.C. Nielsen Co. But to Cohen, everything came down, finally, to the bottom line. He squirmed in his chair. His stomach was beginning to ache. "Listen, Betty. Let's be just a little bit reasonable, for once. Do you know what one of those machines costs?"

"You're damn right I know," Betty shot back. "They cost nothing, that's how much."

"Nothing?" Cohen was incredulous. "What do you mean, nothing?"

"I mean you don't buy the goddamn things, you lease them. And the lease expense is all built right into the price of the production package you sell to the network, so what the hell are you chintzing around for?"

This yenta was too much. "For Christ's sake, Betty, an item's an item. This show's already setting records for the dough that's being spent on it. All I'm asking is for you to give a little on something that's no big deal. Have you talked to Darla about it? I'm sure she wouldn't mind."

"She wouldn't, huh? You know what she said? She said if Cathy Drake wants a van, let 'em go give her one. Is that clear enough?"

Cohen bit his tongue in order to shortstop his instinctive reaction, which was to tell Betty to go fuck herself. With the premier telecast of "The Witches" still weeks away, the publicity the new series was already generating was fantastic. The concept of an adventure series starring two of the most beautiful women in Hollywood had caught the public imagination as few television properties ever had, and the magazines and the columns couldn't give the forthcoming series too much space. Zander and Cohen had never seen anything like it, and for that matter, neither had anyone else. "The Witches" was the talk of the industry, and the UBS Research Department was predicting something approaching a forty share for the first show, with ratings building after that. If they were right, and there was good reason to believe they would be, the lease cost of a second van would be a flyspeck on Cohen's books. Nevertheless, the years he had spent as a CPA, first in the fur business, and then, through his cousin Abe, in television, had conditioned and fine-tuned his almost worshipful regard for money. He rubbed the back of his neck and listened to his stomach gurgle.

"Art? Are you there?"

Jesus. The broad's voice sounded like one of those hags who used to buy and sell second-hand clothing in his old neighborhood when he was a kid on Manhattan's Lower East Side. "Old clothes? Oooh-ld clothes?" the women would wail. The memory came back across the years. He sighed once more. "Yeah, I'm here."

"Well, what about it, for Christ's sake? Are you agreed to keep Cathy Drake the hell out of Darla's van or aren't you?"

Cohen looked out the window. Beverly Hills was a long way from Delancey Street. "Yeah," he said slowly. "I'm agreed. The van is Darla's. We'll get another one for Cathy."

Betty's tone was that of the victorious plaintiff in a tort suit: still wounded by the outrage of it all, but soothed by the balm of the monetary award. "Well, that's better. I'm glad to hear you talking sense for once."

"Okay, but don't let me find you sucking around for anything else, understand?" Cohen's voice rose as he returned to form. "I'm already so far over budget I can't see the top of the hole. And I'm not listening to any more crap about special favors or anything else, you hear?" But Betty had hung up.

Cohen returned the phone to its cradle. "Son of a bitch," he mumbled.

"What's the problem?" Gary Zander had wandered into Cohen's office, coffee mug in hand.

"Frolich," Cohen replied. "That cunt."

"What's she want now?"

"She says Darla has to have her own van. We got to get another one for Cathy Drake."

Zander grinned. "Let 'em use the honey wagons, like everybody else."

"Fat chance," Cohen said sourly. "Fucking show ain't even on the air yet, and already we got two stars on our hands."

"So? What's to complain? The publicity we're getting's fantastic. Every place you look there's a magazine cover with one of them or both of them on it. So who gives a shit if they want to be prima donnas?"

"Yeah," Cohen said. "I suppose so."

"You see the entertainment section of the *Times* this morning? A full page story on 'The Witches.' Fabulous."

"I was just on my way," Cohen said, "to read it." He stood and picked up the newspaper section.

"You know what it says?" Zander was exultant. "That we'll have the number one show on TV. That it's going to be the biggest hit of the new season."

"That's terrific," Cohen said as he moved past his partner. "I'll go read it right now. Because if I don't shit pretty soon I'll explode."

As it turned out, "The Witches" surpassed all predictions. It became, from the first telecast, an unqualified smash. Its share of audience, on the premiere Thursday evening in late September, was a forty-nine, and it built from there. With seventy million television-equipped homes in America, and with an average sixty percent of them watching TV at 9:30 P.M. Thursdays, and with the national average of two and one-half viewers per set, that meant that no fewer than sixty-three million Americans were tuned into "The Witches" during the weekly airing of the series.

No one—not even Gary Zander—had expected it to be as big a hit as it was.

Chapter 28

Darla lay on her back in the king-sized bed in the master bedroom of the Presidential Suite of the Sands Hotel. It was a little after eleven A.M.—early morning by Las Vegas standards—and Mike was snoring loudly through his open mouth.

Darla stretched luxuriously. This weekend was a rare treat. She and Mike had come to Las Vegas the previous afternoon because "The Savage City" was shooting a sequence here on Monday, and for once Darla wasn't involved in any of the action "The Witches" was working on that day in Hollywood. Thus she was enjoying the unusual luxury of a three-day weekend. And adding spice to the occasion was the fact that the scenes Mike's show was shooting here would feature Ted Walters in a guest role. Darla had not seen Ted since the week they had spent together up at Big Sur. For the past several months he had been on tour in Europe. Now the prospect of seeing him this weekend, and possibly finding an opportunity to be alone with him, was delightful to contemplate.

She stretched again and thought about how fast things were happening to her. Although shooting "The Witches" was exhausting, it was also tremendous fun. Instead of being on the edges of a production, watching wistfully while the director handled the principals with care and deference, here she was at last, right in the middle of it. And the show was a fabulous hit. The amount of press interest it had generated was incredible. Every magazine in America, all the syndicated columns and newspaper features, were captivated by the new series. Almost every day the set or the location was crawling with reporters.

Her advertising career was also zooming. And although performing in television commercials was only a means of getting additional valuable exposure, the attention it focused upon her was extremely gratifying. The care given her Superfresh commercials resulted in a presentation of Darla to television audiences in the most flattering manner possible. The attention to detail in those thirty seconds of videotape made each of the commercials an exquisite study of a girl whose natural beauty was remarkable. In them, her hair was perfect, her complexion flawless, and her eyes, her smile, and her winsome personality were all depicted at their absolute best. Magazine polls showed that women liked her as much as men did, and possibly even more. Betty had renegotiated Darla's contract upward, so that Superfresh now paid her at the rate of one hundred and fifty thousand dollars a year.

Before signing the new contract, Darla had been hearing rumors for some time that Superfresh was looking for a replacement for her. At first she had been hurt by this, and embittered. But then, to her wry amusement, all that had abruptly changed when "The Witches" had gone on the air and had become an instant hit. At least she thought it had changed. But in this business, you never knew.

Betty had advised her to be highly selective about accepting offers from other advertisers, regardless of the money involved, and to take only a few, choosing them on the basis of the prestige and the type of exposure they would provide. As a result, she now also worked for Savage, the men's cologne.

In commercials for this company she was portrayed as slinky and sexy, and yet the campaign came nowhere near delivering the impact of the Superfresh advertising. She understood clearly the reasons for this. In the Savage commercials she was the girl who flipped over a man who slathered his chin with the sickly-sweet cologne. The campaign used her strictly as an adjunct to the product.

In the Superfresh advertising, however, it was Darla all the way. Her startling good looks, shown always in breathtaking closeups, provided the impact. Her personality, in all its trusting, little-girl-innocent sincerity, provided the persuasion. And her incredible mouthful of snowy teeth suggested that Superfresh Mouthwash would work miracles. Use this stuff, girls, the message said, and this is the kind of smile you'll have. And although, as the advertising research had revealed, the women of America didn't believe it for a minute, they went into their stores in droves, and came out clutching bottles of Superfresh, visions of themselves as Darla dancing in their heads.

The changes in Darla's relationship with Mike were also remarkable. She was pretty sure that he had continued to screw around with other girls, but the pain of wondering about his furtive dabblings was not nearly as severe as it had once been. She felt it, but it was no longer devastating.

On the other hand, for the first time in her life, Darla had begun to realize the true meaning of freedom, and that was perhaps her most exhilarating discovery of all. She found that she could enter into an affair with a man, even a brief one, and not be hobbled by inhibitions. Her career was rocketing, her love-life was sensational, and each seemed to complement and support the other. The money and the acclaim and the overtures were pouring in, and that made her feel strong and confident and sure of herself in her dealings with men. And because she was learning that she could like a man, and go to bed with him, and experience a deeply satisfying relationship with him that didn't have to be permanent, she had developed a deep awareness of her power as a woman, and it showed in her work. She exuded sex appeal, and in an earthy, natural, but entirely wholesome way. And thus her public life gave strength to her private life, and vice versa.

But nothing was perfect, she knew. In addition to Mike's infidelities, there were countless business problems to contend with. Her poster was doing well, although it was really too early to tell what sales levels it might attain. Her contacts with the advertisers she worked for were a constant hassle. The Superfresh television commercials were okay, but the still photography never did please her. Raymond Sand had shot a couple of the ads, but Darla's opinion was that in this work he had never again even come close to the quality he had achieved in the poster shoot. The agency had then employed a succession of big-name L.A. photographers to make subsequent shots, but none of them had managed to satisfy Darla either. After long back-and-forth conversations and occasional squabbles involving the agency and the client, an ad would finally be produced. Then Darla would pick up an issue of *McCall's* or *Glamour* and see herself smiling seductively from a full page in color over a picture of the Superfresh bottle, and she would hate it.

Invariably, she felt that her hair looked like straw or her mouth was funny, or her skin looked too dark or too light, or there was something wrong with her eyes, or whatever, and there would follow a seemingly endless stream of telephone calls between Darla and Betty as messages were relayed back and forth. Eventually there would follow more meetings and discussions as agency people flew out from New York, and then, after much pulling and tugging, a new ad would be planned and the whole process would begin all over again.

It was not only Darla's dissatisfaction that fed these disputes, she knew, but the client's as well. She gathered that one problem peculiar to print advertising was that an ad simply gave everyone concerned too much opportunity to stare at it and find fault. A television commercial would be on the air for a mere half-minute, then vanish, leaving even an audience as critical as Superfresh management with only an impression of a stunningly beautiful Darla who had been on the tube for a tantalizingly short time. But a magazine ad, in contrast, was something you could hold up and study and criticize and pick at until you were sick and tired of it, after which you could drop it and two days later go back to it and find fault with it all over again. Moreover, there was the static quality of print that added to its invitation to criticize. The picture did not move; it simply lay there, with all its flaws locked in forever, frozen in colored inks for the beholder to grow more and more restless with as time passed. If you didn't like an ad at first blush, given time for study you would grow to loathe it.

The other advertiser and its agency—the Savage people—were worse. They constantly came up with sappy commercial ideas that had Darla mouthing idiot lines while she pretended to be devastated by the stench of the Savage cologne on the male model's face. Darla despised the commercials and fought constantly with the people from the agency, either through Betty or directly, to little avail.

But Darla's contretemps on the advertising side of her career were nothing compared to her problems in the production of "The Witches." In all her life, she had never seen anything to approach the confusion, the inefficiency, and the abrasive interrelationships among the principals, the director, the producers, and the crew, that constituted normalcy in the making of each episode. To begin with, there were the endless struggles between Darla and Cathy. Each was sure that she was the star of the series, and hence treated the other with subtle condescension. Each was immediately and violently jealous of the slightest advantage or favoritism that might be accorded the other. Each constantly sought ways in which such advantages might accrue to her and not to her rival. And each found secret avenues by which to approach the director or the head writer or the producers to curry special treatment. At the same time, each knew how important it was to her own image to maintain an air of mutual admiration and cooperation and even affection with the other.

Consequently their relationship was conducted on two levels. Publicly, and for consumption by the swarms of reporters and feature writers, they were good friends. Privately, and in their sub-rosa maneuverings, they were lionesses competing for the same piece of meat.

In the meantime, the strain on everyone of shooting one full hour episode per week was horrendous. Gary Zander and Art Cohen really had produced the top-rated show on television, and that meant the employment of such factors as exotic locations and elaborate production values and big casts, as well as herculean effort on the part of the director to achieve the highest possible quality in each scene, a working method rare in the medium. It was much more the accepted practice merely to get the shot made, and if the scene didn't play quite as brilliantly as it might have, or if this detail or that was not quite right, so what? They weren't out to make *Gone With the Wind*. What the hell, this was only TV.

"The Witches," in marked contrast, was being shot as nearly as possible according to the production standards of a feature picture, just as Zander-Cohen had promised it would be. The result was a punishing, back-breaking, exhausting schedule that reduced cast and crew to quivering, worn-out bundles of raw nerves by the time the last scene had been shot each Friday night. And as much as Darla loved being part of it, as much as it meant to have this break at last, she was nevertheless completely played out at the end of each week.

Darla kicked the covers off the bed. She turned and looked at Mike's body. The drapes were still drawn; in the semi-darkness, the contours of his muscles, the black hairs on his chest, were only dimly visible. Then she noticed that he was semi-hard. Darla had read that a man normally became fully erect at least three times each night while he slept, and from what she had been able to observe during the years she had lived with Mike, it was true. The trick, she knew, was to catch him on the rise. She reached out stealthily and touched his cock with her fingernails.

Mike stirred slightly and interrupted his snoring with a groan. Darla paused for a moment and smiled in anticipation. It was always exciting to her to creep upon him like this, and lately she had found that this was often the best time to approach him. Coming out of sleep, rested and not fully awake, Mike could be lured into making love quite easily.

Darla looked at her body, then back at Mike's, and that was exciting too, seeing them both together, naked, knowing that they would soon be locked in a passionate embrace. She was in excellent shape, she noted with satisfaction. Her muscles were firm from tennis and swimming, and the sun had burnished her skin to a deep gold, except for the narrow bikini band of white that ran across her pelvis.

Darla moved her hand from Mike's body to her own. She was wet, she discovered as she moved her fingers. Her body was also charged with the restless, almost electric current of energy she had experienced so often lately.

She thought about the times she and Ted Walters had made love, and the mental images that formed in her mind added to the excitement that was rising within her now. She looked down to where her fingers were gently moving and she imagined Ted lying between her legs, his warm mouth pressed against her, his tongue probing, exploring, licking her, lifting her higher and higher. She'd come, she knew, if she kept this up, and what she really wanted now was Mike. She turned to him again and lightly fondled his cock with her fingers.

Mike groaned once more in his sleep, and after a moment of sputtering, his snoring ceased and he lay quiet. To her delight, Darla saw that his penis was growing larger. She bit her lower lip to keep from giggling, and as lightly as she could, she began to move her hand up and down. An instant later, Mike was rock-hard.

Darla leaned over and kissed his mouth as wetly and sloppily as she could. "Mike?" She kept her lips close to his.

"Mm? Wha—?"

"Let's fuck." Hearing her say it, she knew, invariaby turned him on.

"Um-m."

She tightened her grip a little. "Come on, honey," she breathed. "I want your cock. Turn over and fuck."

Mike's eyes fluttered and opened. He looked down at her moving hand.

Oh God, Darla thought, I'm going to come before he even gets it in. She opened her legs, slid her free arm over his back as he rolled over onto her, and guided him into her.

It was sublime. As soon as she felt him enter, Darla gripped Mike's broad back with both arms and held onto him as tight as she could. However she might enjoy other men, in any of the myriad inventive, delightful positions, what she loved most was to have Mike exactly like this, while she lay on her back, her knees partially drawn up, holding him, the huge, strong body over her, taking her, dominating her, using her. She felt his powerful hands reach under her and pull her to him. He plunged deeper into her, and then she was coming. Her orgasm was a hot, shivering flash that swept over her and made her squirm and rock and move her hips as if this climax had a life and will of its own.

As Mike's fetid morning breath roared in her ear and the whiskers on the side of his jaw scratched against her cheek, a small, warm thought appeared in one corner of Darla's mind. This weekend, she decided, was going to be a hell of a lot of fun.

Chapter 29

The center court at the Las Vegas Tennis Club was a jumble of cables, reflectors, scrims, and baffles, a sprawl of equipment dominated by a dolly-mounted 35mm camera. The crew of "The Savage City" went about its work with the studied, casual air of professionals who had worked together for a long time, while in the stands the extras who comprised the audience chattered among themselves, happy to be getting paid for sitting outdoors in the warm Nevada sunshine.

Near the judge's stand Rod Britney was in conference with Mike Brady and Ted Walters, the two principals in the scene he was shooting. Britney wore frayed jeans, an old pair of boots, and a faded khaki shirt. A stopwatch hung from a lanyard around his neck. Brady and Walters wore tennis whites, Walters's shirt decorated with a blue pattern that identified Capri, the Italian sports clothing manufacturer who paid him fifty thousand dollars a year to wear their apparel.

The director's expression revealed his exasperation, although his tone was patient. "We don't have all afternoon, you know. And this really shouldn't be so difficult. All I'm asking is that you keep the rally going as long as possible. I want the sequence to be one take with no cuts, to give the scene authenticity. Later we'll cut away for the special effects." He squinted at the sun. "This light will change in another half-hour or so, and that'll make more problems. So let's get it done. Remember, it should look like you're both playing all out, but the key thing is to keep it going. That should be simple for you, Ted."

The pro grinned. "Sure, it should be."

The implication of the reply was not lost on Mike. He scowled. "Meaning, I suppose, that the reason we're not getting the shot is me."

Walters smirked, and Mike felt his temper rise.

"All right," Britney said. "Let's not go into who's doing what wrong. We'll get this in a breeze if you'll both just bear down and concentrate."

"Yeah, sure." Walters's voice held a note of boredom. He glanced casually up into the stands to where Darla Dawson sat with Sarah Winchester, the girl with whom he was currently living. Both girls waved, and he raised his racket in acknowledgment.

"Come on," the director said. "Let's do it. Places, everybody."

Mike walked to his position at the far end of the court and waited patiently as Walters, the ball boys, and the actors who were playing the officials in the scene went to their stations.

Billy Jackson, the makeup man, approached Mike and patted his face with a sponge bearing tan pancake. "This sun is hell on skin tones," he remarked.

"Yeah." Mike was still smarting from Walters's implication that Mike's ineptness had been holding up the shooting. He stood silently as Billy made repairs.

"Okay," the makeup man said. "That's got it." He smiled. "You look beautiful again."

Mike grunted as Billy walked away. He had no time today for precious compliments from faggots. All he wanted now was to get this scene over with and get into a shower. Working with Walters was beginning to get on his nerves. The tennis player was such a goddamn smartass. Actually, Mike was a pretty fair player himself, and yet they'd been on this setup all afternoon and still didn't have the footage Britney wanted. The concept of the scene was that Mike would be locked in a hard-fought match with a skilled tennis player, and then after a long, exciting rally, Mike would suddenly bring his extraordinary strength into play and blow his opponent off the court.

"Settle down, everybody," the A.D. yelled. "Audience, let's pay attention, and we'll get it this time." He looked carefully around the set and then nodded to Britney.

"Okay," the director said. "Camera."

"Speed," the cameraman replied, indicating that the big Mitchell was rolling at the proper twenty-four frames per second.

"Slate," the director ordered.

The slate man held the board identifying the scene and the take in front of the camera and slapped the sync boards together smartly.

Britney took a deep breath. "Action."

Ted Walters uncoiled his lithe body into his big trademark serve, sending the yellow sphere booming across the net to Mike. The ball seemed to have energy of its own as it caromed off the surface of the court, and Mike found that he had to strain to return it. As the rally progressed, he moved carefully into position for each stroke, concentrating on making his swing as precise and yet as powerful as he could. Even though he knew Walters was merely breezing along, Mike had to marvel at the smaller man's effortless grace.

After six or seven exchanges, just as Mike was beginning to feel confident that Britney would have his footage, the ball suddenly seemed to veer slightly to the right, and when Mike hit it, it went out by a yard.

"Cut!" Britney's voice was heavy with disappointment.

"Shit," Mike said. "I'm sorry." He looked across the net and saw that Walters was barely containing a smug smile. The little bastard. Had he done that deliberately? Hell, he must have. There was spin on that ball, and even if Mike had been expecting it, which he wasn't, he probably wouldn't have been able to return the shot.

"Okay," Britney called. "Give us just a minute here, and we'll go for another one." He squinted anxiously at the sun. "That was going great until that last shot. Try to keep it in, Mike, if you can."

Mike nodded tersely as the director turned to confer with the cameraman, who sat back in resignation on the dolly seat. As Billy trotted over to patch his makeup, Mike noticed that Walters was again grinning up to where Sarah Winchester and Darla were sitting. So that was it. Walters was hot-dogging for that cunt Sarah at Mike's expense, making Mike look like an asshole while the great tennis whiz patiently and kindly put up with his childish fumblings. Maybe what Walters needed was to have his racket stuck up his ass, head-end first. Mike ground his teeth, resolving to stay with him on the next exchange no matter what.

"All right, now," Britney said to the cast. "I have to tell you that if we don't make it this time, that's it for the day. The light won't match the earlier footage unless we get what we need in the next few minutes." He glanced at Mike but said nothing. He ordered the crew into action once again, and Walters's serve came whistling over the net toward Mike.

The tennis professional's moves were as catlike as ever, but this time it seemed to Mike that Walters's stuff was easier to handle. Mike moved back and forth on the court with as much care as he could muster for each shot, readying himself for the returns and then whacking the ball sharply and cleanly. He was tiring rapidly, he realized. The racket felt like lead in his hand, and he could feel the fatigue pains streaking across his upper back. But he didn't let down for an instant, running hard to get into position, giving it all he had. He lost track of the number of exchanges, and at one point he had to stretch to pick up a low shot with his backhand, but he got to it all right and sent the ball arcing back in a picture-perfect return.

"Cut," Britney called. On hearing the director's order, Walters went into a grotesque parody of a tennis player, assuming a comic, spraddle-legged stance that made him look like a spastic ape. A roar of laughter went up from the extras in the stands.

That's fucking done it, Mike thought. He threw his

racket down and started toward the net. I am going to punch that prancing little shit right square in the mouth, he said to himself, and I don't give a goddamn what anybody thinks.

"Beautiful, Mike." Britney smiled. "That last backhand was a beauty."

Mike stared blankly at the director. "Huh?" What the hell was Britney talking about?

"We got more than enough," Britney went on as he walked up to Mike. He shook his head. "You made it look so easy that time. Christ, if you'd played like that earlier we would have had the shot two hours ago."

"Oh, yeah." The muscles in Mike's shoulders sagged and he unclenched his fists. "Glad we got it." He looked at the other end of the court and saw that Walters had gone up into the stands, where he sat chatting animatedly with Darla and Sarah. Mike turned and walked off the court.

The hot shower was relaxing and deeply restorative. Mike let the water beat on his back and shoulders for a long time, soaping and resoaping himself, relishing the soothing effect of the stinging needles of water. He was positive now, as he stood thinking about it, that his conjecture on Walters's play had been accurate. The pro had been toying with him throughout the afternoon, making him look as silly as possible in the eyes of Sarah Winchester while he displayed his own admirable skills. But for Christ's sake, why? Walters certainly must have looked a lot more impressive to her knocking over other pros, guys who could really give him a hell of a fight, than he would have in screwing around with Mike in a make-believe match for a TV program. So why go through all that? There was no doubt whatever that this was exactly what the little prick had been doing, because the minute Walters learned that they were down to their last chance to finish shooting the scene, he let Mike make every return and Britney got his footage. Just like that. So what the hell was going on?

Mike wrestled with the question for several minutes but came to no satisfactory conclusion. What could be so important to Walters about making an ass of Mike?

And why would that be a big deal to his girlfriend? Mike thought about Sarah, a dark-haired girl with a full mouth and a ripe, inviting body. She had been Miss Something-or-other in Michigan and had come to California thinking, like so many girls who had won minor-league beauty contests, that the next step would be acting in movies. Her career went nowhere, but someone introduced her to Walters who spent a night or two with her and invited her to move in. For the last six months or so, she had been on the tour with the pro. As Mike thought about her, a suspicion began to form in his mind. He remembered now that when he had met her the previous evening, she'd been extremely warm in her greeting, holding his hand tight when she shook it, looking directly into his eyes. And when they went to dinner together at the Flamingo, Sarah made a special effort to be attentive to him. Later, he recalled, when he played a few hands of blackjack, she stood close to him at the table, watching him, and he was aware of her lush breasts brushing against him.

Mike was used to girls responding to him this way, and usually thought nothing of it, taking it as his due, knowing that it was an experience common to any star. To be sure, he reveled in it, and when the girl was especially attractive, and the circumstances were right, he took maximum advantage of the opportunity. But often he paid no attention, or when a girl made overtures, he simply kidded with her, teasing her a little, and then walked away from it. But this was different. Mike suspected that, unbeknownst to him, or probably unnoticed by him, Walters's nose had been bent out of joint by Sarah's flirting, and this was the tennis pro's way of getting even. Why, that silly little shit. The more he thought about it, the more certain Mike became that he had found the answer. It burned him to think about it, and yet at the same time the realization that he had figured it out was vastly satisfying. Once you knew where your opponent was coming from, he told himself, you could handle him. He grinned broadly, and turning off the shower, reached for a towel.

Chapter 30

Dick Hazelman had arranged a party that evening at Caesar's Palace. Mike led Darla into the lobby of the hotel at a little after eight o'clock. Mike was wearing white linen slacks and white Gucci loafers, an open-necked white silk shirt from Parini in Rome, and a beige mohair jacket his tailor had finished only the previous week. He knew that the effect of his darkly tanned skin and his muscular good looks against the light, elegantly fitted clothing would be striking. He felt fine now, having enjoyed a brief nap after his shower, and he was looking forward to the evening. The thought of seeing Ted Walters and his girlfriend was especially pleasing to him. Now that he had unraveled the mystery of the afternoon's conduct by the tennis pro, he was no longer outraged, but was even amused by what Walters had been up to. Not that Mike was about to forgive the little bastard and just walk away from it. Hell, no. That wasn't his style. And although he wasn't angry about it, he was a little miffed. Nobody gave Mike Brady that kind of crap and got away with it. What Walters needed was a lesson, and Mike had figured out a perfect way to give it to him. He grinned to himself, relishing his plan.

Mike was aware of the stir he and Darla were causing in the glittering lobby of the hotel. Even here in Vegas, where show business personalities were to be seen easily and regularly, he was something special to the public, and he loved it. To the press, and even to his associates, he pretended to hate the fuss generated by the fans and the autograph hounds, but the truth was that it was deeply satisfying, even thrilling to him, to have total strangers, pretty girls among them, approach him with that goggle-eyed, star-smitten, worshipful expression on their faces, simpering about how they never missed his show, and how wonderful they thought he was, and how handsome, the girls frequently throwing in an offer to prove their fealty in more tangible ways. He liked having Darla on his arm, too. With her rather spectacular appearance, abetted by the great mane of blonde hair and the white evening dress she wore, she set off his presence very well, he knew.

Hazelman's party was in one of the second-floor suites. As Mike guided Darla toward the elevators, a group of teenaged girls, giggling and shrieking, bore down upon them. "Oh, Christ," he said. "Here come the scavengers." He grimaced, but he noticed that one of them, a tall girl with blonde hair done up in the increasingly popular imitation of Darla's, had a very good body. He turned the scowl on his face into a smile as the group bounded up to them.

For a moment, as the kids milled about, waving scraps of paper, clamoring for autographs, Mike didn't get it. They seemed to be ignoring him and directing all their attention to Darla. He stood gaping as the girls chattered excitedly, pushing their pencils and pieces of paper toward his wife, all jabbering at once. He shoved his hands into his pockets and stood to one side as Darla smilingly complied, doing her best to write her name, answer the flood of questions, and acknowledge the compliments at the same time. "I see you all the time in the Superfresh commercials," he heard one girl say, and "Gee, I think you're the most beautiful lady in the world," and "Your hair is fantastic. Is it real, or a wig?" and "Do you think 'The Witches' is going to make you rich?"

When the girls had collected their prizes and were drifting away, giggling among themselves, Mike took

Darla's arm and headed her once again toward the elevators. Her face was flushed, he noted, and her eyes were bright with excitement. Nothing like this had ever happened before, and he didn't know what to make of it. A mixture of feelings—hurt, disappointment, even jealousy—churned in him. But he wasn't going to let Darla know it. "Well, how does it feel?" He smiled.

"Wonderful." Darla laughed. "Absolutely wonderful."

"Pardon me, please?" It was the tall blonde girl with the Darla hairdo. "Could I have your autograph, Mr. Brady, please?" Mike scribbled his name and the girl darted off after her friends.

This time Mike's amusement was genuine. Christ, he said to himself, I am now an afterthought.

The suite Hazelman had engaged was already thronged with people. Mike left Darla in a group that included Bob Backus of "Stellar and Cross," the ABC cop series, and Rena Morena, the Latin singer whose show at the Nugget was a big hit. He strolled over to the bar and ordered a Chivas on the rocks.

"Hey, Mike. How you doing?" It was Britney. The director's concession to dressing for a party had involved putting on a fresh pair of jeans and a clean shirt.

"Fine, Rod." Mike accepted the drink from the bartender and sipped it. "How about you?"

"Okay, now," Britney smiled. "This afternoon was getting a little tiresome, with all that hot sun. I think everybody was feeling a bit frayed. But you really brought it off in that last take," he added. "I can't wait to see the rushes."

Mike nodded. "Glad we finally got it, and I'm sorry I slowed you down."

"No problem at all," Britney replied. "I know it was tough, playing with Walters. Even when he's taking it easy he's hard to stay with. The man is incredibly competitive."

"Uh-huh." Mike wasn't deceived. Britney was being cordially apologetic, his manner and his words obviously intended to be supportive to Mike and to smooth over any abrasion the day's shooting might have caused. But his true feelings had been expressed on the court that afternoon, when he had been struggling to hide his disgust and his impatience with Mike for holding up the scene. All of which made Mike the more determined to revenge himself on Walters. He smiled as he thought of his plan once more. So the tennis pro was jealous of Sarah and resented her interest in Mike? So he'd taken it out on Mike by trying to make him look like a clown in front of the girl? Okay. Mike had his own ways of dealing with that kind of shithead. He smiled at Britney. "It still would have gone a lot faster and a lot easier if I knew what the hell I was doing with a tennis racket."

An expression of wonderment crossed the director's face. "Not at all," he said quickly. "Anybody would have had a hard time with Walters. I'm only glad we got the shot."

"Sure." Mike grinned. "So am I." He knew exactly what was going through Britney's mind. The director was surprised that instead of finding Mike touchy and irritable over the afternoon's ragged efforts, he was finding him pleasant and self-effacing. Well, there was a hell of a lot that Britney didn't know. One mistake nobody should ever make was to take Mike Brady for granted. He swallowed more of his Scotch, feeling assured and expansive as the whiskey made its way into his belly.

"Hey, you guys—this a private party?"

They turned to find Sybil Moscowitz smiling up at them. Sybil was a writer for *People Magazine* whose favor Dick Hazelman was currying by entertaining her and her husband for the weekend here in Las Vegas, and by inviting them to this party, a made-to-order opportunity for an exclusive interview, since they would be the only journalists in attendance. Sybil was a bright-eyed little woman with chopped-off brown hair and rosy cheeks. Her husband Jeff was the photographer end of the team. Hazelman considered a feature in *People* worth more than a piece in most other publications, chiefly because it was one of the best-read of the general magazines among both men and women in the more affluent urban areas of the country.

"Oh, hi," Britney greeted her. He tended to be a little gun-shy of writers, especially since a newspaper story one of them had written a few years earlier had figured prominently in a divorce suit in which Britney's second wife, feral bitch that she was, had stripped him clean. Nevertheless, he made room for the reporter at the bar.

"How goes, Sybil?" Mike asked. "You getting much?"

"Not enough, Mike," Sybil shot back. "Never enough."

"Why don't you try Britney, here?" Mike suggested pleasantly. "They don't call him Rod for nothing, you know." He noted with satisfaction that the director had flushed slightly at the jibe.

"Terrific," Sybil replied. "But if you don't mind, I'll settle for a drink, this time around."

"Sure. What'll it be?"

"Vodka martini on the rocks?"

Mike asked the bartender for the drink, and Britney excused himself. "As long as I can't be of service," he mumbled as he moved away.

"He's scared you're going to write a story about him," Mike said.

"That's refreshing," Sybil remarked. "In fact, it's a totally new experience for me. In my business it's usually the other way around. Especially working for a rag like *People*. It's not only the publicity, it's even become a kind of an in thing to be covered in it. But then, show folks have always been freaky, don't you think?"

"Search me."

"I'd love to," Sybil said sweetly.

Mike laughed as he took the martini from the bartender and handed it to her. "Luck."

She raised her glass to his and tasted her drink. "How did the shoot go this afternoon?"

"You were there. What did you think?"

"If I didn't know you were always kind and loving and even-tempered, I'd say Walters had you pissed."

Mike smiled. He was relaxed and feeling good, and

257

the Chivas was spreading its cheer. No reporter was going to get his goat tonight, not even one with a nose as suspicious as Sybil's. "No comment."

"Meaning he did?"

"Meaning it was hot and dusty out there and I was playing lousy tennis and if I was pissed at anybody it was at myself for holding up the scene."

"Do you really think Walters is as good as he's cracked up to be?"

"I think he's one of the top players in the world. It says so right in *Sports Illustrated*. Must be true, huh?"

"Oh, hey," Sybil replied with mock seriousness. "If SI says so it must be. Time Inc. would never bullshit anybody." She looked at him. "But you know what I hear? That he's slipping a little, and that Dumas is expected to take his ranking away from him this year. Starting by beating him at Wimbledon."

"Couldn't prove it by me," Mike said pleasantly. "Walters could whip me without a racket."

The writer sipped her drink, and Mike knew she was ruminating about what approach to take next. He was an old hand at fencing with the press, and prided himself that he never lost his cool with a reporter or a columnist.

"So how do you think this show will turn out?" Sybil inquired.

"Very well," Mike answered. "It's a good script, and the sports angle is something a little different for the series. I think the audience will enjoy seeing an old jock like me hobbling around the court."

"Think Walters's guest shot will help the ratings?"

"I sure hope so," he said. "God knows we can always use a boost." He glanced around the room, which had become quite crowded with people, among them a sprinkling from the UBS network and various acts working in Vegas, as well as Hazelman's friends and members of "The Savage City" cast. Mike noticed that Walters and Sarah Winchester had arrived and were standing talking in the group that included Darla. The trick, he said to himself, will be to slide Sarah away from her little peckerheaded friend.

"So the ratings have you worried?" Sybil asked.

Mike smiled and shrugged in reply. He asked the bartender for a refill.

"Well, do they?" Sybil persisted.

"What's to worry?" Mike said easily. "Ratings always fluctuate. Ours have been a touch soft from time to time, but by and large we're on one of the most solid shows on television. Matter of fact, if you'll take a look, you'll see that although 'The Savage City' had been drifting a little, we had a three-point share jump in the last Nielsen. That," he said, unable to keep a trace of smugness out of his voice, "is what you call vitality."

"Uh-huh." Sybil leaned close, her chipmunk eyes watching him intently. "I hear the turnaround was due to one thing: Andrea Derringer."

The remark was like a lance driven without warning into his chest. Despite Mike's earlier casual indifference to the writer's probes, this one had gone home, hard. It took all his self-control to remain calm as he answered. "I wouldn't say that."

Sybil Moscowitz had been a reporter for a long time. She smelled blood. "I would. The girl is one of the most exciting new personalities in television, and the public is responding to her in a big way."

Mike drained the Chivas from his glass and signaled to the bartender for another.

"I also hear that UBS is delighted with her and that Peter Fried is personally taking credit for discovering her," Sybil went on.

"Is that so?" Mike countered. "I thought we all had Barry Lieber to thank for that stroke of genius."

Sybil grinned. "You know this business, Mike. If she'd been a flop, she would have been an instant orphan. As it is, she's looking great and everybody wants a piece of the credit."

"Yeah." His voice was flat.

"How do you feel about having her in the series?" Sybil explored.

"Okay. Fine. I'm always looking for new ideas, new factors to keep the show fresh, stimulate viewer interest."

"More name guests, for instance—like Ted Walters?"

Walters again, the turd. Mike looked over and saw that the tennis player was talking earnestly to Darla. Sarah Winchester had become engaged in a conversation with a dark-haired young man Mike didn't recognize. Go ahead, Walters, he said to himself. Ignore your girlfriend and you'll make it all the easier.

"Is that right?" Sybil persisted. "You want more name guests?"

"Yeah, sure," Mike replied. "Don't kid yourself. That has a lot to do with interest in the show, too."

Sybil was not about to settle for this idea. "Sure, but nothing like what Andrea has meant to it. Some people say that she's been more than just a fresh new face— that she's actually earned the series a reprieve."

Mike scowled. What the hell was this? Was he actually standing here defending himself and his series against attack from this pushy little cunt? He swallowed more whiskey. "Reprieve? That's pretty strong language. I think you're just trying to blow this up into a story."

"Am I?" Sybil bored in. "I don't think so. I think Andrea Derringer is a terrific new personality and that she has a kind of animal magnetism that affects everybody, including you."

Once again, the writer had found a chink in Mike's armor. A picture of Andrea formed in his mind as he had last seen her, in the house on Sierra Drive, wearing a yellow silk peignoir, which, typically, she hadn't bothered to close. She had kissed him goodbye and he had walked out to his Mercedes feeling drained, and then halfway down Benedict Canyon he'd wished he could have her all over again. Okay, so Andrea Derringer really did have animal magnetism. More than even Sybil Moscowitz knew.

"Are the stories true, Mike?"

"What stories?" What the hell was she getting at now?

Sybil's tone softened, became almost intimate. "You know, about you and Andrea."

"Shit," Mike snorted. "I don't know what you're talking about." He finished his drink and set the glass down on the bar. "And now, if you'll excuse me, there are some people I have to say hello to."

Sybil smiled happily, obviously pleased at what she had mined. "Sure, Mike. Thanks for the drink."

As he moved through the crowd, various well-wishers greeted Mike, but this time the star treatment tasted like bile in his mouth. He spotted Hazelman talking to Shorty Zoll, the remarkably successful agent who was as famous in the Hollywood community as many of the stars he represented. Mike caught the producer's eye and beckoned to him.

Hazelman hurried over, full of bounce, as usual. "Hi, Mike. Having a good time?"

"Glorious," Mike mumbled. Was this jerk never anything but cheerful?

"Ran into Louise Lasser earlier," Hazelman said. "She wants to stop in later on to say hello. Will you be around?"

"No. I won't." Mike looked at the producer. "You're staying here, aren't you? In this hotel?"

Hazelman looked puzzled. "Yeah, why?"

"You alone?"

"Uh-huh. Brenda is in New York visiting her family. Why?"

"Because I want to borrow your room, or your suite, or whatever the hell you're staying in." Mike stopped a passing waiter and told the man to bring him a Chivas.

An expression of understanding crossed Hazelman's face. "Oh, sure. I get it." He dug into his pocket for his room key and slipped it surreptitiously to Mike. "Seven-fourteen," he said under his breath. "But hey, Mike—be careful, will you? You know that's taking a chance, with Darla right here."

"Don't worry about it," Mike replied, his tone edged with sarcasm. "She's being entertained by your tame tennis player."

At around ten o'clock the double doors at one end of the big room were opened, revealing a sumptuously laden buffet table in an equally spacious adjoining room. Smaller tables for dining had been arranged. As the guests moved into the second room, Mike slid smoothly into the flow of people and took Sarah Winchester's arm. She looked up at him, surprised. "Hey, baby." Mike smiled. "How about having dinner with me?"

Sarah had been talking with the young dark-haired man with whom she had spent most of the evening. She opened her mouth to protest, but Mike ushered her away and up to the buffet table. He handed her a plate. "Hungry?"

"I—guess so." She looked at him speculatively. "Are you always so domineering?"

"Only when I want something desperately," Mike laughed.

Sarah's expression softened and she shook her head. "Really, Mike."

She certainly was pretty, Mike decided as he watched her fill her plate with fresh salmon and avocado salad and artichoke hearts. Good big tits, and a roundness of the hips he liked, and a full mouth that was interesting and alluring. He picked up a plate and followed her along the table.

They sat with Bob Deakin, a UBS executive, and the girl Deakin had brought with him from Los Angeles for the weekend. The girl was impressed to find herself sharing a table with Mike Brady and at first addressed most of her remarks to him, but Mike largely ignored her, displaying his most charming good manners to Sarah. After a time, Deakin and the girl gave up trying to engage them in conversation, leaving Mike to chat intimately with Walters's girlfriend.

Sarah liked Los Angeles, she told him, and was looking forward to getting back there when the current swing of the tour was finished. She wanted to continue her efforts to break into acting, and planned to enroll in one of the schools. Mike gave her some advice on which of them he thought could be most helpful to her career. Without making any definite promises, he managed to convey to her that he thought she had talent, and that he would even go so far as to put in a good word here and there. Sarah was genuinely pleased, and obviously flattered, and she responded to him warmly as dinner progressed.

The wine steward kept their glasses filled, and by the time dinner was finished, Mike was a little drunk. But he was delighted with the success he was having with the girl, and was totally confident that things would work out exactly as planned.

As soon as some of the guests began to leave the tables and drift back into the other room, Mike grasped Sarah's arm. "Let's get out of here for a little while," he said. "This place is stuffy. I could use some air."

They slipped out of the dining room and took the elevator to Hazelman's suite.

As Mike closed the door behind them, Sarah looked around with mild curiosity. "Are you staying here?"

He shook his head. "This is Hazelman's. I just wanted a place where I could get away from the crowd for a breather. Big jams of people get on my nerves." He stepped to a sideboard, on which stood bottles of liquor, mixers, and ice. "Drink?"

"A little one, please. Scotch." She sat down on a deep white sofa and leaned back comfortably.

Mike brought their drinks, a light one for her, a dark amber for himself, and sat beside her.

"We shouldn't be gone too long," Sarah said, tasting the drink.

"Sure. But the peace and quiet is nice, isn't it?"

"Uh-huh. You know, there were a lot of interesting people there tonight. Dick Hazelman must know everybody."

"He makes it a point to try."

"Well, that's good, isn't it?" Sarah asked. "I mean, isn't that part of his business?"

"Yeah, I guess so. But I think he has a natural talent for ass-sucking. A lot of guys have to do a certain amount of it at one time or another, but for Hazelman it's a joy."

"Do you have to do a certain amount of it, too?"

Mike looked at her. "Hell no, I don't. I call the shots, I don't take them."

"Must be nice," Sarah said thoughtfully, "to be in a position like that. I suppose that's where everybody would like to be. It's what most people dream about all their lives, and then they never get there."

"Sure. But the reason they don't is that they usually don't get much beyond dreaming about it. In this life, if you want something, you have to reach out and take it."

"In the beginning you had to, though, didn't you?"

"Had to what?"

"You know, suck ass, as you put it?"

"Never, baby. Never." He drained his glass and stepped over to the sideboard for a refill. "With me it was always a battle, right from the start. When I was a kid in Cleveland I was a street fighter. Then I started boxing in the amateurs, which weren't really amateurs. They were supposed to be, but there were always a few bucks under the table. I ran up a good record, and then I got into the Olympic trials and made the team. I won a gold in Tokyo, and that gave me a reputation. All of a sudden, people knew who Mike Brady was." He returned to the sofa, a little unsteadily, and flopped down beside her.

"Why didn't you go on boxing after that? You must have had a lot of offers, didn't you?"

Mike laughed. "I had 'em by the hundreds. Every creep and his brother wanted to turn me pro and then manage me to the heavyweight title."

Sarah's eyes were wide. "You didn't want that?"

"I didn't want to be somebody's meal ticket while I got my brains scrambled. That's for jerks. But then I was interviewed on a couple of television sports shows and ABC wanted me to be a color man."

"A what?"

"A color man. The guy who's number two on a sports announcing team. The number one guy calls the action, while the color man puts everybody to sleep with a bunch of dumb remarks. You know, during time-outs he says things like 'Yep, ol' Charlie there was a real nifty athlete at Slippery Ass Tech until he got caught blowing grass and going down on the coach's mother.'"

Sarah laughed. "Sounds to me as if you missed your calling."

Mike grinned. "I guess I do have a certain talent for it, at that. But I knew there were a lot bigger things to be had on that tube. When UBS gave me a shot on 'Trailrider,' I grabbed it."

"Weren't you afraid of getting stereotyped as a cowboy? I mean, isn't that what often happens with those western series? I've heard people say that it's a big risk for anybody to get into them for that reason."

Mike swallowed half the Scotch in his glass. "That's bullshit. A good actor, a really strong personality like mine, can do anything and not get tagged with typecasting."

"Do you think so?" Sarah sounded unsure.

"Hell yes, I know so," Mike replied. He thought about it for a moment. "You know who's a perfect example of that, and who's a hell of a lot like me in that respect, as well as in a lot of other ways? The Duke. Good old rough, tough John Wayne. Christ, he's been in as many horse pictures as Roy Rogers. But anytime he wants to do something else, like a war movie where he's a combat officer, or something where he's a cop or a CIA agent, nothing to it. He does it, and he's great. And you know, Duke was a jock too, to start with. Football player."

"I didn't know that."

"Sure. Hell of a good one, from what I'm told. Played at Southern Cal. So anyhow, I knew what I was doing. One season in a supporting role on 'Trailrider,' and bang—my own series. And look what's happened since. 'Savage City' is one of the hottest shows on TV."

"It's true, Mike. You really made it. Right to the top. And without kowtowing to anybody."

"Damn right. But you're wrong about one thing. I haven't got where I'm going yet. Not by a long shot."

Surprise showed in Sarah's eyes. "You haven't? But what more is there? I mean—"

Mike emptied his glass and set it down hard on the coffee table. "I'll tell you the plan, baby." He was feeling expansive, and enormously confident, unaware that the underlying reason for his euphoria was that he was now quite drunk. "What happens next is that I dump this show."

"Dump it?" Now she was genuinely astonished.

"Exactly. I dump it. You know why? Because the time to go out is when you're on top. When you're right up as high as you can go with one thing, it's time to go on to something bigger."

"But what could be bigger, Mike?" She shook her head in wonderment. "The star of your own hit series. What else is there?"

He looked at her with a small smile, as if he was shyly revealing to her a great discovery he had made. "I'm going to do movies," he said softly. "First as an actor, and then I'm going to produce them. That's where the real money is, for a creative talent."

Sarah stared at him. "I had no idea. I mean, I didn't know you had any interest in that end of the business."

Mike flicked a hand deprecatingly. "Who do you think runs the series now? Hazelman? Or that string of jerk-off writers?" He punched his chest, his voice rising. "*I* create these shows, that's who. I plan the story lines, I decide on the creative concepts. Hell, I even come up with most of them myself. What do you think we're doing right now? Putting Walters into one of the 'Savage City' episodes was my idea, because I knew it would turn the audience on to remind them that I was once a jock, and a great one at that. America is nothing but one big arena, you know. Show the people a name athlete and they go apeshit."

"I know," Sarah said, the expression on her face clearly indicating that she was thinking about the experience of living with one of the world's top tennis stars.

But Mike was oblivious to her reactions, enthralled now with his ideas concerning himself and his future. "I want to package my own pictures, as an independent. What I'll do is, I'll set a concept, and then I'll hire writers to do the script according to what I want, and then I'll pick the actors and the director and produce the property. Sometimes I'll star in the pictures myself and sometimes not." He looked at the ceiling. "Give me five years and I'll be one of the biggest men in this business. Not just an actor starring in some fucking television series, but a really big man. Like Kubrick, or even De Laurentiis. And you know why I know it for sure? Because I'm exactly like those guys. I have the brains, and I have the balls, and I also have one other thing. I have the creative ability."

Sarah held her nearly untouched drink in her hands, an expression of fascination and curiosity on her face. She put the glass down on the coffee table and followed Mike's gaze upward, seeing nothing but the smooth, ivory-colored surface of the ceiling. "You sound very sure of yourself."

"I am sure. As sure as I'm sitting here. And as sure as I am that if you want to be something, you have to believe in it yourself, before anybody else will."

"That sounds like somebody I know," Sarah said with a slight smile.

Befuddled by alcohol, caught up in his own self-adulation, Mike didn't grasp what she meant. "Who's that?" he asked thickly.

"Ted, of course. He wrote the book on how important it is to believe in your own ability."

"Did he, now?" There was an edge of nastiness in his voice. He thought about the tennis player and a wave of anger surged through him. The image of Walters standing on the far side of the court, grinning superciliously as he put Mike through the afternoon's humiliating exhibition, was infuriating. The nerve of that lousy little shit. So Walters was jealous? He'd give him something to be jealous about, starting now. He turned and looked at Sarah, his anger turning to lust as his eyes swept over her body. Jesus, she was something. He slid an arm behind her back and kissed her suddenly, forcing his tongue into her mouth.

Sarah started in surprise, and then pulled her face away from him. "Please, Mike. I didn't—"

He grasped her jaw in strong fingers, and kissed her again, his other hand gripping her wrist from behind her while his body pinned her against the sofa. In this position, he knew from experience, a girl was helpless, unable to bring either arm into play to defend herself, while at the same time he was in an attitude of control, with one hand free to do whatever he wished. He chuckled to himself as she twisted her body. This was going to be fun, he decided. He liked the ones that struggled a little before they gave in. It was sporting, like landing a marlin. First the battle, and then she was all yours. It tasted sweeter that way, when you finally got it. He moved his hand downward and slipped it into her blouse. She wasn't wearing a bra, and the heavy, full breast felt firm and smooth in his hand.

Sarah tore her face free. Her eyes were wild and frightened. "Mike, stop. Stop. I didn't come up here for this. Honest. Please let me go. If I misled you I didn't mean to. I—"

Mike grabbed her jaw again and held his face an inch from hers. "Sure, baby. I know. You don't really want to fuck. You don't really want to feel the best cock you ever had." The sound in his throat was a cross between a growl and a laugh. He pressed his mouth against hers, holding it there as she strained unsuccessfully to free herself. He lowered his free hand to her waist and undid the button on her pants.

Sarah's struggling increased, but she was trapped, no match for his strength in any circumstances, but especially in this position. She tried to kick her feet, but Mike swung a heavy leg over and held it between her knees.

She was helpless now. Her muffled protests turned to a groan expressing a mixture of fear and resignation that Mike mistook for passion. He pulled the pants down roughly, leaving them midway down her thighs, and slid his hand under her nylon bikini pants. The touch of the crinkly hair was inflaming to him. Sarah's body began to tremble, which he decided was the result of her rising excitement.

Where to take her? The bedroom? No, it would be a kick to do it right here on the sofa. Continuing to hold her in his vise-grip, Mike reached down and yanked her underpants and pants from her body. Sarah suddenly went completely limp, and Mike grinned to himself.

Okay, I know. Hold out for your virtue, but when that big hard cock is coming at you, that's the time to lay back and love it. He pushed her down onto the sofa, and then climbed astride her.

Sarah's eyes were wide with fear and revulsion. Her mouth quivered. "Mike, please. I'm begging you."

He chuckled again. "Sure, honey, I know what you're begging for. And that's just what I'm going to give you." He undid his belt and dropped his pants and his shorts. "There it is." He grinned.

Staring up at him, Sarah realized that his eyes were fixed on his penis. In an instant the expression on her face was transformed from one of helplessness into that of the trapped animal who knows it must fight if it is to survive. Her lips drew back from her teeth in a grimace as her hands shot out to grip his testicles. Grabbing one in each hand, she squeezed with every ounce of strength her racing adrenalin could pump into her muscles, crushing his balls in a powerful, fear-induced grip.

For a fraction of a second, Mike's alcohol-fogged brain could not grasp what was happening. He was aware only of a violent, nauseating pain. Then he realized what Sarah was doing and snatched her hands from his scrotum. But her hands were large and strong, and when Mike tore them away he wrought further damage, her clamping fingers twisting his testicles, her nails raking the skin of the sack, leaving raw, bloody furrows in their wake.

Mike half stepped, half fell off the sofa, clutching his agonized crotch. "You lousy cunt," he choked out. "I'll fix you." Bent over with pain, swaying drunkenly, he reached for her, but at that moment his stomach convulsed and its contents erupted from his mouth in a burning stream of vomit. He fell to his knees, retching, the slimy mess dripping from his lips and his nose. He fought to gain control, but it was hopeless. His body was wracked again and again by spasms that sqeezed his gut dry, until at last the heaving produced no more than a few thin flecks of yellow dribble.

After several minutes, Mike staggered to his feet. His eyes were tearing, partially blinding him. He groped his way into a bathroom and splashed cold water on his face, finally ducking his head under the faucet.

When he had regained some semblance of control over himself, he wiped his face with a towel and stared at his image in the mirror. His hair was plastered to his skull in long, wet strands, and his skin was flushed to a deep, mottled red. He stood looking at himself for a long moment, his breath rasping in his throat, before he turned and limped back into the living room.

The girl was gone, but Mike hardly noticed. He was still drunk, and his vision was double. Insanely, it reminded him of the image in a camera's rangefinder before it was brought into focus. His head throbbed in a vicious rhythm, each pulsebeat stabbing his cortex like a fiery lance. But the pain in his groin was the worst of all. It was agonizing to walk, but he had to get the hell out of there. He slowly made his way through the door and to the elevator, his steps halting and shuffling like those of an old man, one hand supporting his torn and swollen testes.

When he reached the lobby he put his head down and limped out the front doors to the curb, for once unrecognized. He dragged himself into a cab and told the driver to take him to his own hotel.

Darla was not in their suite. Mike pulled his clothes off as gently as he could, his hands shaking, and fell heavily into bed. He wondered where Darla was. Probably still at that dumb fucking party. Jesus Christ—why couldn't she have sense enough to come back here? Goddamn it, he needed her. His stomach heaved again, but he fought back the urge to vomit. A moment later he descended into a deep, drunken sleep.

Chapter 31

The San Isidro Ranch looked as if it was under seige. The rambling one-story buildings, constructed in the ancient Spanish style of stucco walls and red-tiled roofs, were surrounded by trucks bearing camera equiment, props, wardrobe, portable generators, makeup and dressing rooms, a workshop, an infirmary, and the myriad other items necessary to the operations of a film company on location. The cool green lawns, usually immaculate, were crisscrossed with cables and dotted with litter. To one side of the cluster of ranch houses, in an area shaded by giant oak trees, were parked two General Motors motor homes. The vehicles bore no markings to distinguish them from each other, and in fact no special markings at all, except that in the windshield of each was a small cardboard sign bearing initials: in one, DD; in the other, CD. Thus the crew, and presumably only the crew, would know that each machine was the private mobile dressing room of a co-star of "The Witches," and would know in which one resided Darla Dawson, and in which one Cathy Drake.

The episode they were shooting now at San Isidro required the girls to take on a band of cattle rustlers who operated on a grand and modern scale. They used helicopters to spot their targets and then to herd them into box canyons and other topographical traps, whereupon members of the mob would move in with large trucks containing slaughtering and freezing facilities. The cattle would be rounded up by the choppers and forced into the trucks. Once inside, they would be reduced to sides and quarters while the trucks were en route to distant metropolitan centers, where the illicit cargoes would be sold. It was the girls' assignment, of course, to thwart the rustlers, after a suitable amount of suspenseful chase action, sex, and teasing revelations of various parts of the girls' bodies.

The location was ideal for this story. Originally a Spanish land grant, San Isidro had remained a working ranch continually for nearly two hundred years. So vast were its sprawling prairies and rolling hills that even its cowboys occasionally found themselves lost and too far from home at dusk, forced to build a fire of deadfall pine and to spend the night huddled in a bedroll, their heads pillowed on their saddles. Renting the ranch cost the penurious Cohen a thousand dollars a day, but it was worth it. The place was sprawling and picturesque, and best of all, it was absolutely authentic. Moreover, it was controllable. No unexpected pedestrians or cars or motorcycles were here to come wandering into a shot, and no army of cops was necessary to keep order. And because outside temptations were distant and therefore minimal, it was a peaceful location for the producers, unmarred by crew shenanigans, except for an occasional overly enthusiastic involvement with alcohol or pot, or bouts of bed-hopping.

This morning the crew was set up a mile south of the ranch houses, on the edge of a steep ravine. The action called for Darla and Cathy to ride horses down the seemingly impassable side of the gully, thereby unexpectedly cutting off the escape route of one of the mob heavies. Two stuntmen, both small of frame, one wearing a long blonde wig, the other a long red one, had been engaged to do the actual ride down the ravine slope. Darla and Cathy would be shown galloping toward the edge, and a cut would follow to a reverse-action long shot of what would appear to be the girls leaping into the ravine on their mounts, then struggling to hold them in a long, barely controlled slide down the rockstrewn, almost impossibly steep surface. They had finished the approach shot, and Darla and Cathy sat in canvas-backed chairs drinking coffee and listening to Sal Caretta, the director, discuss the upcoming slide with the cameraman, the A.D., and the two stunt men. After this, the next setup would be a running shot from a camera truck of the girls again galloping the horses, this time along a trail.

"Get the horses set on the edge of the ravine there," Caretta instructed.

The cowboy wearing the blonde wig shook his head. "Can't."

Caretta looked at him curiously. "Why not?"

The cowboy spat. "Horse sits up there on the edge lookin' down that slope, he ain't going to go. He's going to be scared. What you got to do is run 'em so they don't know where they're going till it's too late to stop."

Caretta thought it over. "What if the horses couldn't see?"

The second cowboy, wearing the red wig, spoke up. "You mean blindfold them?"

"Exactly," the director replied. "We did that one time when we had to jump a horse into water."

"No good," Jud Bruner, the cameraman, said. "Camera's too close, there, on the other side of the ravine. You'd see the blindfolds." He sighed. "Which brings up another problem."

"What's that?" Caretta asked.

"We're going to know they're doubles." Bruner nodded toward the two bewigged cowboys. "With them coming at us head-on, there's no way anybody's going to believe that's Darla and Cathy on those horses."

The director scratched his beard. "What if we move the camera down the ravine a ways—make it from a three-quarter front angle?"

Bruner pursed his lips. "Yeah, we could do it that way. But the shot wouldn't be as good. Not as dramatic. The ravine wouldn't look as steep, either, from there."

"Yeah." Caretta studied the Mitchell, set up on an aluminum-and-steel camera platform on the far side of the ravine. A portable bridge, similar to those used by the U.S. Army Corps of Engineers, spanned the chasm just out of camera range. Nearby, the sound man squatted over his equipment. "But at least," Caretta remarked, "we'd get the shot."

"Darla," Cathy said. "Got a cigarette?"

"Sure." Darla dug into the leather musette bag that rested at her feet. "Here you go." She extended a package of Winstons to Cathy and took one herself. Cathy held out a light and Darla inhaled deeply. "God, I'm hungry. Can't wait for lunch."

"Me too," Cathy said. "Must be all the fresh air. How's your weight doing, by the way?" she added solicitously.

"Oh, no problem," Darla replied. "I eat like a bear and yet I never seem to gain a pound." Which is not true, Darla said to herself. But it must be disappointing for you to hear, Cathy dear. "How about you?"

"Same thing," Cathy said. "Even ice cream doesn't do a thing to me."

"Uh-huh." Bullshit, Darla thought. She glanced at the bridge. Jeff Patterson, a young actor who was playing the role of a youthful cowboy who had been coerced into joining the band of rustlers, was crossing over to where Caretta stood conducting the conference with Jud Bruner, the A.D., and the pair of stunt men. Darla sipped her coffee and studied Patterson. He was about twenty years old, she decided, and almost startlingly handsome, in the boyish way she had always found so appealing. He had thick, dark blonde hair that came down over his ears. A lock of it hung down on his forehead and gave him a charmingly carefree expression, even when he was serious. And when he broke into a grin, which was often, the effect was stunning, as if a light had been turned on. His teeth were even and very white, above a well-turned jaw and a thick, athletic neck.

"What's the problem?" Patterson asked jovially, as he approached the group.

Caretta explained the difficulty to him.

Patterson smiled and looked over at Darla and Cathy. "That's easy. You just don't let the girls shave for a couple of days, and the footage'll all match fine."

Both girls laughed, but the five men simply stared impassively at the young actor. This was no time for wise-ass remarks from precocious children.

"Maybe we should scout a new setup," Caretta suggested. "If the ravine's wider farther down it would solve the problem."

Bruner shook his head. "It's not. I've been down there. It's about the same distance across but it gets shallower."

The director scratched his beard again and returned his gaze to the camera. "Shit," he said quietly. "I really want this shot."

Darla put her coffee cup on the ground and stood up, stretching. She ground her cigarette out under her boot and stepped casually over to where the men stood. Out of the corner of her eye she could see that Jeff Patterson was eyeing her admiringly. She put her fingertips into the front pockets of her Levi's. "May I make a suggestion?" she asked shyly.

The men turned and looked at her, a hint of mild amusement in their expressions. "Sure," Caretta said. "What is it?"

Darla spoke in her most ingenuous, little-girl-innocent voice, the one that invariably turned men on. "Well, it seems to me that the simplest way to do it would be to keep the camera right here and let us ride the horses down ourselves."

The men stared at her, and the cowboy wearing the red wig broke into a contemptuous grin.

"Darla!" Cathy said. "You must be kidding."

"I hope so," the red-tressed cowboy said smugly. He looked at Darla. "It ain't as easy as it might look, Ma'am." His tone was that of the respectful male servant, strong, intelligent, and superior, who hopes to prevent his mad mistress from killing herself.

Darla returned his gaze. "I know it's not easy," she said sweetly. "But I can do it. The trick is to dig your heels in and keep your horse's head back. That'll make him sit on his haunches and slide down, and it'll keep him from going over on his nose."

275

The smirk slowly disappeared from the stunt man's face. "It's your funeral. Ma'am."

The A.D. cleared his throat nervously. "Thanks, Darla. Thanks a lot. We'll find another way to do it."

But Caretta was staring at Darla intently. "Do you really think you could do it? I mean, I know you ride well, but—"

"I can do it," Darla said quietly. She shifted her gaze to the cowboy in the red wig. "As well as he can."

The stuntman flushed and looked away. Caretta made no reply for a moment, but merely continued to look at Darla speculatively.

Darla could feel her heartbeat accelerating, although outwardly she maintained a steadfast calm. She could do the stunt—she knew she could. As a kid growing up in Oklahoma she had done crazier tricks on a horse than this. But what was really exciting her now was the prospect of occupying center-stage in a real-life drama. To say nothing of the fact that she would be demonstrating that in a tough, dangerous situation she could be better than most men, and in fact equal to the best— as good as a professional who made his living by taking on assignments like this one. And not only that, but she had Cathy Drake by the short hairs.

The A.D. cleared his throat nervously. He was a nice young man named Larry Keane who wanted desperately to become a director, and who you could tell in the first five minutes you spent with him would never make it. "Hey, Sal," he said to Caretta. "Not really, huh? I mean, that's taking a hell of a chance. Darla gets hurt and the show's up the creek."

Sure, Darla thought. Darla gets hurt and the show's up the creek. But never mind what happens to Darla. That's a proper male way to look at it, you silly son of a bitch. "I'm telling you," she said, "I can do it."

Keane ignored her. "Then there's the insurance," he said to Caretta. "Maybe we ought to check with Zander."

Sal Caretta was not known as a director who played safe. In fact, the reason he had won this choice assignment was that he was brash, ballsy, and willing to gamble to achieve punchy, exciting action. His eyes were locked on Darla. "The lady says she can do it," he said slowly. "And I believe her."

A smile turned the corners of Darla's mouth. "Okay, so let's do it." She looked over at Cathy. "How about it? Shall we show these guys how to ride?"

Cathy's alabaster skin colored, and for a moment she looked confused as she glanced at the horses and then at the edge of the ravine. "Hey, count me out. I'm not the type." She smiled tightly. "And anyhow, my rear end is already black and blue."

Darla shrugged. "Can you make do with one of us?" she asked Caretta.

The director looked quickly at the cowboy who was wearing the red wig. "Sure. Hell, yes. The audience won't even notice him. Especially if you keep your horse a little bit ahead of his." He was enthusiastic now about the idea. His instincts told him this would be a hell of a shot if the audience could see clearly that it was no fake, that these really were the stars of the show, or at least one of the stars, carrying off the hair-raising stunt. Terrific. This was the stuff of which directors' fortunes were made. "Let's go."

By now Cathy had begun to realize just how adroitly Darla had put her on the spot. If the stuntman rode in the shot, Darla would not only steal the scene, but would also come off as the leader in a tricky, highly dramatic sequence. Moreover, if anyone in the audience did bother to look at what they thought was Cathy, they would see that she had narrow-set eyes, a bluish beard shadow about her jaw, huge hands, and knobby wrists. On the other hand, if Cathy actually tried to ride in the shot herself she could wind up in the hospital. She could handle a horse with some competence, but with nothing approaching Darla's skill. Cathy had grown up in California, and motorcycles were her métier. She could run anything from a dirt bike to a hog, and had even competed in hill climbs as a teenaged tomboy. But horses? Jesus Christ.

Darla smiled pleasantly at Cathy, knowing exactly what the redhead was thinking. "Take it easy," she said

277

as she turned away. She was extremely pleased with herself.

"Oh, God," Cathy said good-naturedly, pulling herself up out of her chair. "You really are crazy. But what the hell—anything for the show. Where is the old plug?"

Shit, Darla thought, keeping her smile carefully in place. "Thatta girl, Cathy," she said. "We'll do it better than they ever could." And maybe you'll break your leg, too, with just a smidge of luck.

When both girls had mounted, Jud Bruner took a reading with his meter as Caretta gave them instructions. The stuntmen looked on, their faces sullen.

"We're only going to do this once," Caretta said. "I can't take a chance on going for a bunch of takes. Too dangerous. So if we don't get it the first try, the hell with it. We'll just go back and do it from the longer angle with the stunt guys."

"You'll get it," Darla said. She looked at Cathy. "If it kills us."

Bruner ran back across the bridge to where the Mitchell and the assistant cameraman waited. He dropped onto the small, toadstool-shaped metal seat and squinted through the viewfinder. "This," he said softly, "could be a terrific shot."

His assistant, a cynical young man whose long brown hair was held out of his eyes by a bandanna headband, spat onto the rocky soil. " 'Specially if the broads get their brains knocked out."

Larry Keane led both horses to the spot about fifty yards from the edge of the ravine from which Caretta had said he wanted the girls to start their run. When they were in place the A.D. raised his hand to the director, who had taken a position in the center of the bridge. Caretta held his hand palm-up toward Keane and looked at Jud Bruner.

"Beautiful," Bruner called.

Involuntarily, Caretta glanced down the long, steep surface of the ravine wall. For an instant he wavered, but then his excitement took hold again. He called for camera speed, sound, and slate, and when all was ready, turned his eyes once more toward the A.D. He gestured with his hand and Keane scampered out of camera range. Taking a deep breath, Caretta swung his arm over his head to signal the girls to start their run.

The instant she saw the director begin his arm movement, Darla kicked her horse with both heels and urged him forward with her body, at the same time giving him his head. It was, she knew from years of riding, the sure way to make a horse break into a gallop virtually from his first step. It would also put her ahead of Cathy, so she would be leading all the way down the slide.

As the horses pounded toward the edge of the ravine, Darla felt her excitement rise higher. Peripherally she could see members of the crew watching, and she was aware of the camera across the gully and of Caretta standing on the bridge. But her concentration on taking her horse into the ravine was intense.

When she reached the edge of the chasm, Darla felt the big animal's body stiffen in terror as he suddenly found himself sailing through the air. Gripping the reigns tight with both hands, Darla pulled the horse's head back as far as she could and leaned back in the saddle. As her mount's hoofs hit the slope, she clamped her legs tight against his sides and fought to keep him from leaning forward. His frightened neighing mingled with the clatter of falling gravel, his eyes rolled wildly. As they scrambled and slid down the preciptious incline, Darla cried out exultantly. She could hear Cathy's horse close behind.

When the horses reached the bottom of the ravine they trotted a few steps and stopped, trembling and snorting. Darla leaped from her saddle and went quickly to her horse's head, holding and soothing him. She could hear the excited shouts of the crew from above. Turning to the second horse, she watched with amusement as Cathy slid slowly from the saddle and stood for a moment holding onto the pommel.

"Hey." Darla grinned. "You did great." I'm sorry to say. You missed a great chance to commit suicide.

Cathy's face was chalky. Sweat had darkened the armpits of her shirt. "Dear God, I wouldn't want to do that again." She forced a smile. "But we made it."

Caretta came skidding and stumbling down to the ravine floor, his dark eyes flashing. "Jesus," he yelled triumphantly. "What a fucking shot! That was beautiful. Beautiful." He hugged Darla and then Cathy. A moment later they were surrounded by other members of the crew, all happily shouting congratulations to the girls.

Darla was delighted with herself. She had not only stolen the scene from Cathy, had not only been the central figure in a dramatic situation more tense and perilous than any that could be staged, but she knew at once that she had become a heroine to the crew.

At dinner that night her hunches—and her hopes—were confirmed. The crew talked of nothing but the ravine shot, and how Darla had made it come off. It was, Caretta said, "Life imitating art imitating life." Darla was careful to maintain her usual shy, slightly deferential manner, dismissing the accolades of the crew while inwardly she felt wonderful. Members of a film company were invariably respectful and highly gratified in the presence of courage, especially when the act was a gutsy, selfless contribution to the fortunes of the show, which was exactly how this company saw Darla's role in the morning's shoot. At one point in the evening one of the grips swallowed his third glass of burgundy and inhaled deeply on his joint. He leaned over to Jud Bruner and said, "She put her ass on the line for us, you know it? By me that little broad is okay forever."

Altogether, it was a heady and deeply satisfying time for Darla. That night she made love to Jeff Patterson for the first time.

Chapter 32

Robin Baker walked down Madison Avenue and turned west on Fifty-second Street. It was a Friday in mid-November, one of those crisp autumn days that make New York almost tolerable, and it seemed to Baker that the noontime crowds he passed were happy and relaxed, as if anticipating the coming weekend. Or perhaps, he conjectured, that was merely his imagination, and in fact it was only he who was especially glad to be winding down a hectic week. Tomorrow he'd be attending the Princeton-Dartmouth game, and as an old Tiger guard, his pace quickened at the thought. He and Patty would be joining a large group of friends for the game, and there would be a tailgate picnic outside Palmer Stadium before the contest, and an endless flow of Bloody Marys during, and a round of parties after. Along with other alums, he'd be dropping in at his old club, and by the early hours of Sunday morning it would be pretty drunk out. Princeton had a lousy team, he reflected, the one sour note in the forthcoming festivities. Things weren't the way they'd been when he played, when Kazmaier was the tailback and Princeton was a national power that would play anybody. And beat 'em, too, by God. Now they played in this fruitcake Ivy League and were lucky to beat Brown. Still, the parties would be great, and he'd see more old friends than he could count.

A complete extrovert, Rob Baker was the perfect outside man for an advertising agency, just as his partner, George Barlowe, was ideally suited to the role of inside man. Barlowe's meticulous ways were in marked contrast to those of his partner. Whereas Baker was a bluff, outgoing salesman, Barlowe had the humorless mind of a computer, storing endless reams of facts and figures on the agency's clients' businesses, their financial histories and current market situations. As agency principals, the two complemented each other beautifully, but the man their clients wanted to spend time with socially was Baker.

The 21 Club was crowded, as usual. Mike Beam, the greeter, smiled as Robin walked in. He held out his hand. "Hey, stranger—where you been?"

"Eating in good restaurants, that's where." Baker grinned as they shook hands. "And what are you complaining about? I was here Monday." He pulled off his topcoat and handed it to the hatcheck girl. As he turned around someone slapped him on the back.

It was Dick Dewhurst, publisher of *Cosmopolitan*. "Robin, you look terrific."

"Hiya, Richard. You're looking halfway human yourself."

"Going to TMA?" Dewhurst asked. This was the Toiletries Merchandisers Association's annual convention, always held in a warm climate during the winter months, a week-long round of selling, socializing, and golf, as well-attended by agency and media people as by the manufacturers themselves.

"Sure," Robin replied. "Wouldn't miss it. I hear it's in the Bahamas this year." He moved toward the sitting room just to the right of the entrance, returning greetings from friends and acquaintances on the way. He found John Rawlson studying a painting by Frederick Remington of an Indian brave astride a pony. The Indian was huddled in a buffalo robe, his back turned to the snow-laced prairie wind.

"That's a hell of a painting," the president of the Superfresh Corporation remarked as they shook hands.

"Why don't you buy it?" Robin suggested. "I'm sure Jerry would part with it for the right price."

"I'm sure he would," Rawlson said dryly. "But by the time I get through paying for your advertising program I don't have enough left to give myself a salary."

Robin shook his head in mock dismay. "Things must be really tough." Things were, he knew, in the best shape they'd ever been in. Superfresh sales were going through the roof. But crying poor-mouth had always been Rawlson's style. Come to think of it, that was most clients' style. No matter how rapidly the company's fortunes might be expanding, don't let the agency know about it. The poor bastards might relax for ten minutes. But there were some facts Rawlson couldn't hide. "Just saw the last Nielsens," Robin said. "Looked pretty good."

"Doesn't mean a damn thing. The competition gets worse every day."

The two men climbed the stairway to the second floor, where they were warmly welcomed by Tino, maitre d' of the main dining room. When they had been seated and had ordered a drink, Rawlson asked Robin if he'd be going to the big game on Saturday.

"I sure will." Robin grinned. "Princeton'll kick their ass all the way back to Hanover."

"You look in good shape to play yourself," Rawlson commented.

"Hell, I am. I'm the same weight as I was when I graduated." Robin patted the skin on the top of his head. "Only difference is up here."

"You mean you got smarter?"

Robin laughed. "I mean I got bald. I already was smart."

Their drinks arrived, a vodka martini for Baker, Jack Daniels on the rocks for Rawlson.

"Cheers," Robin said.

Rawlson raised his glass. "Good luck."

As he sipped his drink, Robin glanced around the richly paneled room, recognizing several people he knew. Actually, he much preferred having lunch in the bar to coming up here, always finding the boisterous, casual ambience below more to his liking than the formality of the dining room. But John Rawlson, he knew, liked the upstairs atmosphere, and a client was a client.

"So I should bet on Princeton?" Rawlson asked.

"I wouldn't go that far," Robin parried, "but we ought to win."

"Uh-huh. And maybe you'll get surprised, too."

"You want to M.I.T., didn't you, John?"

"Class of 'Thirty-one."

"Were you in any of their athletic programs?"

The Superfresh president shook his head. "I was too busy studying and trying to get enough work to stay in college. It was during the Depression, and my father died when I was a freshman."

"That had to be rough."

"It was," Rawlson acknowledged. "Kids have it so damned easy today." He drank some of his whiskey. "Christ, I remember some days I didn't have anything to eat at all. I was a chemistry major, you know, and that stink in the lab, working with all those chemicals on an empty stomach—sometimes it made me sick as hell."

Robin smiled. "At least nowadays you don't have to worry about not having enough to eat. Let's get some food."

They ordered Chincoteague oysters, brought in fresh that morning from Virginia, and roast lamb, a heavy lunch that was a favorite with both men.

"Is it true that even back then you had the idea for Superfresh?" Robin asked.

Rawlson nodded. "I figured there was a good opportunity for a mouthwash that didn't taste like poison, and I was right. Just as I saw later on that you could sell Superfresh as a product that not only freshened your breath, but helped to give you a beautiful smile, too. And I was right again."

"I'll say you were. Putting the brighteners into the formula was a stroke of genius. And you were the first brand to use them, right?" Robin knew all about the history of Superfresh, but he also knew that John Rawlson had a fierce pride in his company, and that he liked to talk about it.

"Yes," Rawlson replied. "We were the first. And you know, those dumb bastards in the Food and Drug Administration gave me a hard time about it?"

"Really?"

Rawlson nodded emphatically, his snowy head bobbing. "Can you imagine that? I had to prove to those sons of bitches that the phosphorescents were there only for cosmetic reasons—that they'd simply help make people's teeth look whiter. Of course, there's a whole bunch of toothpaste brands with brighteners. Close-Up, Ultra-Brite, and so on. But we were the first mouthwash. And we're the best, too, by God."

Their food arrived, and as they ate, Baker filled John Rawlson in on the latest ratings on "The Witches." Although the chairman of the agency was not involved with the day-to-day operation of the Superfresh account, he was careful to keep himself fully informed of all its activities, one benefit of which was that he was able to speak knowledgeably to Rawlson of the current situation. "The plan is," Robin said, "that we'll buy time for Superfresh in the program, and that'll turn the show into one big commercial for your company. The audience sees that girl jumping around in the program action, and then when it's time for a commercial, there she is, telling the people to wash out their mouths with Superfresh." This was a shrewd tactic, Baker knew, and he was pleased that the agency's media director had come up with it.

Rawlson thought it over. "You know what else you could do?"

"What's that?"

"You could buy adjacencies in the spot markets, just ahead of the show."

Baker grasped the concept immediately. He looked at the older man with admiration. "Jesus, what a great idea. So in the markets where we buy local spots as well as network, the top fifty markets in the country, we'll have Superfresh commercials just before the show as well as in it." He laughed delightedly. "Christ, can you see that? First, a thirty-second commercial with Darla selling Superfresh, followed by an hour show featuring her and with more of our commercials. God, that's beautiful. The competition will go out of their minds."

"So will the network," Rawlson said. "And as soon as they catch on, they'll see to it that their affiliates jack up their prices on us."

Baker knew that Rawlson was right, of course. Was there anything this old buzzard didn't know? The man had the mind of a thirty-year-old—restless, probing, astonishingly quick to find and implement new ideas.

"So have your media department get on it right away."

"I will." Baker smiled. "That's a hell of a good idea, John."

But the old man was not one to accept compliments. "Uh-huh. So why did I have to think of it? That's what I pay you fellows for."

Baker's smile widened. "Listen, John. Anytime you get tired of running Superfresh, you can come over and be our media director."

Rawlson grinned in spite of himself. "You say the ratings are pretty good, hm?"

"Terrific. Really phenomenal. And the publicity Darla's getting isn't to be believed."

"But not all of it so good, right?"

What the hell had the old man heard now? "Oh, some controversial stuff," Robin acknowledged casually, "but you always hear crap like that about a hot personality."

"I'm not so sure." Rawlson finished the last of his lamb and sat back in his chair. "It sounds to me like there's a lot of trouble in that marriage. Darla and this Mike Brady."

"Maybe, and maybe not. What the hell." He laughed. "There's a lot of trouble in mine." He was about to add, *and probably in yours, too,* but he thought better of it.

Rawlson's face was composed, thoughtful. "I know there's always a lot of gossip, and those rag magazines stir up as much dirt as they can. But I think there's something to this. I hear both of them screw around as much as they want."

Baker wanted to remind his client that this was not

1950, but he held his tongue. "In some ways," he said cautiously, "that kind of story can even be to our advantage. You know, show people are always having affairs. It's part of their lives and part of their lifestyle. To the fans, it just makes them all the more exciting and glamorous."

"Maybe. But too much of it can backfire. I know what you mean about actors, and all their affairs. But it isn't just because they have the opportunity or because it's common in that business, either. It's because they're the most narcissistic people on earth. They don't just want to have adoration—with them it's a compulsive need. They've *got* to have it. And one way to get another helping is to have affairs. More worship. Somebody else to tell them how wonderful they are."

"You're right, I guess," Baker said. "I never thought of it that way."

"Then think about it. Think about actors."

Robin chuckled. "I'd rather not."

"But isn't it true? They're the most self-centered human beings there are. Even when they make love, what they're really doing is making love to themselves."

"Do you think that applies to Darla, too?"

Rawlson raised his eyebrows. "She's an actress, isn't she? So of course it applies to her. And that's why I get concerned about this publicity. It's one thing for her to be leading an exciting life. But it's another one for her to get into some mess that's going to rub off on Superfresh."

"Oh, I don't think there's really much chance of that, John," Baker replied. "And anyhow, there's a good stiff morals clause in her contract."

The blue eyes hardened. "I don't give a damn about her contract," Rawlson said. "What good is a morals clause after the fact? What good is it if she smears our name because she's in the papers in some scandal?" He shook his head.

"Not much chance of that," Baker countered. He wanted to get the hell off the subject. "She's not the type."

"She's not, huh? I hear she screws around plenty."

"Maybe. But I'll tell you one thing—she could screw around with me anytime."

Rawlson's stern countenance softened. "An old bastard like you? What would she want to do that for?"

Baker laughed. "Hell, I don't know. Maybe as a scientific experiment."

"Just to see what would happen, hm?"

"Sure." Robin was relieved. He had succeeded, he felt, in diverting their conversation away from the more serious path it had been following.

But he was wrong. "Have you got her replacement?" Rawlson asked.

Baker shifted uncomfortably in his chair. "I understand we're still looking. Archer tells me Ben Thompkins has screened over a hundred girls."

"So keep searching."

"Sure," Baker replied. "Of course we will. But you know, John, I don't really think there's anything to be worried about."

"Maybe there isn't," the older man said. "But you never know. That's why I want the best girl you can find, all set and ready to step in."

"We'll find her," Baker said. "We'll just keep on looking until we find her."

"We may need her sooner than you think," Rawlson remarked enigmatically.

Baker's eyebrows arched. What did John Rawlson know that he wasn't disclosing? "Why do you say that, John?"

"A hunch, that's all." The cold blue eyes were intense, penetrating. "I have a feeling I know what's going to happen to this girl. Maybe what's already happening. And it's not good. At least, not good for us."

Sometimes, Baker knew, John Rawlson could be abstruse about communicating his thoughts. The trick was to be patient until the older man shifted from hyperbole to an expression of his true feelings.

"You'll see," Rawlson continued. "At first she'll be thrilled with all this success, and she'll be sweet and shy and she'll be grateful to everybody who's helped her. And then, a little bit at a time, it'll start to go to her head. She'll decide she is the new Farrah Fawcett-Majors, and after that she'll start to drive everybody crazy. Just wait and see."

A waiter brought them coffee, and John Rawlson stared moodily into his cup.

Ever the optimist, Baker smiled. "Who knows, John, maybe it won't turn out that way. Not every actress turns into a bitch, you know."

"You're right. Only the successful ones."

"How about a cigar?" Baker suggested. Anything to get off this and onto something more positive.

Rawlson agreed, and a waiter offered choices from three boxes. They selected Macanudos, the rich, heavy Jamaicans, and lit them.

"Your account appears to be running fairly smoothly, for the moment," Baker said. He blew out a cloud of blue smoke. "David Archer doing okay?"

"He seems to be," the president of Superfresh replied. "No complaints."

The exchange was low-key, but both men fully understood its implications. The Superfresh account was now Baker & Barlowe's largest, its billings this year having reached the fifteen-million-dollar level. If Rawlson had spoken negatively of David Archer, however offhandedly, the senior vice-president would be out of his job that afternoon.

"How about Paul Scott?" Robin asked.

"He's okay," Rawlson said. "Not as smart as he thinks he is, but okay. Full of piss and vinegar, and that's good. You need that in an organization. Trouble with too many of my people is, they want to play everything safe. Never want to take a chance. Goddamn it, you can never build anything with that attitude."

"You're right, John."

Rawlson was silent for a moment. When he spoke again, his tone was thoughtful, philosophical. "A company, you know, is like any other human enterprise. It can't stand still. It either grows or it deteriorates. It prospers or it dies. All companies are like that."

"And agencies," Robin said.

Rawlson nodded. "And most of all, people. You take

a young man, a really good one, who starts his career burning with ambition. If he maintains his drive, there's no limit to where he can go. But if he gets to a certain point where he says to himself, okay, I have it made, that's when he's dead. He doesn't know it, and he'd be surprised if you told him so, but that's really what's happened to him. From that point on, he's just riding along, enjoying the privileges that are part of the job and the position, but he's no longer vital, no longer a real contributor. He sits in meetings and thinks about his golf date, or the vacation he and his wife are going to take in Europe, or how to play politics in a way that will keep some other smart young fellow from taking his job away from him, but he's no longer an important part of the organization. When I see the signs of a man changing like that in our company, I don't even discuss it with him. I just move him out. Because once the change occurs, that man's career, and even his life, are over."

Baker had no illusions as to why John Rawlson was telling him all these things. He grinned. "You are looking at the hardest-working young man in New York," he said. "Chairman of the hungriest, fightingest advertising agency in the world."

The corners of Rawlson's mouth turned upward once more in the frosty smile Robin Baker had seen so often.

Robin called for the check and signed it. After a few more perfunctory remarks as they left the restaurant, he wished John Rawlson a good weekend and hurried back to his office.

As soon as he arrived, Baker rang Ben Thompkins. When the agency's vice-president in charge of television production answered, Baker asked him how the hunt for a new Superfresh girl was going.

"Good, Rob," Thompkins replied. "We've seen some great candidates."

"But no new Darla Dawson."

"Not yet, but then you never know. One of the new girls might turn out to be exactly that."

"Yeah," Baker said. "You never know. Tell you what, Ben, I know it's Friday afternoon and all, but I think you ought to get together with me and David Archer right away."

"Sure. I'll be there in a minute."

"And Ben, bring everything you have on the possible new girls for Superfresh. You know, head-sheets, composites, everything." He hung up and called David Archer, telling the management supervisor to come to his office at once.

Baker put the phone down and got to his feet. He looked out the window. The sun had disappeared behind the buildings that loomed skyward from Rockefeller Center, and in the lengthening shadows New York had begun to look cold and blustery.

When both men had arrived in his office—Thompkins carrying a large, thick manila folder—Robin Baker had his secretary bring coffee while he exchanged small talk with them. As his secretary departed, Baker asked her to close the door. He sat down in his favorite leather chair and put his feet on the coffee table in front of the sofa, where Archer and Thompkins sat looking at him expectantly.

"David," the chairman began, "I asked Ben to bring along pictures of all the possible candidates for a new Superfresh girl he could find. I thought the three of us could just sort of riffle through them."

Archer's face was blank.

Baker smiled. "You're wondering why the hell I'm cranked up on a subject like this, aren't you—and on Friday afternoon, for Christ's sake."

"Who, me?" Archer deadpanned.

"I have my reasons, rest assured," Baker said.

"I'm sure you do."

"How many have you got there, Ben?" Baker asked.

"Maybe fifty," Thompkins replied, opening the folders. He withdrew a mass of composites, head sheets, and glossy black-and-white photos of girls.

"Okay," Baker said. "We're going to look through them just to get an idea of what the possibilities might be. And understand I want the fact that I've chosen to involve myself in this project to remain absolutely confidential. As far as anybody else is concerned, things are just kicking along on their usual course. But gentlemen, I'll tell you this." He paused for effect, looking steadily at Ben, and then at Archer. "One of the most important things this agency will do this year—perhaps *the* most important—is to come up with a girl who'll make the world forget about Darla Dawson."

The office was quiet for a moment, the only sounds the ticking of the brass ship's clock that hung on the wall beside Baker's desk, and the muffled din of traffic from Madison Avenue twenty-seven floors below.

Thompkins spoke first. "What is it, Rob—are we going to dump her?"

"No, we're not. Not unless she gets into some mess, or something else unforseen happens."

"Then, what—?"

"I told you," Baker said. "I have my reasons." He got up from his chair and walked slowly around the room, his eyes on the carpet. Finally he turned and faced both men. "Let's just say that we need an insurance policy. And so our job is to find the goddamnedest broad this business has ever seen. Better than Darla Dawson, better than any of them. Do you understand me? I don't just want a pretty face who can't act, or great hair but no brains, or big boobs and a cleft palate—I want it all. The hair, the brains, the face, the tits, the whole fucking business. Do you get it? She's got to have *everything*."

Chapter 33

Derek Wasserman's offices were on Lasky Drive in Beverly Hills. Darla parked her Mercedes in the lot behind the building and took the elevator to the third floor. The blonde receptionist announced her, and Wasserman bounded out into the foyer effusing greetings, kissing her cheek, and holding her arm as he led her into his private office. He asked Darla what she wanted to drink, and got them both Perrier water over ice from the bar that stood in one corner of the large, garishly decorated room.

"So tell me," Wasserman said as he sat beside her on the sofa. "When's the hiatus?"

"Two more weeks." Darla sipped Perrier. "Thank God."

"You mean you're bored already?" Wasserman teased. He was good-looking, in the carefully youthful Beverly Hills mode, his hair stylishly long, his skin fashionably tan, his dark brown silk shirt predictably open, revealing the inevitable thin gold chain.

Darla shook her head. "Not bored, tired. I would never have guessed the amount of work. That damned limousine picks me up at five-thirty, and most nights I'm not home until seven or eight, sometimes nine or ten."

Wasserman nodded sympathetically. "I know—it's

really exhausting." He smiled. "And how do you like the confusion?"

Darla put her glass down. "The confusion," she stated flatly, "is maddening." She looked at him. "I take it it's not so unusual, then?"

Wasserman laughed. "Unusual? It's standard operating procedure. Hurry up and wait. Let's not make this shot as we planned; the site's no good, or the light's changed, or so-and-so is drunk or spaced out on Quaaludes. Or we changed the script last night, didn't anybody tell you?" He laughed again. "Organized mass confusion—that's the history of the film business."

He spoke, Darla noted, as if he were one of the grand old men of the industry, a wise elder who had seen it all. But he couldn't have been more than thirty-one or -two. Nevertheless, he held the reputation of being the best personal manager in the business, especially with women, so good that he was constantly besieged by actresses begging him to represent them. Darla felt she was lucky that he'd been willing to manage her. And yet, she reminded herself, the way her career was taking off, it was a plum for him, too.

"Two more weeks, and then a hiatus, hm?" Wasserman said.

Darla nodded. "They claim they'll be able to stick to that schedule right through. Six weeks shooting, and then a week off."

"Hm." The manager swallowed some Perrier water. "How'd you like to go to New York that week?"

"New York? Really?"

"Sure. There're a million things for you to do, mostly publicity, but also some good business opportunities I've lined up for you. That would be a perfect time to set them. And I've spoken to Betty—the Superfresh people will want to see you, too. But anyhow, a great week in New York wouldn't be too bad, would it?"

Darla smiled. "Not too bad at all."

"And I mean great, too. A suite at the Plaza, limousines all over the place, a couple of shots on the big New York talk shows, a special appearance at the theater, lots of New York shopping, and every day you sleep as late as you like. How does it sound?"

"Like heaven." Darla laughed. "I can't wait."

"Good, I thought you'd be pleased."

Darla picked up her glass. When she spoke again, her voice automatically modulated into the little-girl tone she always used, consciously or unconsciously, when she wanted something. "And speaking of shopping—"

Wasserman held up his hand. "Don't say another word. I promised you a fun Saturday, didn't I? Well, that's just what you're going to get. I have lots of things all arranged for you, starting with a real treat. But first there are some papers I want you to sign. After that, shopping we go."

He got up and stepped over to his desk, returning with several documents and a pen. "Okay." He placed the papers on the coffee table in front of Darla. "If you'll just autograph these for me, we'll be on our way."

Darla glanced at one of the documents as she signed her name in the place Wasserman had marked with an X. It appeared to be a release of some kind. "What are these?" she asked.

"Oh, just a lot of red tape I need in order to have some leeway in setting up deals for you," Wasserman said. "It's standard with everybody I work with."

"You said you had some business things?" Darla asked as she continued to sign her name to the various pieces of paper the manager handed her. "In New York?"

"Sure do. Some of them pretty nice, too."

"Like what?"

"Like a big toy deal, for one. I'll tell you more about it when the time comes. But they're good opportunities."

"What does Betty think?"

"She loves them," Wasserman said. "She'll discuss them with you. And she'll be coming with us on the trip, of course."

"Okay, great," Darla said. She put the pen down. "Now tell me about shopping."

295

Wasserman smiled. "Okay, shopping. But before that, just remember that I've worked out a regular spending program for you, all in coordination with your accountant, and you have to stick with it. The thing is, today is special." His smile widened. "A couple of big items. But don't get carried away, understand. After today, you go right back to five hundred a week spending money, and don't you dare exceed it."

"I promise," Darla said in an obedient tone. Her eyes sparkled. "What's first?"

"First is something you want very much."

Darla's excitement was palpable. "If you don't tell me—"

The manager laughed. "What has four wheels and is *de rigeur* for a major star?"

Darla clapped her hands delightedly. "That sounds like a brand-new car."

Wasserman stood up and took her hand. "You must have been peeking." He chuckled. "I can't imagine how you ever guessed. Come on, we'll go in your old one and leave it there."

The Porsche showroom was busy, but as soon as the sales manager saw Darla he rushed over. He was fawning, almost obsequious. "It's so wonderful to meet you, Miss Dawson. I wouldn't miss your show. You're a truly marvelous actress. Your car is all ready for you, right over here. I hope you don't mind, I put it on our showroom floor, just for today. It's really quite lovely, don't you think?"

To Darla, it was breathtaking. The Turbo Carrera was white, with blue leather. She walked around it very slowly, taking in its sleek lines, its dazzling chrome. How many times had she admired these cars, wishing she could have one of her own, imagining what it would be like if she could drive one home and park it in the garage next to Mike's Mercedes. And now here it was. She had read in a fan magazine once, long ago, that achieving stardom was like having a whole book of beautiful dreams come true. Today she was looking at one of her dreams.

The sales manager showed her the Porsche's gadgets, most of which she was familiar with through having ridden in Ted Walters's, but there were a few innovations, she noted with pleasure. This one had a tape deck built into the Becker Mexico stereo, for example, and Ted's didn't, and her wheels were a little different from his—maybe a little snazzier. She thought for a moment about how surprised Mike would be to see the car, and a tiny thrill coursed through her.

"We'll put your plates on it right away," the sales manager said. He waved a hand toward the bright sunshine. "I'm sure you can't wait to drive it."

Darla turned to Wasserman, her face shining. "Derek, it's beautiful. And it's the exact color I wanted. How did you know that?"

"Like it?"

Darla looked at the car again. "I love it. I just love it."

"I thought you would."

"Do I have to sign anything?" she asked.

"It's all taken care of," Wasserman said. "All you have to do now is drive it. To our next stop, in fact."

A woman customer had been watching quietly. She approached Darla now, a little shyly. "Miss Dawson?"

Darla turned to her. The woman appeared to be in her fifties, slim and well-dressed. "Yes?"

"I'm sorry to bother you, but I just had to tell you how important you are in our house. We all love your show."

"Thank you," Darla replied warmly. "That's always nice to hear."

"The whole family watches, every Thursday night."

"Good," Darla said politely. "I'm glad."

The woman produced a gold pen and a slip of paper from her bag, a brown Gucci. "Would you mind giving me your autograph, please? It's for my daughter."

As Darla scribbled her name, she wondered why adults never simply asked for an autograph, but always had to justify the request by explaining that it was being made with some child in mind. The woman beamed and tucked the prize away in her bag, watching intently as

Darla got into the Porsche, while Wasserman entered the passenger side.

The sales manager shut Darla's door with a flourish. He snapped his fingers and a serviceman rolled open the glass doors of the showroom. A cluster of people had begun to gather—salesmen, customers, shoppers—all smiling broadly. Darla turned the key and the engine came to life with a suitably restrained rumble. The car was not only handsome, she reflected, but also ideally suited to showing off her tan skin and blonde hair. Like a knockout white evening dress, she thought delightedly, only a hundred times better. She slipped the shifter into first gear, and eased the car through the doorway and out into the wide driveway that led to the street.

The tactile sensation of the thickly padded steering wheel, the well-behaved but instant responsiveness of the engine, the crisp newness of the metal and the chrome and the leather, were all in marked contrast to the old rattletrap she was used to driving. The car seemed to transmit power not only to its wheels, but also through Darla's hands into her body, sending a heady sense of authority and control and freedom coursing through her. She owned this beautiful, powerful thing, and she could make it do anything she pleased, make it take her anywhere she wanted to go. It was a better high than grass—almost like making love. As she tooled briskly through the traffic, swinging west on Wilshire and then north on Rodeo Drive, her hair ruffling in the wind, several other drivers recognized her, calling her name and waving. Darla felt glorious.

A parking space had been reserved for them in front of Daignault's. A group which included two uniformed store guards and a policeman, the store manager, Darla's publicity agent, and a photographer, was waiting when Darla eased the Porsche to the curb. By the time one of the guards opened Darla's door, passersby had begun to stop and stare. "Look—look," a teenaged girl cried out excitedly. "That's Darla Dawson!" Within seconds a small crowd had gathered, and the guards had to escort Darla through the excited people into the store. As she passed through the entrance, Darla glanced worriedly over her shoulder at her new car.

Reading her thoughts, Wasserman laughed. "Don't worry, Darla. That's why we have the cop there. He'll take good care of it for you."

Daignault's was a long-time Beverly Hills establishment. Its floors were covered in deep velvet carpet and from its walls hung dozens of tall mirrors in gilded frames. Crystal chandeliers mounting tiny frosted bulbs hung from the ceilings, their twinkling lights reflecting endlessly in the mirrors in a kind of magical asymptote. It was, Darla thought, like a fairyland palace.

Daignault's manager bowed as Darla looked around the place. "It's a thrill, Miss Dawson, to have you here," he said. "I think your show is divine. I can't tell you how it brightens my otherwise drab Thursday evenings."

"That's nice." Darla smiled. As she continued to glance at the opulent surroundings, she suddenly realized that nothing was on display. She was standing in the chambers of one of California's most prestigious and exclusive furriers, and there wasn't a fur to be seen anywhere. How curious.

The manager continued to talk, but Darla tuned him out. She looked through an archway into one of the rooms that opened off the reception area and observed that a woman was sitting in a chair, listening coolly as a Daignault salesperson, chicly clad in a severe black dress, spoke to her. The woman, obviously a customer, was exquisitely dressed and groomed, her aristocratic features serene and composed. Her age seemed to enhance, rather than detract from, her beauty.

As Darla stared at her, the woman slowly turned her head and their eyes met. There was no sign of recognition on the woman's face, but for an instant the merest suggestion of a smile played at one corner of her mouth as something passed between her and Darla, and then she looked away.

With a tiny jolt, Darla suddenly realized who the woman was. Anita Louise. One of the movies' great beauties during the 'Forties and 'Fifties. Darla had seen her work in movie theaters as a child in Oklahoma, and occasionally now when one of her films would appear on late-night television. For reasons she couldn't quite understand, Darla felt a little flustered by the encounter. Had the aging one-time star recognized her?

As Darla continued to look around, Molly Martin, her publicity agent, entered the foyer with the photographer in tow. Molly introduced the man to Darla and Derek Wasserman. "Don't pay any attention to him," Molly said. "Just ignore him and go on about your business as if he wasn't here. The more stuff he shoots and the more candid it is the better." She turned to Wasserman. "You wouldn't believe the calls I'm getting. Every magazine, every newspaper in this country wants Darla, Darla, Darla. I've never seen anything like it."

Wasserman smiled knowlingly. "Of course. What we have here is the hottest star in show business. And maybe the hottest of all time."

"I believe it," Daignault's manager said.

That's a little much, Darla thought to herself. She glanced at Molly and was amused to see that the publicity agent was wearing a stop-the-shit expression. Darla smiled and Molly smiled back.

Darla liked this woman. Molly Martin was a one-time newspaper reporter who had seen everything at least twice. The publicity agent was irreverent, in awe of no one, and fun to be with.

"Well, anyhow," Molly said, "I can place everything I can get. Especially stuff like this, showing Darla shopping, or doing other things magazine readers can identify with. Even though they might find it a little hard to imagine themselves coughing up twenty grand or so for a bunny skin."

"They'd spend it," Wasserman said, "if they had it."

"Oh, sure," Molly said. "Don't get me wrong. Part of the appeal this kind of thing has in print is that the women in the audience love to fantasize, love to imagine themselves in Darla's shoes." She grinned. "Hell, I'd like that myself. All I need is a body transplant."

As they spoke, the photographer shuffled about,

shooting rapidly with a Nikon mounting a 128mm lens, its flash rig drawing power from a battery-pack in his coat pocket.

"Is he coming to lunch, too?" Wasserman asked, indicating the photographer.

"Of course," Molly replied. "More good material. Glamorous star having lunch in glamorous restaurant. Damn right he is. And besides, it'll be good publicity for the Beverly Wilshire, too. They'll want pictures as much as we do."

"Mm." Wasserman glanced away.

"How about glamorous star having lunch in glamorous restaurant with glamorous manager?" Molly asked.

But Wasserman wasn't biting. He pretended to study a chandelier.

"Is seeing me eat a salad really going to be all that interesting?" Darla asked.

"Hey, believe it," Molly replied. "You may think that a lot of what you do is dull and ordinary, but that's not what the fans think. As far as they're concerned, everything about you is fascinating. How you live, what you buy, what you eat, what you read, everything. There's no experience you have that they don't want to know about. Vicariously, they want to follow you everywhere. Hell, they'd love to know what it's like when you go to the can, if they could."

"So would I," the photographer said, popping away with the Nikon.

Molly shot him a hard glance. "Where you working next week?"

"Sorry."

"Then fuck off," Molly said. "I hired a photographer, not a comic."

Daignault's manager became flustered. He was rescued by the appearance of a tall, imperious-looking, gray-haired man, impeccably tailored in a Cambridge-shaded sharkskin suit and a subtly figured silk tie. The man looked like somebody a studio would cast in the role of Prime Minister of England.

"May I present our president?" The manager succeeded in sounding both proud and servile at the same time. "Mister Cedric Carruthers." He bowed to Carruthers. "Sir, I pressume you know who this is," he said, indicating Darla.

"Oh, yes, quite,." Carruthers replied in a crisp British accent. "Miss Dawson. Pleasure."

Darla smiled. "Thank you."

"And Mister Wasserman," the manager said.

As the two shook hands, Darla noticed a delicate gold identification bracelet on Carruthers's wrist. Her eye also caught the expression on the Daignault manager's face as he beamed upon Carruthers adoringly. I get it, Darla thought. A daddy fag, to keep the baby fag all warm and snuggly.

The manager looked vaguely at Molly and the photographer, who had continued to shoot steadily. "And these are, un—"

"Molly Martin," the publicity agent said. "And the lightning bug there is our photographer."

Carruthers glanced at the pair distastefully, as if they had farted in concert. Returning his attention to Darla, he bowed slightly. "We at Daignault's are delighted to be of service to you, Miss Dawson. If you'll step this way, please, I'm sure we can make you quite comfortable."

The room into which Carruthers led Darla was similar to the one she had seen Anita Louise sitting in. The president showed Darla and Wasserman and Molly to French provincial chairs upholstered in apricot velvet, leaving the photographer to wander about on the periphery, occasionally resuming his flash-popping.

Apparently Carruthers decided that Darla was worthy of his personal attention. He dismissed the store manager, who backed out of the room, crestfallen.

"Marie," Carruthers called out. *"Viens, depeche-toi!"*

A thin, middle-aged woman wearing a black dress hurried into the room, and Darla realized that the well-cut jersey was a uniform among the female Daignault personnel. Carruthers introduced her to Darla, and then issued commands in French.

As the woman scurried to do Carruthers's bidding, Molly grinned. "Hey, some class, huh?"

The Daignault president chose not to hear. He bowed once more to Darla. "May we offer you coffee, Miss Dawson?"

"That would be nice," Darla replied. Carruthers tugged on a bell cord, and in a moment a maid, formally clad in gray silk with apron and cap of white lace, entered with a butler's tray bearing a silver coffee service with china cups and saucers. A napkin-covered plate held hot croissants.

As Darla, Wasserman, and Molly sipped coffee, Marie returned, carrying a fur. It was a full-length silver fox.

"I don't really quite know your interests or your preferences, Miss Dawson," Carruthers said. "And so I thought it would perhaps be most effective if we were to explore them together as we present some of our creations. The coats we'll show you are made up, of course. If you were to find something that strikes your fancy, it would naturally be fitted for you to perfection. Or if you prefer, we would create one to your order."

"How long would that take?" Darla inquired.

The Prime Minister pursed his lips as he pondered his reply. "Depending, of course, upon the availability of the skins, I would say an average of perhaps two months."

"I think," Darla said quickly, "I'd rather have something that's already made up."

"Of course," Carruthers responded. "I quite understand. Perhaps a magnificent silver fox would appeal to you?" he inquired politely.

Darla looked at the lush fur draped over Marie's arm and then returned her gaze to Carruthers. The man's autocratic features were composed, impassive, and yet there was something in his eyes. Darla realized that she was being tested. She looked at the fur once more. "I don't think so," she said slowly. "Blacks and grays don't really go that well with my coloring."

Carruthers's voice, like his face, was carefully expressionless. "Does Madame have something in mind?"

All right, Darla thought. It's time, Mister Carruthers, for you to know I'm not kidding. You want Katy Hep-

303

burn, you're going to get Katy Hepburn. She set her coffee cup down carefully on the butler's tray and leaned back comfortably in her chair. "I wish to see," she said, "a range of choices in the brown end of the color spectrum, moving from the dark to the lighter shades.

"Also," she continued, "I am not interested in anything as ordinary as silver fox, whether or not its color is suitable. You may start with sable."

To her satisfaction, Darla witnessed a barely perceptible change take place in Carruthers's manner. The furrier bowed and spoke rapidly in French to Marie, who scurried out, bearing the silver fox. Darla heard Molly's low chuckle of approval. "All *right*."

The next hour was, for Darla, the realization of another of her most cherished dreams. She reviewed a breathtaking array of furs, ranging in color and texture from the honey beige of stone marten to the pale off-white of ermine harvested just as its natural owners had begun to change to their summer hues. To most of them, she reacted either with a nod of restrained approval or with a slight frown of rejection. Only three or four aroused sufficient interest for her to try them on.

Finally she sighed. "You've been very kind, Mr. Carruthers, but I haven't seen anything I'm really that pleased with. Is that pretty much everything you can show me?"

"I believe you've seen nearly everything in the color range that interests you, Miss Dawson," Carruthers said. He bit his lower lip thoughtfully, holding his chin in his right hand and propping his right elbow with his left palm. "Although," he hesitated, gazing at the ceiling, "there is one thing we haven't shown you that is rather, well, spectacular."

Aha, Darla thought. Here comes the dynamite. She felt a twinge of excitement. "And what is that?" she asked calmly.

"Why, it's a mink," Carruthers replied. "But a very unusual mink. I think you might find it somewhat pleasing." His manner was that of the sommelier who presides over a wine cellar in which are stored five thousand bottles of the rarest vintages, and who suddenly remembers where he has a 1925 Chateau Lafite Rothschild.

Darla nodded, her reaction a show of polite interest.

"It's something rather, ah, special," Carruthers said.

In this language, Darla thought, special means expensive as hell. "All right," she said crisply. "I'll see it, please."

The instant Marie returned to the room, for perhaps the twenty-fifth time that morning, Darla knew that she was looking at one of Daignault's big guns. The coat was a ripple of muted gold, as if the animals from which it had been made were creatures of some distant planet, guardians of a sun goddess. When the coat was unfurled, the impact of the deep, incredibly rich texture was stunning.

"It's rather pretty," Darla said evenly. "I think I'll try it on."

As Marie slipped the fur over Darla's shoulders, Molly said, "Goddamn."

Even Wasserman was impressed. "Beautiful, Darla."

And beautiful it was. Darla turned slowly, pretending to study her image in the mirrors objectively. The color of the fur was deeper by a shade than her hair, and the resultant blending of golden tones was worthy of Rembrandt. She slid her hands into the pockets and the coat responded like a live creature, cuddling her lovingly. The photographer's Nikon flashed furiously.

"I think," Darla said, "that this one might do." She studied her image in the glass. "In fact, I believe I'll take it."

Carruthers knew his business. "I must compliment Madame," he said, his tone now respectful. "You have chosen what is probably the most outstanding design in our entire salon. It took two years for us to assemble a sufficient number of perfectly matched furs to create this coat. The animals are all mutant mink, you see, and most rare and difficult to produce. Naturally, the coat is one of a kind. There is simply none other quite like it to be found anywhere in the world." He clasped his hands before him. "And if I may say so, it will require hardly

305

any alteration. It appears as if it were created for you, Miss Dawson, and for you alone."

"Mmm." Darla could not take her eyes away from the sweep of mirrors.

Derek Wasserman cleared his throat. "Say, ah, I hate to bring us back to reality, but I have to raise a question. What's the price?"

Carruthers's imperious gaze fixed upon the talent manager. "The price? Of course, it's—"

"I am not interested in the price," Darla interrupted. It was *Philadelphia Story*, and Katy Hepburn did not muck around with such shit. "You and my manager may discuss that in private, Mister Carruthers. I want the coat delivered to my home on, say, Tuesday, which gives you time to make whatever slight alterations you say are necessary." She made a dramatic gesture of looking at her watch. "Now if you'll take measurements, or whatever, I believe I have an appointment for luncheon."

"Right on," Molly said with undisguised admiration.

When they were once again in the Porsche, sliding briskly through the southbound traffic on Rodeo, Darla glanced over at her manager. "Now you can tell me."

"Tell you what?" Wasserman asked.

"How much it cost, of course. The coat. And incidentally, how much this car was, too."

"Well, now. I was beginning to think you didn't acknowledge that anything as crass as money existed."

"Oh, I know about it." Darla laughed. "I just don't want it to get in the way of my enjoying myself. Not ever again."

A yellow Maserati Ghibli passed them, heading in the opposite direction, and the man at the wheel waved. "Hi, Darla!" he called.

As the Maserati flashed by, Darla got a brief impression of the driver—young, dark, good-looking. She smiled and returned the wave.

"Who was that?"

"I don't know," Darla replied. "Isn't it marvelous?"

Wasserman grunted.

"So how much?"

"Your car was thirty thousand and change. And the coat, my dear, was fifty-five thousand dollars."

Darla was awestruck. She had known, vaguely, that a new Turbo Carrera would cost somewhere in the neighborhood of the figure Wasserman had given her, so that had been no surprise. But fifty-five thousand for one fur coat? Even a fur coat whose ancestry was as rare and noble as the Lord High Fag had described? Wow! And what a hell of a thrill. That made buying it all the more delicious.

Wasserman misread his client's silence. "I think that in the future you should check with me on what the spending parameters are. That way we can avoid embarrassment, and we can also keep things a little more sane. We don't have to take the coat, you know. I can always tell Daignault's you've changed your mind."

Darla's reply was instantaneous and fierce. "Don't you dare," she hissed. She swung the Porsche into the drive of the Beverly Wilshire Hotel and brought it to a stop. As the doorman approached the car, Darla turned to her manager. "It's Saturday morning, and I have just spent something around eighty-five thousand dollars, and I never had so much fun in my life. I bought that coat because I wanted it. Now let's have some lunch. I'm hungry."

Chapter 34

The Beverly Wilshire was actually older than the Beverly Hills Hotel, but it had never attained quite the level of prestige enjoyed by its rival to the north. Refurbished at a cost of twenty million dollars, the Beverly Wilshire was now luxurious, even grand, and the management was dedicated to raising its rank to a point equal to, or if possible higher than, that of the Beverly Hills. The key to achieving such a goal was, of course, no secret to anyone in the business, because the status of any hotel is always determined by one factor: the status of its guests.

There had been a time when the Beverly Wilshire was frequented primarily by tourists, drummers, and conventioneers, catering even to veterans' organizations, whose members believed that a year or two spent in the armed forces entitled them to assemble annually for the rest of their lives. They wore funny hats and stayed drunk for the duration of their convocation, dropped paper bags filled with water out of their hotel windows onto pedestrians on the sidewalks below, and in general displayed their boorishness to the world at large.

In recent years, however, all this had changed. The Beverly Wilshire was now even preferred by a growing number of distinguished visitors to Los Angeles, for a variety of reasons. Some, like the King of Sweden, found an inverse snobbishness in favoring a hotel other than the Beverly Hills. Others, bruised at some point in the past by the failure of the Beverly Hills Hotel to recognize their importance and to treat them accordingly, were now regulars at the Beverly Wilshire with a we'll-show-them kind of loyalty. And finally, there were those who comprised yet another group of status-seekers—people who thought that by patronizing the Beverly Wilshire they were doing the newest in-thing.

In any event, when a television or motion picture star chose to do business with the Beverly Wilshire, whether as a guest of the hotel or merely to dine in one of its rooms, the management saw to it that the luminary was treated with a deference to be found in none of the other inns comprising the Big Four in Beverly Hills. This was especially true if that star employed the services of a skilled publicity agent, and there was no better such agent in the industry that Molly Martin. When Darla pulled up in her new Porsche, it was as if a member of one of the world's royal families had arrived. She and her group were shown at once to the El Padrino, one of the hotel's dining rooms.

"Wouldn't this have been better in a private room?" Wasserman asked loftily when they had been seated.

"Hell no," Molly replied emphatically. "The more people who see Darla in a place like this, the better. And also it makes a more effective picture layout. See, the women who read the magazine want to get the effect of Darla being admired by a lot of other tony-looking people in a posh place. They identify with that, and it's another thing that they like to kind of imagine themselves doing. But if we shut her up in some private room someplace, it doesn't have all that interest going for it, you see?"

"No," Wasserman replied sulkily. "I don't."

Darla listened to the exchange calmy. What Molly had said made eminent good sense, she decided, and her intuition told her that Wasserman's reaction was due in one part to his cultivated snobbishness, and in another part to his resentment at Molly's giving him a didactic lecture on the workings of publicity. There wasn't much, Darla realized, that Wasserman would be willing to admit he didn't know about any aspect of the business. "Who's doing this story?" she asked Molly.

"Sandra Becker," the publicist replied. "For *McCall's*. I've worked with her before. She's okay, but a little too snoopy about some things. You just have to keep your guard up with her. You know, be as open and cooperative as you can, but if she gets into things you don't think are any of her business—you know, things you don't want showing up in the piece—just tell her so."

"Okay," Darla replied. "Anything else?"

"Yeah. Remember what we talked about for your public image. You're the perfect wife, delighted to have a successful career, but a little ambivalent because you're really more interested in your marriage than in any other thing. You rush home from the studio every night to cook Mike's dinner yourself."

Darla laughed. "Come on, Molly—who's going to believe that crap? Dedicated wife, sure. But rushing home to cook dinner?"

"You'll be amazed," the publicity agent said. "That's exactly what *McCall's* would love to tell its readers, and exactly the kind of shit its audience loves to wallow in."

Darla shrugged. "Okay, if you say they'll buy it."

She glanced around the room, and realized with a start that virtually everyone in the place was staring at her. This was something she hadn't gotten used to, and it always surprised her to find herself the absolute center of attention.

The maitre d' approached their table and bowed. "Your guest has arrived, Miss Martin." He turned and held a chair for Sandra Becker.

Molly made the introductions. The magazine writer was dark-haired, homely, intense.

They ordered drinks and made small talk; Molly inquired about the writer's trip out from New York and the hotel's treatment of her.

"Super," Becker replied. "I've got a great room that looks right down on the pool, and the manager sent flowers. Really makes me feel welcome."

Molly nodded. "They do it right. Especially when

they know it's going to do them some good. Their P.R. people are tops to work with."

The drinks arrived, and when the salutations had been exchanged and the first sip swallowed, Becker got out her notebook. "We'll jump right in," she said, "if that's okay. I'll just make notes right through lunch." She looked at Darla. "Molly said you don't like to have interviewers who use tape recorders."

Before Darla could answer, Molly said, "I'm the heavy there. I don't like writers to use them with Darla. Makes it a little harder to manage the piece sometimes, especially if there's something she happens to say that she wouldn't want on the record."

Becker drank some of her Bloody Mary. "It's okay with me." She smiled. "*McCall's* wants pretty tame stuff anyhow. Nothing about Darla's secret foot fetish, or her heroin habit."

Darla laughed. "Or even my struggles with smallpox?"

"Not even that," the writer replied. "What we do want, though, is as much as we can get on your relationship with Mike, your views on marriage and children, and so on. So let's go right into that subject area, okay?"

"Sure," Darla said. "What can I tell you?"

"Well, let's start from the beginning." Becker picked up her pencil. "How did you and Mike meet?"

"Blind date," Darla answered. "Arranged by a publicity agent." She smiled across at Molly. "You know what they're like."

"Do I ever," Becker said. "What was the occasion?"

"Hollywood party for the kickoff of a series, the western Mike got his start in. The network wanted a girl for him to escort, and presto! there I was."

"How'd you like him?" Becker asked. "Was it love at first sight?"

Darla made a face. "The opposite. I couldn't stand him. Thought he was the most conceited thing I'd ever run across. I couldn't wait for the evening to be over with."

"So how'd you happen to see him again?"

311

Darla was surprised to experience a trace of nostalgia as she recalled those events that now seemed so long ago. "Well, I really wasn't expecting to," she said. "I had a little apartment I was sharing with another girl on La Brea in Hollywood, and Mike started calling me a day or two later. I told him I wasn't interested, you know, came right out with it, but he was insistent. Even sent me flowers. Finally I said okay, it was about a week later I guess, and he took me out to dinner."

"Love at second sight," Becker said.

Darla laughed again. "Not quite. In fact, it was even worse than the first time."

"Oh, my." Becker scribbled on her pad. "The plot thickens. So how did you two ever get together?"

"Went to another party, about two months later, with a guy who was just, you know, a friend. Mike was there, and when he saw me he made a fuss over me, and we spent a lot of that evening talking together. I realized then that I'd been wrong, that he wasn't really so much conceited as he was just sure of himself, and sure of what he wanted."

"Which was you, right, Darla?" Wasserman interjected.

"Eventually," Darla said. She thought about it. "Actually, I guess we were already in love that night, and didn't know it. The next day I couldn't stop thinking about him. The things he'd said, his ideas. Somehow that night he loosened up, wasn't trying to impress me at all. We just talked and talked about everything, as if we were old pals, and I liked the way he thought about things. In some ways he's old-fashioned, and in others very modern, even progressive."

"Like what?" Becker inquired.

"Well, like he has lots of political ideas that sound like my father back in Oklahoma. The people in elected offices ought to be more accountable to the voters who put them there, and people on welfare who can work should have to, and so on. But at the same time he always supports liberal causes, always supports the Democrats. And that's so like him. Mike takes a tough stand on everything, but inside he has a great big heart."

"What happened next?"

"He called," Darla went on, "that next day, and asked me to dinner again. And that night we went out to Santa Monica and had spaghetti and red wine in this little place and we were totally relaxed together. It was wonderful."

"Then you knew?" Becker asked.

"Then I knew," Darla replied. "I was head over heels in love." She smiled, remembering. God, was that ever the truth. She'd never been so happy as in those first wonderful carefree days with Mike.

Becker scribbled. "So when were you married?"

"Not for two years," Darla replied. "We lived together, but we didn't marry for—" Suddenly aware of what she'd said, she shot a glance at Molly.

"Better not use that, Sandra," the publicity agent said.

"Hey," Becker replied. "We're out of the Dark Ages, haven't you heard? Everybody's doing it."

"Nevertheless, don't use it," Molly ordered.

Becker shrugged. "Okay. So what are the interests you two share?"

"Oh, we're both physical culture nuts. We run together sometimes. You know, jog. And we play a lot of tennis, and we swim. Then there's our home. We're always doing things to it, changing this room or that one, shopping for furniture and stuff, especially antiques."

"Do you cook?"

Darla drank some of her Perrier water. What the hell, she thought. "Oh, yes. All Mike's favorites. I usually rush home from the studio so that I can get there before he does and get dinner going."

Becker's pencil raced across the paper.

My God, Darla thought, she really is buying it.

"What are some of those dishes? You know, his favorites?"

"Well, he loves anything Italian. Eggplant parmigiana, lasagna, manicotti." She looked at Wasserman, whose expression lay somewhere between boredom and nausea.

"Isn't that hard to do? You know, get things like that together when you're so short of time?"

"Yes, it is." Darla thought fast. "But I can often do some of the basic preparations before I leave in the morning, while I'm waiting for the limousine to pick me up."

"Sure," Becker nodded. "What else does he like? How about seafood?"

"Loves it," Darla replied. "He's a nut on cracked crab with mustard sauce." A picture suddenly rushed into her mind of the last time she had actually prepared that dish for her husband. She had worked so hard to make that a perfect evening, and it had been such a disaster. She saw Mike's alcohol-flushed face distorted in anger, felt the sting of his hand as he struck her, saw his huge body looming over her as he forced her down onto the bed.

Becker leaned forward. "I said, does he like wine?"

Darla suddenly realized she had missed one of the writer's questions. "Oh, sorry. Yes. Yes, he likes wine very much. We both do. But we almost never drink it during the week. We usually share a bottle at dinner on the weekend."

"You know what?" Molly Martin smiled. "All this talk about food has me ravenous. Why don't we order, okay?"

"I thought you'd never ask," Wasserman said.

"How about another drink?" the photographer suggested.

"How about you take a picture," Molly replied. She signaled the captain, who practically leaped to her side.

They ordered, Darla requesting a salad as usual, shrimp this time, as Sandra Becker continued to press her with questions.

"How do you feel about children?" the writer asked.

"Love them," Darla answered. "We both do. And we're looking forward to starting our family just as soon as we can. Unfortunately, that'll have to wait a little while, because we're both so busy right now."

"Boys or girls?" Becker smiled.

"Both," Darla said. "Any kind's fine with us. We just want children, and the more the better."

The writer's eyes narrowed a fraction. "Would you say Mike is a very loving person?"

Molly interrupted. "She means how is he as a stud, don't you, Sandra?"

"No," Becker replied innocently. "I was only—"

"Sure," Molly said. "The answer is, sensational. He has a two-foot schlong, okay? Now let's stay on the track."

Darla laughed. "He's a very loving person," she said to the writer. "Tender and considerate, and very mindful of my needs. He's a wonderful man to live with."

Becker made furious notes. "Ever quarrel?"

After a moment's hesitation, Darla said, "Yes, sometimes. But it never really means anything. We do some yelling and get things off our chests, and then we forget about it. I honestly think it's good for us, sometimes."

Then food arrived, and as they ate the writer asked for a sketch of Darla's childhood in Oklahoma, her early family life, and for other fill-in material.

"What are your views on women in society today?" Becker asked over coffee.

Darla sat bolt-upright. This was something she could really chew on. "I think we're finally coming into our own, and it's about time. I believe a woman can do anything a man can do, and she has every right to make her own choices as to how she wants to live her life."

"In other words," Becker led her, "you think women should have the same kind of freedom men have?"

"Absolutely," Darla said. "A marriage should be a totally sharing relationship. The work, the home, all of it. A woman should be able to have a career if she wants one, and when the house is to be cleaned, that's every bit as much her husband's responsibility as it is hers."

"Is that how your marriage operates?" Becker asked.

"Yes, it is," Darla answered. "We share it all. The only reason I cook Mike's dinner is that I want to. It gives me pleasure to do something he enjoys and appreciates."

"How do you feel about open marriage?" The writer's eyes narrowed again, fractionally.

"That's a personal matter that's entirely up to the couple," Darla said. "It's not my idea of what marriage is all about, but at the same time I respect other people's right to live that way if it's what they want."

"Do any of your friends have that kind of an, ah, understanding?"

Darla caught a faint scowl of warning on Molly's face, but she plunged ahead. "Yes, they do. And that's just what it is—an understanding. They recognize each other's right to come and go as they please, and they don't ask questions. For Mike and me it would be wrong, but for some people it's the only way they can have a marriage."

"So you're not all that put off by the so-called swinging Hollywood life?"

This time a faint alarm bell rang in the back of Darla's head. "I'm neither put off by it nor attracted to it. That kind of life simply holds no attraction for me. I love my husband and we have a very close realtionship, and that's all that matters."

Realizing she'd get no further on this tack, Becker tried a new direction. "Your work on 'The Witches' is grueling, I imagine. Long hours, so much to get done in so little time."

Darla nodded. "We do one a week. It's tough."

"I'm sure it is. And how," Becker inquired, "do you get along with Cathy Drake?"

Darla was ready for this one. She had long since learned to expect it in interviews. "I'm Cathy's biggest fan. She's a fine actress and a wonderful person, and I'd always do anything I could to help her." Including, she said to herself, cutting her throat.

"Does she feel the same way about you?"

"I'm sure she does," Darla replied. Especially the throat-cutting part.

"And that," Molly said, "is just about all we have time for. Sandra, it's been terrific. You've got everything you need for a great piece."

"You're right." Becker looked at Darla admiringly.

"You know, I've interviewed a lot of terrific women, but I have to tell you quite honestly that I admire you more than just about any of them, including the great Jackie O."

Darla was genuinely moved. She put her hand over the writer's. "That's very sweet of you, Sandra. I really appreciate it a lot."

"I'm the one who's appreciative," Becker replied. "You've made my job easy."

"Sure," Molly said. "Now you've got nothing to do but enjoy yourself for a couple of days, compliments of *McCall's* and the Beverly Wilshire Hotel. You can work on your tan, and at night you can cruise the bars on the Sunset Strip. Might even get laid, if you play your cards right."

Becker laughed. "Sounds glorious."

The photographer's Nikon flashed. "Maybe we could have a drink later," he said to Becker.

"Keep your hand on your f-stop," Mickey said. But Darla noted that Becker had smiled warmly at the photographer in response to his suggestion.

As they made their exit from the hotel, the Beverly Wilshire management bowing and gushing, the crowd Darla was beginning to expect as a matter of routine began to assemble. The doorman held the door of the new Porsche open, and as Darla entered the car, a teen-aged girl broke away from the crowd and darted up to her.

The girl was overweight, sweaty, and clad in dirty jeans. Darla had a fleeting impression of a pimply face wearing a determined expression, and then suddenly she felt a sharp pain on the left side of her head. She cried out in stunned surprise.

The girl had gripped a handful of Darla's hair in her meaty fist. In her other hand she brandished a pair of scissors. The blades flashed, and the girl held the mass of amputated hair aloft, triumphantly.

Molly Martin reacted first, reaching Darla and the girl in one bound. She punched the teenager in the stomach. "You little shit!"

The girl scrambled off into the crowd, which had

broken into laughter and cheers. She was clutching her gut but still hanging onto the booty.

Darla was in a state of shock as she slumped in her seat. There was a momentary flurry as the hotel people surrounded her, with concern and worry on their faces.

"Miss Dawson, are you all right?" the manager asked, his face pale. "Shall we call a doctor?"

Darla shook her head. She felt for her hair, her hands fumbling at the place where the scissors had done their work. "No, no, I'm all right."

Derek Wasserman took his seat beside her, open-mouthed, an expression of confusion on his face. God, Darla thought. There is nothing like having a man around in an emergency. She waved off the solicitous group around the car and slammed the door. The engine burst into life and Darla roared away.

She dropped Wasserman in front of his office, turning off his flustered remarks. For once, she thought grimly, he doesn't sound like such a know-it-all. Fifteen minutes later she was home.

Maggie looked up in surprise. "What happened to you?"

"Nothing." Darla strode through the front hall. "Nothing at all."

"You all right?" the black woman asked solicitously. "Can I get you anything?"

"No, I'm fine, really." Impulsively, she put her arm around Maggie's plump shoulders.

"You sure? You ain't sick or nothing?"

"No, I'm all right. I just want to be alone for awhile."

"Okay," Maggie said doubtfully. "No phone calls?"

"No. Nothing." Darla walked into her bedroom, unbuttoning her blouse.

"You want your messages?"

"They'll keep," Darla said. She shut the door behind her and pulled off the rest of her clothing. In her bathroom Darla swung the hinged mirrors so that she could see her head in profile. Christ, what a chunk that horrible little bitch had cut out of her head. Bobby Benbo would choke when he saw it. She fumbled with the hacked-off ends, trying for a minute or two to disguise

318

the damage by combing over it. But she was unsuccessful. She gave up, finally, walked back into the bedroom, and flopped down on the bed.

She wondered where Mike was. She hadn't seen him in two days. Or was it three? Jesus, talking to that writer had been a farce. Like some kind of phony session with a psychiatrist—pretending to express all her thoughts and emotions, baring her soul. Except that it was all bullshit. Instead of describing things as they were, she had detailed them as she would want them to be. What a sad, hypocritical little sham. All so that the ladies in the *McCall's* audience could lift up their heads from their own dreary, miserable lives and read about what a beautiful experience Darla Dawson was living in the world of glamour and success, secure in the powerful love of her devoted husband.

Darla fumbled in the drawer of her bedside table for the bottle of Nembutal. She swallowed one and rolled over, burying her face in a pillow. Suddenly she was racked by uncontrollable sobs. She cried for a long time, until the barbiturate took hold and she slid from her misery into a deep, dreamless void.

Chapter 35

Mike Brady pushed the Mercedes hard through the gathering dusk, ascending the climbing turns of Laurel Canyon at the limit of the car's ability to hold the road. The tires shrieked as he wound the heavy convertible through the curves, the big V-8 howling at something over 5,000 RPM. He passed car after car in the dense, homeward-bound traffic, taking absurd chances, paying no attention to the blare of horns and the flashing of headlights as other drivers protested his recklessness.

Cynically, tiredly, Mike reflected that even this was no longer fun. There was a time when fast driving had rated a close second to screwing as his favorite sport, but tonight he felt no elation, no exuberance at whipping the 450 SL flat out up the serpentine highway that rose from Hollywood through the sere hills to Mulholland Drive. Just before reaching the top of the ridge, he turned off onto the hidden promontory where his house perched and pulled the Mercedes into the driveway. To his left was one of the most spectacular views in all of Southern California, a panorama of purple hills and shadowy valleys. At the outermost reaches lay the city of Los Angeles, a dark plain where a galaxy of lights twinkled, seeming to stretch to infinity.

Mike saw none of it. His back was laced with pain, and his head ached fiercely, as if a demon were tightening a steel band around his skull. He noted dully that

Sally Dane's Toyota was parked in the driveway. Sally was Darla's secretary, hired at Wasserman's suggestion to help cope with the flood of mail, phone calls, appointments, and endless trivia that inundated the actress. Even when he was at his hottest, Mike thought sourly, he had never needed a secretary. He touched the button on the transmitter mounted under the Mercedes's dashboard, and the garage door lifted open. He eased the convertible inside and turned off the ignition. God, but it had been an exhausting day. Correction. An exhausting week, an exhausting year. This was the first time he'd been home since—when, Sunday? He needed a shower and a drink and about twenty hours of deep sleep.

As he got out of the Mercedes, Mike wondered if Darla was home. Her car was here, he observed. Or was it? In the darkness something looked different. He snapped on the overhead light in the garage and stared at the white Porsche. For a moment, he didn't get it. Whom did he know who owned a brand-new white Turbo Carrera? He studied the sleek coupe for a few seconds, and then he caught sight of the license plate, and it was like a punch in the gut. His feeling of fatigue deepened as he turned off the light and touched the button that would close the garage door.

In the kitchen Maggie was scrubbing vegetables in the sink. She looked up and smiled a greeting as Mike entered from the back hall. "Evening, Mr. Mike. Welcome home."

Mike grunted. He opened the refrigerator door and peered inside, almost reflexively, not even aware of what he was looking for. He shut the door and started toward the bedroom.

Darla appeared in the doorway of the kitchen. She was wearing white pants and a pale green cashmere sweater. Even in his state of exhaustion, Mike realized that she looked radiantly beautiful. She smiled tentatively. "Hi, Mike."

"Um."

"I was hoping you'd be here for dinner."

"Yeah."

"Mike?"

"What?"

"How do you like it?"

"How do I like what?"

Darla smiled her little-girl smile, her eyes bright with excitement. "How do you like what?" she mimicked him in a low, teasing voice. "How do you like my new Porsche, of course. Didn't you notice it in the garage?"

"Yeah, I noticed it."

The smile slowly faded from Darla's face. "Well, didn't you like it? Don't you think it's beautiful?"

"I think it's the most beautiful fucking car I ever saw in my whole silly goddamn life. I think nobody in the world has got a car as nice as that, okay?" His voice rose. "You must really love the son of a bitch." He pushed past her, walked down the hall to their bedroom, and slammed the door behind him.

The shower made him feel a little better, but not much. He resorted to the trick he had learned in his boxing days, alternating the shower from hot to icy cold and back again, over and over, and it helped some. But when he had toweled dry, the fatigue was still there, deep within his bones, and the demon still held his head in an excruciating grip of steel. He pulled on a pair of jeans and a cotton sailor's sweater and walked into the study.

Darla was sitting at her desk, on which stacks of paper were piled high. Sally Dane occupied a chair beside the desk, her notebook opened on her lap. She waved a hand. "Hi, Mike. How's it going?"

"Terrific." He looked at the stacks of mail.

"We're getting them by the thousands," Sally said. She was pretty in a more or less standard, snub-nosed blonde way. An alumna of UCLA's School of Theater Arts, Sally had lucked into this job because her father, an engineer at NBC, was a friend of one of the lighting men who worked on "The Witches." "If I didn't have help from UBS's publicity department I could never handle it," Sally went on. She was bubbling with excitement. "Every day the count gets higher. Today alone we got over four thousand letters. Isn't that fantastic?"

"Yeah. Fantastic." Mike glanced at Darla and saw that she had looked up from a letter and was watching him coolly. Something about her hair looked odd. It seemed to be thicker on one side than on the other. "What'd you do to your hair?"

Involuntarily, Darla touched the left side of her head. "It was—" She stopped and blinked several times. "It just needs washing." She returned her attention to the mail.

Mike stepped to the bar and poured himself a stiff Chivas over ice, no water. He looked at Darla. "Drink?" She shook her head.

Mike took a long pull of the Scotch, the whiskey burning his throat and his belly, but warming and relaxing him. Immediately, it seemed, he felt less tired. He lit a cigarette and the image of the new Porsche came back into his mind. He felt a pang of guilt as he thought about his reaction to it. So his wife had herself a new car, and a nice one, at that. So what was he so upset about? She'd earned it, hadn't she? Along with all the other things that were finally coming her way. Was that bad? What the hell was the matter with him, anyway? He turned on the TV and flopped down onto the leather sofa.

A film clip loomed onto the television screen, a fuzzy picture of a trailer truck that had gone off one of the freeways and caught fire as it overturned. It lay on its side in the ditch, still belching black smoke. An announcer made excited voice-over remarks about the wreck, but Mike did not listen. He looked at the picture of the smoldering hulk for a few seconds and then glanced at the two women, who continued to work on the piles of mail.

He swallowed more of his Scotch and picked up a copy of that morning's *Los Angeles Times* from the coffee table.

He leafed idly through the newspaper, dwelling with half-interest on Jim Murray's column, which was devoted largely to conjecture on the Rams' chances to win a divisional title during the upcoming season, and then flipped to the entertainment pages. He looked at the movie ads, finding nothing much of interest, and was about to put the paper aside when an item in a box caught his eye. It was by somebody named Feldman, a writer he'd never heard of. SAVAGE CITY'S BIG GUN A DERRINGER, the headline said. Mike scanned it twice, the hairs on the back of his neck prickling as the meaning of the word-play sank in. He took a deep breath, and very slowly began to read the piece.

> She came, they saw, and according to every measure from TVQ to the Nielsen ratings, Andrea Derringer has conquered. The tall, leggy beauty not only has given the staggering Mike Brady series a desperately needed shot in its aging arteries, but she has just plumb run away with the show. Although it's strictly a no-no to mention such things within earshot of the super-sensitive ex-jock, word has it that Andrea, and Andrea alone, has saved "The Savage City" from TV's boneyard. What next? Nobody at UBS, least of all Peter Fried, is saying, but the options are pretty clear. One, revamp the show around Andrea, with Mister Muscles reduced to the well-earned role of second banana; or two, junk the series altogether, and Brady along with it, launching Andrea into television's stratosphere in an altogether new vehicle, designed especially to showcase the beautiful lady's formidable talent. Our choice? The latter. TV's rating competition is nothing less than total war, and you don't fight with popguns when you have a howitzer on your side. Or to put it more precisely, when your Derringer is the biggest gun of all.

Jesus Christ. Mike looked again at Darla, who went on poring over the impossible stacks of letters. He swallowed the last of his Scotch and returned to the bar, refilled his glass, without ice this time, and emptied it in one long gulp. Now the whiskey seemed to have no effect upon him. He put the glass down on the bar and walked aimlessly out of the room, into the hall, and through the living room out onto the patio.

It had become totally dark, and the distant lights of Los Angeles shone more brightly. The night air was fresh and clear, and a slight breeze had come up. Mike stood still, looking out to the south and seeing nothing, only dimly aware that the flagstones felt cool beneath his bare feet.

For God's sake, what was happening? What the hell was going on? Was this reality, or some crazy dream sequence, like the ones you sometimes saw in an old movie on TV? For the first time in his life, he was up against a problem he didn't know how to cope with. Was that shit in the newspaper anywhere near true? Or was it just another piece of gossip, barely fit to wrap the garbage in? Numbly, he forced himself to face the realization that in just those few short lines, Feldman, whoever the fuck he was, had put into focus all the fears and suspicions and anxieties that had been creeping about in the back of his mind like so many evil genies, ducking in and out of the shadows of his thoughts.

The question was, what to do? Problems were something you took action against—difficulties were what you solved with your balls and your fists. But what did you do when you couldn't even settle on what your target was, couldn't even identify your enemy? His first reaction was that he should lash out; go in slugging. A picture of Dick Hazelman's tan, smiling face came into his mind and he wanted to smash it. But what good could that do? And Arnold Gross, his dumb shit of a Harvard lawyer who thought he was such a goddamn genius and whose annual fees were a fucking fortune, what had he done to prevent this, except to mouth a lot of fancy phrases, more like some asshole psychiatrist than a lawyer. Wouldn't it be satisfying to throw that smug prick right through the window of his plush office? And Fried? It wasn't really the UBS program boss's fault either, although the son of a bitch had had a hand in it.

All right, the thing to do was to take action. But how? He'd call a showdown, force Hazelman and Fried and UBS to the wall. And yet somehow, he wasn't as sure of his ground as he always had been—

wasn't so positive what the outcome would be if he were to set an ultimatum, if he were to bring this mess to a climax. In the end, that would possibly only hurt him worse, and Andrea too.

Andrea. Christ, this wasn't her fault. She was only doing what anybody would do, trying to make the most of this break, this big opportunity in her career. And God knew it was true that she *had* helped the show, had given it a boost when, as much as Mike hated to admit it now, it had really needed it. Andrea. Jesus—she was the only sane, reasonable one in this whole situation. And the only one he could trust, too. That son of a bitch of a writer, implying in his snotty, smartass article that Andrea had deliberately upstaged him, when the truth was that the kid adored him, had always turned to him for advice and counsel, practically ignoring Britney's ideas, depending mainly on Mike for help with interpretation, for guidance in anything from playing her character to planning a difficult scene.

As he thought about Andrea, Mike was surprised to realize that the mental picture of her beautiful face, with its large, dark eyes, the wide mouth and the high, elegant cheekbones, actually made him feel better—gave him the only suggestion of a pleasant experience he'd had all day. He turned abruptly and strode back into the house.

In the bedroom Mike lifted the phone and dialed. He listened impatiently to the buzzing in the earpiece, then heard the click of an answer at the other end.

"Hello?" Andrea's voice was low, husky.

"Hey, love."

"Mike, how are you?" There was genuine pleasure in the rich tones.

"Great—but I need to see you."

"Okay. Is something wrong?"

"No, I just want to see you."

There seemed to be a faint hesitation before Andrea replied. "Sure. Tonight?"

"Yeah, tonight. Now."

"Just a minute." There was a muffled sound as Andrea apparently held her hand over the phone and said something to someone else. She came back on. "Wonderful, darling. Please come as soon as you can."

Mike couldn't help himself. "What'd you do," he asked testily. "Get rid of the company?"

Andrea chuckled softly. "If that's jealousy, I'm delighted. But I have to confess that I was only giving Margarita the night off. Unless," she teased, "you'd rather have her stay around?"

Mike laughed, feeling foolish. "Be there right away," he said, and put the phone down.

Maggie looked up, blank-faced, as Mike walked through the kitchen and into the back hall. "Tell my wife," he said, "that I can't stay for dinner. That I had to go out."

Andrea's house was totally dark, except for the light beside the front entrance. Mike parked his Mercedes in the driveway and walked up to the door, hearing Andrea's yappy little Lhasa Apso bark as he approached. He pressed the bell.

Andrea was wearing pants and an open-necked white silk shirt, as she usually did in the evening, the thin material clinging to her full breasts and revealing her large nipples in an erotic definition that turned Mike on like an electric switch. Her scent was a mixture of musk and Replique as she pressed her body against his and slid her tongue into his mouth.

The effect she had on him was incredible—soothing and exciting at the same time. He felt himself respond, as he always did, to her sensuality. "Jesus," he whispered, "but I want you."

Andrea lay her head against his chest. "I want you too, darling but not right this minute."

"Why not?" He was suspicious, as always, and a little jealous, when she was ever anything less than totally responsive to him.

Andrea looked up, her great gray eyes filled with concern. "Because you're distraught, somehow—upset about something."

"I'm a little—uptight. I—"

"Mike, please," Andrea said softly. "You don't have

to tell me. I just want you to be completely relaxed and at ease. If you feel like talking, fine. But if not, you musn't feel you have to. It's enough for me just to have you here."

"Yeah, of course. That's what I love about you."

"Come on." She led him by the hand to the sofa and gently pressed him into a seat. She smiled. "First thing you need is a nice, quiet smoke." She opened the cigarette box on the coffee table and held it out to him. The box contained several joints. "I rolled these right after you called. It's Colombian, good and fresh."

The marijuana calmed him, eased his tensions. Mike pulled its smoke as deeply into his lungs as he could, and exhaled slowly. His thoughts immediately became clearer, less jumbled, and his headache, he noted, was diminishing, nearly gone. In its place was a faint buzzing sensation he found quite pleasant. Good old grass. And especially good old top-quality dynamite Colombian grass, the best in the world. He grinned at Andrea. "Stuff's great."

She smiled. "I thought you'd like it. Makes you see things in a better light, doesn't it?"

"Yeah, it really does." He looked at the joint in his fingers. "Should be required smoking for anybody in a tough job. If Nixon had blown one of these now and then he'd probably still be president."

"God forbid."

He laughed. "I'm with you."

"I hear ABC is buying that book by John Erlichmann—*The Company*, I think it's called. They're going to turn it into a miniseries. All about how a maniac president gets himself thrown out of office."

Mike snorted. "Isn't that some crock of shit? All those bums are making a fortune by spilling their memoirs into books or TV or both. Nixon's supposed to be pulling down over a million for the Frost interviews, and they say Swifty Lazar is getting him two more for his book."

Andrea was wide-eyed. "That much?"

"Sure. And not only that, but Paramount wants the rights. Beautiful, isn't it?"

"Crime does not merely pay." Andrea smiled. "It makes you rich."

"It's the small-time crime that doesn't pay," Mike said. "Just like in anything else, you've got to go big if you expect to make any real money."

She nodded somberly. "You're right, of course. Just as you always are."

Mike grinned. "Not always. I was wrong once. I think it was in 1968."

Andrea laughed appreciatively.

He dragged deeply on his joint. "Actually, I stole that line. And from Peter Fried, of all people. I was in his office a while back, and he had a little sign on his wall. It said, 'I am never wrong. The only time I was wrong was when I thought I had made an error, and I was mistaken.'"

Andrea laughed again. "That's funny. That's really funny."

"Yeah. But in Fried's case I'm not so sure. I think he's probably serious."

"Maybe he is," Andrea replied. "But you must admit he has quite a track record."

"Yeah, he has. But that doesn't make him the fucking genius he thinks he is, and that he tells the world he is. It just lets you know what assholes the program guys at the other networks are. By comparison, Fried is a combination of Einstein and William Shakespeare."

"Must be exciting," Andrea said. She blew a stream of smoke toward the ceiling. "Having all that power. Being in charge of hundreds of millions of dollars worth of programming. Being able to bring on a new show or snuff out an old one with just a flick of your finger."

Mike looked at her. Andrea's lips were parted, and her eyes were shining, as she stared at some distant fantasy. "That turns you on," he said. "Doesn't it?"

Andrea nodded. "Sure. Power always turns women on. Which is why some of the greatest lovers in history have been rather ugly men. Napoleon, for example, or Lord Nelson. They were irresistible to women because they were able to take life and shape it any way they wanted to. They lived as they pleased, and did whatever they wanted. They were driving, relentless, the superior male animal."

Despite himself, Mike had to agree with her. "Aristotle Onassis," he said quietly.

"Exactly. The head of a frog on an ape's body. What an incredibly ugly man. Yet all he had to do was beckon and women couldn't get into his bed fast enough."

"Except Jackie."

Andrea laughed. "Except Jackie. What she couldn't get into fast enough was his bank account."

Mike's cigarette was less than a half-inch long. He disdained roach holders, believing they made him look silly. He dropped the butt into an ashtray and lit a fresh joint, dragging hard. His headache was completely gone now; he felt great. His spirits were soaring the way they always used to, and the way they so rarely did these days. Christ, but it was wonderful to feel like this—strong and clear-headed, able to cope with any goddamn thing, excited to be in the presence of this ravishing, sensuous woman who knew and appreciated him so well. His problems with "The Savage City" and his career? Hell, he could handle them with ease. He'd think it all out later tonight. But first, he had something much more interesting to deal with. "And what about me?" he asked. "Is it my power that turns you on?"

Andrea stared at him almost reverently. "Oh, God, yes," she whispered. "Your power, and your strength, and your intellect, and your fantastic maleness. You're the ultimate man, Mike—a gigantic, stainless steel cock."

Mike could hear her breathing, could see the magnificent breasts rising and falling, the nipples distending the thin white material of her blouse. He tossed his roach into the ashtray and reached for her.

"No," Andrea said. "Not yet." She got up from the sofa. "I want you, Mike—so much I'm ready to come, right now. But I want this to be marvelous for you, the best you've ever had." She slipped off her blouse and her pants and stood before him.

As many times as Mike had seen this woman naked,

the sight was invariably stunning to his senses. Andrea was statuesque, lush, ripe. And she was also in perfect condition, her tawny skin smooth and sleek over firm muscles. Mike stared at the beautifully turned legs, the dark patch between her thighs, the curve of her belly, the wide, roseate nipples, and then his eyes locked with hers and he could hear the blood roaring in his ears.

Andrea's mouth curled in a half-smile. "Take off your clothes, Mike. But don't get up, and don't touch me. I want to do it all."

He pulled off his sweater and pants, his gaze riveted to the dark gray eyes.

"That's lovely," Andrea said. She turned and opened a drawer in a table behind her. When she again faced him she held a small silver box in one hand, a tiny silver spoon in the other. She smiled again, her eyes glittering, as she approached him. Slowly, gently, her hands very steady, she dipped the tiny spoon into the powdery white contents of the box and extended it toward him. "Plug one side," she commanded.

Mike obediently lifted a finger to his right nostril and held it shut. Andrea carefully placed the bowl of the spoon directly under his left nostril, and pressed it lightly against the opening. "Snort, baby."

He inhaled sharply. The sensation was a tickling that also slightly stung his membranes.

Andrea refilled the spoon. "You are about to enter stage two of this rocket ride. First a little pot, and now a double-do of coke. Then I'm going to send you right into orbit." She again extended the spoon, and Mike repeated the inhalation process, this time through his right nostril.

The cocaine took hold, the rush at first a deliciously warming glow, and then an instant later a fantastic expansion of his senses. His thoughts became as clear as dry air, and his ability to think with incredible quickness was a marvel to him. Physically, he felt infinitely powerful, as if his muscles had become charged with some kind of super-adrenalin that was racing through his body. At the same time he seemed remarkably calm, in total control of himself, completely in charge of this situation, this woman, his mind, his body, his life. There was nothing he couldn't handle, no imaginable set of circumstances he couldn't deal with as if it were child's play. He looked at Andrea with this strangely cool, superior objectivity, studying her body almost with detachment as she dipped the tiny spoon into the mystical white powder, carefully inhaling it into one nostril and then the other.

Christ, but she was beautiful. And he possessed her. Just as he could possess anything that might seem desirable to him, no matter what it was. She was his, to dominate and to use, physically, spiritually, in whatever ways it might amuse him. And now, if she wanted to please him by assuming the active role while he was passive, why, that was rather charming. He would indulge her, allow her to play out her fantasies while he enjoyed her little game.

Mike watched with interest as Andrea approached him. He knew from the expression on her face, from the half-open lips and the hot intensity in her eyes, that she felt the cocaine rush, that she was astride it, soaring to impossible heights, riding the magic surge. He grinned. "I prefer coke to Pepsi."

Andrea threw back her head and laughed. "It's the real thing."

"Jesus, but I feel marvelous."

Andrea bent over him. "That's wonderful, darling, but I'm going to make you feel even better. Much better, in fact. Better than you've ever felt."

"Prove it to me."

Andrea laughed again, deep in her throat this time. Quickly, but as lightly and gently as a warm breeze, her fingers began to play over his body. She stroked him, brushing the hair on his chest and his thighs, pausing occasionally to draw her nails slowly across the flesh on the inside of his elbows and the girdle of muscle on his lower belly. As her hands did their work, Andrea's hair touched him also, the tactile sensation arousing each nerve end, kindling in him a powerful passion. Despite himself, Mike began to tremble.

Triumph lighting her face, Andrea pressed her hands

against his chest and pushed him down on the sofa, where he lay staring at her, his breath rasping in his throat. She lifted one of his feet in both hands and began to suck his toes. Again Mike's nerves sent wildly erotic messages racing to his brain, the sensation closely akin to orgasm, as he felt himself on the brink of but not quite reaching climax. He clenced his teeth and closed his eyes as Andrea's mouth slowly worked its way up his leg, her tongue flickering, exploring, probing, teasing, tickling, while her nails stroked and touched him. She traced the inside of his thigh with her lips, and he felt her fingers hold his cheeks wide apart. She waited for an instant, then suddenly plunged the point of her tongue into his anus.

"Jesus," Mike moaned.

The tongue flickered, dipping and licking and just as suddenly, it stopped. Then Andrea's hot, wet mouth closed on Mike's penis. She did not move her head, but simply held it there, sucking.

Mike came in a wild burst, his semen spurting onto Andrea's tongue, into her throat. She still did not move, but continued to hold him in that grip until at last the blood drained from his cock and it became flaccid. Only then did she release it.

Andrea looked up at him. "Like it?"

"It was incredible."

Andrea purred. "It was only the beginning, darling. I have lots of other wonderful things to show you. Enough to make you happy all night long."

And she did. Until the sky to the east became gray and then faintly yellow, Andrea played Mike's body and his emotions. Finally he could no longer think or feel or move his muscles. Totally exhausted, he sank into sleep.

He had not, as he had told himself earlier he would, thought his problems through to satisfactory solutions, nor had he thought about them at all. In fact, he had not even noticed a number of objects lying about the room, which, if he had looked at them carefully, might have reminded him of his troubles. One of these was a handkerchief, hand-rolled of Irish linen, on which the initial H was embroidered. Another was a copy of the *Los Angeles Times*, folded open to the amusement section. Mike saw none of these things. And when he opened his eyes again, shortly before noon, they had been removed from the room.

Chapter 36

Betty Frolich opened lunch at Chasen's with two martinis and a serving of hot cheese canapés. She followed that with an endive salad and a crab quiche, accompanied by several cups of coffee. For dessert she had a Napoleon and more coffee.

Mal Meyer stared at her in awe. "Jesus Christ. How can you eat like that?" While watching Betty consume her food, Mal had eaten a chicken salad and drunk a small bottle of mineral water.

"Pressure," Betty explained. "It always does this to me. When things are smooth and easy, I diet. I work like hell on it, too. But when everything's hectic, when the pressure is really on, like now, that's when I eat a lot. Compensation, right? If you're into amateur psychiatry."

Mal shook his head wonderingly. "Right now something must be squeezing the shit out of you."

"It is," Betty said. "I represent the hottest talent in Hollywood. Maybe the hottest of all time. And believe me, I feel it. Everybody in the world wants to jump on board this train. Darla is going nowhere but up, and in the meantime the deals come in by the bale. I can't even remember half of them."

Mal grinned. "Is that a hype?" He was in his early fifties, fleshy and balding, but the smile transformed his face, giving it a much more youthful appearance, recalling the athlete he had been at Dartmouth.

"Sure," Betty rejoined, "if you want to see it that way. But I have to tell you, I really don't care. Take you, Mal. You want to make a movie starring Darla. You know how many other guys want to do the same thing?"

"Two thousand?" Mal asked innocently.

"Hey listen," Betty said. "You think that's a joke. I wouldn't be surprised if there were at least that many."

"Uh-huh. That's nice." There was an unmistakable dryness in Meyer's tone. He was a rarity in Hollywood, a successful producer with an Ivy League background. He looked and dressed the part of the top-level studio executive, suntanned and expensively casual, and he always spoke in hip, moderately scatological argot, but his accent and manner were still Dartmouth.

Betty drained her fourth cup of coffee. "I mean it. There's a stack on my desk right now that's this high."

"I know you mean it," Meyer said. "But if you took out the ones that are just bullshit, and the ones that are dreams by some guy who figures if he can get you to bite he can make himself a fortune off Darla's career, then how high would the stack be?"

"Plenty high," Betty insisted stubbornly. "And I'll bet you'd know most of the guys who are making offers. Some of the most respected people in the business."

"Okay," Meyer said. "And then let's take out the ones who don't have the money. How does your stack look now?"

"Money my ass," Betty said. "If you've got Darla, you can get the money."

"Don't kid yourself." Meyer smiled. He was obviously not only unruffled by this jousting, but was even enjoying himself. "The bankers are no longer a bunch of stuffy Wall Street dummies who don't know anything about the business. They know it takes a great deal more than a name talent, even a hot name talent, to insure that a picture will make money. Unless you have a producer with a damn good track record, you can forget it, even with Darla."

"Say, what do you want from me?" Betty asked. "You ask me to lunch, and I go, even though this place isn't what it used to be, ever since Dave died." She swept a pudgy arm in a gesture that was a dismissal of the red leather banquettes and the mahogany paneling and the cheerful, well-dressed patrons. "And now you want me to defend myself because Darla's hotter than a pistol."

"I don't want you to defend yourself," Mal replied pleasantly. "What I do want is for you to realize what a hell of an opportunity my interest represents to you and to Darla." He smiled. "And Dave Chasen may have died, and this place may have gone downhill a little, but somehow you forced yourself to eat a fairly respectable lunch. Like a starved bricklayer, for Christ's sake."

"I told you, it's the pressure."

"Okay, it's the pressure." Meyer signaled a waiter. "I think Miss Frolich would like more coffee," he said as the man scurried to their table. He returned his attention to the agent. "Look. We've known each other for a long time, and I don't have to try to con you about who I am and what I can do. Let the record speak for itself. Thirty-two pictures in a little over twenty years, and more than half of them have been real moneymakers. You know what that makes me?" He laughed, a short, high-pitched bark. "It makes me a freak. Or as our more reserved banking friends would say, a man of unusual accomplishment in this industry."

"So what am I supposed to do—kiss your feet because you're offering Darla a picture? You seem to forget, there's also a little matter of a contract with UBS."

Meyer nodded patiently. "I know all about the contract. And so do you. Getting out of it might take a little doing, and Peter Fried might huff and puff until he gives himself a hernia, but it still could be broken. Right, Betty?"

The agent sipped coffee, measuring Meyer shrewdly over the rim of her cup. "Maybe."

"Yeah," the producer said, knowingly. "Maybe. But let's go on. So of the four factors necessary to make a successful picture nowadays, we've already got three, right?" He held up a meaty hand and ticked off his points by snapping erect a finger to enumerate each. "Star, producer, and money. So what does that leave?"

Betty shrugged, affecting boredom. "I don't know. Some luck, maybe? Mazel tov to us all."

"Not luck," Meyer went on, patiently. "It leaves a story." He held up a fourth finger. "That's the fourth factor. And it's also the one that a lot of very smart people, including myself, think is the most important of all."

Betty snorted. "Writers are a dime a dozen."

"Sure they are. But the good ones cost a little more than that. Which is why they don't write for television. No offense, Betty, but yours is an asshole medium."

"Mine?" The agent's voice rose. "What do you mean, 'mine'? I'm responsible because TV is shit?"

The producer laughed in his high-pitched tone. "Of course not. I mean it's the medium in which you do most of your work, right? Commercials and shows, TV is mostly what you're involved with."

Betty was aware that this was a subtle putdown, and maybe not so subtle, come to think of it. In this most status-conscious of all worlds, movies ranked far higher than television among people in the business. Part of what the producer was doing, she knew, was reminding her of what the score was. Betty might be a successful agent, but her experience was mainly limited to television, which was to movies as the Toledo Mudhens were to the New York Yankees. Mal, on the other hand, was a producer with a solidly based reputation as a profitmaker. In the entertainment industry, that was infinitely more important than creativity or artistic skill. A picture might draw critical acclaim, might win an award at Cannes, might even attract audiences in respectable numbers. But in the end, the ruthlessly pragmatic men who made the important decisions would evaluate a movie by one criterion alone: did it make money? In their eyes Mal Meyer was a winner, by the only standard worthy of consideration.

"So a story is important," Betty admitted grudgingly. "That much I'll grant you. But I still say getting a good one is no mystery, either. You buy a novel, you hire a screenwriter who knows how to turn out a script, and what's the big deal? Right now some of those offers you're sneering at without even knowing what they are have got pretty damn good properties attached to them. Bestsellers, even."

"Like what?" Meyer asked.

Betty set her cup firmly into its saucer. "Like *Torrid Passion*, by Cornelia Woodward."

The producer groaned and rolled his eyes ceilingward.

"God almighty."

"What the hell do you mean, 'God almighty'?" Betty asked indignantly. "Do you know how many copies that novel sold?"

Meyer shrugged, as if the subject wasn't fit for discussion.

"Well, I'll tell you how many, Mr. Smartass," Betty went on. "If you'd like to know. It sold two million, three hundred thousand in paperback alone. Now tell me that's a big nothing." She curled her thick lips in disdain.

The producer looked at her calmly. "There are novels," he said patiently, "and there are novels. The thing you're talking about is very handy for hanging in the john, especially if you have diarrhea. You know why? Because it has a lot of pages in it. About six or seven hundred, as I recall. Outside of that, I can't think of anything to recommend it."

Betty opened her mouth to protest, but Meyer silenced her by holding up his hand. The producer spoke as if he were lecturing in a school for retarded children. "It's what we call a formula novel, Betty. Cornelia Woodward simply writes the same shit over and over again. Sometimes she calls it *Torrid Passion*, and sometimes she calls it *The Primitive Heart*, and sometimes she calls it some other fucking thing, but whatever the title is, a certain type of women buy it, not because they're going to get something new, but for the opposite reason—they know they're going to get more of the same. They know they're going to get exactly the same jerk-off they got last time, and that's fine with them." He went on before she could interrupt. "A movie, on the other hand, has to have a hell of a lot more going for it, if it's going to make it. Based on a novel? Sure, you bet. Provided the novel is a good, solid idea and reasonably distinctive. It doesn't have to be unique, but just unusual enough so that it has a handle. By that I mean that it can be described in a line or two, and no more. *Jaws*, for example. A monster shark pops up off Long Island and bites the ass off a bunch of people. *The Exorcist*. A little girl is possessed by the devil." Meyer turned a hand palm-up. "You see? Then too, the novel should have sold well, because then it'll have the additional value of having helped create a market for the picture. In a sense, it's advance publicity."

"Okay," Betty protested. "So I know all that. What do you think, I'm stupid? I told you in the first place, you start with a novel, right?"

"Wrong," Meyer answered. "You start with a story. It doesn't have to be a novel. Sometimes it's an original, like *Star Wars*. Good story, good handle. Western set in outer space with a lot of dynamite special effects. Right? *Star Wars* is well on its way to becoming the biggest box-office grosser of all time."

Betty was a little irritated by all this condescension. "Okay, I read *Variety* too."

Meyer ignored her pique. "And in *Star Wars*, Lucas did it backwards. First the movie, *then* the novel. Same as with *Love Story*. Rich college hockey player marries poor broad who dies. Always the good story with a handle."

"All right, all right." Betty sighed. "I've got to get back to my office. What's your deal, Mal? For Darla?"

Meyer smiled. "A first-rate story, an original, written especially for Darla. A top director and the best possible production values. And I'd release the picture through International."

"The deal, Mal, the deal. For Darla?"

"A million dollars," Meyer replied softly.

Betty stared at the producer thoughtfully. "A million dollars."

Meyer nodded.

"Plus, I assume, a percentage of the gross."

The high-pitched laugh was almost a bark. "For a girl who's doing her first starring role? A *percentage*, on *top* of a million dollars?" He laughed again.

"First starring role, who gives a shit?" Betty said. "This is Darla Dawson we're talking about, Mal. And you know it."

"Well, of course I know it," the producer acknowledged. "Which is why a million dollars for one picture—her *first* starring role, I point out again—is a hell of a deal. After all, I don't have to remind you that Darla isn't exactly Elizabeth Taylor, or even Jackie Bissett, if you want a current comparison."

"Jackie Bissett" Betty snorted contemptuously. "A pair of tits and a wet T-shirt."

"Plus considerable skill as an actress and a proven box-office draw," Meyer countered.

Betty gathered up her handbag, checking to see that it contained sunglasses, keys, and whatever. "Thanks for lunch, Mal. I've got New York calls to make."

The producer smiled benignly. "Sure, love. I enjoyed it. Let me know if there's any interest."

Betty looked at him. Ten percent of a million dollars was a nice round figure. "The story. You said it'd be an original."

"Right."

"About what?"

"About Darla. Her own career."

The agent's face registered genuine surprise. "You mean really based on her?"

Meyer nodded calmly. "It's a hell of a story, you know? Model zooms to the top of show business while she carries asshole actor husband on her back. She's flying up while he goes into the crapper. It really is a hell of a story."

Betty sniffed. "I doubt she'd go for the idea, but it's interesting. I still think there are some very good novels around."

Mal Meyer knew his business. "Sure. And say, by the way," he said casually. "I guess I should also check in with Derek Wasserman, right? Isn't he more or less handling everything with Darla these days?"

Betty's lunch turned instantly to cement in her stomach. "No." Her tone was acid. "He's not. And if you hope to make this deal, Mal, you'll continue the discussions through me, and nobody else."

"Sure, love." Meyer smiled. "When?"

The agent slid out of her seat as the captain pulled the table away, and got to her feet. Son of a bitch, why had she eaten so goddamn much? Pressure or no pressure, she couldn't keep this up. "We're going to New York next week. I'll be in touch when we get back."

Meyer nodded. "I'll be in New York next week myself. Why don't you call me? Maybe bring Darla over for a chat?"

"Maybe. Depends on the schedule." She watched warily as Meyer got up.

"Terrific," the producer said. "You can get me at the Pierre."

Esther looked up as Betty walked heavily into her office and sank into her chair. The agent's desk was a mound of white. A few of the papers had slid off the pile and fallen to the floor. The phones were ringing, as usual. Even with the two extra girls Betty had put on in the last few months, it was impossible to keep things sorted out. "How was lunch?" Esther asked.

Betty belched. "Lousy."

"You have a lot of calls," Esther said. "You want them now?"

"No. Get me Ben Thompkins in New York." Betty kicked her shoes off and looked disinterestedly at the vast heap of papers. Absentmindedly, she pulled her aching right foot across her left thigh and began massaging it. Her conversation with Mal Meyer returned to her mind. A million dollars. Ten percent of a million dollars. In one shot. Movies. For one stretch of fifteen years, Elizabeth Taylor had made not less than a million dollars a year. But as Meyer had said, Darla Dawson was not Elizabeth Taylor. Well, how the hell did he know she wasn't?

"He's on," Esther called.

Betty picked up her phone. "Ben? How are you, dear?"

"Terrific, Betty. How are you?" He sounded very upbeat.

"A little frantic, to tell the truth. You should see my desk. It's literally piled high with offers for Darla."

"Yeah. Well, you always were a shitty housekeeper, Betty. You really ought to get organized."

Betty felt a small flash of anger, but she suppressed it. "Now I assume everything is all set for our discussion with Mister Rawlson?"

"Sure. You're on at eleven on Thursday, the nineteenth."

"Okay, that'll be fine. But I have to warn you, Ben. The numbers are going to be pretty heavy."

"Uh-huh. We can discuss it."

"Would a little advance warning help?"

Ben laughed. "Hey, nothing's going to surprise me, Betty. Darla wants ten jillion dollars and the Mona Lisa, right?"

"I'm serious," Betty said calmly. "The new contract will be totally different from anything in the past." To her satisfaction, there was a long pause before Ben responded.

"What do you mean?"

"I mean that from now on, you're going to have to pay Darla real money."

"Real money? What kind of shit is that? We're already paying her a fortune."

"It may be a fortune by your standards, Ben. But not by ours. A hundred fifty thousand a year is nothing in today's market. Even for an ordinary top model, let alone a real superstar like Darla."

"Darla's already a superstar?"

"You bet your ass she is."

"Hey, Betty, come off it, will you? I mean, we all love the lady and wish her well, but there's a big difference between a superstar and a superblast of publicity. And as far as the money's concerned, she's getting big bucks right now—as big as any headliner."

343

"That's not exactly accurate, Ben. Even a beginner like that kid, what's her name, Margaux something, is getting a million bucks."

"Her last name is Hemingway," Ben said dryly. "Her grandfather once did some writing."

"You don't have to get sarcastic."

"And that million bucks has got a lot of air in it. What's more, it's spread over several years."

"Okay, what about Candice Bergen? She couldn't carry Darla's makeup case, and that perfume company is dumping money all over her."

Ben sighed. "Candice Bergen is an established movie actress, Betty. Now tell me, because I can't quite remember the figure, just how many pictures has Darla starred in?"

"I'll tell you where I've just come from," Betty answered. "I've just come from a meeting with one of the top independent producers in Hollywood, a guy with maybe the best track record in the history of pictures for making not just hits but moneymakers, and you know what he's begging me?"

"To go down on him in ragtime?"

"I'm serious, Ben. He's begging me to take two million up front, *plus* a percentage of the gross. And you know what else?"

"What else, Betty?"

"He's having the story written by one of the foremost novelists in the world. Not just some screenwriter, but a novelist of the first rank."

"What's his name?"

"Can't tell you that, Ben. But I will tell you that his contribution completes the four factors you need for a successful picture."

"The four what?"

"The four factors," Betty said patiently. "Star, producer, money, and a great story."

"Uh-huh."

"You're dealing with a superstar, Ben. And the tab will be appropriate."

"I'll bet it will. What do you have in mind?"

344

"That's what we have to discuss," Betty replied. "In New York."

"I can't wait."

" 'Bye, Ben."

When Betty put the phone down, she pulled her left foot across her right thigh and massaged it.

"You want some coffee?" Esther called.

"No. I want some bicarbonate of soda." She went on massaging her foot. A picture of Derek Wasserman's smoothly handsome face came into her mind and she belched again.

Chapter 37

United Airlines Flight Six took off for New York from Los Angeles International Airport at 8:45 A.M. The equipment was a wide-bodied DC-10, and the flight was heavily booked, as usual. Darla's entourage consisted of her agent, Betty Frolich; Derek Wasserman, her manager; Molly Martin, her publicist; Sally Dane, her secretary; Lee Merriwell, her makeup artist; and Bobby Benbo, her hair stylist. The group occupied the first eight seats of the forward end of the first-class compartment. Betty sat with Molly, Wasserman with Sally Dane, and Lee Merriwell and Bobby Benbo sat together. Darla rode in the first window seat on the port side of the aircraft. The aisle seat she used for her handbag.

Whenever United, or any major airline, was flying a VIP, one cabin crewmember was assigned primary responsibility for seeing to it that everything went smoothly, and that the luminary's every wish was, if humanly possible, granted at once. On this flight, the crewman responsible for Darla was the steward, an engaging young man named Chet Delford who had graduated two years earlier from the University of Southern California's School of Business. Delford was used to handling celebrities, but even he was excited about having Darla Dawson on board.

As Flight Six made its left turn on the climb out over the ocean and swung east, reaching for its eventual cruising altitude of forty thousand feet, Chet sat with Marcy Fernald, one of the stewardesses, and waited impatiently for the captain to turn off the seat belt sign so that he could move about the cabin, and especially so that he could ask Darla if there was anything she needed.

"She really looks fantastic," Marcy said. Marcy was a well-built little brunette from Oak Park, Illinois, who had become a stewardess in order to meet interesting men, visit exciting places, and get as far away from Oak Park as possible. She lived on East Sixty-third Street in Manhattan and had been on the choice Coast run for three months, during which time she had met more interesting men than she could count, or even clearly remember. New York and Los Angeles had proved to be two of the most exciting cities anyone could imagine, and Marcy never thought about Oak Park at all, except when her mother called to nag and to express her worries about young girls who were crazy enough to live in an evil, nigger-ridden city like New York.

"Who's that?" Chet responded casually, pretending he didn't know to whom Marcy was referring.

"Darla Dawson, of course," Marcy said. "Don't tell me you didn't notice."

"Oh, sure, I noticed," Chet said. "I just didn't know who you meant. I'm not trying to be blasé, but on this trip I'm always playing nursemaid to somebody or other. A lot of the time I feel more like I'm a P.R. agent than like I'm flying for an airline."

"Uh-huh." From her aisle seat in the aft part of the first-class cabin Marcy couldn't see Darla very well, catching only an occasional glimpse of the famous mop of honey-colored hair. "You know, I think she's even more beautiful in person than she is on TV."

"Really?"

"Sure. A lot of them aren't, you know. Sometimes I'm amazed to see somebody famous and their skin isn't good, or they're really not as pretty as in the movies or on TV, you know? But she looks even better than on television. The minute she walked on board, I thought, Oh, wow! What I wouldn't give to look like that."

"Yeah, sure. I know what you mean," Chet said. "But I'll tell you something. I think a lot of it is just who she is. I mean, sure, she's got all that wild hair, and those teeth, and that unusual rosy tan color and all, but you put it all together and she's just another flashy showbiz blonde. Actually, I think plenty of girls are a hell of a lot better looking, but they're not on TV, and they're not Darla Dawson, and so nobody pays all that much attention, you know?"

"Um. Maybe," Marcy replied. From the angle of Darla's head, Marcy could see that the actress was looking out the window, probably staring down at the San Bernadino Mountains. Marcy wondered what Darla might be thinking about.

"You, for instance," Chet went on. "You don't have that kind of Las Vegas look, but I think in a lot of ways you're classier than she is."

Marcy turned to him, obviously surprised and delighted. "Hey, Delford, I like your style."

Chet shrugged. "It's just the truth, that's all."

Marcy patted his arm. "Well, it's nice to hear. There's nothing like getting your ego boosted once in a while."

"Any time." Chet smiled. It wasn't so hard, he thought, when you knew how. He would give his left arm to go to bed with Darla Dawson, and the odds against that ever happening were, he knew, something better than ten thousand to one. But Marcy was a nifty little piece, and the flight engineer had told him she gave good head. One Marcy Fernald in bed was worth a whole gaggle of Darla Dawsons on TV, or even Darla in person on Flight Six, acknowledging his obsequious ministrations with a condescending smile. "Maybe we could have dinner tonight, in New York," Chet said. "If you're free."

"Sounds great," Marcy replied. "I'd love it."

"Good." Chet smiled again. "I know a terrific Italian place on Forty-seventh Street."

"Okay, you've got a date. I wonder who all those others are."

"What others?"

"The other people Darla Dawson came on board with."

"Oh, those," Chet said, affecting boredom. "They're just her, like, you know, staff. One's her manager, another one's her agent, and the two fags take care of her hair and makeup."

"Really? Oh, wow."

Chet was slightly mystified. "What's so great about that? It's not like they were anybody important."

"Are you kidding? It's the same as being, oh, a princess, say. Every place you go, there's somebody to see that everything is just so, everything's done for you, all the things like seeing that the hotel is just right, and your theater tickets are all arranged, as well as making all your business deals, and taking care of just everything, so you never have to think about anything. All that, and your own hairdresser and makeup guy, so you're always looking fantastic."

"Mm-m. I suppose," Chet said.

"That way she has time for everything," Marcy remarked wistfully. "Her career, and being married to Mike Brady , and all those affairs she has, too."

"What affairs?" Chet asked suspiciously. What did Fernald know that he didn't?

"Oh, you know. She's got a couple going all the time."

Chet snorted. He didn't know why, but he didn't much like the idea of Marcy knowing things like this when he didn't, even if it was all a lot of unfounded gossip, which it probably was. "That's mostly crap," he said loftily. "You hear that all the time about anybody famous."

"Maybe you do," Marcy said. "But in her case I think what I hear is true. 'Specially when it's coming from a couple of personal friends of mine."

"Oh, yeah? Who's that?" Chet's tone was grudging, but he was fascinated with the prospect of learning who, besides Mike Brady, was actually getting some of America's most famous blonde.

"Well, one of them in Jeff Patterson."

"That young guy in 'The Witches'? Ah, that's silly."

349

Chet scoffed. "Hell, he must be ten years younger than she is."

"So? What's wrong with that?"

Something in Marcy's tone warned Chet to be careful. He didn't want to mess up what promised to be a good time over something as inconsequential as Darla Dawson's love life, no matter how juicy it might be to contemplate. "Nothing's wrong with it. I just meant if it's true."

"It's true, all right," Marcy said. "Debbie Carter flies for Northwest, and she was on a flight to Vail, and Darla was on the flight, going out there to shoot a commercial for Superfresh—you know she's the Superfresh girl."

"Yeah, I know," Chet said, trying to squelch his impatience.

"It was something where she's skiing, you know? Maybe you've seen it on TV."

"Uh-huh." Why was it a girl could never just tell you straight out whatever the hell she wanted to tell you?

"Well anyhow, Darla gets on the flight in L.A. and she's got several people with her, just like this, I guess, and Debbie said Jeff was with her. So they sit together, and all the way out they're necking like crazy, and finally Jeff gets a blanket and puts it over them, and Debbie said she kept sneaking looks at them, and what went on then was really wild. She swore they were making it under the blanket."

"Really?" Despite himself, Chet found this fascinating to envision. "Was she sure? Debbie, I mean."

"Listen, we've all seen stuff like that go on, 'specially on night flights. Haven't you?"

"I, ah, sure. Of course I have. Plenty of times." Chet didn't care to be outdone in matters of worldliness, especially by a stew.

"Anyhow, then Debbie had a layover there for a couple of days, she wanted to go skiing, you know?"

"Yeah."

"And she saw Darla and Jeff everywhere together, including they were staying together at the lodge."

This was a little more than Chet could take. "Debbie was hiding under the bed, huh?"

Marcy's tone was cool. "She didn't see them in bed, no. But she did see them sitting in the lounge together, in front of the fire one night late, and they were all over each other, just as if nobody else was there. And then they went upstairs together."

"Humph. Doesn't prove anything."

Marcy looked at him. "Yeah. Well, the seat belt sign is off. If you'll excuse me, I have things to do."

"Sure, catch you later." Shit, he said to himself, I hope I didn't fuck it up. What do I care who Darla Dawson shacks up with? He got out of his seat and walked down the aisle to inquire if there was anything he could do to make the actress's journey more pleasant.

In the inboard seat behind the row in which Darla was sitting, Derek Wasserman stretched the muscles in his arms and his back. He glanced at Sally Dane, who occupied the seat beside him. Sally was holding an attaché case open on her lap before her, working with the inevitable stack of letters it contained. "How goes?" he asked with mild interest.

"Okay," Sally said. "I'm just getting these sorted, deciding which ones get answered by us."

"How many do?"

Sally tapped her teeth with her ballpoint pen. "Oh, I don't know. I guess maybe one-fourth of them. Most of those I answer and sign Darla's name." She laughed. "I'm getting so I can write it better than she can."

"What about the rest of them—the ones that neither you or Darla answer?"

The secretary shrugged. "I send them to UBS Publicity. Some of them they answer with a short note that has Darla's name printed on it, and some of them they just dump. Especially the weirdo stuff."

"Weirdo?"

"God, you should see what some people write. It would make you blush to read it."

This was turning out to me more interesting than Wasserman had expected. "Like what?"

351

"Oh, a lot of icky personal stuff," Sally replied. "And some of it is just—you know, nuts?"

"But what do they say, for instance?"

"Oh, a lot of—well, here. Read one." She shuffled through the stack of letters in the attache case and selected one, handing it to Wasserman.

The letter was written on cheap, variety-store stationery.

Dear Darla,

You don't know me, but I feel like I really know you. Although not as well as I'd like to, do you know what I mean? Ha ha. I watch The Witches every week, and even though Cathy Drake is a very pretty girl too and sexy and all I don't hardly take my eyes off of you for the whole hour. I have to tell you Darla and I hope you won't mind this and you'll understand cause after all I'm a man and you're a woman but I have to tell you that you've got the best pair of boobies I ever saw really, not so big and all but just nice and after I get through looking at you for an hour you can imagine what shape I'm in. I can't stand up right away in front of the TV with my wife in the room you know? Ha ha. Well anyhow, I bet you'll get some kick out of this, but I bought one of them terrific posters of you, and I hung it up in the bathroom and sometimes after the show I go in there and I kind of imagine what it would be like with you, cause I'm not just a fan I'm really crazy about you and even though you never met me I have this real feeling about how we'd be together. Sometimes in bed with my wife I close my eyes and pretend it's you which is not easy because my wife runs a little on the fat side. Well Darla if you ever get to Gary, Indiana I hope you'll look me up because I think I could give you the biggest surprise you ever got in your life if you know what I mean. My wife says with what I got I could be in a zoo or a museum or something.

Lots of luck to you and kisses from your biggest fan,

                    Charlie Zybryszki.

When he finished reading, Wasserman looked at Sally.

"See what I mean?"

"Holy shit," he said in genuine awe. "Are many of them like this?"

Sally curled her lip in an expression of conjecture. "We get a certain number of weirdos every day. Not really all that many, actually just a handful. But when they're strange, they're strange. Compared to some of them, that one's nothing."

Wasserman read through the letter again and handed it back to Sally. "I'll tell you one thing Mr. Zybryszki said that's correct."

"What's that?"

"He could be in a zoo or a museum or something."

Sally laughed. "He didn't even say it. His wife did, right?"

"Yeah, you're right. You know, somebody ought to keep a file of this stuff. Just in case." He frowned. "You never know when some nut might try to make some trouble. Could be a good thing to have this stuff on hand."

"Maybe. But you'd have to have a vault to put it all in. And anyhow, most of it is just harmless fantasizing."

"How do you know?"

"Oh, I took a couple of psych courses at UCLA, and we learned that most people indulge in sexual fantasies at one time or another, some more than others."

"Yeah, but do they write them down in letters and then send them to somebody they don't even know?"

Sally giggled. "No, most of them don't, but some do."

"So I see. Mister Zybryszki sounds like quite a case."

"Hey, like I said, that one's mild, compared to some. Once in a while we get one that's really freaky. If you saw one of those, you'd be sure we ought to turn them over to the cops."

"Then why don't you?"

The secretary frowned. "That's up to UBS to worry about. And you know what they'd say about it."

"Yeah. Don't make waves."

"Right on. But there's something else, too. I was talking to Molly about it one day. And that is, if those real rags got hold of it, like the *Star* or the *Enquirer*, they could blow the whole story into something nasty. They thrive on that stuff, you know."

"Yeah, but none of it's Darla's doing. She didn't ask those creeps to write her letters."

"No, but why make a fuss? A silly letter never hurt anybody."

Wasserman remained skeptical. "Maybe, and maybe not. Let's say Darla makes a personal appearance someplace near where one of those crazies lives. He might try to get to her, some way or other."

"I doubt it," Sally replied. "And anyway, our security is pretty good. Between UBS and the agency, she's kept pretty well insulated when we go anywhere."

"What does Betty think?"

"Oh, she just laughs it off."

"Yeah, well, sometimes I think Miss Frolich could take her responsibilities a little more seriously."

"Meaning?"

"Meaning she ought to be paying more attention to the biggest star she ever lucked into being around, instead of just taking her for granted all the time."

Sally Dane was twenty-three years old, and dazzled by her job. Understandably, she was also fiercely loyal to Darla. Any threat to Darla's career or well-being, however slight it might be, was automatically a threat to Sally's shiny, tinsel-draped, jet-paced new world. She looked closely at Darla's manager. "You think Betty's not paying as much attention to Darla as she should?"

Wasserman shrugged. "How could she be? You know that damned Holloway Thomas Agency is nothing but a factory. If you asked Betty how many people she was involved with over there, actors as well as actresses, she wouldn't even know."

"Yeah, well, maybe. But remember she got Darla her first big break."

"*Darla* got Darla her first big break," Wasserman said knowingly. "All Betty's done ever since has been to sit there and collect a big fat ten percent of everything Darla earns. That's some ride, when you consider how little she does to earn it."

"Okay, and forgive me for asking," Sally said, "but after all, aren't you sort of doing the same thing? And besides, you weren't even there at the beginning."

Derek Wasserman's handsome face assumed a sober, thoughtful expression. "There's a big difference, Sally. I manage only a few people, and every one of them is a big star. I turn away dozens of girls who beg me to manage them, because I don't ever want to be just some guy who handles talent by the dozen, the way so many agents and managers do. I've given Darla tremendous help since she's been with me, and you know why? Because I've really dedicated myself to her, totally committed every facet of my abilities to helping her become the biggest star the industry has ever known."

Sally nodded. "I know you've done a lot for Darla, Derek."

"And I'll tell you something else. I'd never even suggest this to her, but sooner or later she's going to realize she'd be doing much better if I were responsible for all aspects of her career."

Sally looked puzzled. "Could you do that? I mean, there's some legal thing, isn't there?"

Wasserman flicked a hand. "That's nothing. That is, sure, in California a theatrical agent has to be licensed, and you're not supposed to be both a manager and an agent. But that wouldn't be hard for me to get around. And Darla would be saving a hell of a lot of money."

"By just paying you your fifteen percent and not ten more to Betty?"

"Exactly. Darla wouldn't be shucking out as much money, and I'd be making more for her because I'd be more effective if I didn't have Betty draped around my neck. We'd all be better off."

"Yeah," Sally said quietly. "All except Betty."

"You want what's best for Darla, don't you, Sally?"

Was that a kind of veiled threat? Sally wondered. Something in Wasserman's tone implied that she'd better stay on his side. She wasn't sure, really, just how much influence the manager had with Darla, but why take chances? "Of course I do, Derek. You know that." And come to think of it, wouldn't it be terrific if she could play a part, somehow, in doing something really good for Darla? If Wasserman was right, and it seemed logical, Darla would be saving a great deal of money by putting everything through him. Sure, it would be sad if Betty got screwed in the process, but this was show business, and people had to look out for themselves, didn't they? Golly, one thing was certain—it was all so exciting.

In her aisle seat in the first row of the starboard side of the jet, Betty said to Molly, "I hope you're keeping the agenda straight. I have a feeling this could turn into a circus, unless you run it with a strong hand. You know Darla."

"Sure." The publicity agent smiled. "I do indeed. Can't say no to anybody. Interviews, talk shows, they're all okay with her."

"Exactly." Betty shook her head in wonder. "It amazes me sometimes, you know? How little affected she is by all this. In most ways, she's no different from the simple little kid she was when I first picked her up."

"You've done a lot for her, haven't you, Betty?"

The agent curled her lips in a philosophical expression. "Yeah, I guess I have. You might say I packaged her, really. The hair, the way of talking and presenting herself—I did all of it. To say nothing of getting her the deal with Superfresh."

"What happened there?" Was it the usual rat race with a million girls trying for it?"

"Oh sure, the standard procedure. But I knew the agency guy. Ben Thompkins is an old friend of mine—V.P. in charge of production for Baker & Barlowe. Based in New York. I put the word in to Ben and Darla had it wired before she ever walked into the casting session." Betty smiled wistfully. "Nothing against Darla, but she's kind of forgotten all that."

Molly shook her head knowingly. "They always do, somehow. Even Darla. But still, as you say, she's taking all the madness surprisingly well."

"I think that's one of the things that makes her so appealing. She had a basic naiveté that isn't put on. I mean, I taught her how to dress, and how to handle herself, and how to use her hair almost as a part of her personality. But the underlying Darla comes through as clearly as ever. I saw to it that she never lost that."

Molly swallowed the last of her club soda. Like most reformed alcoholics, she consumed a great deal of liquid, mostly coffee or unsweetened carbonated beverages. "She really is naive, isn't she?"

"And how. It worries me, sometimes."

"You're afraid somebody might con her?"

Betty sighed heavily. She was wearing a St. Laurent safari suit, and it was already rumpled and sweat-sodden. "Somebody has."

It was obviously difficult for Molly to maintain an air of nonchalance. "Who?"

"Oh, I hate to say anything, and I expect you to keep this confidential, of course."

"Of course," Molly said. "That's understood."

Betty lowered her voice. "Well, very frankly, I'm afraid our dark-haired friend is giving her a good screwing, and not the kind a girl would prefer."

"What dark-haired friend?"

There was a hint of impatience in Betty's reply. "Young Mister Wasserman, of course."

"Really?" Molly's eyes were wide.

"You bet he is."

"How?"

Betty held up a pudgy finger to emphasize each point. "First, he's collecting fifteen percent of everything she makes. And that's on top of my modest ten percent. Next, keep in mind that he doesn't make her most important deals, I do. Third, he's a johnny-come-lately who jumped on board when I'd already brought

Darla up to stardom. Fourth, from what I gather, he keeps her in the dark on half the shit he's got her involved in. He tells her, It's a good thing, bubula, and don't worry about it. Fifth, I've overheard just enough to know that a lot of his wonderful negotiations are no more than saying yes to the first asshole offer that comes along. Darla could be doing as well if Sally Dane was her manager."

"Then why'd she take him on in the first place?"

"How the hell should I know? Maybe she thought it was the thing to do. You know, part of being a star."

"That doesn't sound like Darla."

"No, it doesn't. But there the son of a bitch sits. With his hand in her purse."

"I hear he's got some stuff lined up for this trip."

"Yeah," Betty growled disgustedly. "A doll deal and a game deal, and they both suck."

"Are you sure?"

"Hell, yes, I'm sure. The doll is seven and a half percent and the game is five. Any schmuck could walk right in off the street and get that."

"No shit?"

"Of course. Standard royalties, both of them." She smiled suddenly. "Although at that they're better than what her dumbass husband got."

Molly leaned closer. "You mean he didn't even get that much?"

Betty put a hand over her mouth to choke back a laugh. "I mean that schtummy got nothing."

Molly looked skeptical. "Hey, come on."

Betty's eyes were bright. "You think he's so brilliant, huh? Well, let me tell you a little secret. Right in Mister Brady's contract there's a clause that says the property reserves all licensing rights to any character that appears in the show as well as the show itself."

"Jesus Christ," Molly said softly.

"Exactly. You know all those dolls of Mike Brady as the detective in 'The Savage City'? And you know the 'Savage City' game that Milton Bradley produces? And the toy pistol and the T-shirts and the poster? Well, the world's greatest businessman doesn't get one fucking dime out of the whole megillah."

"Oh, wow."

"Uh-huh. But guess who does."

"The package, right?"

"Right. And UBS. No wonder Dick Hazelman loves Brady. That shithead is a moneymaking machine for him." She smirked. "Or was."

"*Was* is right," Molly said. "I hear Mike has really had it. Either Derringer takes over the show or Fried gives her a new one of her own. They say she laid it right on the line. Two choices, and in both of them Mike gets flushed down the drain."

Betty guffawed. "At last a role he's ideally suited for. The Ty-d-Bol man."

Both women laughed. Molly blew her nose and wiped her eyes with her handkerchief. "I'll bet Hazelman never gave Derringer those bum license deals."

"You bet your ass he didn't," Betty replied. "But for that matter, who ever heard of anybody pushing her around, let alone Hazelman. It took her about ten minutes to chew that jerk up and spit out the pieces."

Molly slowly shook her head. "I just hope nobody like him ever gets his hooks into Darla."

"I keep telling you," Betty said, "somebody already has."

"God, I hope not. I mean, are you sure?"

Betty snorted. "Okay, you figure it out. How does the record look so far?"

"Yeah, but Christ, Betty, you've been with Darla a long time. Like you said, right from the beginning. Couldn't you do anything? You know, talk to her straight?"

"How? What would I say? You think I'd crap on somebody she hired? You know me better than that. I don't play that way."

"Yeah, but somebody ought to tell her."

"Uh-huh." So this shiksa bitch was finally grasping the idea. "Maybe someday somebody will." Betty turned and beckoned to a stewardess. "I'm hungry, honey. And thirsty. Bring me a martini, very dry, straight up, with an olive. And a sandwich, any kind."

The stewardess smiled pleasantly. "We'll be serving lunch in a little while. Can't wait until then?"

"Not possibly," Betty said. "I'm starved. Make the martini with Beefeater's." She sat back in her seat. God, what a life. She had to work her ass off every minute, even when she was on a goddamn airplane.

In the seat directly behind the agent, Bobby Benbo looked at Lee Merriwell and smiled. "Makes me nostalgic, going to New York."

"Why?" There was a note of suspicion in the makeup artist's tone. The active role-player in their relationship, he knew Bobby was inclined to be coquettish, and the thought invariably angered him. When he occasionally caught the hairdresser actually flirting, he flew into a rage.

"Oh, nothing really," Bobby said. His great liquid eyes were dreamy. "It's just that I once had a very beautiful affair there." He looked up at the ceiling of the cabin. "It was this time of year, too."

Merriwell clamped his jaw shut. A spot of color rose in each cheek.

"That's what's so exciting about New York," Bobby went on. "You just never know what's going to happen there."

Chapter 38

As the DC-10 descended into the New York area, the captain banked the big jet to the right, out over Staten Island, and then back to the left as JKF approach control handed Flight Six over to the tower. The port wing dropped, and the sight that lay before Darla was dazzling. The late afternoon sun bathed the stone towers of Manhattan in a pinkish glow, the light glinting on a million panels of glass, reflecting from the World Trade Center, the Empire State Building, and countless other lofty structures, as brightly as if the most glamorous and powerful city on earth had indeed been built from blocks of gold.

Darla realized that this was far more than a routine trip. In her violent and sudden rush to the top, this visit to New York represented a march triumphant, the enterting of a conquered city by a newly crowned queen. She smiled to herself. What a beautifully turned description, she thought. With talent like that, you ought to be writing Molly's bullshit. Darla pulled a mirror from her handbag and studied her face. Amazing. Aside from those maddening tiny wrinkles under the eyes, she looked as fresh and youthful as a twenty-two-year-old, and God knew she felt no older than that. As she dropped the mirror back into her bag she realized her pulse was racing, the feeling of anticipation as strong as when she had been a high school cheerleader on her way to a big game, or when she was entering the gaily decorated gym on the night of the junior prom.

"Beautiful, isn't it?"

Darla turned to Molly who had taken the seat beside her. The press agent's dark hair was freshly brushed and her blue eyes were shining. "Sure is," Darla agreed. "And exciting, don't you think?"

"Boy, I'll say," Molly replied. "For all the dozens of times I've made this trip, that sight never fails to turn me on. The dirtiest, crummiest town I ever saw, and far and away the most fun."

Darla looked out the window again. Off to the left she could see the Statue of Liberty, startling in her coat of oxidized green, and just abeam was the spidery network of cables from which hung the bed of the Brooklyn Bridge. God, Darla thought, Molly's right. The theater, and the shopping, and the restaurants, and the business deals, and the relentless, frenetic pace. There would be the television talk shows, and on the weekend, the finals at Forest Hills. A picture of Ted Walters's face came into her mind, and she felt a bittersweet twinge. Then she thought of Jeff Patterson, and the thought was a small delight. Jeff had become a delicious toy, hers to savor and to play with when she felt like it, and to toss aside when it bored her. And then, as if she had been saving it for last, just as she had saved the cherry on a sundae when she was a child, she thought of Dante Corelli, and a thrill rushed through her. She saw the square jaw, the darkly handsome, masculine good looks, the elegantly tailored clothes, and then in her vision the clothes disappeared and his powerful arms were encircling her and she could feel the thick mat of hair on his broad chest tickling her breasts as he drew her close to him.

The steward approached, checking to see that Darla's and Molly's seat belts were fastened, and Darla returned the young man's smile. He was a cute young thing, puppylike in his eagerness to please, in his begging for a pat on the head, even physically resembling a playful dog, with his stock mustache and his fashionably long locks. He's a schnauzer, Darla thought. No, a Yorkshire terrier. It had been fun to flirt with him during the flight, and she could imagine what fantasies must have gone through his mind.

"Is everything okay, Miss Dawson?" the steward asked. "Do you need anything?"

"Everything is just fine," Darla replied. "You've really been terrific, and I'm very grateful. What's your name?"

"Delford. Chet Delford."

"Well, thank you, Chet," Darla said. "I want to remember that." She gave him her biggest smile, the 24-karat dazzler.

The steward flushed deeply. "We, uh—I," he stammered. "You're welcome. If there's, ah—excuse me." He moved down the aisle.

"Get any on you?" Molly asked.

Darla was puzzled. "Any what?"

"Well, he obviously came all over himself. I wouldn't want him to mess up your dress."

Darla laughed. "Who's meeting us?"

"A whole contingent. You have passed through stardom and into the beyond. Now you are an event."

"Really? That's sensational. Do I get a discount on a cup of coffee?"

"Honey, if you want coffee, there are guys in this town who could buy you Brazil."

"Sounds interesting. I never owned a country."

Molly pursed her lips. " 'Course, they might want you to do a thing or two for it."

"Listen," Darla said. "For Brazil I might do a thing or three, even. As my grandma used to say, if you're going to sell it, sell it dear."

"Your grandma knew what she was talking about. My trouble has always been my generosity. I can't resist giving it away."

Darla smiled her understanding. "A lot of us have that problem." She studied the press agent. "Ever been married?"

Molly shook her head. "Never. Closest I ever came was to be a mistress, and believe me, there's some difference."

363

Darla was intrigued. "A mistress? Really? How fascinating. Was he rich and powerful?"

"He was rich and powerful and a four-barreled prick. Kept me for five years and then cut me off as if I'd all of a sudden contracted leprosy."

"That's lousy."

"Sure is," Molly agreed without rancor. "Or was. At first, I thought the whole thing was nifty. A nice apartment that didn't cost me a nickel, presents, clothes, once in a while a trip. But on Christmas and Thanksgiving and all the other important days, zap. He was home with the wife and kiddies. It took me a long while to realize that I was never anything but a receptacle. Or to put the metaphor precisely, an ashcan."

Darla nodded sympathetically. "Doesn't sound quite so glamorous, when you describe it that way."

"It's not," Molly said. "Because when you get past the women's lib bullshit, when you stop kidding yourself and face the truth, we're all the same. What we want is a husband and home and kids and a loving relationship. We want to be the woman to a man. And no matter what Bella or Kate or any of those others would have you believe, that's where it all is."

The big jet touched down on the runway without a rumble. As the DC-10 taxied to the ramp, Darla thought about what Molly had said, and felt a pang of remorse. For all the trouble and the jealousy and the abuse, she had powerful feelings about Mike, and even though those feelings had become twisted and misdirected, she felt them whenever he came into her mind. Which was less and less frequently, she thought wryly.

And yet, damn it, why should she feel guilty? She had tried and tried to be a good wife, tried to go along with Mike even when he was at his impossible worst, putting up with his faithlessness and his harsh, sometimes even brutal, treatment of her. Yes, of course it was true that he was going through what was undoubtedly the most difficult time of his life. But there again she had tried, offering sympathy and understanding, getting nothing but a kick in the teeth in return.

Was Molly right? That all a woman really wanted

was that *Better Homes and Gardens* crap? Not so long ago Darla would have agreed absolutely. But now? She wasn't so sure. When she tried to think the concept through she came to no satisfactory conclusion, but only wound up confused and—what? Something else that she couldn't quite identify. She thought about it, and slowly realization dawned. She *did* agree, basically, and there was the conflict—a conflict she resented emotionally, and even, when she forced herself to face it, intellectually. Because what it came down to was that Darla was having the time of her life. She was Shirley Temple, wandering around the Good Ship Lollipop. And instead of candy canes and chocolate sodas, there were handsome men and fast cars and jets and stacks of money and the roar of applause. She'd wanted it all, all her life, and here it was. More and more and more of it. And instead of diminishing, instead of the supply threatening to run out, it was actually growing larger all the time. The more she enjoyed, the more there was to enjoy. She took a deep breath and pushed Mike and that whole tawdry, depressing business out of her mind. Look out, New York—here comes Darla.

She felt Molly's hand on her arm. "I think," the press agent was saying, "this is where we get off."

"Hm? Oh, I'm sorry," Darla said. "I was sort of lost in thought."

"Your privilege, honey." Molly stood up. "But they're holding the passengers for you."

As Darla got to her feet and looked aft in the cabin, she suddenly realized what Molly meant. The steward and the stewardesses had snapped lines into place and were making the other passengers wait, so that Darla could be the first to step off the jet. They were all craning their necks and gawking, struggling to get a better look at her. Nearby, her entourage, Betty and Derek and the others, were beaming. God, even getting off an airplane had become something special. She smiled, and picking up her handbag, made her way to the door. She thanked the crew, who mouthed a smiling chorus of replies, and stepped out onto the ramp with Molly just behind her.

All along the corridor, other travelers stopped to stare at Darla, a few calling out hellos, or excitedly directing someone else's attention to her. When she passed the security area, the scene was pandemonium. Flashbulbs popped, and a score of reporters crowded around her. There was even a UBS remote news unit, the operator pointing one of the new minicams at her.

"Welcome to New York, Darla. How do you like it?"

"How long do you plan to stay?"

"Is it true you're quitting TV for the movies?"

"How do you get along with Cathy Drake?"

"Are you and Mike really having problems in your marriage?"

"What are your views on sex and violence in television?"

Molly pushed her way in front of Darla and held up both hands. "May I have your attention, please? May I have quiet, for just a moment? Will you shut the hell up, please?"

When the babble had subsided, Molly said, "Miss Dawson really can't answer all these questions now. We're due at a taping session at the network shortly."

Groans of protest arose.

"Hold it," Molly went on. "But Miss Dawson has graciously consented to say just a few words."

Remembering Molly's earlier coaching, Darla led off with her friendliest smile. "First of all, I want to say thank you for the wonderful welcome. I love New York and it's always a thrill for me to come here, especially because everyone's always so nice to me and because there are so many exciting things to do and to see. I expect to be here for about a week, maybe a little longer. Then I have to get back to California, because 'The Witches' starts shooting again soon. I know there have been rumors about my quitting the show, but that's all they are, rumors. Cathy Drake is a good friend of mine, and a fine actress whose work I admire very much. As far as my future plans are concerned, I can't say. Sure I'd like to do movies, but—" She smiled her coy, little-girl smile. "Nobody's asked me."

A roar went up.

"About Mike," Darla went on. "We're just as happy as we ever were, and that's very happy. He's a wonderful husband and a great guy and I love him very much. As far as our having problems in our marriage goes," she grinned at them, "don't believe everything you read in the newspapers."

Laughter greeted this, and then the tide of questions rose again.

At a signal from Molly, two security guards joined with several New York Transit Authority policemen to make a path for the group. Familiar faces loomed close as Darla followed the cops, and she recognized Ben Thompkins, David Archer, and Paul Scott from Superfresh's advertising agency.

Thompkins was his usual friendly, easygoing self. "Hey, sweetie—weclome to New York." He kissed her cheek as they walked along, the other two men smiling greetings. Paul Scott was carrying a large bouquet of red roses that he presented to Darla.

"Beautiful," Darla exclaimed, cradling the roses in one arm. The splash of scarlet against her blonde hair and her bronzed skin and beige silk dress formed a vivid contrast.

"Hope you had a good trip," Scott said.

"It was fine. Nice and easy." Darla didn't much care for this man. There was something vaguely repellent to her about his too-smooth good looks and his slightly unctuous manner. She liked the other one, Archer, a little better, but she didn't really trust him either. He seemed to be merely an older version of Scott, a bit more dignified, with the touches of gray hair at his temples, but certainly stamped from the same mold. Of the people she'd met in the advertising business, the only one she much liked was Ben Thompkins. As head of television commercial production for the agency, he'd always seemed to understand and respect her, and had always gone out of his way to treat her as a person, rather than as a piece of property.

It was amusing, when she bothered to think of it, how so many people had changed in their attitude toward her. At first, to the Baker & Barlowe staff members, she had been just another model. But then, as her career had begun its ascendency, rapidy climbing to its present height, they had treated her more and more deferentially, until now they were as ass-kissing sweet to her as they were to their clients. And for that matter, as far as the people at Superfresh were concerned, she had no real feeling for them, either. They were all made of papier-mâché too—all, that is, except one. She had never in her life, in Hollywood or anywhere else, met a stronger, more forceful man than old John Rawlson. She would be seeing the Superfresh president on this trip, and even though she was now a full-blown star—a superstar, if you wanted to believe Molly's hype—she always felt anxiety at the prospect of seeing the old man, and then was invariably unnerved in his presence. She pictured him in her mind's eye, with his ruddy cheeks and his shock of snow-white hair, and his cold, all-seeing blue eyes, and her feeling of awe was heightened.

A trio of black limousines was drawn up at curbside. The first in line was a Rolls-Royce, taller and more stately than the two Cadillacs parked close behind it. A black-uniformed chauffeur saluted smartly and held open the door of the Rolls.

"Hey," Darla said as she approached the huge car. "That's my style."

Thompkins grinned. "First-class all the way." He steered Darla into the Rolls and then helped Molly get in. "We're going to the Plaza," he called out to the others. "You'll be following us in the Caddies." He ducked in after the two women.

"They can follow me, too," Betty yelled. She bulled her way into the Rolls, and the chauffeur slammed the door behind her. She and Ben occupied the jump seats; Molly and Darla sat behind them.

"Is the baggage taken care of?" Darla asked.

"Will you stop worrying about crass details?" Molly smiled. "I keep trying to get you to understand you are now one of the world's great ladies. You do not occupy your mind with such drek—that stuff is all done for you. All you have to think about is being your beautiful, charming self."

"Hey, by the way, Darla," Betty said, "you really ought to have a personal maid. Especially on a trip like this."

"Oh, I really don't need one. I can get my packing done pretty fast, and besides, Sally gives me all the help I need."

"It isn't just that," Betty said. "I mean, somebody of your stature doesn't wash out her pantyhose or wonder where she put her yellow sweater."

"Betty's right," Molly interjected. "It's more than just convenience, it's another part of your image. But on both counts, you ought to have one."

Ben had listened to all this with a faintly amused smile on his face. "There's another thing," he said to Darla now. "Which I'm sure your manager will tell you. And that is that in your tax bracket, hiring a maid will cost you practically nothing."

"Right on," Molly said.

Betty snorted. "Hell, I've got a better idea. Let the network provide you with a maid. That way, it costs you *absolutely* nothing. And the way my accountant always explained it to me, something that costs you absolutely nothing is better than something that costs you practically nothing."

Thompkins laughed. "Good thinking, Betty."

Fascinating, Darla thought. All these people not only want to be part of my life, they all want to run it for me, too. The trick is to sort out who really wants to help me, and who just wants a piece of the action. There was a time I thought I knew who wanted what, but now I'm not so sure. The only thing I am sure of is that they all *want*.

Darla looked out the Rolls's window. "Where are we?"

"Queens," Ben replied. "We're going to go through the Midtown Tunnel. That's fastest, this time of day."

"Are the others still with us?" Darla asked.

"Sure," Ben said.

"I'll say they are," Betty said, looking back through the rear window. "With a Rolls-Royce and two Cadillacs, this outfit looks like a Jewish wagon train."

When the cars pulled up in front of the Central Park South entrance to the Plaza, Darla was surprised to see a horde of teenaged girls, squealing and waving placards, milling about on the sidewalk. The placards read *Darla we love you!*, and *Darla Fan Club N.Y. Chapter*, and *Darla's the Greatest!*

"Hey!" Molly exulted. "Look at that turnout!"

As the doorman held open the door of the Rolls, Ben got out first and took Darla's hand. He helped her out of the car, and as she emerged, the howling of the teenaged girls increased to the level of screeching. Several policemen and hotel personnel held the girls back as Ben led Darla through the crowd and up the red-carpeted steps into the lobby. Darla was aware of cameras clicking, and she was startled to see that every one of the girls was wearing a Darla hairdo. It was bizarre.

The manager of the Plaza introduced himself and made a short welcoming speech, as several other staff members stood by, wreathed in smiles. Darla had never been in the Plaza before, but one glance told her that the place was full of old money. The carpeting and the marble and the chandeliers looked more like movies of grand hotels in London and Paris than anything she had ever seen in America. And for that matter many of the guests, looking on with restrained interest, appeared vaguely European. The expensive cut of their clothes was in marked contrast to the kind of mod, Las Vegas inspired *kitsch* you saw people wearing in even the best of the Los Angeles hotels.

The manager bowed, and Darla was ushered into an elevator and whisked up to her suite. It was on the top floor of the hotel facing east, looking out at the General Motors Building, and beyond that, the 59th Street Bridge.

The suite was spacious and elaborate. The floors were covered with rich Chinese rugs, their soft pastel colors beautifully complementing the damask-covered walls and the Louis XIV furniture. A marble fireplace stood at either end of the living room.

"Not bad, huh—your highness?" Molly grinned.

"Not bad at all," Darla replied. There were vases of fresh flowers everywhere she looked. Suddenly she realized she was still carrying the bouquet of roses Paul Scott had given her at the airport. Now she didn't quite know what to do with them.

"Here," Molly said. "Let me take those." The press agent spotted an empty vase in the foyer and stuffed the roses into it. "Most of the rest of these are from UBS. The big one over there is from Peter Fried himself, yet."

Darla made a brief tour of the suite. There were two large bedrooms, each with dressing room and bath, a smaller sitting room, and a pantry. When she returned to the large sitting room, the others had assembled, and two waiters were opening bottles of champagne under the watchful eye of one of the assistant managers.

"Hey, who's sleeping where?" Betty asked no one in particular.

"Darla and Sally have the bedrooms in this suite," Molly said. "The rest of us are scattered around."

"If you'll just let us know when you wish to go to your rooms," the assistant manager said, "we'll escort you to them. Miss Dane has checked everyone in."

The waiters served champagne and Derek Wasserman raised his glass and said, "I propose a toast to the most beautiful and talented star ever to take New York by storm." There were cheers, and they smiled at Darla over their glasses. The wine was cold and tingling and delicious, much drier than any Darla had ever tasted.

David Archer stepped close to her. "You've never looked lovelier, Darla. I can't tell you how pleased we are to have you in New York. Mister Rawlson asked me to tell you he's thrilled that you're enjoying such well-earned success, and that he's very proud that you're representing Superfresh. He's looking forward to seeing you while you're here."

"That's very nice. Please tell him I'm looking forward to seeing him too."

There were a few more perfunctory remarks from the agency people, and then Ben Thompkins put his empty glass down with an air of finality. He leaned over and kissed Darla. "So long, sweetie. We'll get the hell out of here and let you get some rest. It's great to have you in New York." Archer and Scott added their goodbyes and the three men left.

A moment later a knock sounded and Sally Dane opened the door, revealing a short, remarkably ugly girl whose appearance was made even more grotesque by her Darla hairdo, the streaked blonde tresses framing an oily lump of a face. She wore jeans and a T-shirt imprinted LOVE DARLA. The girl was fat and braless, her nipples pushing out the O and the L on the T-shirt. She was chewing gum furiously, an expression of excitement in her tiny, close-set eyes. Sally started to close the door, but Molly called out, "Hey—it's okay. Let her in!"

The girl strode into the foyer and on into the sitting room, making straight for Darla. "Hi, I'm Heather Fink," she announced. She shook Darla's hand vigorously. "President of the New York chapter of the Darla Dawson Fan Club," she added proudly. "Geez, what a terrific pleasure. For me, this is really the high point of my life, you know?"

"It's nice to have you here," Darla said. "What did you say your name was?"

"Heather," the girl replied. "Heather Fink." She had a pronounced Bronx accent. "We really turned them out, didn't we?" she said exultantly.

Molly greeted Heather warmly. "How're you doing, Prez?"

"Hiya, Molly?" Heather gave Molly the same energetic handshake. "What do you mean, how'm I doin'? You saw 'em, didn't you? Must of been a couple hundred kids I had out there. I told you I'd have 'em here."

A waiter approached with a tray.

"Geez, champagne," Heather said admiringly, taking a glass. "I thought it would be like this, you know?" she remarked to Darla. "I mean, I figured you'd live like

372

this. And why shouldn't you? The most popular TV star in the world!" She raised the glass ceremoniously. "Here's to you, Darla. Welcome to New York from me, on behalf of all your fans." Heather raised the glass to her lips and then hesitated, obviously becoming suddenly conscious of the problem presented by the cud of chewing gum in her mouth. Her eyes darted from side to side as she briefly sought a place to deposit the wad, and finding none, swallowed it with a noisy gulp. She smiled broadly and emptied the glass.

She looks like an over-sized chimpmunk, Darla thought.

"How long you going to be in town?" Heather asked.

"I plan to—" Darla began.

"We're leaving tomorrow, probably," Molly interrupted. "You know, one of those quick turnarounds? It's the business, right, Heather?"

"Oh yeah, geez, I understand," Heather said to Darla sympathetically. "You don't have time for nothing, hardly. I was hoping you could make a meeting of the chapter we're having tomorrow night. Can you imagine the reaction, if you was to walk in? In the flesh? They'd go out of their minds."

"I'm really sorry," Darla said, picking up her cue.

"It's okay, really," Heather said. "Anyhow, you want to get back to Mike, right?"

"Uh, right." Darla smiled.

"Geez, I can understand that too," Heather sighed. Her expression became slightly lascivious. "Wow. Imagine making it with Mike Brady whenever you felt like it." She closed her eyes, obviously imagining it.

"Yeah, okay, Heather," Molly said. "Hey, it was great of you to organize this terrific reception." She took the girl's arm and began gently steering her toward the foyer.

"Sure, anytime, Molly," Heather said. "There's nothing I wouldn't do for Darla. I mean, nothing. You know?" She turned back as Molly continued to walk her out. "See you, Darla. Good luck. I'll try to get out to California next year."

"Wonderful, Heather," Darla replied. She gave a small wave.

Molly handed Heather a manila envelope. "There you are, Heather. A hundred bucks plus ten personally autographed photos. And here's an extra twenty for doing such a great job." She stuffed a crumpled bill into Heather's fat little hand and eased her through the door.

"Jesus Christ," Betty said.

"Did you ever?" Derek Wasserman laughed. "She was really something else."

Lee Merriwell began flexing his jaws in an exaggerated imitation of Heather Fink chewing gum. "Hey, listen, sweethot," he intoned nasally to Bobby Benbo. "In the entiah world, I'm the biggest Dolla Dawson fan, yet."

"Oh, no, you ain't, sweethot," Bobby rejoined, flexing his own jaws wildly. "T'll have you know I got Dolla's name tattooed right on my ass."

"Molly," Darla asked, a little petulantly, "did I understand that right? Did you really have to pay her to organize that, uh, demonstration?"

"Of course not," Molly replied soothingly. "That was just a little thank-you gesture, a couple of bucks to make up for Heather's expenses. I told you not to worry your head about such things. That's what you've got me for."

"Oh, my." Derek shook his head. "Heather Fink, president of the New York Chapter."

"Hey, don't knock it," Betty said. "What we have just seen is reality, in the flesh. When you scrape away the Nielsen ratings and the TVQ and all the rest of it, what have you got? Heather Fink, bless her."

"I guess you're right," Derek said. "The 'Witches' audience is not exactly Jimmy Carter."

"The hell it isn't," Molly said. "He's in there, too. He likes girls, I know he does. Said so himself, in *Playboy* or *Penthouse*, or one of those skin books."

"Damn right," Betty agreed. "And how about that raunchy brother of his, Billy? That one's probably got a TV set in the bathroom."

The waitress and the hotel's assistant manager stood

wide-eyed, silently observing all this. Suddenly aware of their presence, Molly called out, "Hey, thanks a lot, you guys, but we can take care of ourselves from now on. We'll call and ask the desk who's where. Thanks a lot, okay?" She gave each of them a bill as she saw them out. As she was about to close the door a bellman arrived with a dolly piled high with luggage.

"Oh, right this way," Sally Dane said to the man with the bags. "Just follow me."

"What time are the UBS people due?" Darla asked Molly.

The press agent looked at her watch. "You've got another hour, so you'd better start getting ready. No use rushing."

"What's this?" Betty asked.

"Dinner at the Americana," Molly replied. "Tom Jones is opening there tonight for a week and then after that he's taping a UBS special. A couple of UBS execs and their wives are taking Darla to the opening."

Betty nodded. "A double hype, huh?"

"Those are the best kind," Molly said. "Hey, incidentally, and before I forget—everybody meets right here at nine o'clock tomorrow morning for a briefing on the schedule. There're four thousand things have to be done on this trip, and I want everything to be smooth. Darla's got the movie meeting and the toy meeting and also an audience with the king, Peter Fried at UBS. She can't be in two places at the same time, so let's get everything nailed down tomorrow morning."

Darla headed for her bedroom.

"Hey, Darla," Lee Merriwell called out. "Yell when you're ready for us, okay?"

The bath was heavenly. Sally had filled the huge tub with great creamy stalagmites of suds. Darla lay in the hot, fragrant water, feeling the tension and the fatigue slowly leave her body. God, she thought. How I've looked forward to this trip. She could hear muffled sounds of laughter coming from beyond the bedroom door as the others continued to work on the champagne.

Sally walked into the bathroom, a pale green silk

dress over one arm, a rust crepe de chine over the other. "Want to choose one of these, Darla? Or neither?"

Darla thought about it for a moment. The pale green was classier, the rust sexier. Let's see, she ruminated. The type of crowd that would be attending an Americana opening was about the same as one that would appear for a similar function at Miami's Fontainebleau. That made the choice easy. What she needed tonight was the bombshell effect; the Marines hitting the beach. She pointed to the rust. "That one."

Sally disappeared, and Darla lay back in the suds once more. She no longer felt tired, but was looking forward to the evening, inwardly delighted to contemplate the stir she would cause when she stepped into the glittering supper club. Tonight would be fun. In fact, the whole trip would be a wonderful, frenzied, adventurous release from the grind of shooting that damned show. For these few days, she'd have herself a ball. There were so many things she wanted to do, so many things she wanted to buy. There would be no getting up at five o'clock to get ready for the limousine, no hurry up and wait, no freezing in the predawn on locations and no sweating under the relentless glare of the studio lights, no dragging herself into the house at eight or nine or ten, sometimes too exhausted even to eat, no forced pleasantries with Cathy Drake, no worrying about what Mike was doing, where, and with whom. The hell with it, all of it.

Sally reappeared with a glass of champagne and two envelopes. She placed the glass on the edge of the tub and handed Darla the envelopes. "Mail yet, already," she said in a Heather Fink accent.

Darla laughed. "You'd better be careful, or you really will start to sound like a New Yorker."

Sally clapped her hand over her mouth in mock dismay. "Heaven forbid!" She darted back into the bedroom.

Darla opened the first envelope and withdrew a card of white parchment on which the words "United Broadcasting System" were engraved. To one side, in smaller letters, was Peter Fried's name. The message on the card was neatly typed.

Dear Darla,

Welcome to New York. UBS is honored to have you here, and we'll do everything we can to make your stay as pleasant and as productive as possible. I'm looking forward with great pleasure to our meeting.

Cordially,
Peter Fried

Darla studied the card for a moment. Strange, she thought. She had only met Fried a couple of times, and then only briefly, but still, this didn't sound like him at all. The network program head was rather flamboyant and garrulous, and anything but polite. This note seemed courteous and restrained. Even the signature was written in a tiny hand. Probably a canned statement, Darla decided. She pictured Fried sitting at his desk, barking at a secretary, "Hey, send this broad the welcome letter." She dropped the card over the edge of the tub.

The second envelope contained a piece of plain notepaper. On it was written in scrawling, boldly masculine script:

Darla, love—call me when you get to New York. Number is 759-6681. Can't wait to eat you up. And down. And sideways. Love, D.

It was tantalizing to think about. A tingly, highly erotic sensation spread through Darla's body as she contemplated a tryst with Dante Corelli. She slid deeper into the hot, fragrant water, until her chin was barely above its whipped-cream surface, and carefully placed the note on the edge of the tub. Lifting the glass of icy champagne, she held it aloft and said aloud, "Ladies and gentlemen, this calls for a toast. Here is to me." She giggled and drained the glass in one long swallow. New York, New York. A hell of a town.

Chapter 39

The bell rang and the sound stage grew quiet. Britney called for action and Mike began his move. The scene required him to walk to stage center, where a table and chairs stood. A box lay on the table. Mike was to begin opening the box, whereupon a shot was to fired offstage. He was then to hit the floor and rolled out of range of the off-camera sniper.

Mike picked up the box and realized that his hands were shaking. He tore at the paper wrapping, his fingers feeling thick and clumsy. He was aware that sweat was beading on his face. The shot sounded, and he dropped the box and fell to the floor. After the first complete roll, his head began to spin wildly. He lay flat and pressed both hands onto the surface of the stage, breathing hard.

Britney called for a cut, and walked casually over to the table. Out of the corner of his eye, Mike saw the director signal to his assistant.

"Okay, everybody," the A.D. called. "That's it for today."

Mike got to his feet slowly, the dizziness abating slightly as he did.

Britney leaned against the table and studied his script.

"Sorry, Rod," Mike mumbled. "I'm just not feeling too great."

Britney shrugged. "No problem. It's the end of the day, anyway. We can pick this up in the morning."

"Yeah," Mike said. "Thank God we've got a hiatus coming up. I really need some time off."

"Uh-huh."

Mike started toward his dressing room.

"Mike?" Britney called.

"Yeah?"

"I'll be over in a minute," the director said. "I'd like to talk with you."

"Sure." What the hell was this, now? He'd said he wasn't feeling well, hadn't he? If there was anything he didn't need, it was a heart-to-heart with Britney. What he did need was to be left alone.

Inside the dressing room, Mike took a bottle of red-and-yellow capsules from a drawer and popped one of the capsules into his mouth. He washed it down with a cup of water from the cooler and slumped into a chair. The rush started almost immediately, and by the time Britney knocked on the door Mike had already begun to get himself together.

The director walked into the room. He straddled a straight-backed chair and lit a cigarette.

"What can I do for you, Rod?" Mike was back in control now. He glanced down at his hands. Almost completely steady.

Britney blew out a stream of smoke. "I won't beat around the bush, Mike. Frankly, I've been worried about you."

"Oh? Why is that?"

"A number of reasons. Your performance lately, for one thing. I really—"

"Hey," Mike said sharply. "I told you I wasn't feeling so hot today, didn't I?"

"It isn't just today."

Brady leaned forward, his temper rising.

Britney raised a hand. "Easy, Mike. I'm not being critical. I'd just like to be able to say what's on my mind, because I think it could be helpful. I'm not here to fight with you. I really am concerned."

Mike slumped back into his chair. All right, he said

to himself. The best way to handle this is to let him speak his piece and then get him out of here. "Okay, Rod. So talk."

Britney dragged on his cigarette. "For the past few weeks, I've seen you undergo a real change. At first, I chalked it up to your just being tired, too. Hell, we're all kind of wrung out. But the more I've seen, the more I've come to realize that this is something else. You're—like a different guy."

"Different how?"

"Different in that you don't have the forcefulness, the strength I'm used to feeling when I'm around you. You know, it's just not—" He raised his shoulders and dropped them in an exaggerated shrug "—you."

"Yeah. Well, the rest will do us a lot of good."

"I hope so, Mike."

"Sure. I'm going to get plenty of sun and plenty of sleep, and I'll be back here full of charge."

The director crushed his cigarette in an ashtray. "You also ought to get yourself straight."

Mike was shocked and surprised. And instead of anger, he felt something now more closely allied with fear. "What the hell do you mean by that?"

Britney's gaze was steady and direct. "You know what I mean. You're on something, and it's not booze. And it's part of what's chewing on you, turning you into somebody who isn't Mike Brady."

Mike started to protest, but nothing came out.

"You want to know why I'm saying these things to you? Okay, two reasons. One, this show has done a hell of a lot for me. And originally the series was built around one guy's personality. You haven't been easy to work with, in fact the opposite, most of the time. Nevertheless, I feel that I owe you something. Two, I don't like what's been happening to the show, as well as to you."

Mike shook his head, as if to clear it. "The ratings are okay."

"You mean they're better than they were. But they're still not at the same levels as, say, a year ago. And in this business you don't get many second chances."

"You're blaming it all on me, huh? What am I, a miracle worker? Every series has its ups and downs."

"Yeah." Britney's gaze was unrelenting. "And so do people. Right now you're in a slide, Mike. And I'm saying to you, turn yourself around. You get straight, and get going again, and that'll do more for the show than anything else possibly could."

Mike stared at the director. "Did Hazelman put you up to this?"

Britney grimaced. "God, no. In fact, he'd probably be good and pissed if he knew I was saying some of these things to you. After all, a lot of the changes in the show were his idea in the first place."

"When you say changes, you're talking about Andrea, aren't you?"

"Yeah, I guess I am."

"So what's wrong with her? You ask me, she's done a lot for the show. Gave it a new angle, some new interest. And you know something? I was against her coming in, at first."

"I remember."

"But then I saw how she could help the show, and she has."

Britney stood up. "Sure, Mike. But ask yourself this. Has she helped you?"

Brady stared at the director. He realized that his dizziness had returned. "Do me a favor, will you, Rod? Get the hell out of here."

"Yeah. I was just leaving." Britney turned and left the dressing room.

Mike sat back in his chair. He looked at the drawer where the bottle of pills was. It was hard to think clearly about what the director had said. Christ, was he really turning into a junkie? Hell, no. He was just under a lot of strain and sometimes he needed to get himself calmed down, needed something to help him over the rough spots.

He ought to go home tonight. He ought to go home and get a good long sleep. He really felt lousy. But with Darla not there, he didn't much like the way it felt to be rattling around with only Maggie in the house.

Darla. What a crazy twist their life together had taken. Or a twist not together, he reflected. All of a sudden her career was going through the roof. And his?

Oddly, he had found himself thinking about her often, and missing her. That was a laugh, wasn't it? After years of ignoring her, of taking her for granted, now he wished he could talk to her, ask her what she thought about what was happening to him. But hell, he couldn't do that, even if she were home, without revealing a lot of things he wouldn't want her to know about. And yet he kept thinking about how good it would be if they could just sit together and talk.

The door opened and Andrea Derringer walked into the dressing room. She smiled. "How are you, honey?"

Mike looked at her. "Hi. I'm fine. Little tired, but okay."

"I know what you need. You need some fun. How about getting cleaned up and we'll have dinner—maybe LaScala or someplace. Come on."

Mike got to his feet. "Sure. Sounds good."

Andrea kissed his lips lightly. "Beautiful."

"You know, I've been thinking."

"Yes?"

"We've only got a few more days of shooting before the break. As soon as we wrap it up, I'd like to get away, go somewhere really private."

"Oh? Where, for instance?"

"I'm not sure," Mike replied. "But just the two of us. Maybe somewhere up in the mountains. I could use some rest and some fresh air."

Andrea's face wore a slightly derisive expression, but Mike didn't notice. "That could be lovely," she said.

"Yeah. I think so too." He started toward his bathroom. "Be with you in a few minutes."

"Take your time," Andrea said.

Chapter 40

The limousine swung down Lexington Avenue and stopped in front of Bloomingdale's, where a New York City policeman and two of the store's uniformed guards awaited its arrival.

A private detective, assigned by UBS to look after Darla, sat in the front seat. He was a former New York cop, a big, rumpled man with a red face, named Murphy. "Okay," he said over his shoulder to the women who sat in the passenger compartment. "You wait here for just a minute, please." He got out and stepped over to speak to the cop and the two guards.

"Sometimes all this fuss is a big nuisance," Darla remarked. "It'd be a lot easier if I just tied my hair up and sneaked in here alone."

Molly shook her head. "Not worth it. There are more nuts per square inch in this city than anyplace else on earth. Why take chances if you don't have to? And besides, I've got the *Post* here, waiting for you."

Darla looked at the publicist. "For me to what?"

"You know," Molly said. "Redhot TV actress shops Bloomingdale's, her favorite New York store."

Darla smiled. "That's wonderful, Molly. I've never even been inside the place."

"So what?" Molly laughed. "It really is a very good store."

"This is a crock," Betty said. "For publicity like this, Bloomingdale's should pay through the nose."

"They don't get too excited about such things," Molly rejoined. "A lot of famous people shop here all the time."

"Maybe," Betty said. "But I still think they ought to do something for Darla."

Murphy opened the door of the car and helped the women out onto the sidewalk. A female writer from the *Post* and a photographer greeted them. A small crowd of pedestrians began to gather.

"Stay next to me at all times, Miss Dawson," Murphy said. "Wherever you go in the store, just be sure I'm alongside."

"How about if I want to go into a dressing room?" Darla asked innocently.

The security man grinned. "I'll wait outside the door."

Shopping in the huge store took nearly two hours, and Darla realized when the tour was over that she hadn't nearly seen it all. She bought a light blue pants suit by Mic-Mac, to the delight of the sportswear buyer, a set of glasses for the bar at home, and a big, squashy leather hassock. She ogled the exquisitely decorated furniture display rooms on the fifth floor, poked around in the boutiques, paid $51.90, including tax, for a two-ounce jar of something called Nefertiti Skin Cream at one of the first-floor cosmetic counters, and signed autographs until her arm ached.

From Bloomingdale's they went to Saks, where, under similar security protection, Darla bought a short jacket of Russian raccoon, and several pairs of soft leather gloves.

"That stuff ought to keep you nice and warm in L.A.," Molly teased.

"Oh, I know I don't have much use for it," Darla laughed. "And I could find a jacket just like this in Beverly Hills. But God, this is fun! I just love to spend money."

They had lunch at LaGrenouille, the small, chic restaurant on Fifty-second Street whose owner went to such enormous pains to see that his crystal and silver and linens were always immaculate, that his flowers were never more than a few hours from cutting, and above all that his sauces were at least the equal of those produced by the kitchens of La Tour D'Argent in Paris, where he had trained for so many years in his youth. They were the guests there of *Vogue Magazine,* one of whose editors put Darla through a set of questions that had become so routine that she knew what they would be even before the editor asked them.

Later, as the limousine crawled through the midtown traffic, Betty said, "Sometimes I don't know how you do it, Darla—keeping your patience through all that crap. But you've got so you're as smooth as a statesman."

"Stateswoman," Molly corrected.

"Statesperson," Darla countered, then laughed. "But I'll confess that sometimes I feel like telling the whole, unvarnished truth." She went into a mock interview. "Yes, indeed, I hate to cook. The maid does it. If my husband comes home hungry, that's tough. He can go to the refrigerator or wait till the maid puts dinner on, just like I do. My favorite foods are not all that fancy French junk, either. I love chicken enchiladas, even though they give me gas."

Molly was convulsed.

Darla made a crazy face. "Do I think Cathy Drake is a good actress? No, I don't. In fact, she stinks. What's more, she has a wart on her ass. I've seen it."

Even Betty was laughing now.

"And what do I think about Arnold Schwarzenegger? The same as any other woman. I wonder if he has muscles in his prick."

From his front seat Murphy turned and poked his head back into the passenger compartment.

"Hey, what's all the laughing about?"

"Just girl talk," Darla replied, and Molly and Betty went into further peals of laughter.

Looking mystified, Murphy turned back to face front, shaking his head.

In the lobby of UBS's West Side studio, Molly said to Darla, "This may be your big chance to say what's really on your mind. Dreyfus always does a number on his guests."

"I think that's lousy," Betty said as a guide led them toward the elevators. "Running an interview show like it's some kind of inquisition. And on Darla's own network, too. I think Gary Zander or Peter Fried or somebody ought to tell this jerk to buzz off."

"Just look at the ratings, if you want your answer," Molly said. " 'The Morning Show' is trailing 'Today' by around eight points, which is enough to give Ed Wechsburg and those other UBS geniuses cardiac arrest. They'll do anything to get those numbers up, and if it's going to take making the show controversial, so be it."

Dan Dreyfus was a bright-eyed, pleasant-looking young man of the Dick Cavett type, voluble, well-educated, highly intelligent. Formerly an actor and a nightclub comedian, he had gotten his start while still an undergraduate at Cornell, and after several years of increasingly successful TV appearances had been rushed into this show in a desperate effort to bolster the program's sagging Nielsens. He was the fourth host of "The Morning Show" that year. The format was a combination of news and interviews, a kind of hash that lay somewhere between "Today" and CBS's "Morning News." Most of "The Morning Show" was telecast live, interspersed with bits like this one, videotaped in advance, and with filmed and taped news clips. Partly as a habit ingrained during Dreyfus's nightclub days, and partly because it gave the show a sense of presence that UBS theorized made it more interesting, this was one of the few shows originating in New York that played before a live audience.

"This morning 'The Morning Show' welcomes the young lady who has become a show business phenomenon," Dreyfus burbled into the camera, "moving from obscurity to the very top of television in an amazingly short time. Let's welcome the very lovely Miss Darla Dawson!"

The audience dutifully beat its palms while Darla smiled into the camera. The red light told her it was taking her, and she swiveled in the modernistic, cup-shaped plastic chair she occupied on the stage and waved to the audience.

Dreyfus wasted no time in boring in. "How does it feel to be on top, Darla? Are you worried you could go down just as fast as you came up?"

"It feels great to be in a successful series like 'The Witches,'" Darla replied, holding her smile in place, "and I'm not worried about anything. I'm having too much fun."

"Some people say your husband is having a lot of fun, too, when you're not around," Dreyfus said.

The audience gasped. Darla had expected some bold probing, but this was surprising, even from a smartass like Dreyfus. Nevertheless, she'd be damned if she'd lose her cool. "He'd better not be," she replied, playing it as a joke. "Or he'll hear from me when I get home."

But Dreyfus knew this would be a juicy theme, the kind of thing the home audience, as well as the one in the studio, would eat up. "Oh, come on now, Darla. You can't say it doesn't bother you. Mike Brady is a handsome guy, a star in his own right, and everybody knows he has girlfriends." He paused, and then drove home his big shot. "Andrea Derringer, for instance."

Darla heard the audience gasp again. She decided that Dan Dreyfus was detestable. "How do you get information like that?" she asked sweetly. "By sneaking around in the dark?"

The audience guffawed, and Darla was gratified to see just the slightest flicker of uncertainty cross Dreyfus's face. That's it, she told herself. Turn it around on him. You'll have the audience right with you.

"Word has it," Dreyfus resumed, "that you like to play around yourself, now and then. What about you and young Jeff Patterson, for instance?"

"What about it?" Darla replied. "I've worked with Jeff. He's a nice boy and a fine tennis player. I like having him for a partner because he makes me look good."

"Sure," Dreyfus said sarcastically. "I'll bet he does. And Ted Walters? Your relationship with him isn't that much of a secret, you know. What would you say about that?"

"I'd say it proves tennis is my favorite sport," Darla replied sweetly, and the audience applauded. She was glad to hear their encouragement, but her temper was near the boiling point. She thought about how nice it would be to stick her finger into Dreyfus's eye.

The host returned to the attack. "Many television critics believe that your co-star, Cathy Drake, is not only prettier than you are, but a far more talented actress as well. What's your opinion?"

This was the nastiest phrasing of a question of this kind Darla had ever heard, but at least it came as no surprise. And as Dreyfus was expressing it, Darla thought she noticed a trace of femininity in his manner. Now that was something to work on.

"They could be right," she replied earnestly. "Cathy Drake is a good friend of mine, and I think she's beautiful and terrifically talented." She widened her smile. "But what do you think? You do like girls, don't you?"

The audience got it instantly, and responded with a roar of laughter, mixed with scattered applause. "You tell 'im, Darla," she heard someone call out. This time Dreyfus looked distinctly uncomfortable, Darla noted with satisfaction.

The young man made a quick recovery, but he was obviously stung, and not at all pleased with the direction the interview had taken. "How do you feel about women's lib?" he asked next, a trace of a sneer on his face. "Are you for it or against it?"

Again Darla knew immediately what Dreyfus was up to. He was trying to get her to polarize the audience, to take a stand that would please one half of the viewers and anger the other half. Well, screw him. "I don't believe in putting labels on anything," she replied thoughtfully. "But I do think that women who struggle for their rights need all the help and encouragement they can get. What's more, the best men in the world are the strong ones who offer women understanding and support, because they're sure of their masculinity and don't feel threatened just because somebody wants to be treated like a person and not like an object."

Dreyfus's eyes narrowed. "Do you think women ought to have status equal to that of men in everything? In business, say, or government?"

"If an individual is qualified, why not?" Darla replied. "But the criterion should always be ability, not sex." She put all the sincerity into her voice she could muster. "And anyway, government could stand to have more of its members seeing issues as women do. If it had been up to women, ninety percent of the wars in history would never have been fought."

The audience rose to its feet, cheering, and Darla acknowledged their response with a gracious, unsmiling nod. She glanced at Dreyfus, whose gaze was venomous.

"We'll return to 'The Morning Show' in just a moment," Dreyfus said cheerfully into a camera, "right after this."

As the limousine pulled away, Betty slapped her broad thigh triumphantly. "Whee! I loved it. You shoved it right up that fag bastard's ass."

"Do you think he really is?" Darla asked. "I thought maybe, but I wasn't sure."

"Is he!" Betty rejoined. "I'll guarantee you that one squats to pee."

"You know what's beautiful?" Molly giggled. "He has to sit through that whole thing all over again, when the show goes on the network tomorrow morning. There's nothing he'd love better than to dump it, but he can't. Darla's the hottest interview on TV, and on top of that the audience was eating right out of your hand. The only one who'll hate that bit is that shithead Dreyfus himself."

Darla smiled happily. "Hey, I really did handle him pretty well at that, didn't I?"

"Damn right you did," Molly exulted. "You were sensational."

"What's on for tonight?" Darla asked. "I can't keep track of this agenda."

"Tonight's a big one," Molly replied. "Dinner with the president of UBS and his wife at their home with a few friends, and then to the ballet at Lincoln Center."

"That's nice," Darla said, without enthusiasm.

"Be patient," Molly told her. "Tomorrow night you have off."

"I know," Darla said. "And believe me, I can't wait. I wish I could have the whole damn day to myself."

"Uh-uh," Betty admonished. "Tomorrow we meet with Mal Meyer himself, the man who wants to give you a million dollars."

"Is that for real?" Darla asked. "I mean, no fooling. Is he serious?"

Betty was mildly exasperated. "Of course it's for real. I've been working on it for I don't know how long. Mal Meyer is one of the most important independent producers in the business."

"I know that," Darla said. "What I'm asking is if he's really serious about making a movie with me. I mean, I know we have a lot of offers and all, but that one would really be something."

"It's for real, all right," Betty said. "You'll see. But I do think we ought to make this just as small a meeting as possible. Mal doesn't like a lot of folderol. Should be just you and me going."

"I can't do that, Betty," Darla said. "Derek is my manager and he should be there. And anyway, I don't think one more person would be any problem."

"Maybe," Betty answered. "I just wouldn't want to see anything get screwed up."

When they arrived at the Plaza, Darla hurried to her suite to get ready for the evening ahead. First she'd bathe, and then take a two-hour nap, in order to look her absolute best, and then Bobby and Lee could go about giving her a dynamite hair and makeup job. She felt a little awed by the prospect of attending a private dinner at Harold Kallit's home, even though she had met the UBS president on two earlier occasions and he hadn't been the least bit intimidating, not nearly as formidable as Peter Fried, the program chief, for instance. Nevertheless, Harold Kallit, with his mild manner and his accountant's appearance was one of the most powerful men in television, one of a handful of executives who ruled the multi-billion-dollar industry with an iron fist.

As Darla soaked in the tub, Sally Dane sat on a chair beside her, a folder spread open on her knees, and read through Darla's messages. "Derek left a bunch of stuff for you; the most important thing is about the guy who's president of the Bando Toy Company. It's a deal Derek has been working on for months, he said to remind you. Guy's name is Steinman and he wants to make a doll of you."

"That's nice." Darla yawned. "I was hoping somebody would."

"No, this is for real," Sally said. "Derek said it could make you a fortune. He wants a meeting with the guy tomorrow or the next day."

"Uh-huh. What else?"

"Let's see, more on the business side. Capitol Records called, and La Fleur, the cosmetics company." She flipped through her papers. "And a lot of other stuff that's just junk. You can look through it when you get time."

"Any personal messages?"

Sally grinned. "You thought I'd never get to those, huh?" She held out a small envelope. "This came with the roses in the living room."

Darla opened the envelope and read, *"Dinner tomorrow night, honey. Can't wait. Love, Dante."*

"And Ted Walters called, says to please call him at his hotel. I have the number. Also Jeff Patterson called. Says to tell you he misses you, and would it be okay if he came to New York?"

In answer, Darla merely sniffed and went on bathing. After her bath and her nap, Darla put on gold and white evening pajamas, and when they had finished with her, Bobby Benbo and Lee Merriwell were delighted. "Marvelous," Bobby kept breathing over and over, his eyes bright. "Absolutely marvelous."

"The most beautiful girl in the entire universe," Lee agreed.

In the end, the evening turned out to be rather dull. The Kallits' apartment, a sumptuous duplex on Sutton Place, was furnished in a mixture of English and French antiques, its walls resplendent with the works of Cezanne and Monet and Dufy and Renoir. Darla found the place breathtaking. Her fellow guests, on the other hand, were considerably less stimulating. They were older, a half-dozen couples, the men in their dinner jackets all somehow resembling each other, short and broad and balding, powerful-looking physically as well as in the sense of wealth and influence they exuded, smoking long, thick cigars and conversing, mainly among themselves, about market prices and politics and people Darla had never heard of. The women, too, spoke a language of their own, their predictable gossip interspersed with references to charities and social events.

There were a few perfunctory questions from the women about her career, and admiring glances from the men, who studied her body as they might that of a thoroughbred horse. But except for these, Darla found herself not much involved with the group. In a subtle way, Darla understood, Mrs. Kallit was letting her know that pretty young women who were employed by her husband's network were, after all, still only employees, no matter how famous or fascinating the public might consider them.

After dinner the group was transported in a fleet of limousines to Lincoln Center, where they saw Swan Lake. To Darla, this was by far the most enjoyable part of the evening. The huge auditorium, aglitter with lights and packed tier upon tier with handsomely garbed people, was dazzling to see, and the production of the famed ballet was superb. Best of all, there was no need for her to make small talk, and she had only to sit in her deep, comfortable seat and watch the marvelously talented and beautifully costumed dancers perform, while the familiar strains of Tchaikovsky's score swept over her in waves.

It was also, she realized, virtually the only time she had had since her arrival in New York that was her own, time that she could devote to her own thoughts. Her mind was filled with a jumble of impressions, a giddy whirl of pictures, recollections of things that were happening to her at what seemed to be an ever-accelerating pace. To her mild perplexity, she also kept thinking about Mike, wondering what he was doing, wondering if he was with someone else.

When Darla got back to the hotel she suddenly realized that she was tired, in spite of the nap she had taken earlier, and that her feet hurt. She said goodnight to Murphy, and went into the pantry and searched the refrigerator for something to drink, settling finally on a can of Budweiser. The place was quiet, the low hum of the air-conditioning system muffling the few street noises emanating from Central Park South and Grand Army Plaza more than sixteen floors below. She swallowed a few sips of the beer and wandered into her bedroom, pulling off her clothing as she went.

Sally Dane's bedroom was connected to Darla's. On an idle impulse, Darla gently opened the door and peered inside. In the soft light of a lamp, she was greeted by a wholly unexpected sight. Sally and Derek Wasserman lay naked on the bed, sleeping soundly, Derek snoring through his open mouth. Several thoughts flashed through Darla's mind, some of them erotic. Carefully, quietly, she closed the door and got into her own bed. It took a long time for her to get to sleep.

Chapter 41

Cathy Drake ran along the beach, her feet splashing in the nearly spent waves that rolled gently onto the white sand. The sky was a deep cloudless blue, and the morning sun felt warm and pleasant on her tan skin. Up the beach to her left the palm trees of the Kahala Hilton waved gently, and straight before her in the distance Diamond Head rose out of the sapphire Pacific like a storybook mountain.

Cathy felt wonderful. She was in perfect shape, she reflected with pleasure, her belly flat, her muscles finely toned. She knew she looked sensational in the white string bikini she was wearing, and all along the beach, heads turned to stare as she jogged by. This trip was a marvelous idea, she thought to herself. There was no place in the world she would rather spend "The Witches'" shooting hiatus than Hawaii.

She ran past the crescent of beach to the point that extended out into the ocean, and ducked into a small grove of trees. Lying there on a beach towel was Sal Caretta. The director was also deeply tanned from the sun, his skin the color of saddle leather. He was wearing a swim suit that barely contained his genitals, and he was reading a paperback novel. Cathy dropped down beside him.

"How you doing?" Sal asked. "Enjoy the run?"

"It was great. Nothing like it to keep you in shape."

"Then it's what I ought to do," he said, patting his stomach. "But running's a bore. I'd rather swim."

"So swim," Cathy said. "Come on." She got to her feet and ran back toward the beach. Caretta dropped his book and followed her.

They swam out about a hundred yards, and then rolled over and floated alongside each other.

"I think," Caretta said, "that I have died and gone to heaven."

"Isn't it beautiful?" Cathy looked up at the cerulean sky. "The water's so warm, and the air is perfect. I love Hawaii."

"And I love you," Caretta said. He put one hand under her and gently rubbed his middle finger against her.

"Don't do that."

"Why not?"

"Because I might be forced to rape you, right here in the ocean." She reached into his bikini and squeezed his cock.

"It's a question of who rapes whom," Caretta said. "Come on, I'll race you back."

Cathy laughed. "Let's go."

They were both good swimmers, and they went back in using the modern windmill crawl, their arms flashing in the bright sunlight. Cathy reached the sand a stroke ahead of Caretta, and then both of them ran laughing back to the grove of trees. They flopped down onto the beach towel.

Sal wrapped them in the towel, still breathing hard, and then he kissed Cathy, holding her body against him, one leg thrust between hers.

"Wow," Cathy said. "You're really ready. I can feel it."

"It feels even better inside."

"Think we can do it here?"

"Why not?" Caretta reached down and slid Cathy's bikini pants off, then kicked off his own. He put his hand between her thighs and began to caress her. Cathy trembled and pressed against him. He slipped a finger into her, moving it gently in and out while he explored her mouth with his tongue.

Cathy grasped his cock. It was hot to her touch, and she could feel it throbbing. She slid her hand back and forth on it and Caretta groaned.

"God," Cathy breathed. "I want it."

Caretta rolled over on top of her and Cathy arched her back and guided him into her. She closed her eyes and pressed her lips to his neck, tasting the salt on his warm skin, moving her hips to the sensuous rhythm of the breaking waves. "That feels so good," Cathy whispered. She gripped his back and bucked under him, grinding and twisting.

Caretta's voice was hoarse. "Beautiful, just beautiful." He drove into her as far as he could.

"Sal, give it to me. Harder."

"Oh, Jesus, here it comes," Caretta said through clenched teeth. "Now." His body tensed and shuddered.

Afterward they lay beside each other panting, still wrapped in the beach towel. Cathy felt totally relaxed, as if her body had become weightless. She looked at the brilliant blue sky, and her gaze slid down to the horizon. A sailboat was out there, a sloop. It was carrying a huge red-and-white spinnaker, and it was scudding rapidly before the wind. That's the way it's done, she thought to herself with a smile. You need some luck, like when you're catching the wind. But what you do with it is up to you. She turned to Caretta. "That was lovely," she said.

He smiled. "That's why they call me the best fucking director in the business."

"You *are* a good director," Cathy said. "And you know something? That's the main reason the show's a hit."

"Hey, really? You mean that?"

"Of course I mean it," Cathy replied. "Sure, everybody's turned on by the idea of the two sexy girls, but the truth is that you need a lot more than that to make a top-rated series."

Caretta was pleased. "Well, now," he said. "I didn't think anybody had noticed."

"I noticed, and I've told Gary Zander so. I think you ought to win an Emmy for what you've done with it. I don't think anybody's ever put more into a series than you have. The real creative force behind 'The Witches' is you, Sal."

"An Emmy. Wouldn't that be something?"

"It sure would. And you deserve it."

Caretta rolled over onto his stomach and looked at her. "And you know something else? You deserve an Emmy yourself. For best actress in a series."

"Oh, forget it," Cathy said. "I think either Darla or Andrea Derringer will wind up with that."

"Don't be so sure," Caretta said. "Derringer comes off too close to what she really is for people to like her that much. She's a first-class bitch, and it shows."

"And Darla?"

Caretta shrugged. "Cute, sexy, and not very talented. She isn't nearly the actress you are."

Cathy lifted her head and kissed him lightly. "That's sweet of you, Sal."

"I mean it."

"I know you do. It's one of the things I love about you. You're always so supportive."

"Don't kid yourself," Caretta said. "People know it when they see the two of you. There's only one real actress in the series, and anybody can see that."

"I hope you're right."

"I am. And I'll tell you something else. You know I have a hell of a lot to do with how a scene is constructed and how it plays. In the final analysis, the star of 'The Witches' is going to be you, sweetie. I guarantee it."

"Oh, Sal, you're wonderful." Cathy kissed him again.

"Hey, what do you say we go up to the bar?" Caretta said. "I think a piña colada would be just about right."

"Terrific." Cathy reached for her bikini bottom. She pulled it on and got to her feet.

The sun was higher now, and a slight breeze had come up. The palm fronds rustled in the warm air, and the sound of music and laughter drifted toward them from the hotel. Cathy smiled to herself. Things were going exactly as planned. She took Caretta's hand and they started up the beach toward the bar.

Chapter 42

The Pierre seemed to Darla to have the same kind of moneyed, old-world charm that characterized the Plaza, and yet it was different, somehow; perhaps a little less imposing, not quite so grand, but every bit as elegant. As she walked through the ivory-and-gold-paneled lobby, her feet soundless in the deep carpeting, she was again struck by the differences between the first-class New York hotels and the ones in Los Angeles. Compared with this, L.A.'s Century Plaza was merely a multi-storied, slightly gauche motel. She entered an elevator, the security man, Murphy, ahead of her, Betty Frolich and Derek Wasserman trailing behind, and was whisked to the seventeenth floor.

A good-looking but severely dressed blonde opened the door to Mal Meyer's suite. "Hi, I'm Sharon Peterson. If you'll just come in and sit down, please, I'll serve you some coffee. Mister Meyer will be with you shortly." The group entered the suite, except for Murphy, who slouched in the hallway.

Darla sank into a comfortable armchair and took in her surroundings. There was a marble fireplace, *de rigeur,* apparently, for a suite in a good New York hotel, at least in the older ones, and the furniture was what she would call French Provincial, except that it looked a little fancier than that. Yet it wasn't quite as formal as the stuff in the Plaza. Damn it, she just had to learn more about such subjects. Furniture and art, paintings and sculpture—now that she could afford really nice things, she ought to know something about them.

"Cream and sugar, Miss Dawson?" the blonde asked politely.

"No thanks," Darla responded. "I just like it black." She studied the other girl. About her own age, she decided. Excellent figure, well set off by the trim black pants and black sweater she was wearing, and her face was quite striking, despite the fact that she was doing nothing to help it. Her hair, dark ash in color, was pulled back into a bun, and she wore heavy horn-rimmed glasses, and no makeup. Maybe that's so everybody will think she's strictly business, Darla thought, amused. She sipped her coffee and listened without interest as Betty and Derek chatted idly with Sharon Peterson about their journey from Los Angeles.

"We came in on United's Flight Six," Derek was saying. "The best thing about it was that it was fifteen minutes early."

"We were on TWA," Sharon said. "And it was okay. They're really all pretty much alike, don't you think? That is, the American ones all are. Only the European lines are different. Or at least some are a lot better than others."

"I'll say they are," Betty said. "But the way I'd put it is, some are a lot worse than others. Last time I went to Paris I was on Air France. Christ, what an airline."

Sharon smiled. "Air Chance."

"Exactly." Betty sniffed.

One of the doors leading off the living room opened and Mal Meyer walked in. "I heard you," he said to Betty. "Disparaging my favorite airline."

"Hello, Mal," Betty said. "What's to like about Air France?"

"Cute broads," the producer replied. "And they never run out of champagne. You must be Darla," he said, turning his attention to her. He smiled and extended his hand. "How are you?"

Meyer wasn't quite what Darla had expected, if indeed she had formed any clear picture of what this man might be like. He was wearing a blue-and-yellow silk paisley robe and apparently nothing else. His handshake was firm and his smile was friendly. Darla returned the smile. "I'm fine, Mal. How are you?"

"Terrific." He patted his ample belly. "Lost ten pounds since I've been on this fucking diet, four of them in the last couple of days." He flopped into a chair and waved a greeting to Derek Wasserman as his secretary brought him a cup of coffee.

"How long are you planning to be in New York, Mal?" Betty asked.

"About a week," Meyer answered. "You know, the usual shit. Argue with the banks, see a couple of plays, talk to some publishing houses." He smiled again. "Order some shirts, catch the finals at Forest Hills."

"Publishing houses?" Betty asked. "Are you into publishing?"

Meyer sipped coffee. "In a way I am. The publishers are finally waking up to what concepts like marketing a book mean."

"I don't get it," Betty said. "That's their business, isn't it?"

"It is," the producer replied. "But they don't know it. Most of them live in the nineteenth century. They think there's something holy about publishing a book, for Christ's sake, instead of understanding that it's a business, just like any other business."

"So how do you get involved?" Derek asked. "Buying movie rights to novels?"

"Right," Meyer replied. He waved a hand toward a pile of books on the writing desk. "I read all the time, looking for new properties. You wouldn't believe how some of those publishing characters can louse up what ought to be a successful book."

"Like how?" Betty asked.

"Like no promotion, to cite the worst offense," Meyer replied. "A publisher spends thirty or forty thousand dollars to advertise a new title and he acts as if it's a fortune. Do you know how much advertising forty thousand dollars buys in the real world?" He snorted. "A fart in a windstorm."

Betty shifted in her chair. "How much should they be spending?"

"At least a hundred, hundred fifty thousand," the producer said. "And that's just advertising. There also ought to be that much or more spent on P.R. You know, personal appearances by the author on TV talk shows, book club luncheons, interviews with newspaper columnists, advance hype on the movie—all that stuff."

Betty leaned forward. "And if a book gets that kind of promotion it can really go, huh? Provided, like you said, that the book is okay to begin with?"

"Absolutely," Meyer said. "How do you think Jackie Susann knocked out those best sellers one right after the other? Sure, she always turned out a good book to start with—and don't misunderstand me, when I say good I mean commercially viable. But then there was a very strong advertising program, and a hype you wouldn't believe." Meyer threw his head back and emitted a short, high-pitched laugh. "Christ, did that broad know how to hustle a book. She knew more than the fucking publishers ever did. And not only that, but she herself was a big part of the push. A lot of writers, you know, can't talk. At least not in front of an audience or in front of a television camera. The guy comes on wearing a lumberjack shirt and a beard, and he sits there with his thumb up his ass while the interviewer struggles to get two words out of him. But Jackie!" Meyer slapped a broad thigh. "Here is this tall, great-looking number, poised, smooth, wearing beautiful clothes, and two beats into the interview, she's running it. From then on the interviewer is a wooden dummy who talks if and when she wants him to. Of course, that was her background, you know, she was an actress and a model before she ever started writing novels. But that was another thing. The broads in the audience, the women in this world who buy the books, they looked at Jackie and they said, Hey! This is for real. She's been there. If she writes it, that's the way it really is. So then they bust a fallopian tube getting to the bookstore. Jackie's books sold in the millions, and turning out a moneymaking picture on a base like that was a breeze. The same broads lined up at the box office with their tongues hanging out, and the ones who were too dumb to read came along because they'd heard about it. Jackie knew exactly what they wanted, and exactly how to give it to them."

Betty's eyes narrowed. "So the best way for Darla to make her debut as a star in a movie would be in a picture based on a best-selling novel. Right?"

Meyer looked at the agent for a moment, and then laughed his high-pitched bark. He wiped a tear from his eye. "Jesus, Betty, you really are too much. You thought, aha! Now I've got him by the balls, right? Well, as I think I explained to you the last time we talked, it's the story that makes the picture, whether it's written by Harold Robbins or Aesop."

"But still," Derek said to Meyer, "if Darla were to make her first big starring appearance in a picture based on a best-selling novel, that would be the right way for her to make that start, wouldn't it?"

Meyer shrugged. "That would be one way. And as I explained to Betty the last time we talked, it'd be a good way. But it wouldn't be the only way."

"But I have to tell you, Mal," Wasserman said, "as far as I'm concerned, it *would* be the only way. I couldn't consider letting Darla do a picture based on anything less than a bestseller."

Darla saw Betty stiffen. "I think it's something we have to talk about," she said icily.

Mal Meyer glanced at Betty and then back at Wasserman, a small smile playing at one corner of his mouth.

He knows exactly what's going on between those two, Darla thought. He's probably seen it a thousand times. And he thinks it's funny.

"What I was thinking about," he said, "is a story that would be more or less based on your career. It wouldn't be a peek kind of thing at all. Not some cheap exposé of your love life, although of course there'd be a very important love theme in it. What I think would be extremely compelling would be to tell the story of what it's like emotionally for a girl to go to the top in this silly business in a very short time." He looked at her, measuring her reaction. "You know how interested the public is in this general subject area."

"Yes," Darla said. "I know."

"A lot of people think they understand what it's like," Meyer went on. "But of course they don't at all. They think it's all glamour and excitement and just one wonderful thing after another. But the truth is that for every rung of that ladder you climb, it costs you plenty. The disappointments, the physical work, the emotional exhaustion, they're all a pure bitch. I think a picture that showed the truth about that could be tremendous. And all my instincts tell me that with a really first-rate script on that theme, a picture starring Darla Dawson herself, would have people knocking the theaters' doors down."

Darla sat silently for a moment, thinking about what the producer had said.

"It seems to me that—" Wasserman began, but Darla cut him short by raising her hand.

"You know, of course," Darla said to Meyer, "that I'm under contract to UBS."

Meyer nodded. "Sure, I know it. But contracts can be broken. In a lot of cases, they *should* be broken. There was a time when the movie studios used them to put people in bondage. I remember when Warners had Natalie Wood on a piece of paper for seven years at about what you'd pay your maid. Less, for Christ's sake. And now the networks are doing the same thing, and in some ways it's a lot worse." Without looking at his secretary, Meyer held out his cup in her general direction and Sharon quickly got to her feet and refilled the cup.

"You think about it," Meyer went on, "and you'll see that for what you're giving UBS, you're getting screwed. For pure hard work, you're in a medium that compares to the old 'B' movies. Every five or six shooting days, they turn out a new one, right? And then after six weeks of squeezing your brains out, they give you a week or two off. During which you're expected to do guest shots, and make publicity appearances, and what-the-hell-ever. And then you go back to busting your gut for six more weeks. And what are you getting for it?" He held up a meaty hand. "Don't tell me, because I already know. It's around five thousand per episode, right? So they shoot twenty-six new shows a year, and you make a hundred thirty thousand dollars." He paused. "Now a lot of people would say, what the hell. You only work half a year, what could be wrong with that?"

"I'm sure that's exactly how they'd see it," Darla said.

"Okay, but look at it this way," Meyer continued. " 'The Witches' is the top-rated show on television. And mostly, it gets those ratings because of Darla Dawson. Right? Sure. You know it, and I know it, and you can be goddamn sure the network knows it, too." He looked at her closely. "Have you ever stopped to think what 'The Witches' means to UBS in terms of grosses? Well, let me tell you about it. There are six minutes of commercial time per show. That's twelve thirty-second commercials that UBS jams down the viewer's throat every Thursday night. Average cost to the advertiser? Seventy thousand bucks a pop. And there are fifty-two weeks in the year. Let's say the show gets pre-empted a couple of times and that there's a total of fifty telecasts. Try that on your pocket calulator."

"It's a lot of money," Darla said.

"The gross," said Meyer, "is forty-two million dollars a year. Less what it costs those gonifs Zander and Cohen to produce the show." He laughed. "And you can be damn sure that's something short of forty-two million. Then take out network operating costs and whatever the hell else the accountants can dream up to confuse the IRS, and when you get all through it still takes a large truck to haul the profits to the bank. My educated guess is that UBS's take is around fourteen million."

Darla was fascinated. She had heard these figures, or close approximations of them, discussed before, but never in this context. She had never attempted to equate her importance to the show and her compensation from it with the series' overall revenues.

Meyer drained his coffee cup and set it on the table before him. "So now look at your hundred thirty grand a year."

Darla took a deep breath. "What you're saying is absolutely true, Mal. But remember, only a short time ago, I was a nobody running around on casting calls, no different from ten thousand other girls in L.A."

"Uh-huh. And so all of a sudden, pow. You're the hottest thing in the business. But let me ask you this." His voice softened. "How much time have you got?"

A jumble of thoughts flashed through Darla's mind. She saw a closeup of the tiny lines under her eyes, each one microscopically deeper than it had been a year ago. She saw herself lying on her back each morning, her legs feeling heavier as she bicycled them in the air. She saw the date of her dreaded, monumental thirtieth birthday, now only a few months away. And then, crazily, she saw Cathy Drake's smooth, unlined face. "I really don't know," she replied. "But I expect that in a couple more weeks I can start going after character parts."

Meyer grinned appreciatively. "Terrific. And hey, no offense. That was just my smooth, unsubtle way of telling you to get it while you can. You hang around TV long enough and one day you wake up nowhere. You've given that fucking tube everything you've got, and what's it done for you? It's paid you back a fraction of what it's made from you, and zap! You're an old lady." He leaned forward and scratched his bare foot. "You know, the numbers show you that TV is a hell of a moneymaker. It really is. But not for the talent, comparatively speaking. It pays you a lot, but nothing compared to what it makes off you. It's the greatest revenue producer in the history of entertainment, but the guys who make the money from it are the ones who own it— not the entertainers. That's why the best advice I can give you is get the hell out of TV and make movies. If you've got what it takes, and I think you have, that's where the big dough is."

The telephone rang and Sharon Peterson answered it.

She covered the mouthpiece with her hand. "Ralph Saltonstall at the Chase."

Meyer nodded absently. "Tell him I'm in the shower. I'll meet him at his club—what is it, the Union?—for lunch at one o'clock."

When Sharon had relayed the message into the telephone, the producer smiled at his visitors. "And now, everybody, having enthralled you all with my boundless wisdom, it's time for me to get into my overalls." He scratched his jaw. "I may even shave, in honor of the Chase Manhattan Bank."

"What kind of timetable do you have, Mal?" Betty asked. "Provided everything is agreeable, and we can work out a satisfactory resolution of Darla's contractual obligations to UBS, when do you think you'd actually want to go into production?"

"Before the end of the year," Meyer replied. "Getting under way before January first would have favorable tax implications." He smiled at Darla's manager. "Right, Derek?"

Wasserman nodded. "Yes, of course."

Meyer got to his feet and stretched. "Jesus, I'm hungry." He patted his belly. "When I go off this goddamn diet I'm going to put it all right back on again in one shot at La Cote Basque." He looked at Darla. "How about you, honey—you don't look as if you have any trouble with weight."

Darla laughed. "Don't kid yourself. I have to work on it."

"So what do you do?" Meyer asked. "Jog? Tennis? Both?"

"Both," Darla replied. "Plus another trick a tennis player friend of mine taught me. I jump rope. It's one of the most strenuous exercises there is. Just a few minutes of it at a time, a couple of times a day, can do wonders for you." She stood up, and Meyer looked at her body with frank admiration.

"Well, hey," Meyer grinned. "If that's what it does for you, I'll sure give it a try. Who's your friend—the tennis player?"

"Ted Walters," Darla answered. "Do you know him?"

"I've met him at the club," Meyer replied. He laughed. "Ted Walters—the world's greatest diplomat."

Darla smiled. "Not quite."

"You going to catch any of the matches at Forest Hills?" Meyer asked.

"I hope so," Darla said.

"The finals should be terrific," Meyer remarked. "This is the real showdown year between Walters and Dumas. And as an authority on tennis, and a shrewd bettor, I expect to lose my ass, as usual."

Darla laughed. "Never bet against Ted Walters or the New York Yankees."

"When do you think we might have a slightly more definitive talk?" Derek asked the producer.

"I don't know," Meyer replied casually. "Whenever you have a better idea of Darla's situation with the network and the series, you know?"

"I'll call you," Betty said, "when Darla and I have discussed it further."

Meyer stretched again. "Yeah, sure. Call me anytime. But if you're interested, you better not screw around too long. I've got a lot to do before the end of the year if we're going to make a picture. In the meantime, I've got other things going."

"So have we," Derek said, a touch of superciliousness in his tone. "In fact, we have a number of very good offers."

The producer grinned. "Yeah. So Betty tells me."

Wasserman opened his mouth and shut it without speaking.

There he goes again, Darla thought, as she studied Meyer. He doesn't miss a trick.

As they filed out the door, Meyer shook hands with Darla warmly. "Nice talking to you."

"Thanks, Mal," Darla replied. "I enjoyed it too."

"Hope we can get together."

Darla smiled. "May I ask you something?"

Meyer continued to hold her hand. "Sure. What is it?"

"Did you go to Harvard?"

The high-pitched crack of laughter filled the room. "Harvard? Hell, no. Dartmouth. And my senior year we whipped Harvard's ass twenty-one to nothing. Game was at Cambridge, too. I scored twice."

"I'll bet you were shy and modest, even in those days," Betty said.

Meyer ignored her. He bent down and kissed Darla gently on the tip of her nose. At the same time, he gave her buttocks a pat. " 'Bye, love."

As Darla walked through the door she realized she hadn't minded the pat at all. Somehow it had instantly brought Dante Corelli to mind. And tonight, she reminded herself, would be the night.

Chapter 43

Ted Walters was tired. It had taken him nearly three hours to dispose of Arturo Estranza, the doggedly patient, soft-stroking Spaniard from the Costa del Sol, the man sports writers called "the human backboard." Ted's fatigue was more a result of frustration than of his physical labors on the court, because Estranza played the kind of tennis Ted loathed. The Spaniard had no real game of his own, no attack modus, but simply played a persistently passive style, waiting for his opponent to make the mistakes that were, for the world-class boomers who dominated the modern game, inevitable. Typically, Walters had refused to alter his play in the least for this match, although had he done so, had he played a more canny, mixed game, he might have had less trouble with the short, swarthy young man.

Beaten now, Estranza was exhausted. His shoulders sagged in the sweat-sodden white shirt he invariably wore, although the tradition of whites-only had long ago been swept aside at Forest Hills as at all the other great tennis centers of the world, including the stuffiest of them all, Wimbledon. Face streaming, black hair a wet mat above his craggy brow, legs trembling, Estranza was still a gentleman. His broad brown face broke into a toothy grin, and he trotted gamely to the net to shake Walters's hand as the crowd roared its approval of his sportsmanship and his unbreakable courage. "Nice match, Ted," he panted in heavily accented English. "You make me run so hard."

"I make *you* run?" Walters said as they walked off the court together. "Crazy fucking spic, you like to wore my legs off."

As he stood mopping his face with a towel, Ted thought of the audience's reaction to the match. Typically, they had not applauded him for winning, but had cheered Estranza for giving him a battle. When Ted had forced them to yell with sheer excitement as he made a seemingly impossible return, or when one of his patented thundering shots had gone down the line at something over a hundred miles an hour, just ticking the inside corner in a breathtaking display of precision that contradicted his awesome power, their reaction was grudging as well as involuntary, and he knew it. And when one of Ted's shots had gone out, or when Estranza had trickled one of his cheap, pisspot lobs just barely over the net and Ted had stretched his gut running but could not quite get to it, then the crowd was savagely exultant, deeply gratified to see the detested, arrogant Walters lose a point. Well, as always, he had one reaction to all that. Fuck 'em.

The loudspeaker boomed the official score of the match, but Walters did not listen. He looked around the ridiculously small stadium, with its capacity of only fourteen thousand, checking the crowd for beautiful women out of long ingrained habit, wondering as he always did when he played here how this place had ever become the mecca of American tennis, the site at the end of each summer of the most important tournament in the United States, and one of the two most important in the world. Besides its Lilliputian dimensions, the stadium's layout was lousy, its facilities for everyone from the players to the officials to the sportswriters were hopelessly inadequate, and to top it all off, the one thousand or so members of the West Side Tennis Club did not much give a damn whether this prestigious event took place here or not. As a matter of fact, as several of them had let Ted and the other pros know, they resented the whole business, being forced each year to give up their club for two weeks to a horde of subway-borne riffraff who, to their disgust, had developed a rapidly increasing interest in a game which for nearly a century had traditionally belonged to people of the upper classes alone.

Television had had a lot to do with those changes, Ted thought as he looked up at the platform mounted midway up one side of the stands, on top of which two cameras and their operators crouched like some battery of space-age artillery. Television had brought changes in many things having to do with how people lived and what their interests were. And yet now there was a whole generation of adults who had never known a time when there was no TV. In fact Ted Walters was one of them.

"You did okay," Jack Mansfield, his manager, said.

"Yeah." Ted swished water around in his mouth and spat it out. "But it took too goddamn long to blow him off. The guy's not that good."

"So, then, why not listen to me once in a while?" Mansfield asked patiently. "If you'd played him the way I told you to, you would have been out of here an hour ago." The manager had silver hair and a face deeply wrinkled and grained like old, worn leather from years of playing in the sun. He had competed here himself some twenty-five and twenty-six and twenty-seven years earlier, against men like Seguras and Kramer and Pancho Gonzalez, and for a tiny fraction of what a top pro made today, but Ted had never heard him express the slightest resentment of that. Discussing it once, late one night in a London pub, he had merely sloughed it off in response to Ted's question. "It was just timing, like with a lot of things. I played before the money was big, but I've got nothing to complain about. Tennis has been good to me."

Ted grinned at Mansfield now. "What the hell would I want to listen to you for? That would make it too easy, wouldn't it? Then I could win without even trying. This way keeps me honest."

Mansfield's face remained sober as he draped a jacket around Ted's shoulders, but a smile played at the corners of his mouth. "You better take it easy tonight. Get some rest for a change. You're going to need it when you come up against the big boys."

"You're trying to tell me something, right, Jack?"

"I'm trying to get you to realize that everybody here has got just one ambition, and that's to knock you off. And I'll tell you something else—Dumas has never played better in his life than he's playing now."

"That supposed to scare me?"

"Nope. I only want you to take this seriously and to play smart, instead of just tough."

"Stop worrying about me, will you, Jack?" Ted teased. "And stop hinting that I ought to sleep alone, just because I'm in some Goddamn tournament. Christ, if I listened to you I'd turn into a monk or a fag or something."

Mansfield slung a bag of gear over his shoulder. "I didn't say anything like that."

"You didn't have to."

"Let's get to the showers," Mansfield said, "before you get cold. And as long as you mention it, sleeping alone now and then wouldn't hurt you, you know. This is a game of stamina today, as much as anything else. The guy who can run the longest and the hardest is going to win."

Walters swallowed some water and turned to leave the court. "So if I lose you can blame it on Sarah, okay?" He shook his head. "All you old guys have got weird ideas about sex being bad for you. Hell, a few years ago Joe Namath won the Super Bowl on a diet of Jack Daniels and cunt, and here you go harping on me just because I get lonesome at night."

A gaggle of club officials, well-wishers, and sportswriters crowded around Ted as he began making his way out of the stadium toward the clubhouse. That was another thing about this crazy, dilapidated old dump, he thought. You have to walk a couple of hundred yards right through all the fans and tennis groupies and assorted nuts just to get to the showers. Give me L.A. or Vegas or Phoenix anytime. Or damn near anyplace else, for that matter.

People shoved scraps of paper and pencils under Ted's nose. He ignored them, continuing to push his way through the crowd, paying no attention even to the girls, all of them young, many of them pretty, who implored him to notice them, to respond to them. There had been a time when he would occasionally get involved with them, the crazy kids who seemed to think there was something magical, even spiritual, about going to bed with a famous athlete or an actor or a rock star. But no longer.

Two security guards were just ahead of Ted and Mansfield, leading the way, and one was close behind, but they were not very effective against the determined crowd. "How you think you'll do tomorrow?" A fat man in a red sports jacket shouted into Ted's ear. "Terrific," Ted mumbled.

"Ted, Ted, tell me your hotel and room number," a girl screeched.

Ahead of them, Walters saw what looked like a delegation of some kind, coming across the grass. "What the hell is this?" he growled to Mansfield.

"I don't know," the manager replied. "But I see a TV camera."

Indeed, Ted observed, one of the men in the group carried a minicam. There were also several guards and a girl, and Ted vaguely recognized a couple of the other men as club officials. It was clear that whoever they were, Walters was their objective.

"Goddamn it," Ted said to Mansfield. "There weren't supposed to be any interviews until I could at least take a shower."

"Don't blame me," the manager replied. "I never gave any permission for this, whatever the hell it is."

When the two groups met, bystanders crowding close, the man holding the minicam pointed it at Ted and the others pressed in on him, one of them a young man in a bright yellow jacket with a large patch on the breast inscribed *UBS TV SPORTS*. Ted looked at him distastefully, and at the West Side Tennis Club officials, both of whom wore badges proclaiming their status, and who grinned at him like idiots. He could feel the muscles in his legs stiffening a little now, and the sharp fatigue pains beginning to shoot across his back.

The young man in the UBS jacket poked a microphone into Ted's face. The mike looked like a short black baseball bat. It was connected by a wire to a leather case apparently containing a tape recorder that hung from the man's shoulder.

"Great match today, Ted," the young man said.

Walters made no reply, but simply glared at him.

"How do you feel?" the UBS man persisted. He had a black mustache and black hair and black eyes and large, even white teeth that made him look to Ted something like a cross between a squirrel and Mark Spitz.

Ted sighed. "Beautiful. And if you don't mind, I really want to get into a shower."

It was as if he hadn't spoken at all. The young man smiled with his mouthful of teeth and said animatedly, holding the mike close, "There are a lot of excited fans of yours here today, Ted, and one of them just can't wait to meet you."

At this the club officials and another man, a short, greasy-looking type, pushed in closer, shoving the girl in the group tight against Walters. The girl was strikingly pretty, with dark hair and a dazzling smile. A large corsage was pinned to her dress.

The UBS man poked the mike between Ted and the girl and announced in a triumphant voice, "And here she is, Ted. Joanie Roberts, the newly crowned Miss New York State!"

Ted looked dully at the girl and then at the smiling UBS men. "No shit?" he said into the mike.

The UBS man looked momentarily confused, and the others seemed embarrassed, except for Miss New York State, who burst out laughing.

"It's okay, Eddie," the UBS man said to the cameraman. "We'll make a new start." To Ted he said, "Hi, Ted, how're you feeling?"

"Plenty fucking tired," Ted told him. "And if you don't get out of my way I'm going to stick that thing up your ass and you can record yourself taking a crap." He

416

pushed his way through the group and continued his struggle to get to the clubhouse.

The West Side Tennis Club never made any concession to the world-ranked players who competed in its annual tournament. The players used the same lockers and the same showers as the members, all of them mingling together in a forced cameraderie enjoyed by few of the members and none of the competitors. Ted strode up to the crowded clubhouse, a half-timbered stucco structure which had been erected in 1924, when the club moved from the West Side of Manhattan, from whence came its name, to what was then the semibucolic expanse of Forest Hills. He ignored the greetings, remarks, and catcalls of the people who jammed the dining tables set out on the terrace, entered the old building, and climbed the stairs. Pulling his shirt off as he went, he finished undressing when he reached the lockers on the second floor.

There was the usual jocular chatter in the shower as several players jibed at one another. Estranza was already there, and he grinned as Ted stepped into the steaming room.

"You did okay today, huh?" a man said to Ted. He had gray hair and blotchy, reddish skin that hung in loose folds from his belly.

Walters ignored all of them, simply standing still as the hot water beat on his skin, his face upturned to the jet, feeling the heat slowly soak into his stiff, tired muscles, his aching joints. There was a blister on his right big toe and it stung as the water coursed over it. Ted cursed the shoes he had worn that afternoon. They were too new and too little-used to be worn in a match like today's. He thought about the match itself then; he was still wound up mentally and emotionally, unable to push it out of his mind. He knew from years of experience in competition that there was only one way to do that, only one way to forget about the day's play, and that was to let it run its course in his memory, replaying shot after shot, volley after volley, until at last it would leave him alone.

Half an hour later he walked out of the shower feeling great. The big toe was still a little sore, but a dab of Polysporin and a Band-Aid would fix that. As for the stiffness and fatigue, he had flushed them away with gallons of steaming water, had washed them down the drain, and he was no more tired now than he would have been if he had spent the afternoon lying in a hammock. The match, too, was gone, exorcised from his mind by his mental replaying of it, and in its place was an enthusiasm for the evening ahead, even an eagerness for the next day's match. His ability to rebound like this, he knew, was due principally to two things: he was young, and he was in superb condition. What he did not acknowledge, on the other hand, was that this almost magical faculty would not last forever. He could intellectualize the idea, true enough, but emotionally he could not grasp it, could not accept the thought that a time would come when he could not pound an opponent into the clay or the grass of the Har-Tru and then raise hell all night and be fresh and ready for another match the next day. Sometimes, practicing with Mansfield, he would be amazed by the brief flashes of power and deftness the older man could occasionally call up, as if he had reached back into his youth for what few dregs of greatness remained there, as if he was playing from memory, as if for a fleeting moment Mansfield's hair was black and his belly was flat and his legs were as strong as Walters's, as if it was 1950 and he was laying his big serve straight down the great Jack Kramer's throat. But then Ted would force the manager to run, and would roar with laughter as a moment later Mansfield became again a middle-aged man, shaking his head, sweat dripping from his chin, fighting for breath. But identify with that? Understand that someday he, Walters, would be in his fifties, unable to go at full tilt for as long as he pleased? Impossible. That was something that could never happen.

Ted toweled dry as he stepped to his locker. He pulled on pants and a sports shirt, then carefully administered to his abraded toe.

"Great match today, Ted," a club member said.

418

"Thanks," Walters replied, without looking up.

"Hope you have a good day tomorrow," the man said.

Ted did not reply to this, but concentrated on sticking a Band-Aid over the reddish hole in his toe.

"Hope you fall on your ass," a second voice said in a heavy French accent.

Walters looked up, feigning surprise. "Dumas? You still here? I heard you got eliminated by that Doctor What's-her-name. The one who had her cock amputated."

Despite himself, Dumas flushed deeply as several bystanders guffawed. "Smart shit," he mumbled.

"Hey, that's very good," Walters said. "After you learn English, you learn tennis, huh?"

"I learn *you*," Dumas countered. "Wait and see."

Ted grinned. He hadn't lost his touch, his ability to get Dumas highly pissed without even trying. The French star looked to be in great shape, he noted, a little huskier, a little more mature than the last time he'd seen him. The man's jaw seemed squarer, and the dark brown eyes appeared steadier, their owner more sure of himself when he fixed you with them. He would be some handful, Ted thought, enjoying the idea, relishing the prospect of facing the frog again. He sat down on a bench and pulled on socks and loafers as Dumas moved away.

Mansfield dropped onto the bench beside him. "The reporters are waiting," he said quietly. "Let's get out there and get it over with."

"Or let's skip the whole fucking thing," Ted replied.

The manager shook his head. "You can't do that, and anyhow, those guys are working for a living, just like you and me."

"So?" Walters stood up. "I didn't ask them to be sportswriters. And besides," he needled Mansfield, "if they were worth a shit they'd be real reporters." He moved toward the press area.

As with virtually every other facility of the West Side Tennis Club, the room in which interviews took place was inadequate. In fact, it was not even a room, but a

419

partially enclosed second-floor verandah just off the locker room, overlooking the terrace and the grass courts, an improvisation, actually, for this purpose. No more than fifteen feet square, it was jammed to its limit with writers and photographers. Patiently, for him, Ted entered the verandah, Mansfield trailing, and moved to its center. As soon as they saw him, the reporters, two or three females among them, began to pour out a stream of questions.

Walters held up both hands and looked at the floor, his mouth clamped firmly shut, holding the attitude until the babble finally subsided. When the room became reasonably quiet he looked up, dropping his hands. "Okay, here's what we'll do. So we're not here all night, I'll point to you, one at a time, and you can ask a question. Okay?"

"Who are you," a man from *Sports Illustrated* cracked. "The President?"

"I didn't know he played," Walters answered. He pointed at Cal Josephson of *The New York Times,* and nodded.

"How come you had such a tough time with Estranza today?" Josephson asked.

"Man plays a very controlled game," Walters answered. "He makes you run, forces you to make mistakes. Smart tennis player." Out of the corner of his eye he saw Mansfield nod approval. He pointed toward another writer, a man he did not recognize.

"Crumanski won today," the man said. "So you play him tomorrow. How do you think you'll do?"

"Okay, I hope," Walters replied, straight-faced.

"What I mean is," the man persisted, "your record against him is spotty. He's beaten you a number of times, but never in an important tournament. Do you think he has a chance tomorrow?"

"Sure he does," Walters said. "Hell, yes. Crummy is a very emotional guy, and sometimes he gets too high, too up, and he blows a match he should win. Technically, he's as good as anybody in the game."

"Including you?" somebody asked.

"Sure." Ted nodded. "Like I said, he's as good as anybody. Trouble is, he's a pop-off."

"Also like you?" another voice asked.

Walters smiled. He was feeling damned good, and Crumanski was a friend of his, and he was looking forward to dinner with Sarah and raising a little hell. "Sure, just like me. We are two of the world's great motor-mouths."

They laughed appreciatively, and then Bill Vance of the *Daily News* asked the question that all of them wanted to hear Walters answer.

"You think you can beat Dumas?"

Ted shrugged, affably, having anticipated the question as much as his audience had. "I've beaten him before."

"Sure," Vance countered. "But you haven't played him in some time. He went out of Wimbledon with an injury, but now he's going great."

"Beautiful," Ted said. "If we both make the finals, should be a good match."

A laugh went up at this. Virtually all of the world's top tennis players were in this tournament, but nobody, among the press or the fans or the players themselves, had any illusions about who the two finalists would be. Barring injury or some fluke upset, Walters and Dumas would be at each other's throats, going all out for the money, the glory, the number one world ranking. Fuck the other guy, leave him for dead. This was the game's ultimate showdown, the heavyweight championship bout.

"A lot of people think Dumas has more stamina than you have," Vance probed.

"At what?" Walters answered innocently.

They laughed again, including, Ted noted, the women reporters. One of them was kind of cute. Well-built, athletic-looking herself. Probably with some ladies' magazine like *WomenSports*. He pointed to her.

The girl asked a trite question. "Do you think women players ought to get the same recognition and the same prize money as men?"

Walters looked her straight in the eye. "Absolutely," he said earnestly. "All my life, I have been a very big tit man."

The men howled, the women looked indignant, and Jack Mansfield covered his face with his hand. The interview was over.

Downstairs on the terrace, Ted found Sarah Winchester sitting at a table with a group of players and their wives and girlfriends. They were a handsome group, suntanned and healthy and happy, enjoying a drink together, laughing and bantering. They were glad that the day was over and that they could relax now in the beginning of the evening, absorbing the ambience of the crowded clubhouse, appreciating the breeze that swept toward them from across the expanses of manicured grass, the courts as cool and green as emeralds in the last rays of the sun.

Ted pushed into a seat next to Sarah. "Hi, love."

She kissed his cheek lightly. "I thought Estranza was going to wear you out," she greeted him. "I was worried about you."

"Never fear," Ted replied. He waved in response to the greetings from the others at the table. Crumanski was there, and Bill Stoddard, and Deseaux, and their women. Stoddard's girl was some chunk, Ted was reminded as he smiled at her. A pair of boobs that wouldn't quit, and an invitation written all over her face every time she looked at him. What the hell was her name? Jean, he remembered. She was from Texas. Well, now, he'd get to her, sooner or later.

A waitress hurried by and Ted grabbed her arm. She was a cute blonde, obviously a college girl in a summer job that would end shortly. "What's your name, honey?"

"Connie," she smiled.

"Okay, Connie," Ted said. "Your assignment is to see that there is never a time when I don't have a cold beer in front of me."

"Count on me," Connie replied pleasantly, and scurried off.

"It's a drag joint," Crumanski was saying in his barely understandable English. "Only what is unusual is it's both kinds. The women are men and the men are women and nobody knows what anybody is. What is more, nobody give a shit."

"Where is it?" Stoddard asked.

"Greenwich Village," Crumanski replied. He was dark-skinned and shaggy, his uneven features constantly scowling, even when he was in a good mood. "You should go there," he said to Stoddard. "In that place, even you could get laid."

Stoddard smiled happily. He was from Florida, a tall, good-looking boy, invariably good-natured. "That's wonderful, Crummy," he drawled. "I'll make a note of it."

Walters laughed at their chatter, their endless needling, feeling relaxed and expansive. Connie brought him a frosty bottle of Michelob, and he drained it in one long gulp, ordering another before the girl could so much as move away from the table.

"How do you feel?" Sarah asked him solicitously. "Are you tired?"

"Hell, no. What's to be tired from?" Ted liked Sarah, found her comfortable and easy to take, a great convenience on the tour because she was a good lay who didn't bug him, and she was always friendly and even-tempered, suffering silently when he went into one of his occasional black moods, supporting him unflinchingly even when he was at his most boorish, holding her tongue while he insulted anyone who came within striking distance, including her. She had also learned to look the other way when Ted occasionally got himself involved with another girl, a random piece he would stumble across, to be enjoyed briefly in whatever part of the world he might be competing in, a girl who would be forgotten as soon as he climbed into an airplane for the next tournament, wherever it might be.

Connie returned to the table with another beer and this one Ted drank slowly, looking around at the crowd on the terrace, at the well-dressed men and women, many of whom were staring at him, a phenomenon that had long ago become commonplace to him. He glanced at his watch, the solid gold Rolex that had been one of the prizes he had won at Cannes the year before. Almost seven o'clock. Damn, he was getting hungry. Tomorrow, Crumanski. He smiled as he thought about the terrible-tempered one who sat across from him now, trading jibes with anyone who would listen. Tomorrow. Would Darla come out tomorrow? He thought about her, saw her face before him, smiling up at him, saw the mass of blonde hair, the startling violet-blue eyes, cool and yet friendly, heard her speak to him in that crazy way of hers, a baffling combination of naive, innocent kid and world-wise, sophisticated woman. Jesus Christ—would he ever get over this? Mooning after that broad like some silly, love-struck teenager? Counting days until he'd see her again, thinking about the times they'd made love, aching with the memory of what it was like to be inside that beautiful body. Damn. He couldn't believe that a woman—any woman—could make him feel like this.

Connie was back again, this time with a folded sheet of paper that she handed to him. Walters took it from her desultorily. This was another thing he was used to: the scribbled invitation from some female or other who wanted to share his bed. He unfolded the paper and scanned the words on it.

To his surprise, the message was printed in a bold, masculine hand. *Very important you talk with me at once. I am in the bar. Frank DiNero.*

Frank DiNero? Who the hell was Frank DiNero? It took Ted several seconds to connect the name with a face, an identity, but then he had it. DiNero—Mr. Dark Glasses, the Vegas gambler who had tried to proposition him. What was DiNero doing here now? Attending the matches, of course, just as a lot of other gamblers were. What was so surprising about that? Walters crumpled the paper into a ball and thrust it into a trouser pocket.

"What is it?" Sarah asked, smiling. "Invitation from a fan?"

"No." Ted hesitated. "It's nothing. Just a guy I

know." He decided to ignore the note, at first. But a minute later his curiosity got the better of him. Feeling ambivalent, but wondering what DiNero thought was so important, Ted got to his feet and walked casually into the clubhouse.

The gambler was easy to spot, standing in the crush at the bar looking slightly out of place in this crowd, his face nearly obscured by the inevitable sunglasses.

Ted pushed his way in until he was alongside DiNero. He didn't look at him, but held his gaze forward, as if, like the others there, he was trying to attract the attention of one of the harassed bartenders. "What's up?" he said.

"I got something for you," the gambler replied.

"What?"

"The deal we talked about."

Ted froze. What the hell was this? He kept his eyes straight ahead.

"It's set," DiNero said.

"I don't know what you're talking about," Ted growled.

"Yes, you do," DiNero said. "One big one, already there, in your name. After the final, all you got to do is pick it up. I'll tell you how, after."

"After what, for Christ's sake?"

DiNero's voice lowered to the point that it was barely discernible over the babble in the crowded bar. "After you lose."

Ted clenched his teeth. He wanted to slug the gambler, to bust his mouth for him. But he couldn't, didn't dare. Wouldn't that give that goddamned mob of reporters something to write about. "Get out of here," he hissed. "Get the fuck out of here."

"Sure," DiNero said. "I was just leaving. But remember. It's set."

"Out," Ted commanded.

"You'll see," DiNero said. "You'll see." He melted away in the crowd.

"Problem?" Sarah smiled when Ted returned to the table.

"No problem," he replied tersely. Goddamn it, he could kill that slimy son of a bitch. What the hell did he mean, "You'll see"? He finished the last of his beer and then abruptly stood up, pulling Sarah with him. "Catch you guys later," he said to the group at the table. "I'm hungry." He made his way from the terrace, leading Sarah by the hand. From joyful exuberance, his mood had gone to black, unreasoning anger.

Chapter 44

Darla showered and put on fresh bikini pants, then sprayed antiperspirant under her arms. She dabbed Joy on her neck and her breasts, and admonished herself for her schoolgirl nervousness as she stood in front of the full-length mirror and giggled like a damned fool. "You are an idiot," she said aloud to the image in the glass. "You are too short to be a top model, and in fact you are too short to be any kind of a model. Your tits are too small, and you're getting old, and how the hell did you ever get to where you are, anyway? But for that matter, where are you? I'll tell you where. You're in the most exciting city in the world, and you're about to explore it with one of the most interesting men in the world, and tomorrow you can worry about wrinkles and calories and pounds and whether your bosoms sag, and tonight, the hell with it." She put on a pale lemon-yellow silk dress and slipped her feet into ballet slippers and stared again at her reflection. "Okay," she said. "What we need now is for nobody in this goddamn city to know I'm Darla Dawson." Carefully, she tied her hair into a coiled mass on top of her head, and then she pulled a large straw hat down over it. There, she said to herself. Garbo, by God. Aloud, she muttered, "I want to be alone." And giggled again. To top off her disguise, or at least her means of assuming anonymity, she put on dark glasses. More than the costume itself, the notion of dressing up in something special, something mysterious, added greatly to her excitement, her sense of expectation.

Darla told Bob Murphy she wouldn't be needing him and took the elevator to the lobby. To her delight, the men who passed her studied her face and her body with appreciative expressions, but none showed any sign of recognizing her. Even the women, who gave her the usual close scrutiny, failed to realize who she was. There you are, she told herself. Take away the Darla Dawson hairdo and what have you got? Just another dope with hot pants looking to have a hell of a good time in New York with a fascinating guy.

As many times as she had imagined seeing Dante again, as many times as she had tried to envision his appearance, the actual sight of him standing in the lobby waiting for her nearly took her breath away. His skin had been tanned by the summer sun to a deep brown color, and his teeth looked even whiter than when she had seen him last. He seemed taller to her, too, and bigger, and yet just as trim, and she noticed that his thick, carefully groomed, jet-black hair was a little longer. He wore an open-necked sport shirt, a thin gold chain gleaming at his neck, and a straw-colored linen sports jacket. The instant he saw her, he broke into a broad grin, and as he held open his arms to her, Darla thought she had never seen a more attractive man.

"My disguise didn't fool you a bit," she said as he held her against his hard, muscular body.

"That's because I'm not a sight hound," he said. "I'm a scent hound. I'd know your unique combination of Joy and pussy anywhere."

Darla punched his arm. "Dante! You are lascivious."

"Right," he agreed. "Aren't you glad?"

"To tell you the truth," Darla replied as he took her arm and guided her toward the doors onto Central Park South, "I was counting on it."

The evening started in high gear and never slowed for a moment. They went to the Heliport Club atop the Pan Am building for drinks and to watch the dazzling panorama of New York on a summer evening as twilight turned to night with a million lights twinkling and gleaming, sipping Stolichnaya so cold it was viscous, so cold it made Darla's throat ache as she swallowed it.

"It's the only real Russian vodka sold in America," Dante explained. "And the reason you can get it here now is that the Russians made an exchange agreement with Pepsico. Can you imagine that, for Christ's sake? They send us the best vodka in the world so that they can drink Pepsi-Cola."

"Everybody to his own taste," Darla said, feeling marvelously silly, "as the man said who kissed the cow."

Dante looked at her with mock seriousness. "What the hell do you know about kissing cows? Have you been messing around behind my back with some cow?"

"Don't knock it if you haven't tried it," Darla retorted.

Dante's voice softened and he placed one large hand on her thigh. "Tonight we try everything."

Darla felt herself responding to his touch. My god, she thought, control yourself. The night's just getting started.

From the Heliport Club they went to Maxwell's Plum, and stood crushed among the crowd of jaunty singles who cruised the bar looking for action. The sound level in the place was fantastic, Darla thought, an unrelenting roar of conversation punctuated with the clink of glasses and high-pitched laughter. "Is it always like this?" Darla asked. She had to shout so Dante could hear her question.

He shook his head. "This is unusual. Most of the time it's a hell of a lot busier."

Darla looked wonderingly at the funky decorations, the light from the Tiffany lamps casting a multicolored glow in all directions, and at the boisterous young people who moved in search of one another, the women as aggressive in their prowling as the men. "How do you know so much about New York?" she asked Dante.

He bent and spoke into her ear so that she could hear above the din. "It's really more or less my base now. I spend more time here than any other place."

"Do you have an apartment?"

"Yes, a suite in the Waldorf Towers." He pulled her against him. "Want to come up and see my collection of genuine Mongolian dildos?"

"Not until you feed me." Darla laughed. "And by the way, I'm starved. When do we have dinner?"

"Dinner? Already? How can we have dinner when we're not even drunk yet?"

From Maxwell's they went to Thursday's, which to Darla's astonishment was even louder and more crowded. She stood on tiptoe and Dante cocked his head to hear her. "Are there any quiet places in New York?"

"Christ, I hope not," he rejoined. "Quiet places aren't good for you. They remind you that someday you're going to be quiet forever, whether you like it or not. Give me a noisy joint anytime. Complete with bawdy wenches in low-cut dresses and the booze flowing in rivers."

A young man standing next to Dante was staring at her, Darla suddenly realized. Having long since discarded the dark glasses, she wondered if she had been recognized. The young man was tall and slim and wore a droopy mustache. Darla was about to change her position, to turn away from his gaze, when she grasped that he wasn't actually looking at her at all, but was merely glassy-eyed drunk.

The young man roused himself and leaned unsteadily toward Dante. "Hey, pal, how'd the Yankees do?"

"They won." Dante smiled. "Three to one."

The young man nodded somberly. "That's terrific," he said. "That's really terrific." He was silent for a moment, reflecting, no doubt, on the satisfaction of a New York victory. He looked at Dante again. "Who'd they play?"

Dante grinned. "Red Sox."

"New York is a baseball town, isn't it?" Darla remarked to Dante. She liked their having to press close to each other to be heard. Dante's smell was a wonderful combination of soap and after-shave lotion and man.

"New York is an everything town," he replied. "It's a

baseball town, and a basketball town, and a football town, and a soccer town, and a town where you can find any sport that turns you on. Hell, there are even cockfights in New York, if you know where to go."

Darla was surprised. "Cockfights? I thought they were illegal."

"Since when does legality have anything to do with it, except to speed up the action?"

"I've never seen one," Darla said. "A cockfight."

"God almighty." Dante sighed. "You have indeed led a provincial life."

Thirty minutes later a cab deposited them in front of a tumble-down tenement building in East Harlem. A group of ragged youths was playing cards on an up-ended packing crate in the yellow gleam of a street lamp. Dante called one of the boys aside and spoke to him briefly. The boy nodded and said something in a lilting Spanish accent. Darla saw Dante slip some crumpled bills into the boy's hand and then they followed him down the street and into an alley. They stopped in front of a door and the boy knocked softly. When the door opened a crack the boy spoke into the opening and Dante passed another bill and they were quickly inside.

Darla saw that they had entered a huge basement room, dank and musty, lighted by a single cluster of bulbs that hung from the ceiling. A large crowd of Latin-looking men surrounded a circular pit under the lights, the glare casting fantastic shadows that flickered across the swarthy faces. Many of the men held money in their hands, folded bills clutched between the fingers of their fists. Their speech was a babble of Spanish, rapid and highly animated. It seemed to Darla that they alternated between shouting and arguing and laughing, hostile and menacing one instant, friendly and jovial the next. The air was heavy with acrid tobacco smoke from the slim dark cigarettes many of the men were smoking, and the place stank of the smoke and the men's sweat and a fetid mixture of garlic and stale food. Some of the men drank a colorless liquid from bottles.

Dante nodded toward the circular pit and Darla followed his gaze to where a grinning man with a gold tooth stood holding a fighting cock next to his face. The bird was reddish brown, its comb and wattle as red as fresh blood, its black eyes snapping in its feral head. The man whispered something to the bird and then raised his clenched right fist and shouted a phrase in Spanish. At this a roar went up from the crowd and across the pit a second man appeared, also holding a fighting cock. This bird was lighter in color, and looked to Darla to be slightly larger than the other.

For the next several minutes a confusing procedure took place, which Darla understood was somehow ritualistic, as one of the handlers and then the other would hold his bird aloft, and then would place the creature onto the sand surface of the pit, each move underscored by shouts from the crowd. As this routine unfolded, the excitement among the men increased, until the tension in the vast, gloomy room seemed at the breaking point, and the sound became a roar.

Fascinated, Darla shivered. She was grateful to feel Dante's arm encircle her as they watched the men and the birds in the pit. Now the men were fastening curved knives of gleaming steel to the cocks' spurs, and the shouts of the crowd seemed near frenzy as the tempo of their wagering increased.

A third man, tiny and brown, looking himself like one of the fierce fighting birds, entered the pit and spoke briefly to each of the handlers. He raised his hand, holding it poised for a moment like a guillotine blade at the apex of its travel, and then swung it downward. At this the handlers released the cocks. They flew at each other in a blur of feathers and flashing steel blades.

The earlier excitement was nothing to what took place now. The men screamed unendingly, shaking fists in the air, pounding each other on backs and shoulders, their eyes riveted to the battle in the pit. The birds whirled and slashed at each other in a maelstrom of fury, and Darla found that despite the wave of nausea that swept over her, she could not look away.

The larger bird, the lighter-colored one, suddenly

slowed in its attack, staggered drunkenly, and flopped onto the sand, a dark, glistening stain spreading slowly among the feathers of its breast. The bird's handler sprang to it and scooped it up. He held the bird's head to his mouth and sucked at its comb as the crowd continued its frenzied screaming. To Darla's horror, the man then opened his mouth and took the mortally wounded cock's entire head inside it, holding it there for several seconds.

Miraculously, the battered bird seemed to recover a little. The handler quickly returned it to the floor of the pit and leaped back. There was a brief flurry as the reddish brown cock rejoined the battle, and then the wounded bird lay dead, a bundle of ragged, blood-soaked feathers.

"I think," Darla whispered into Dante's ear over the screams of the spectators, "I may get sick."

Outside, the fresh air was cool and clean and the relative quiet of the street was almost eerie. The young men continued to play their game of cards on the improvised packing-case table, and it occurred to Darla that leaving the cockfight was like awakening from a strange dream. She could hardly believe what she had seen moments earlier.

Dante led her to the nearest corner and a minute later flagged down a cab. "Go to the Carlyle," he instructed the driver as he settled onto the seat beside her and slammed the door. He looked at Darla's pale face and grinned. "I believe we could use a drink."

"You must be crazy," the cabbie said over his shoulder as they rattled southward on Lexington Avenue. His accent sounded to Darla exactly like Heather Fink's. "Coming up here at night."

"How about you?" Dante responded. "You were here too, weren't you?"

"So I'm crazy too," the man said. "Take your life in your hands every time you come up here. 'Specially after dark. Lot of cabbies won't do it, you know? Somebody wants to go to Harlem, black or Spanish Harlem, either one, forget it. Liable not to get back, you know? Some of these guys, the junkies, they'll kill you for a couple of bucks. Enough for a fix, you know? That's all they want."

Dante put his arm around Darla and held her close.

"I been driving a cab in New York thirty-three years," the cabbie went on. "Was a time when a lot of people liked to go up to Harlem at night, go to places like the Cotton Club, Small's Paradise, you know? Hear the music, bands like Lucky Millinder and Cab Calloway, everybody always had a good time and never no trouble. Now you come up here and you don't know what the hell is going to happen." Hearing no response from his passengers, he settled into a morose silence as he steered the clattering vehicle around and over the potholes that pitted the surface of the streets.

Darla felt Dante's arm stiffen as he drew her closer to him and then his mouth found hers and her heart beat faster. She opened her mouth and sucked his tongue as it slid across hers, and she felt her excitement grow as his hand cupped her breast and his thumb began to slowly caress her nipple. "Dante," she whispered. "It's so good to be with you again."

"Even at a cockfight?" he teased.

Darla laughed. "Yes, damn it. Even at a cockfight. Ugh! What an experience."

"I told you you can find any sport you want in New York," Dante said. He moved his hand down her body. "Including my favorite, which is called groping in the back seat of a cab."

"Two can play at that one." Darla giggled. She reached down and squeezed him.

The cab stopped and Darla struggled to compose herself hurriedly as Dante paid the driver. A uniformed doorman took her hand and helped her to the sidewalk, then Dante took her arm and guided her into the hotel. They turned into a pleasant room that looked like a supper club, and a smiling captain showed them to a table.

Darla looked around at the crowd. They varied in age from very young to very old, but there was a sameness about them, an air of superiority, of bored restraint, that seemed to say, New York is our city, but we don't mind if you enjoy it, too.

A slim, good-looking black man was playing the piano and singing. He was doing Cole Porter, just finishing "Night and Day" and segueing into "I Get A Kick Out Of You" as Darla began to listen. He handled the great standards with mastery and insouciance, as if he had written them himself.

"That's Bobby Short," Dante said.

Darla nodded. "I've heard of him. He's good, isn't he?"

"Yeah, terrific."

"The Carlyle," Darla ruminated. "Why is the name familiar to me?"

Dante shrugged. "Maybe because it was headquarters for the Kennedy family for a long time. They kept an apartment here."

"Oh," Darla said, "that's it. Now I remember. I read about how President Kennedy would come to New York and stay here."

"Exactly," Dante said.

A waiter bowed.

"More vodka?" Dante asked.

Darla shook her head. "I think I'd like some Scotch."

"Two Chivas, on the rocks, with a little water," Dante said to the waiter, and the man hurried away. "Jack's big problem was giving the Secret Service guys the slip," Dante said to Darla.

"Why did he want to do that?"

Dante laughed. "Why do you think? Because he wanted to get laid. He was one of the biggest cocksmen ever. Certainly the biggest who ever made it to the White House. He had broads stashed all over the place."

Darla was wide-eyed. "Really? Are you sure?"

"Damn right I'm sure. You know Helen Lansberry?"

"The singer? I know who she is. I have some of her records, in fact."

"Uh-huh. And she's in one of our posters," Dante said. "She knew the prez, and very well. Told me a lot about what a baller he was."

435

Darla shook her head in wonder. "That's amazing."

"Why is it?" Dante said. "He was human, just like all the rest of us."

"I think," Darla said mischievously, "some of us are a little more human than others."

Dante smiled and brushed his lips lightly against hers.

The waiter served their drinks and they touched glasses.

"Here's to the swingers of the world," Dante said.

"I'm not sure whether I like the idea or not," Darla said as she felt the Scotch warm her belly.

"What idea?"

"Oh, you know. The President of the United States having affairs. Sure, I know what you said is true. A man is a man, and I guess President Kennedy was certainly as much of a man as any, and yet, I'd always want somebody in that position to be a little more—straight, I guess."

Dante lifted an eyebrow in amusement. "Like Nixon, for example?"

Darla grimaced in mock horror. "God, no."

"Exactly," he said. "So given a choice, I'd take a guy like Kennedy anytime, even though, if you pushed aside the charm and the style, his actual record stank."

"It did? Why?"

"The Bay of Pigs, The Berlin Wall, and sending the first troops to Vietnam," Dante replied. "Those are the things that are the real Kennedy legacy—the truth of what we have to remember him by. And if you want to know, he wasn't above making deals with some of our people, either."

Darla felt a cold chill pass through her. She sipped her Scotch and looked at Dante. Part of the great attraction he held for her, she knew, was the dark, secret part of his life, the danger it represented. Like a tiger, she thought. It's beautiful to look at, and part of its beauty is that it's strong and fierce and it can kill you.

He grinned at her now, his teeth very white in his tanned face, as if he had read her thoughts precisely, or even as if she had spoken them aloud. "It's part of what I love about you," he said. "You're the biggest thing in show business, and just one inch under the surface you're an absolute square."

Darla returned his smile, and squeezed his leg under the table. "Am I now? A square, huh?" She moved her hand up a little. "You'll see how square I am. That is, if I can keep from passing out for lack of nourishment."

Dante laughed. "Okay, baby. I'm starved, too." He signaled the waiter for a check, and a few minutes later a taxi took them twenty blocks south, to midtown Manhattan.

The restaurant was bustling and cheerful, full of fresh flowers and people who seemed to be enjoying themselves enormously. "This is lovely," Darla said as they walked in. "Is it French?"

Dante looked at her in dismay. "French? You go out with a wop and you expect French food? An Italian can't live on that stuff. Tonight you find out what it's like to really eat."

"Where are we?" Darla asked. "What's it called?"

"Mario's Villa D'Este," Dante replied. The maitre d' greeted Dante like a long-lost brother, shaking his hand warmly while with his left hand he gripped Dante's shoulder. The two men exchanged a few words of rapidly spoken Italian, and then Dante turned to Darla. "This is my friend, Miss Dawson," he said proudly as the man's eyebrows rose in recognition. "But it's a secret, you understand?"

The maitre d' bowed, his face instantly regaining its composure. "If you will come this way, Mr. Corelli, I have the best table in the house for you and your sister."

Darla had never enjoyed a meal more. There was a marvelous air of festivity, the kind that can be found in an Italian restaurant as in no other, and Mario's was one of the best. They began with clams oregano, hot and spicy, and a bottle of Frascati. The wine was round and mellow, golden in color, more fullbodied than the California or the French wines she knew.

"It's a peasant wine," Dante told her. "And it goes all the way back to the time of the Romans, as many of the Italian wines do."

Darla savored its flavor. "It's different," she said. "I like it very much."

Dante smiled, obviously pleased. "Italian wines are like Italian food, and they are both like the Italian people. Maybe not so refined as some, but more real—hearty and full of life and full of fun."

"That's wonderful," Darla said. "Because that's just how I feel tonight."

They had zuppa di pesce next, rich and flavorful with bits of whitefish and snapper and vegetables, and then an entree of veal cannelloni, the pasta as thin as paper, as delicious as anything Darla had ever tasted. She ate ravenously, to Dante's delight, and drank glass after glass of a bold red wine.

"What's this one?" Darla asked.

"Valpolicella." He smiled. "I gather you like it?"

"I love it," Darla said. "And it's making me woozy, which is wonderful." She took another bite of cannelloni. "This is heavenly," she remarked. "And I'm sure there isn't a calorie in it."

"Not a one," Dante replied. "And anyway, calories are something you think about tomorrow, or maybe the next day."

When the dishes had been cleared, a waiter moved a dessert cart to their table. It was stacked high with impossibly rich-looking confections, puddings and pastries and cakes.

"I couldn't," Darla said. "I would love to, but I just couldn't."

"There is always a way," Dante said. He spoke to one of the waiters in Italian and the man bowed and pushed the cart away. The waiter was back in a moment, this time with a table bearing a brazier and some utensils. He lighted a fire with a flourish and then with swift, deft movements, whipped eggs and wine together in a bowl over the brazier.

"What is it?" Darla asked.

"Zabaglione," Dante replied. "It's really very light,

and I think you'll be glad you had just a tiny bit of room left. The wine is Marsala, which of course is a dessert wine. Practical, hm? And also very Italian." He grinned. "You want dessert, you make it with dessert wine."

"Of course." Darla laughed. "Perfectly logical."

Dante had been correct, she decided as she tasted the first spoonful of the hot, creamy-smooth substance. She smiled at him. "It's very light and very delicious and I'm glad I saved just the tiniest bit of room."

They finished the meal with the strongest espresso Darla had ever experienced, and with thimble-sized glasses of Strega.

"My God," Darla exclaimed as she sat back on the leather banquette. "I wouldn't have believed I could do it. No wonder Italian women get rounder as they get older."

"That's not the reason," Dante said.

"What is it, then?"

"It's Italian men," he replied. "They get wiser as they get older. Then they realize that speed is not so important as comfort." He gave her side a tiny pinch and Darla jumped. "That's why you never see an Italian with a Wasp mistress." His handsome face expressed disdain. "All those bones, sticking into you."

"Is that so?" Darla said indignantly. "Well, I wouldn't want to offend you, Mister Corelli."

"Or bruise me?" he grinned.

She kicked him lightly under the table.

From that point on, the night became for Darla a kind of blur. Dante took her to a place on West Fifty-fourth Street called Eddie Condon's, where they drank more Scotch and listened to blaring, joyful Dixieland jazz. From there they went to a private club whose interior was an eerie set of angled walls clad in stainless steel, with colored lights mounted in the ceiling that flashed in an erratic pattern. The effect in combination with the pounding beat of recorded music induced something close to hypnosis, and the air was so thick with marijuana smoke you could get high just from breathing it. Sometime later they moved on to what looked like an old-fashioned saloon, jam-packed with people eating hamburgers and drinking, seemingly oblivious that the time was something close to four o'clock in the morning.

"What is this place?" Darla asked.

"It's called P.J. Clarke's."

"Oh, I've heard of it." Darla looked around. "It's kind of famous, isn't it?"

"Kind of," Dante said. "It's a New York tradition. At least, you're liable to see most anybody in here, from Andy Warhol to Jackie O, especially when it gets late."

They ordered mugs of draught Heineken and Darla found the cold beer soothing and refreshing, despite the fact that she had consumed as much alcohol that night as she ever had at one time in her life. "Is it old?" she asked. "Or did they just make it look like this?"

"Oh, it's for real, all right," Dante said. "This was a typical joint when the Third Avenue El ran right outside the door, there. The original reason it got to be an 'in' place was that *Lost Weekend* was shot here. You know, the picture where Ray Milland played a drunk?"

"Sure," Darla said. "I've seen it on late-night TV."

Dante nodded. "Milland won an Academy Award for the part. Then everybody started coming here." He smiled. "But I doubt that many people know that now, or that they care."

"So how do you know it?" Darla teased. "Do you collect trivia?"

"Of course. That's why I'm so big in the poster business. We produce a lot of trivial shit for people to hang on their walls."

"Dante!"

"Well, not really," he grinned. "Some of it's pretty good. Take yours, for instance. We must have sold several hundred copies by now."

"How would you like to get hit over the head with a beer mug?" Darla asked him.

"Not too much." He leaned over and kissed her gently. "The truth is, your poster is only the greatest seller of all time. Number one in the history of the business."

Darla was delighted. "Really? That's wonderful. How many copies?"

Dante looked at her. "Don't you read your royalty statements?"

Darla shook her head. "Derek Wasserman takes care of all that stuff. He's my manager. Looks after everything."

"Uh-huh. And who looks after Derek Wasserman?"

"What do you mean?"

"I mean, you have somebody else, don't you?"

"Well, my agent, Betty Frolich, of course."

"No," Dante said. "I mean somebody else who knows what's going on with your business."

Darla thought about the question. "Well, there's my accountant. But Derek oversees that too. He hired him, in fact."

"Yeah. And who's your lawyer?"

"I don't have one," Darla said. "That is, anything like that I need, Arnold Gross takes care of. He's Mike's lawyer, and he's very good. At least, I'm told he is."

"Yeah." Dante looked at her steadily.

"What is it?" Darla asked. "You act as if something's going on behind my back."

"There is," Dante said. "I promise you there is. I don't know what, and I don't know who's involved, and I don't know whether it's anything bad that could hurt you. But I'll tell you this, honey. Anybody who's where you are, and who's going up the way you are, has got a lot of people hanging on for the ride."

"Somebody else was telling me that," Darla said. "Just today."

"It's the truth," Dante said. "Which is why you need your own lawyer. A good one. The best you can get. And then you know what you'll have? You'll have at least one person you can trust, and who is professionally qualified to give you the advice you need, and who can head off somebody else who's trying to screw you. And somebody always will be, I guarantee it. If not straight out, then indirectly, while they're trying to get something out of you for themselves."

Darla considered what he was saying. It was true that the people around her were constantly bickering, constantly trying to maneuver her into doing things that she wasn't always so sure were in her best interests. "Maybe you're right," she said.

"You can be damn sure I am," Dante replied. "And you know how I know? Because Star Graphics has become the biggest factor in the poster industry. Of the top-selling twenty posters right now, I'd say that we produced fifteen of them and every one of them is a picture of a person or a group of people who are stars in show business. I see the same thing over and over again. In most cases," he said, putting his hand on hers, "I don't give a damn. But in your case, I care very much."

Darla nodded, knowing instinctively that what he had told her was true, that she needed advice from someone whose only purpose was to see that her business affairs were handled as well as possible. There had been a time when she was willing to leave virtually everything of a legal nature to Mike, but for some time now, she had questioned whether his judgment had been all that sound. After all, his own career wasn't doing so well, and as far as Arnold Gross was concerned, Mike did nothing but complain about what he charged was the lawyer's ineptitude. And Derek Wasserman? She thought of the number of times her manager had shoved papers in front of her to sign, and how, like a fool, she had gone right ahead and scribbled her name on them without even understanding what they were. Could she trust Derek—really trust him? Probably about as much as she could trust Betty Frolich. But how much was that?

"So tell me," she said to Dante. "How many copies have you sold?"

"Of your poster? All told, as of the beginning of this week, just over four million. Our price to the trade is a dollar, so your ten percent so far has amounted to a little more than four hundred thousand dollars. When you get back to L.A., be sure you check those figures."

"I will," Darla said. And to herself she said, you'd

better be damn sure you do. She leaned over and kissed Dante's cheek. "And now tell me something else, please. Are we going to sit here and talk business for the rest of the night?"

Dante laughed. "That wasn't exactly what I had in mind."

"I hope not," Darla said.

He held her hand to his mouth and kissed it. "I love you, Darla. And I don't want tonight to be over."

"I know."

"It's almost as if a night like this is some kind of magic—as if it didn't belong to the rest of time."

Darla smiled. "I love you, too, Dante. I feel you're one of the few people in the world who's really on my side, who isn't just one of those hangers-on you were talking about." She looked around the crowded barroom, and then returned her steady gaze to his face. "It's strange, isn't it? You want something so desperately, more than anything you can imagine, and then when you get it, you don't know what to do with it, or even why you wanted it so much. I still want to be on top, higher than I am now, higher and higher. But I no longer know why I want to, or what I'll do when I get there. The thing is, I already feel that somehow I've lost something, somewhere along the way."

Dante nodded understanding. "I think," he said, "that I want to make love to you, very much."

Dante's suite was on one of the top floors of the Waldorf Towers. Looking toward the sunrise with Dante's arms around her, Darla could see a great ship crawling slowly up the East River, and beyond that a panorama of tall buildings and smokestacks trailing white plumes, and on the horizon long streaks of pink and red and gold as dawn came to Manhattan. She felt his hands cup her breasts, and then all the passion and desire she had fought to control that night flooded through her in an exhilarating and dizzying surge. She turned and pressed her body against him.

They made love for hours, urgently at first, and then gently, but never leaving each other alone, spending the emotion and the hunger that each had been storing for the other over the months since last they had been together, and when finally Darla fell into the deep sleep of exhaustion, her body still entwined with Dante's, the morning sun was high, its warm glow streaming across them as they slept.

Chapter 45

The lounge in the Regency was nearly deserted. Always busy in the late afternoon and early evening, it tended to lose its crowd as the night wore on, and although the handsome hotel on the west side of Park Avenue was heavily booked every day of the year, its bar usually became quiet and sleepy by midnight.

At a small, dimly lit table, Betty Frolich sipped her fourth or fifth martini since dinner—she couldn't remember which—and stared at Margot Simmons through red-rimmed eyes. Margot looked lousy, Betty decided. The former actress's face was not merely thin, but gaunt. Her eyes seemed to be sunken into her head, with purplish circles under them, the pupils glazed with fatigue, or grief, or both. Betty sipped at her drink again and shivered, grateful for its effect upon her obese body. In their accepted role, Betty well knew, martinis were an excellent aperitif, the most sophisticated of alcoholic beverages devised for the purpose of whetting one's appetite. But they were the agent's customary drink for an entirely different reason: there was nothing more powerful, more numbing to the cortex, than a solid belt of gin. The remainder of the cocktail—the token drops of vermouth, the ritual twist of lemon, or the less sophisticated olive—were mere trappings, there for show, for demonstrating nicety. What Betty wanted, and

445

what alone was important to her, was the shot in the head that juniper could deliver like nothing else.

"Sometimes I get to the point where I don't think I can handle it," Margot said. "I look at what's happened to my life and I think what the hell." She was drinking Scotch on the rocks, steadily, with greater determination even than that with which Betty was consuming gin. She raised her glass and swallowed half its contents.

"I know," Betty said. "I know exactly what you mean."

"I thought when I married Donald Krause I finally had it made," Margot said. "I thought I'd finally got to a point in my life where I could take just about anything more that fate, or whoever the hell it is who calls the shots, could hand out. The kids were in pretty good shape, I was in a position where I didn't have to sit around and slobber because I was a has-been actress, I didn't have to feel that my life was over because I wasn't an ingenue any more, or because of a couple of busted marriages. I had something to do that I couldn't only handle, but that I could actually be a success at."

Betty sipped her martini. She had arrived at a state of near-anesthesia, the blissful, semi-aware drifting that any gin from Beefeater's to Ralph's Markets' nine-dollar-a-half-gallon special induced in her.

"I just never would believe what losing him could do to me," Margot said. Her mouth trembled, and she looked for a moment as if she might begin to cry again. Instead, she shuddered and got herself back under control. "And I still can't really believe he's gone."

"I know," Betty said. "It must have been a terrible shock."

Margot shook her head. "Terrible. Just terrible. We were at the Princess in Acapulco, did I tell you that?"

"You said he was on a golf course," Betty remembered.

"We were staying in a villa," Margot went on relentlessly, as if forcing herself to relive the event. "Don loved the place because the course was always so green and beautiful, and the ocean was right there."

"I'm sure it was lovely," Betty said. Jesus Christ, she

was sorry. But did Margot have to lay it out for her, chapter and verse, wallowing around in the details like a pig in shit? Everybody had their troubles, and everybody knew what it was like to lose somebody they loved.

"I just couldn't believe it," Margot said. "I kept thinking that if we could get him to a hospital, or if we could fly a heart specialist down from Houston or L.A., you know, crazy ideas like that, we could save him."

Betty nodded and drank more of her martini.

"Instead, this Mexican doctor, he wasn't even the house doctor, he was there with his family on vacation, he kept shaking his head, and then I just kind of fell apart, you know? I finally got it through my head that Don wasn't just sick or hurt or anything like that, he was dead." Margot drew in her breath through clenched teeth and drained the last of her Scotch.

Betty nodded again, numbly.

A waiter materialized at their table.

"Two more," Betty ordered, and the man disappeared.

"I was so glad to hear you were in New York," Margot said. "When I read that Darla Dawson was in town I figured you'd be with her. My oldest boy lives in New York now, did I tell you? I've been visiting him and his wife."

"Yes," Betty said. "You told me."

"I should get back to Milwaukee," Margot said. "But somehow I just can't face it. Without Don I don't give a damn what happens to Krause Beer."

A few minutes of morose silence followed. Then the waiter returned with their drinks.

Betty sipped hers, the fresh martini cold and brittle in her mouth.

"It must be nice for you," Margot said reproachfully, "to have Darla making such great strides in her career."

"It's wonderful," Betty replied. She didn't really want to talk about Darla, or for that matter anything else, at this point. She would have much preferred to float along in her martini haze, content that the gin was doing its work, and that as a consequence the business,

447

and the whole world, for that matter, could go fuck itself. But she grasped that if she didn't pick up the conversational ball, Margot would lapse into a further lugubrious recounting of her husband's unexpected death. She squinted across the table. "But at the same time," she went on, "this kid has turned into a very large pain in the ass."

"Is that so?" Margot asked politely, but without interest.

"It's amazing to me how fast she's forgotten what I did for her," Betty said.

"That's something you could never say about me," Margot said. "I never for a minute forgot what you did for me. If it hadn't been for you, I never would have met Don."

Oh, no, you don't, Betty thought. We're going to leave poor Don in peace. Aloud, she said, "Almost as amazing as how fast she came up."

Margot sniffed. "I don't see much talent there, as an actress."

"You won't," Betty said. "No matter how hard you look. She made it because she's pretty, and sexy, in some kind of a dopey, cutesy way that turns guys on, and because I steered her as carefully as anybody I've ever handled."

"Uh-huh."

"I got her the Superfresh assignment, you know," Betty went on. "And that's really what started her. I figured that she'd be exactly right for it because she was different from the other little pussy cunts who run around the business all looking exactly alike. And you know why she looked different? Because I taught her how to style her hair that way. That big crazy mess that looks like a cat slept in it? All my idea, because I knew it could be a trademark for her. At first everybody laughed at it, said it looked old-fashioned. But did I know what I was doing? You bet your sweet ass I did. Now everybody imitates it."

Margot nodded dully.

Betty sipped gin. "Then the poster. She actually resisted me on that. Didn't want to do it at all, can you imagine? But it's making her a fortune. Which reminds me, I have to check some figures when I get home."

"What figures?"

"Royalty figures," Betty replied. "I'm having a little trouble getting reports out of the *gonif* accountant Derek Wasserman keeps in an attic someplace."

"Who's Derek Wasserman?"

Betty sighed. "He's the *schmuck* manager Darla hired. After what I've done for her, she goes and hires a *manager,* for Christ's sake. Fifteen percent to that prick, while I get ten, and what does he do? Moves in after I make the deals, after I get things set. Little Jack Horner sticks his thumb in the pie and pulls out money that belongs to me."

Margot shook her head. "That's typical."

"Right," Betty agreed. "The bastard is into everything. Including, I have a feeling, Darla's secretary."

"So what's new?" Margot said. "You can't trust anybody."

"Isn't that the truth." Betty's speech had become noticeably thicker. "Not anybody."

"What are you going to do about it?"

"Plenty. You know I got Darla the lead in 'The Witches,' only the hottest show on TV."

"Uh-huh."

"Well, now I'm about to take her out of it. The goddamn network is making a bundle out of that show you wouldn't believe. And if they think I'm going to sit around and watch them get rich while they throw us a bone—you know, some lousy token raise—then Peter Fried can go play with his joint."

"What's the contract say?"

Betty snorted. "The contract calls for a silly little increase the second year, which is bullshit, because the last thing she could deserve is a small raise. If the show is lousy it goes off the air and she gets nothing. But if the show's a hit it stays on and she deserves a real hike, right? That's fair, isn't it? Damn right it is. But either way, it can't come out that all she should get is a little bump. Either it's what she's worth or it's nothing."

"Yeah," Margot said. "You're absolutely right. So what are you going to do, then?"

"Movies," Betty told her. "I lined up the biggest deal you ever heard of, with one of the top producers in the industry, and that little shit Wasserman had nothing to do with it."

"How much?"

"Two and a half million up front," Betty said. "And on top of that I'm pretty sure I can get a percentage of the gross. We're still negotiating."

Margot shook her head. "That's a good deal, Betty. Even for you, that's a good deal."

"And how it is."

"What about her advertising?"

Betty drained her glass. "That's another place she has me worried. I've got her a hell of a contract with Superfresh, where she makes a load of money for doing next to nothing, and now she's threatening to blow it."

"Why would she do that?"

"How the hell do I know why? An ego trip, maybe, I don't know."

"Any way you can get her to see things differently?

Betty signaled the waiter for another round. "Yeah, I think so. I set up a meeting with the whole crew. The client, the agency, everybody. When Darla sees them all applauding, I think she'll come around. Meantime, I've got to be careful, because I'm about to sign another deal with them."

"With Superfresh?"

Betty squinted at Margot. "I can trust you, can't I, Margot." It was a statement, not a question. "I know I can."

Margot put her slim hand over the agent's fat one. "Of course, Betty." Margot's speech was also becoming sloppy now, although if Betty had heard anything different about it, or if she'd thought about any change in Margot's enuciation, she would have ascribed the slurring to an emotional reaction from her old friend. As it was, she was too drunk to be aware of any such nuances.

450

"I've found a kid who'll make everybody forget about Darla."

It took a moment for this to sink in. "You mean you're handling Darla's *replacement?*"

"Sh-h-h." Betty held a thick finger to her lips, conspiratorially, although they were by now virtually the only customers in the lounge. "She's not a replacement. Not yet, anyhow. The company wants another girl, somebody younger, for some new product. So if Darla walks out, I've still got, you know, insurance."

"You want to be careful," Margot said. "Or people will say you're disloyal to Darla."

The agent sneered. "Disloyal? After what I just told you about how she's reacting to the success I made for her? You talk to me about disloyal?"

Margot nodded. "Yeah, I see what you mean."

The waiter brought them a fresh round. Betty raised her glass unsteadily. "Here's to the future," she said dramatically. "If there is one goddamn thing I've learned in this world, it's that a girl has to look out for herself." She took a long pull at the martini. "Believe me, nobody else gives a shit."

Chapter 46

The atmosphere in the Superfresh Corporation's conference room was tense. Stanley Brinker, the company's advertising manager, looked at his watch at intervals of less than one minute. Al Monahan, the marketing director, pulled papers from a manila folder and pretended to study them. Robin Baker made occasional attempts at small talk, to which no one responded with more than a grunt. David Archer and Paul Scott stared impassively at the ceiling, or the walls, or out the windows, willing to look at anything except each other. Ben Thompkins, B&B's vice-president in charge of commercial production, drummed his fingers softly on the surface of the conference table. Philip Strauss, the agency's research director, sat beside Thompkins. The only man in the room who appeared totally relaxed was John Rawlson, president of Superfresh, an anomaly inasmuch as he was the one person whom the others present would never dare to keep waiting.

"It's ten-thirty," Brinker said to David Archer accusingly. A highly political man, Brinker never opened his mouth without having first considered the strategic implications his words were to have. "If they're not here in another five minutes, I think we should hold the meeting some other time. Mister Rawlson and the rest of us have more important things to do than sit around waiting for a model." By expressing these thoughts to

Archer, Brinker was deferring to Robin Baker, the head of the agency, but condescending to Paul Scott, who everyone knew was willing to try anything short of assassination to take over Archer's job. At the same time, Brinker was demonstrating dedication to his boss by showing his indignation that the agency had the gall to waste John Rawlson's precious time. It would also be evident that he, Stanley Brinker, would much rather be hard at work than sitting here.

"I think you're quite right, Stanley," Archer replied. "We could all spend our time in better ways." The consummate diplomat, Archer was used to boardroom repartee. First, he knew, one should agree with the client; second, the tension should be relaxed. His handsome face, stern and lean below the carefully groomed black hair touched with silver at the temples, broke into a grin. "But let's give the lady her due. After California, New York traffic must be an awful shock."

A chuckle went around the table, and Baker launched into a story about the time he had a box at Yankee Stadium for the opening game of the World Series and had to listen to the first four innings on the radio in a taxi, gnawing his knuckles in frustration.

John Rawlson listened to their exchanges with mild amusement. He was not in the least deceived by Brinker's remonstration; he knew precisely what the advertising manager's motives were, just as he knew that Brinker was not what he pretended to be in several other respects. For example, Brinker's manner was not exactly prudish, but he was certainly strait-laced, and around the company's offices was considered stuffy. Yet Brinker had been having affairs with other men's wives for years. Although Stanley Brinker would have had a seizure if he had learned that the Superfresh president had any knowledge of these liaisons, the fact was that John Rawlson knew all about them.

As a matter of fact, Rawlson mused as he looked at the men sitting at the conference table, there were things about every one of them that they would be startled to learn that he knew. There was Archer's drinking, for instance. And Scott's affair with that copywriter,

453

Tippy something. And he knew that Al Monahan, his marketing director, was secretly looking for another job.

"It is now ten-forty," Stanley Brinker announced in a loud voice. "I suggest we—"

The double doors of the conference room swung open and one of John Rawlson's secretaries stepped in and said, "Miss Dawson and her group are here. May I show them in?"

Rawlson nodded, and a moment later Darla swept into the room.

She looked radiant, the old man thought as he took her hand. She seemed smaller physically than she appeared on television, but even more startlingly beautiful. Her face was tanned and looked relaxed and rested, the marvelous violet-blue eyes clear and luminous, framed by the astonishing mass of blonde hair that was imitated everywhere now, but which remained so uniquely hers.

"I'm glad to see you again," he greeted her warmly.

"I'm glad to see you too," Darla replied, holding his hand, her face lighted by the famous smile, her teeth incredibly white and large and even. There was a warmth about her, a strength of presence, that reached out and touched people. It made them like her and want to be close to her and to protect her, somehow. "I'm sorry we're late," she said. "New York is such a confusing place, and the traffic is terrible, but you know what the truth is?" Her smile widened and her tone suddenly changed and she sounded very young and innocent. "I just overslept. Will you forgive me?"

John Rawlson grinned. "Of course I will. How could I not?"

Darla squeezed his hand and waved toward Molly Martin, Betty Frolich, and Derek Wasserman. "I think you know everybody?"

There was a flurry of small talk while Darla and her group were seated, and the secretaries served coffee.

"Darla, we're very happy to have you here today," Paul Brinker began the meeting. "We wanted to tell you how pleased we continue to be to have you represent Superfresh, and also to tell you something of our future plans."

"Thank you," Darla smiled. "I'm glad to see everyone again, and there are some things I wanted to say to you all, too."

"At the same time," Brinker went on, "I have to tell you that there are some problems. And I think that just to set the record straight, we ought to tell you what those are right now, so that no one has any misunderstandings." He cleared his throat and glanced around the table before continuing.

He's enjoying this, John Rawlson reflected. Brinker is not only the man in charge in this meeting, but he has an audience that includes a famous actress, the head of the agency, and me.

"During the past couple of years, we've had good growth in the Superfresh brand," Brinker said. "Sales have increased substantially, and there's no question that the advertising has made a contribution to those increases, and that having you represent the brand has also helped."

I would call that something of an understatement, if I were Darla Dawson, Rawlson mused. He watched her face closely, but the actress gave no indication that she found fault with Brinker's remarks.

"Nevertheless," Brinker continued, "sales increases are meaningless if profits don't keep pace. After all, the name of the game is money, and the Superfresh Corporation's ultimate responsibility is to its stockholders. Simply posting sales gains is not enough. We must also show commensurate increases in our earnings." He paused again.

Come on, man, get on with it, Rawlson thought.

"And that brings us to our number-one dilemma," Brinker said dramatically. "Superfresh sales may have increased, but the expense of achieving those sales has risen astronomically. For example, television time costs have more than doubled since you began to work for Superfresh, Darla. Magazine space rates have also gone way up." He glanced at the agency men. "And production costs in both TV and print are out of sight."

Betty Frolich leaned forward, her fleshy arms resting heavily on the conference table. "Wait a minute," she interrupted. "What has this got to do with us? So everything has gone up. So what? I also have to pay more for a pound of coffee when I go food shopping. What does that have to do with the fact that you've got the world's number-one TV personality for what anybody in the business would call bargin rates?"

Stanley Brinker flushed. "What may be a bargain to some people certainly wouldn't be called that by others. Especially if you look at those fees in terms of how they affect our business."

"From everything we can see," the agent shot back, "your business is doing great. If you can't control your costs, that's your problem. It sure as hell is not ours."

Brinker's face darkened further. "Controlling costs is exactly what we're struggling with. Since it *is* a problem that affects all of us, we're trying to get you to look at it from our perspective. In the hope," he added indignantly, "that we can all have a clear understanding as to how we should be formulating our plans for next year."

"I'm sure Darla and her associates will be sympathetic to these problems," David Archer said smoothly, "but this is not the time or place to get into an argument. All we really wanted to do this morning," he smiled at Betty, "is to give everyone a kind of status report, and to tell you about what we hope to achieve from this point on."

"Fine," Betty said testily. "Let's go. But don't waste your breath crying poor-mouth. If you're trying to set us up for some rinkydink increase in next year's contract, you can forget it. If you want Darla on Superfresh next year, you're going to start paying her what she's worth."

John Rawlson studied the agent as she spoke. Very intense, he decided. And probably a compulsive eater.

"We're not here to negotiate," Robin Baker remarked hastily. "This is just a friendly get-together so we'll all know what's going on and also have a chance to say hello to Darla." He turned to Scott. "Paul, why don't you show everybody some of the new layout ideas now, as well as a couple of the new storyboards."

The younger man sprang to his feet. "Fine, Robin."

He stepped to the presentation panel which ran the length of one side of the room. A number of pieces of foamboard rested on the shelf there, their contents sides turned to the wall. Scott lifted one. "The idea of the new ads," he said in the deep voice in which he took such obvious pride, "is to make each of them look like a poster. We want to present Darla and her great smile as forcefully and dramatically as we can. And here is the first in the new series." With a flourish, he flipped the piece of foamboard around, revealing the layout mounted on it.

"Hey," Molly said, "that's dynamite."

Scott smiled. "We think so too."

"Maybe her head could be turned a little," Wasserman said, "to give the shot a little more personality."

"These are only rough layouts," Archer interposed. "Just to give everybody an idea."

"Let me show you some of the others," Scott said, reaching for another board.

As the discussion continued, with various people in the room remarking on the magazine layouts and the concepts expressed in the television storyboards, John Rawlson paid almost no attention to the advertising materials, all of which he had seen previously. Instead, he looked at Darla's profile with interest.

She would be how old now? Thirty? Yes. Just thirty. What an excellent age for a woman. Still youthful, but with her beauty ripened by maturity, reflecting a poise and a sophistication not to be found when she was younger. He looked at her slim, straight nose, at the full lips and the gently curving chin, at the long, beautifully turned throat, at the line of her breasts, pressing enticingly against the gossamer silk of her blouse.

"Okay, Paul," David Archer said as Scott concluded his presentation of the proposed new advertising, "thanks very much." He smiled. "That will give you a pretty good indication of where we're going, and I think it's fair to say that the new campaign will be even more impactful than what we've had up to now."

"Very good," Stanley Brinker added. "And now,

Darla, and everyone, I'd like to thank you for visiting us this morning."

Darla nodded. "I'd like to thank you too, for having us. And there's also something I'd like to say."

Brinker and the others smiled, a little indulgently. It was clear that despite Darla's newly obtained prominence as a famous television personality, perhaps the most widely photographed woman since Jackie Kennedy, none of them took her very seriously, or thought of her in any role other than that of the pretty model who decorated Superfresh advertising.

"I've been thinking," Darla began, "about what we were talking about earlier. You know, about how I've helped Superfresh and what the company pays me and all. And I haven't just been thinking about it today. I've been studying it for quite a while."

Rawlson noted that Brinker's face had assumed an expression that was not only amused, but supercilious. To a lesser extent, the others among the Superfresh and agency people were looking at Darla the same way.

"I understand what you mean when you say you have a problem with rising costs," Darla said, addressing this principally to Brinker. "Of course it's not easy to cope with. And the last thing I'd ever want would be to have me make a whole lot of money and then to feel that it was too much, that it just made me a big burden, you know? I really think that above everything else, whatever I get for working for Superfresh ought to be fair."

As Darla spoke, Rawlson observed, the smile slowly disappeared from Stanley Brinker's face. The advertising manager leaned forward. "That's very nice to hear, Darla," he said earnestly. "That's really very nice to hear."

"So I'd like to tell you how I'd like to work with you in the future."

The room became quiet.

"Darla," Betty said, "I think—"

Darla silenced the agent by raising her hand. "What I would like to have from now on," she continued, "is a percentage of the profits."

Now there was no sound whatever in the large, paneled room.

"That way," Darla said, her voice calm and sincere, "I'd always be getting exactly what I was worth. No more and no less. If profits went up, my share would go up. And if they went down," she completed the thought with an exaggerated shrug, followed by the little-girl smile.

She's adorable, Rawlson thought. That is precisely the right word for her. Adorable. He looked at the faces of his colleagues, their expressions ranging now from disbelief to shock.

Darla seemed not to notice. "I'm sure you all want to think that over and, you know, discuss it," she said. "And then you and Betty can work out exactly what the percentage ought to be, and all that. Meantime, thanks for having me. I just love all of you, and I love Superfresh, too." She turned on the big one, the smile that Ben Thompkins called the laser beam. Of the Superfresh group, he was the only one who returned Darla's smile, his face twisted into a grin of genuine amusement.

Darla stood up, and as she did the others all got hastily to their feet, everyone suddenly talking at once.

When he said goodbye, John Rawlson looked directly at Darla's eyes, and the response he saw there was unmistakable. He understood her, he realized, far better than the others did. And somehow, he felt, she understood him too. Impulsively, he bent down and kissed her on the mouth.

After Darla and her group had left the room, several heated discussions ensued at once. Rawlson listened to the babble for a few moments, and then he cleared his throat. At this signal, which they had long since learned to recognize as an indication that he wished to speak, the men grew quiet and looked at him expectantly. He smiled. "Well, Stanley, what did you think of Miss Dawson's proposal?"

The advertising manager twisted uncomfortably in his chair. "It's a very unorthodox idea," he said cautiously.

"I know that," Rawlson said. "But what did you *think* of it?"

Brinker licked his lips nervously. "It's something we'll have to, ah, give a lot of thought to." His voice trailed off.

Rawlson nodded. He looked at Baker. "Robin? What's your view?"

"Stan's right," the agency chairman said. "We've got a tremendous property in Darla Dawson, and the brand's doing great. No question that she's put a hell of a lot of sock in the advertising. Whether this idea of hers makes any sense I just don't know. But I do know I wouldn't want to lose her."

"Mm." Rawlson looked at Monahan.

The marketing director rubbed his nose. "I don't see how we can afford to let her go. Our business has never been better. As far as giving her a percentage of the profits is concerned, that might not be a bad idea. The trick would be to make the percentage so small it wouldn't matter."

Rawlson swung his attention to Archer. "David?"

The man's usual composure seemed to have vanished. "I wouldn't want to lose her either. That could put a serious crimp in our plans for next year. And I would hate to see somebody else pick her up."

The blue eyes fixed upon Scott. "Paul?"

"It would have to be approached very carefully," the younger man replied. His voice seemed even deeper than usual. "For example, what the percentage would net out in actual dollars, given certain sales levels, and so on."

Rawlson looked at Ben Thompkins, who smiled disarmingly.

"Whether it makes sense from a business standpoint I haven't the faintest idea," the producer said cheerfully. "But I have to say the lady sure has a lot of guts." He laughed, and Robin Baker glared at him.

Rawlson nodded again and looked at Philip Strauss, who returned his gaze. "And what do you think?" he asked the research director.

Strauss hesitated. "I think," he said at last, "that

Darla has meant a great deal to Superfresh; she's done an outstanding job. But advertising is a tool, and a model is a tool, no matter who she is. People don't buy Superfresh because of Darla Dawson. They buy it for reasons that range from their acceptance of the advertising claims to their satisfaction with the product. What Darla does is to get us greater awareness of the advertising and its message, and she adds credibility and impact. But a percentage of the profits? That's a pretty big demand."

Rawlson sat silently for a moment. He looked at the faces of the men, all of whom were staring intently at him. He got to his feet. "Your answers," he said, a faint smile at one corner of his mouth, "were about what I expected. You can tell Miss Dawson that we will pay her a large increase in her compensation for the coming year." The smile disappeared. "You can also tell her that under no circumstances will we give in to what she's asking. Is that clear?" He stood erect, his blue eyes cold and steady in his ruddy face. His gaze swung to the windows in the north wall, and for a moment he looked out across Central Park, lush and green in its thick foliage, the trees shimmering in the late summer heat.

Rawlson turned back to the men in the room. "Nothing is forever," he said.

Chapter 47

The house was a sprawl of redwood and glass at the very top of the mountain. It was hidden from the road by a stand of pine, but the view from the opposite side, looking down the valley and to the peaks beyond, was beautiful. Mike stood on the deck that ran the length of the structure and gazed at the steep, forest-clad slopes. The air was crisp and clear, and at other times in his life he would have felt refreshed and invigorated to be in this place. Today he simply felt drained.

The shaking of his hands had grown worse. He studied them, making a conscious effort to keep them still, but found that he couldn't. He had to grip the redwood railing to prevent their trembling.

How long had he been here—a week, two weeks? It was hard to think clearly. For that matter, it was hard to think at all. He couldn't seem to get his mind to work properly. Somehow, he told himself, he had to get things sorted out.

Hearing a sound from within the house behind him, he turned and entered the living room.

Andrea looked up, startled. "I didn't know you were out there."

Mike saw that she was wearing a light raincoat. "You're going somewhere?"

The gray eyes were cool and steady. "As a matter of fact, yes. I'm leaving."

"Leaving? You didn't say anything about leaving."

"I'm saying it now, Mike."

"But how—?"

"I called a taxi to come up from the village. It just got here."

"Hey, listen. What the hell is this?"

Andrea shrugged. "Seems clear enough to me. It's goodbye."

"Goodbye? For Christ's sake, if you wanted to go home, why didn't you tell me? I would have—"

"I wanted to leave alone, Mike. And that's what I'm going to do."

As confused as he was, the jumbled thoughts in his mind began to mesh. "Well I'll be damned." Andrea attempted to move past him, but he blocked her path. "You know, I'm finally beginning to get it. I'm finally beginning to understand what's been going on."

She made no reply.

"You must think I'm the biggest jerk on earth. And I guess that's just what I am."

"You've got your problems."

"Problems? Jesus, I'll say I have. And I know now where a lot of them have been coming from."

Andrea's voice was flat. "Don't blame me for what you've been doing to yourself. Having a good time is one thing, but burning yourself up is something else."

"Burning myself up? God, Andrea. You were the one who was always right there with the speed and the downers and whatever the hell else you could stuff into me."

Her mouth curled in derision. "So it's my fault, huh? What kind of a man are you?"

Rage boiled up in Mike's chest. He clenched his fists, but as he did his head began to spin wildly. He slumped into a chair.

"Can't make it, can you?" Andrea taunted. "Can't even beat me up. Can't solve this one by using your fists or by pushing somebody around. You know what I think, Mike? I think you've had it."

He looked up at her. "You lousy bitch. You really played me for a sucker."

She walked to the door and opened it. There was a slight smile on her face as she returned his stare. "With you it was easy." And then she was gone.

Mike sat in the chair for a long time, trying to sift through the impressions in his mind. Looking back over these past few days was like recalling a nightmare. He saw pictures of himself with Andrea, spaced out on drugs, dancing with her, wrapped in her arms in bed, laughing hysterically at nothing, popping pills and more pills.

Then he forced himself to think about what had happened during the recent couple of months. And that was even uglier. The show. His position in it. Britney had tried to tell him, but he wouldn't listen. Andrea was right about one thing. She hadn't done this to him—he'd done it to himself. All Andrea had done was to give him a good hard shove.

And now what? What the hell was left? Christ. If only he could talk to Darla. She'd be the one sane element in this revolting mess.

He pulled himself out of the chair and crossed the room to a telephone. He flopped down on a sofa and lifted the instrument. Darla wasn't in L.A., wasn't home. Where was she? New York. But where? God, it was hard to think. He glanced at the coffee table in front of the sofa. There was a bottle on the table. A bottle of red-and-yellow capsules. He put the phone down and picked up the bottle. He shook out several capsules and stuffed them into his mouth.

It was getting dark, he realized. He lay back on the sofa and waited for the methaqualone to hit him.

The bed was bathed in soft light that filtered in from the living room beyond. Music drifted in also, cool modern jazz figures, a trumpet playing upper-register riffs against a piano-and-bass obbligato. Ted Walters propped himself on one elbow and gazed at Darla's body, his emotions a mixture of admiration and wonder.

What the hell, he told himself. If you took it all apart, what was it? Arms, legs, tits—so what? He'd had dozens, hundreds even, that were as good, maybe a few even better. There was that ballerina with the Royal Ballet company in London. Or the swimmer on the French Olympic team. Christ, what a body that one had had. And others, so many he couldn't begin to remember them all, some encountered for only a few hours, suddenly becoming a lustful, exciting part of his life, and then as suddenly gone. Jesus, it was easier to recall tennis players he'd faced than broads he'd balled. So why did Darla do this to him? What was the magic, the stunning impact of being with her, of making love to her until he felt totally drained, more spent than he would have thought possible, only to find some reserve hidden deep within his body from which to draw the strength to do it again, just one more time? And what was it about her that made him want to be with her, to put his arm around her, to enjoy the easy camaraderie, the low-key kidding that was their way of expressing to each other that underneath the fame and the stardom that each had achieved, Ted in his world, Darla in hers, they were just a couple of kids who had lucked out, who were not actually touched by it all, who were no different, really, from anybody else?

For a long while Ted had resented this tie to Darla, this emotional bondage in which she seemed to hold him. He had wanted to be free of her, free to enjoy with his old, reckless abandon the bounteous joys that life held out to him. He hated mooning after one girl like some teenaged asshole, never able to get her out of his thoughts, never able to find in anyone else the indefinable attraction that produced the bittersweet longing he felt for Darla, and for Darla alone. But then he had decided that for all the misery, it was worth it. He would rather have it this way, seeing her sometimes at intervals of as much as three or four months, than not see her at all. He leaned over and gently kissed her cheek.

Darla smiled up at him. "I know," she teased. "You're starved. You want three hamburgers and a mug of beer and then a bowl of coconut ice cream."

Ted shook his head. "I'm beyond all that. I only used

to get that hungry when I was young. But now, since you've stolen my youth and left me broken in body and spirit, I don't have the strength for nonsense like food."

"Poor boy. So what do you live on?"

"Pussy. With maybe a little warm milk and cinnamon toast."

Darla pushed his face away playfully. "You haven't changed a bit, Ted Walters. You are rude and raunchy and from what I hear, a lousy tennis player."

Ted grinned. "Who told you that—Dumas?"

"Don't laugh. I read in *The New York Times* he might beat you."

"Uh-huh." His tone was scornful. "And what did the story say about the odds?"

"I don't know. I don't remember."

"It says I'm favored six to five on the Vegas line," Ted said. "And you know what? That's a steal. Sell your jewels and bet all the money on me."

"I thought you said you were broken in body and spirit."

"Only when it comes to screwing. As a tennis player I am still the greatest in the history of the game."

"The paper said you even had trouble with that little Spaniard, what's his name—?"

"Estranza."

"Right. So if Estranza made a monkey out of you, how could you hope to handle a much younger, faster player like Dumas?"

"Listen, Darla. Are you being a worse smartass than usual, even?"

"I'm just quoting the paper," she replied innocently.

"Well, for your information, *The New York Times* is full of shit. As are all newspapers, and most of all the sports sections. They love controversy, and they love colorful characters, especially the ones they can get the public pissed off at."

"So you're suggesting that your delightful personality is merely a distortion that was created by *The New York Times*?"

"Damn right. The fact is, I'm a charmer. Courteous,

kind, and mindful of others. The Boy Scouts of America want me as their mascot."

"That's wonderful, Ted. But what if Dumas does beat you?"

He pretended to be annoyed. "Hey, what the hell is this? You trying to shake my confidence?"

"It would take a bomb to shake your anything."

"Is that a hint?"

Darla giggled. "Certainly not. If you lose tomorrow, you do it all by yourself. I don't want you to go blaming it on me."

"But actually, you'd be secretly proud, right? Behind every great man stands a great woman, looking down at his beat-out body and saying, Poor Charlie. He just couldn't get it up any more."

"Doesn't sound like any of the men I know," Darla said. "At least any of the ones I've known up to now."

A pang of jealousy burned in Ted's chest. Well, of course she has other guys, he thought. And she's married, too, for Christ's sake. Nevertheless, the thought of someone else kissing that mouth, of someone else lying between those legs, was maddening. It was also, he realized to his surprise, highly erotic. He took her hand and placed it on his swelling penis. "Walters may be down," he growled, "but he is never out." Darla giggled again, and he stifled her laugh with a sloppy kiss, his tongue sliding wetly into her open mouth.

She had become instantly aroused, he perceived. Her nipples were stiffening, and her breathing had deepened, and he could feel a slight tensing of the muscles in her arms and her belly and her legs. He bent and kissed her breast, drawing his tongue slowly back and forth across the nipple until she began to moan softly and to move her hips a little in a way that was inflaming to him. He put his hand between her legs and caressed her, stroking her firmly but gently, feeling her very wet and warm, and she moaned and moved her hips a little faster.

"Put it in me, Ted," Darla whispered in his ear. "Put it in me. Now."

Walters entered her tenderly, marveling that he could, and that it could be like this, as exciting as if they hadn't already spent hours together. Darla grasped his shoulders and Ted pressed his mouth down on hers and they moved together in a slow, exquisite rhythm, their bodies joined in an incredible, unending kiss, floating in space, aware of nothing but each other, soaring together, giving, loving, feeling.

He had no idea how long it lasted, how long they lay totally joined. But when he came it was like surfing off Maui, only a hundred times more thrilling, climbing to the top of a gigantic tropical wave, higher and higher, reaching for the very peak, and then hurtling down the other side in a dizzying rush, every nerve in his body tingling with the sensation, every sense straining with the power and the force of what his body was giving of itself.

Afterward, it took a long time for his breathing to slow, for the pounding of his heart to subside even a little. He suddenly felt cool, and his senses told him that his body had become wet with sweat and the artificial breeze of the air conditioning system was making him feel chilly. He rolled off Darla's inert body and was instantly asleep.

He had no idea where he was when the bell rang, or even what the bell was, or where it was coming from. He was only aware that there was a ringing, an insistent clangor that wouldn't leave him alone, wouldn't let him stay where he was, warm and comfortable, struggling to sink back down into the depths.

"I think you'd better get that."

It was Darla's voice, he comprehended. "Yeah."

"Come on, Ted. Better answer it."

He shook his head, understanding, finally, that the origin of the insistent pealing was the telephone. "Who the hell's calling?" he mumbled. He pulled himself over toward the instrument and fumbled for it. "Yeah?"

"Ted? Ted, it's me, Sarah." Her voice sounded small and distant and frightened.

Instantly awake, he swung his legs over the side of the bed. "Hey, what is it—something wrong?"

"I'm in trouble, Ted. I'm in a lot of trouble."

"What trouble? Where are you?"

Sarah began to cry. "I don't know where I am. But a man is here and he won't let me go, and he's hurting me. Ted, I can't—"

He heard muffled noises and then a male voice crackled metallically through the receiver. "You remember what I told you, Walters? It's all set. A million bucks in an account in your name in Liechtenstein. You get the account number after you lose tomorrow. Then all you have to do is go pick it up."

"Lose tomorrow?" A surge of rage swept over Walters. He leaped to his feet. "Fuck you, lose tomorrow. Listen to me, you son of a bitch!"

"No, Walters. *You* listen. You're going to play it like you're told, or the way you get your girlfriend back is I mail her to you, a piece at a time."

"What!"

"Yeah. So you play great tomorrow, right? But Dumas plays just a little bit better."

Walters's voice fell to a whisper. "Jesus Christ."

"That's right. You think about it, you decide to be reasonable, right? Here, wait a minute."

Walters heard more muffled sounds, and then Sarah's voice again. "He—he's hurting me, Ted. He burned me with cigarettes. And he made me—do things." She began to sob.

DiNero's voice came back on. "Remember, Walters, it's all set." There was a click and then silence.

Walters dropped the telephone onto its cradle. He felt numb and nauseous and he couldn't think.

"Ted." Darla was wide-eyed. "What is it? Sarah's in trouble?"

Walters sat down on the bed and nodded slowly.

"How? Where is she? And who wants you to lose?"

He stared at her, his heart pounding, a headache suddenly throbbing above his eyes. "A gambler. A mob guy from Las Vegas named DiNero. He says he'll—kill her unless I lose tomorrow."

"Where is she?"

He shook his head. "I don't know. She said he was hurting her. Burning her with cigarettes, and Christ knows what else."

Darla bit her knuckles. "Oh, God."

"Yeah." He stood up and rubbed his face. "What the hell can I do? I can't go to the cops. He'd kill her for sure, then. And that would be the end of me, too," he added ruefully.

"Is he—are they in New York, do you suppose?"

"I have no idea. I guess so. Sarah left word today that she was going to be visiting friends tonight, back tomorrow. But I suppose that was a fake."

"Do you know this man?"

"No. That is, he tried to talk to me a couple times in Vegas, tried to get me interested in a deal where he'd put money in an account in some European country if I'd drop a big match. I just walked away from him. Then he showed up at the West Side right out of the blue and told me it was all set. He says I get a million bucks if Dumas wins tomorrow."

Darla shook her head. "And now he's got Sarah."

The pounding over Ted's eyes increased in tempo.

"You said his name was—DiNero?"

"Yes. Frank DiNero."

Darla got off the bed and headed for the bathroom.

There was a carafe on one of the tables in the bedroom. Ted unstoppered it and gulped ice water. The cold liquid burned in his stomach, increasing his nausea. He returned the carafe to the table, pulled a robe out of the closet, and put it on. Sarah's voice repeated its terrified cry in his mind. *He's hurting me, Ted. He burned me with cigarettes. And he made me—do things.*

Christ. He'd never been in a jam like this, never felt so helpless. He saw Frank DiNero's face in his mind's eye: the oily black hair, the thin mustache, the black lenses of his glasses huge and shiny like the eyes of a fly. God, if he could only get his hands on the son of a bitch.

The bathroom door opened and Darla returned to

the room. She had dressed in slacks and a blouse, and had tied a scarf over her head.

Ted stared at her. "What are you going to do?"

"I have to go," Darla replied. She took his hand. "Maybe I can help, I don't know. I'm going to try."

"Hey," he protested. "You can't—"

"Yes I can," Darla said.

"Will you come back?"

"No. Not tonight. And tomorrow morning I have a meeting I have to make. But you'll hear from me. And I'll be at Forest Hills tomorrow afternoon."

"Darla—"

"No, Ted. It has to be this way." She kissed him quickly and left.

Chapter 48

It was after five A.M. when Darla reached the Waldorf. She phoned Corelli from the lobby and then took the elevator to his suite. He greeted her at the door wearing a silk robe, showing no surprise at her unexpected visit. Darla fell into his arms, struggling to hold back the tears, and it took Dante several minutes to get her calmed down. He led her into the kitchen and made a pot of coffee, and when they were seated at the table over steaming cups she told him the entire story of the trouble Walters and his girlfriend were in. Dante pressed her for details, urging her to recount several times what had happened. Finally he told her he would do what he could, but he could not be positive that he would be able to locate Sarah Winchester.

Darla looked at Corelli's face in an attempt to fathom his feelings, but the dark features were impassive. She could imagine how he was taking this, knowing instinctively that there would be a conflict of emotions within him. No matter how much he had urged her to turn to him if she ever needed help, she was aware that his attitude toward her ran a great deal deeper than friendship, and that this evidence of her involvement with Walters would have its effect on him. Corelli was in cool control of himself as always, but at the same time, she knew, he was a vital, passionate man. She hated to do this to him, and yet, what choice did she have? There was no one else she could go to. She finished her coffee, feeling leaden, worn out.

When she returned to the Plaza, Darla tried to rest, but sleep, as she'd expected, was out of the question. Finally she got up and went into the shower. She stayed there for a full thirty minutes, employing the trick Mike had taught her of alternating between hot and cold blasts of water, and it helped. She still felt tired and tense when she emerged from the shower, but at least she'd be able to cope. She picked up her watch and glanced at it. After ten, and she was due in Peter Fried's office at ten-thirty. She dressed hurriedly, tossing instructions to Sally Dane, and with Bob Murphy leading the way, hurried to her limousine. As she settled into the car's deep cushions, she tried to make herself relax, to push Ted's problems out of her head and to concentrate on the upcoming discussion. The prospect of a private meeting with the UBS program chief filled her with apprehension. Here we go, she told herself. Straight into the lion's den.

Peter Fried was a hungry young man. After college theatricals an NYU, he had landed his first job in broadcasting as a page at NBC. His rise there was meteoric, and like William Paley, James Aubrey and Fred Silverman before him, he became a celebrity in his own right. Extremely quick to learn, he was fiercely ambitious, willing to work fifteen and sixteen hours a day, driven by his desire to head a major broadcasting company. He had defined his goal almost immediately upon joining the network. Unlike the other bright young men who were his contemporaries, to whom such exalted positions as V.P., Network Sales, or V.P., Network Operations, seemed as distant and as unreachable as the stars in some remote galaxy, Fried had charted his course all the way to the top, and then had set about getting there with a fury. Talented, even gifted, in his ability to conceive and shape and select program content that would attract television audiences in greater-than-average numbers, he had perceived early that for him the ultimate gratification would be not merely to be responsible for some or even all of what a network put on the air, but to run the entire billion-dollar operation.

Within seven years, Fried became program chief of NBC-TV. It was a rise even more rapid than that of Fred Silverman or Jim Aubrey, in itself an achievement which made him a legendary figure in the industry. But to the intense young man, the job was at first merely a steppingstone, and then, quickly, a frustration. NBC was an extraordinarily successful enterprise, the oldest of the broadcast companies, and also the stuffiest, members of its top management seeing themselves as belonging to a very exclusive club, admission to which was to be gained not only through ability, but also by reason of background, family connections, and political maneuvering. To Fried, the notion of struggling for at least ten more years merely to get into the charmed circle was unthinkable. He jumped to the rival UBS network, whose traditional position in the bitterly contested ratings race had always been dead last. At UBS he not only was paid three hundred thousand dollars a year, which was nearly twice the rate of his compensation at NBC, but also enjoyed other financial benefits he had not previously known, such as stock options, which provided an opportunity to amass considerable amounts of what tax-conscious executives in the industry called "keeping money."

Far more important than any other consideration, however, Fried knew that in the rough and dirty world of an also-ran network, performance here was everything. Boost the ratings, and the sky was the limit. Push UBS into a position of leadership, or even one of serious contention, and he would have a clear shot at the top job. His sixteen-hour work days went to seventeen and eighteen, and his already strained family life all but disappeared. He had married a nice girl who worked in NBC-TV's programming department, and they had a daughter whom he now almost never saw. What he did see, to perhaps a greater extent than anyone else in America, was television. There were sets in his office at UBS on which he could watch the shows on various channels simultaneously, and they were almost never turned off. There was a set in the limousine the network assigned him, and a sprinkling of others throughout his Fifth Avenue apartment, including a bracket-mounted Sony next to his shaving mirror. There was never a moment in Peter Fried's waking hours when he was not occupied with some aspect of television programming.

In less than two years, he lifted UBS's ranking not merely to a level of importance, but to one of dominance. As a result, he was labeled a genius, and held in absolute awe by the broadcasting, advertising and entertainment communities. His face peered out from the covers of a number of national magazines, the eyes blazing with a dark light as they remained fixed upon a goal that by now had become obvious even to the black man who shined his shoes each morning. To the trade he was more of a star than most of the talent with which he decorated his network's programs. Word had it that in very short order Peter Fried would become the chief executive officer of UBS, and that nothing short of cosmic collision would prevent him from getting there.

A secretary showed Darla into Fried's office and closed the door behind her. He was on the phone, which gave Darla a chance to take in her surroundings. She sat down opposite his desk and looked around. The desk was vast, its surface covered in black marble. Stacks of memos and manuscripts and letters had been organized into neat piles. Darla observed that as Fried spoke into the phone, his eyes roved back and forth over the bank of television receivers mounted in the wall to his left, their audio turned low. On one set an old Gene Kelly movie flickered, on another Popeye cavorted, and on another a soap opera unfolded drearily. On still another there was what appeared to be a travelogue of some kind, footage of smiling natives in a jungle village.

It was incredible, she reflected, that any one man could have so much power in a communications medium as important as television, and especially a man as young as Fried. He appeared to be no more than forty, his long, dark hair adding to the impression of youthfulness. His face was unlined and relaxed. Only his eyes, staring intensely at the television monitors, gave any hint of the driving ambition that impelled him.

Darla looked out the window to the west and south, and although she was nervous and apprehensive, she marveled at the view. Fried's office was on the fifty-third floor, and it occurred to her that this was the highest she had ever been in any building. In the distance she could see the Hudson River, and beyond that, the smoke-smudged flatlands of New Jersey. To her left, looking south, rose the towers and spires of the New York skyline, the twin towers of the Trade Center looming higher than all the others.

Fried put the phone down. "Hello, Darla." He did not get up.

"Good morning, Peter," Darla replied. "It's nice to see you again."

"Nice to see you, too," he said perfunctorily. "I hope you're enjoying New York. Want some coffee?"

"No, thank you." She smiled, forcing herself to appear comfortable and relaxed, although this was the opposite of how she actually felt. Since leaving Ted Walters's suite hours earlier that morning she had consumed countless cups of black coffee. The thought of drinking another now made her slightly ill.

Fried smiled back, a tight, mechanical curling of his lips, but his eyes did not change their cold expression. "I know your agent and your manager are probably pissed off at me for not including them in our little get-together, but when I want to talk with an artist about his or her career, that's who I talk with. Nobody else."

Darla nodded.

Fried touched a button on the intercom on his desk and spoke into the instrument. "Hold all calls." To Darla he said, "It's great that you're doing so well. I don't ever remember anybody getting up there so fast."

"I've been lucky," Darla said.

Fried nodded. "Yes, you have. But you've also made your own luck. And you've made 'The Witches' the top-rated show on television. Sure, it's a great premise—two gorgeous girls, a lot of sex, and Cathy Drake is terrific. But above all, the show is a hit because you're in it.

You've got star quality like nobody I've seen in a long, long time."

"Thank you."

Fried's eyes fixed on the television monitors for a few moments, then swung back to Darla. "What I wanted to talk to you about this morning is your future. I don't have to tell you that television is a voracious medium. It eats talent up. People come out of nowhere, suddenly they're hot, and just as suddenly, they're gone. The Smothers Brothers, Flip Wilson, Goldie Hawn—the list is endless." He stared at her. "I don't want that to happen to you."

Darla made herself smile. "I don't want that to happen to me either."

"So I'm going to do something about it," he said. "I have a plan for your career."

Darla was aware of the program executive's penchant for taking charge of people as well as projects, of his compulsion to tell writers how to write, directors how to direct, producers how to produce, and actors what roles to play. Even so, she was taken aback. "I think the person who has to decide what direction my career should take is me, Peter," she said quietly.

He seemed not to hear. "What I want you to do is to spend another year in 'The Witches.' That'll be good for you, and good for the show. After that, I want to spot you in different dramatic roles, done mostly as specials."

Darla looked calmly at the program chief. "I think," she said, "that I may have other ideas. And so might some other people. After all, the show is the property of Gary Zander and Art Cohen, isn't it?"

Fried seemed mildly surprised. "Zander-Cohen? They're nothing but a production company. They do what I tell them to do."

The man's chutzpah was hard to believe. "What kind of dramatic roles are you talking about?" Darla asked.

"Serious stuff," he replied. He waved a hand at the bank of television monitors. "Not the shit you're doing now. 'The Witches' is the kind of show that doesn't last anyway. It's a skyrocket. Up it goes, big bang, and then

477

nothing. It'll have one more year of good ratings, and that'll be the end of it."

"Why's that? A lot of the critics think it could go on for a long time."

He shook his head impatiently. "No substance. And no real characterization. The audience wants people, characters they feel are real. 'The Witches' is just a showcase for a couple of pretty girls, one of them with a lot of charisma. But as far as portraying characters anybody could care about, forget it."

"But there are plenty of shows that have that kind of weakness," Darla said.

"Nothing that stays on the air," Fried replied. "I don't care what kind of garbage you're talking about, if it's got good characterization, it'll draw. Take 'All in the Family.' The rednecks who watch that thing don't just identify with Archie Bunker—they *are* Archie Bunker. They love it when he talks about niggers and spics because that's how they feel about niggers and spics."

"That can't be true," Darla said. "City people watch westerns, but they're not cowboys. Don't tell me they identify with the characters in those programs."

"City people do *not* watch westerns," he countered. "The longest-running series in the history of TV was 'Gunsmoke.' Ran on CBS for twenty years. Still pulled good ratings when they yanked it. So you know *why* it went off? Because the audiences who made up those ratings were a bunch of farmers and hillbillies. They watched because Matt Dillon and Chester and Miss Kitty were *their* kind of folks. But nowadays, advertisers and their agencies are too smart to swallow just the raw numbers. What they're buying when they buy television time is an audience made up of people who'll buy their products. And who buys products? People of above-average income and above-average education. Young, up-scale homemakers. Those people live in cities and in affluent suburbs. They sure as hell don't live on farms. Advertisers want shows that do well in the top fifty markets. Beyond that, they don't give a shit. So what pulls in those top markets? Cop shows, with plenty of violence and sex. Comedies, especially dirty comedies. And that's it. Even the freak stuff, like 'Roots,' pulls for exactly the same reasons. Violence and sex. People watched it because they thought they were seeing a kind of lurid exposé—you know, what *really* went on there on the plantations, with the owners abusing the niggers, the massah going down to the slave shack after dinner for a little piece of poontang, all that crap. But mostly it was a lot of cobbled-up bullshit." He laughed, a short bark that conveyed more sneer than humor. "You take the business of the slaves worshipping Allah. That was in there because that's what blacks do *today*. The truth is that at the height of the slave trade, most of the traders were Arabs, and they were the blacks' mortal enemies."

"You're a cynic," Darla said evenly.

"I'm a realist," Fried replied. He studied Darla's face for a moment. "I see things as they are, and not the way a lot of milksop would-be intellectuals wish they were. They think television is some mystical force that's going to improve the poor slob viewer's life, provided *they* are in charge of what the viewer is permitted to watch. They have all kinds of brilliant plans for TV. First, they'd knock off the stuff people are hooked on now—the crime shows and the sex and the raunchy comedy. Then they'd make all the kid shows educational. Cut the sports shows down to maybe one football game or one baseball game a week. And then they'd fill up the time with all these good things that would enrich the viewer's life. Nighttime programming would be symphonies and ballets, and instead of series written by guys like Hyman Goldberg and Bert Speller, there'd be plays by Chekhov and Moliére and Shakespeare, and for modern stuff maybe a shot of Tennessee Williams or John Osborne once in awhile."

Fried rose from his desk, a fist clenched. "*They* know what that poor dumb viewer needs, by God. He needs *culture*. And with television, you can stick culture right up the viewer's ass. You can make television a gigantic electronic enema that washes out all the crap and leaves the viewer full of pure thoughts and appreciation of music and poetry." He stared at Darla. "And you know what the viewer would do? He'd *revolt*. He wouldn't just protest, or stop looking at the tube—he'd come in here and storm UBS and the other networks and he'd burn them and lynch the program heads until he got back his TV shows. Because whether we like it or not, television has already become just what Aldous Huxley predicted in *Brave New World*, even before TV was invented. It's a device for keeping the masses' emotions under control by providing them with a vent. It's the coliseum, brought right into your living room. Instead of sitting up there in the sixty-fourth tier, bombed out on vino, watching the lions chew the Christians' balls off, the TV audiences suck on Budweiser and catch Kojak beating up on a junkie." His voice rose. "Do you really think there's a difference, for Christ's sake? Do you really think there's a difference?"

Darla sat quietly, not answering his question.

Fried slowly sank back down into his chair. "Yes," he said. "I'm a realist. Which is why I know exactly how to use you to get the most out of your character. And how to build your character into something even more powerful than what audiences think they see now." He picked up a telephone and punched a button. "Feed that bit from 'The Witches' into monitor one," he commanded. He put the phone down and said to Darla, "This is something I picked up about a month ago when I was watching your show. I want you to see it now, so you'll understand the kind of thing I'm going to do with you." He turned to the bank of monitors, and flipped a switch. All the receivers went off except one. "Watch."

Darla stared at the tube, fascinated, as a picture loomed into view. Fried turned up the audio, and Darla recognized the sequence as one that had been shot many weeks earlier, on a desert location fifty miles northeast of L.A. In it, Darla had been held hostage by an escaped murderer who was on his way to wreak vengeance on his former wife, who he felt had betrayed him while he was in prison. In the scene they were watching, Darla soothed the man and turned his rage into an understanding that by destroying his former wife he would also succeed in destroying himself, whereas he could still hope to salvage some part of his life if he would give himself up and work toward a parole. To Darla's amazement, she saw that she had actually displayed considerable skill in acting her part. She glanced at Fried, who was watching the picture with an intensity she had never seen anyone display in looking at a television set.

When the scene ended, Fried turned to Darla, his face flushed and exultant. "You see what happened there? You took this savage male animal and turned him into a teddy bear. He went from despising all women, and especially that bitch of an ex-wife of his, to a guy who's falling in love with you. And it's believable as hell. You led him from hate to hard-on in just a few minutes."

"Okay," Darla replied quietly. "So?"

"So that's exactly the dramatic relationship I want to develop in plays, specials, TV movies I'll have you doing after 'The Witches' is off the air." He brought his fist down onto the desk. "You see? A guy who looks at a scene like that falls in love with you a little himself. And you know one of the things that bit has going for it?" His eyes were bright with excitement. "It's that every man, even today after all these millions of years since we climbed down out of the trees, still has inside him the urge to rape. A man looks at that scene, where the escaped con has complete mastery over you, where he can do anything to you he wants, and the man in the audience identifies. A fantasy is going on in his head. Boy, he's saying, would I love to have Darla Dawson in that shack, where she'd have to do anything I wanted her to do. I know what *I'd* make her do, he says to himself. And women? They like it because it shows how you handle this guy with your brains and your womanliness, how you turn him around for his own good, and then if they have a little fantasy, imagining that you probably get laid in the process, well, that's okay, too. In fact, that's terrific. Because they're identifying too.

481

And you know what all of that does? It shows me exactly what I'm going to do with you." He waved his hands as he spoke, his eyes glittering.

"No," Darla said. "You're not."

Fried looked at her without comprehension. "What?"

"I said," Darla replied, "no, you're not."

"What the hell do you mean, 'no, you're not'? I'm not what?"

"What I mean is," Darla said firmly, "you're not going to use me, as you put it, at all. My life and my career belong to me, and what I do with them is up to me, and to me alone."

Fried stared at her for a long moment, and then he threw his head back and laughed. When he leaned forward again, his face had regained its customary hardness. "What's this? Temperament, for Christ's sake? If it is, you can save it for Gary Zander, or that asshole director of his. But when you deal with me, you keep one thing right up in the front of your head." He gestured toward the telephone. "One call, and that's the end of you, if that's what I want. I pull the plug, and zip. Darla Dawson vanishes. For awhile, people say, Hey! Where the hell is Darla? We want Darla. Then a little later they say, Gee, whatever happened to what's-her-name? And then a little while after that you know what they say? *Nothing*. So don't tell me what you're going to do. In this business, I tell *you* what to do."

"No," Darla said. "You're wrong." She took a deep breath. "It's my life, and only I decide what to do with it. The longer I sit here and listen to you talk, the more you help me to realize how right I am. And how wrong you are." She waved a hand toward the television monitors. "Sure, a very short time ago, I would have given anything to have a leading role in a network series. Wow, little Darla Dawson, the big star on television. Well, do you know what getting there has taught me? It's taught me to understand myself, and to understand other people, as I never thought I could. Nothing is black and white, I learned, but only shades of gray. And some of those shades are a lot darker than others. You, Mister Fried, are one of the darkest."

"Hey, listen—"

"No. You listen." Darla stood up, her eyes blazing. "You hold in contempt everybody who wants to make television something good for all of us. And do you know why? Because the truth is, you hold *everybody* in contempt. The people who watch TV are pigs, so feed them garbage. The people who want to improve TV are fuzzy-headed intellectuals, so sweep them aside. The fact is that you don't own the air, it belongs to all of us. Yet you and a grubby little band of men seem to think it's your private property, and that you can litter it with as much junk as you please and the poor dumb viewer is supposed to just say thank you and beg for more. Well, I'll tell you one thing you're right about. The viewers *are* capable of revolt, but not for the reasons you think. And if they ever do storm in here and lynch you, and I hope they do, it'll be because they absolutely will not stand for one more minute of the crap you dump into their living rooms. To you, and the people like you who run television, it isn't an entertainment medium, it's a toilet. When I act again, and to my surprise I'm learning that I can, it won't be on TV." She turned and started toward the door.

Fried leaped to his feet. "If you walk out that door," he shouted, "you're finished."

"You mean finished with TV," Darla replied.

"Christ," he snarled. "Don't tell me you're as stupid as that idiot husband of yours."

Darla stopped, surprised. "Mike? What does this have to do with him?"

A sneer curled Fried's mouth. "He's destroyed himself. And don't tell me you didn't know it. He let that cunt Andrea Derringer run away with his show and she took his balls along in the bargain. And now he's washed up. Do you hear what I'm saying? For that dumb shit, it's all over. And I don't just mean his career, either."

Darla felt a flash of apprehension. "What are you saying?"

"I'm telling you that Mike Jock-head is a wreck. He's

spaced out on drugs, broken down mentally and physically. Hell, he may be dead, for all I know."

Darla was stunned. "You're a revolting man." She turned again toward the door.

"I have a contract," Fried roared.

"Take it," Darla said, "and shove it."

She stepped through the door and slammed it behind her.

Chapter 49

The penthouse was on Fifth Avenue, overlooking Central Park. When Corelli arrived, a butler met him at the private elevator and showed him into a paneled library, where a man sat at a desk. He rose when Corelli walked in, nodded briefly, and extended his hand. The man wore a gray sharkskin suit. He was tall and slim, his black hair and black eyes in marked contrast to his pale skin. "Dante. How are you?"

"I'm all right, Ciro," Corelli replied. "How are you?"

"Fine, fine." The slim man waved at a pair of deep leather chairs. "Sit down. Get you anything?"

Corelli shook his head. "No thanks." He looked around the room. There was a deep Aubusson carpet, and heavy draperies framed the floor-to-ceiling windows. The bookshelves were lined with leatherbound volumes. The library might have been that of a business tycoon or a prominent lawyer.

The man smiled as he took a seat beside his visitor. "You know, that was quite a surprise you handed us."

"Oh?"

"Yeah. Quite a surprise. And also a favor."

"How is that, Ciro?"

The slim man pursed his lips. "You got any idea what the handle is on Forest Hills nowadays?"

"Ah," Dante said. "I see. Now I get it."

The other smiled again. "Yeah. Tennis is no nickle-dime operation anymore. Not when you got international stars and all that TV coverage. A lot of money gets bet. So something like what this guy DiNero is trying to pull off could cost quite a bundle. Some people could get burned pretty good."

"Yes."

"Which means that now we got two reasons to find the son of a bitch. Yours and ours."

"Uh-huh."

"Trouble is, we don't have much time."

"I know."

"So all you can do is keep your fingers crossed while we try to locate him."

"That's what I wanted to see you about," Corelli said. "I wanted to ask you something."

"Sure. What is it?"

"If you find him, I want to be there. I want this guy myself."

The slim man raised his eyebrows. "What for?"

"It's—something I have to do. It involves a friend of mine."

"The girl he's holding?"

"No. Somebody else."

The man regarded Corelli coolly. "Why get involved? We got people who are specialists. It's their business, you know?"

"I know, but this is important to me."

"It's also out of your line."

"I can handle myself."

"Sure, sure. I don't doubt it."

"Look, Ciro. You said I did you a favor. Okay, do me one."

"Yeah." The slim man's gaze held steadily on Dante's face. "All right, you got it."

"Thanks."

Ciro's expression softened. "So how's it going otherwise?"

"It's going very well."

"What about the new thing—the record album jackets?"

"Excellent. Even better than I'd hoped."

"How many recording companies you supplying now?"

"Fourteen." Dante was aware that the other man knew precisely what the number was, that he knew it as well as Dante did.

"Uh-huh. And how many jackets you figure to produce this year?"

"Should be over twenty million."

"Very good." Ciro crossed his legs and tapped the toe of his Gucci loafer with a forefinger as he thought about this. "Should be only the beginning, you know? I mean, we control a lot of the talent, so it's only a question of time before the recording companies are doing business with you on an exclusive basis."

"I'm sure they will be."

The slim man tapped his toe. "And at that point, the prices go up."

"Of course."

"Okay." Ciro got to his feet. He put his hand on Dante's shoulder as he walked him to the door. "I'm glad everything's doing all right. And, uh, about the other thing. There's no guaranteeing we can find him, you know? So just sit tight, and wait to hear from us."

Ted Walters sat on a bench in the locker room of the West Side Tennis Club, wearing only socks and a jockstrap.

"Jesus Christ," Mansfield said. "You look awful."

Walters shrugged. "I don't feel too good."

The manager shook his head in exasperation. "Are you going to tell me what's wrong with you, for God's sake?"

Walters sighed. "Jack, I can't. I just can't. It's something I can't discuss."

Mansfield raised his hands and opened his mouth, as if he was about to lose his temper, but then he composed himself and sat down on the bench beside Walters. "Listen, kid," he said quietly. "All I want to do is help you. There's nothing you can tell me about that's going to surprise me, no kind of mess you're in I haven't been in myself. Whatever trouble you got, I'm not going to get mad at you for it. All I want is to give you a hand. But there's no way I can do that if I don't know what's going on."

"And there's no way I can tell you, Jack. Don't you understand me? I can't tell you."

Mansfield scratched his head. "Let me ask you straight out. Can you play? I mean, if you're sick, you're sick. I can—"

Walters raised a hand. "No. I'll play. I have to."

"You have to? What do you mean, you *have* to?"

"Don't ask me, Jack. I feel lousy, but I have to play and there's nothing I can do about it. And that's it." He rubbed his face with his hands.

The manager got up from the bench and stood looking down at Walters for a moment. He shook his head and walked away.

In her suite in the Plaza, Darla dialed her telephone number in Beverly Hills.

Maggie answered after the second ring. "Brady residence."

"Maggie, it's me."

The maid's tone expressed pleasure and affection. "Hey! How you doing? You lighting up New York? I saw you on TV!"

"I'm doing fine," Darla said. "But I'm in kind of a hurry, Maggie. Everything okay there?"

There was a pause. Maggie would know exactly what Darla meant. "He ain't been home, honey. I ain't heard nothing of him since you left."

"Okay, Maggie, thanks," Darla said. "I'll call you again soon. Meantime, if you hear anything, call me, okay? You have my number here."

"Sure I will. Promise."

" 'Bye, Maggie, and thanks." Darla put the phone down. She went to the front door of her suite and opened it. Bob Murphy was standing in the hall. Darla told the security man to come into the sitting room and to take a chair. She offered him coffee, which he declined. She looked at Sally Dane, who was gazing at Darla and the detective with obvious curiosity. "This is private," Darla said to her secretary. "I'll call you when we're through talking."

Sally's expression reflected a mixture of surprise and mild annoyance. She turned without answering and walked out of the room.

Darla came directly to the point. "I need your help," she said.

Murphy nodded. "Sure. Anything I can do, Miss Dawson, just ask."

"I need some information," Darla told him. "About my husband."

"Okay."

"He's in California. Does your company have an office in Los Angeles?"

"No, but there's an agency there we're affiliated with. We work through them when we want something in L.A., and they work through us when they want something in New York."

"I see."

"What kind of information do you need?"

Darla looked at the detective's homely face. It was calm, impassive. He's probably heard this a thousand times, she thought. Wife wants to know where her loving husband is shacked up, and who with. Nevertheless, she hated being in this situation, feeling cheap and tawdry, besmirched and lowered by having to probe. At the same time, a sense of deep anxiety gripped her, a sense of foreboding that told her Mike was in trouble. There had been something about the way Fried had spoken that had been so ominous, so definite, as if he had been alluding to a disaster that had already taken place. She took a deep breath. "I want to know where my husband is, and—what he's doing."

The detective's face showed no reaction. He reached into his jacket pocket and withdrew a ballpoint pen and a small notebook. "There are a few questions I'll have to ask. Then I'll get in touch with L.A. right away."

"How soon do you think you might hear something?"

"We'll get an initial report fast," Murphy replied, "even if it's negative. But then they'll give you the complete details as soon as they can locate him. They're a good outfit, Miss Dawson. We've worked with them for years. And this kind of thing is pretty much, well, routine."

"Yes. I'm sure it is."

Murphy shifted in his chair. "Okay. What I need to know is everything you can tell me about your husband's habits, his work, his club if he has one, and like that. We'll start with where you live."

Darla answered Murphy's questions mechanically, her mind a jumble of worry about Mike and Sarah Winchester and Ted Walters, her senses reeling from anguish and fear that derived from not knowing. She was begining to feel numb from tension and exhaustion. Her eyes burned, and the events that had occurred since the previous evening made it seem to her that she was living a nightmare. God, dealing with something you understood could be hard enough, but this made her feel so hopeless, so drained. It was horrible. She bit her lip to hold the tears back, forcing herself to respond to the detective's questions as completely as she could.

"Okay," Murphy said at last, "I guess that'll do it for now. Oh, and sorry to bring this up, Miss Dawson, but it's company policy. The fee for this work is five hundred a day, plus expenses."

Darla waved a hand wearily. "Yes, of course. Whatever it is, it's all right."

"I need to have an authorization signed by you," Murphy said. "Or Mister Wasserman could sign it. He's your business manager, right? I'll have one sent over."

"No," Darla said. "I'll sign it. And the bill is to go to me at the home address I gave you, marked 'personal.'"

Murphy closed his notebook. "Of course, I understand. I need to telephone, and we'll get things going right away."

"Use that one," Darla said, pointing. "And thank you." She rose and crossed to the door to her bedroom. When she entered the room, Sally Dane was standing looking at her. Darla had a distinct impression that the girl had been eavesdropping on her conversation with Murphy.

"Not too much time," Sally said hastily, as if to cover her embarrassment, "if you're going out to Forest Hills."

"I'm going," Darla said, unbuttoning her blouse. Despite the long shower she had taken before her meeting with Fried, she felt grubby. "Draw me a bath," she instructed. "Hot, and put in a lot of Joy bath oil." She tossed the blouse aside and unzipped her pants and stepped out of them. Someplace, she told herself, way down deep, you're going to have to find the strength. But you're going to find it.

Chapter 50

The telephone in the living room of Dante Corelli's Waldorf Towers suite rang shrilly. He lifted the instrument. It was one of Ciro's men.

"Corelli?"

"Yes."

"We located your friend. Go down to the Lexington Avenue entrance to the hotel and cross the street. Wait there. We'll pick you up in ten minutes."

The car was a nondescript Buick sedan, several years old. It slid to the curb and Dante got into the back seat. The man in front on the passenger's side was the one who had telephoned him. The man nodded briefly in greeting and returned his gaze to the street ahead as the car pulled away. The driver was somebody Dante did not know.

The southbound traffic was heavy. The Buick turned east and then north, and in a few minutes they crossed the Fifty-ninth Street Bridge into Queens. Dante looked at his watch. Less than an hour. He was suddenly aware that his mouth was dry. "How'd you locate him?" He directed the question to the man in the passenger's seat.

"He left a girlfriend in Vegas," the man answered casually. "He dumped her and she was pissed."

Hell hath no fury, Corelli reflected.

The man in the front seat put it differently. "Never trust a cunt," he said over his shoulder.

"She told you where he is?"

"Yeah. At least where she thinks he is. It ain't all that far from the tennis club."

Corelli looked at his watch again. "Has he got anybody with him, do you know?"

"One guy," the man in front replied. "But he's nothing. I know him from Brooklyn, before he went to Nevada. When he finds out we're onto him, he'll shit. Especially when he sees it's me."

"Won't he tip DiNero?"

"Maybe. But maybe not when he sees who it is. DiNero could be something else, though." He looked back at Corelli. "You got a piece?"

"Yes." Dante could feel the 7.65mm Beretta nestling against his side in the specially-made holster pocket of his custom-tailored suit.

"You want I should go in with you?" the man asked.

"No," Dante replied. "This is something I have to handle."

The man nodded briefly and turned front once more.

The Buick swung south off Queens Boulevard and slowed as it made its way through the quiet neighborhood of row houses. "Should be in the next couple of blocks," the driver said. It was the first time Corelli had heard him speak.

Ted Walters stood beside the table on which Jack Mansfield had laid out his gear and looked around the stadium. This was it—the ultimate in the world of big-time tennis, the tournament that had always meant more to him than any other, and yet instead of the sense of savage exultation he should be experiencing now, he felt that he wanted to die. For the first time in his life, he was up against something he couldn't handle, and more than anything else, more even than the rage and the frustration, he felt deep shame. He had betrayed Sarah, and he had betrayed himself. He had betrayed Darla, who had believed in him, and he had betrayed the millions of people who followed him, a few with love and more with hate, yet who nevertheless respected him for what he was: arrogant, flip, outrageous, but stroke for stroke the best tennis player alive.

The stadium was packed. Many of the fans here today were the ones who had waited until this match, the men's final, before turning out. They came from New York and L.A. and Dallas and Las Vegas and Rio and London, and the wangling for tickets to this teacup of a stadium took some doing. Ted recognized many of them as his eyes swept the stands. He looked up at the pair of UBS television cameras on their platform midway up one bank of seats, the red lights gleaming atop each, and then he looked over at Dumas.

It was true that the Frenchman appeared bigger, stronger, more mature. He had gone from diffident teenager to self-assured young man, the lithe muscles rippling smoothly under his bronzed skin, his face broader, more purposeful beneath the white band that held his long dark hair off his forehead. Dumas returned Ted's gaze, his brown eyes cold and steady, his expression no longer one of awe but of truculence.

The loudspeaker boomed the announcement of the match, but Walters did not hear. His mouth was cottony and his legs were trembling. Jesus Christ. How did you go about throwing a match? It was nothing he had ever even thought about. What would he do—keep it close to make it look convincing? That was a laugh. He would have had enough trouble with the goddamn frog under the best of circumstances, let alone in a mess like this. The way he felt, Ted knew Dumas could blow him off the court even if he were going all out. He took his position and as he did he saw Darla make her way into a seat, causing a flurry of interest among the fans as they recognized her. God. His stomach convulsed, and he forced himself not to vomit.

The Buick rolled slowly down the narrow street, the driver peering out his window at the numbers on the houses. Finally he gestured with his head. "That's it," he said. A man was sitting on the front steps of the house, reading a newspaper.

"We got lucky," the man in the front of the car said to the driver. "Go on by, and then turn around and park down there where you got a good view. Keep it running."

When the car was in position, the man beside the driver turned back to Dante. "I shouldn't have no trouble with this jerk. But if I do, you'll see it, so come on in fast. Now sit tight and keep your eyes on me." He got out of the car and walked toward the house at a casual pace.

Dante reached into his jacket and fingered the Beretta nervously. He looked at his watch again and swallowed. There was little time left. The match would be starting in minutes.

Dante watched as Ciro's man walked up the sidewalk. When he was directly in front of the house, he suddenly darted up the walk and stood over the reader sitting on the steps. Ciro's man kept one hand in his jacket pocket, and with the other held a finger to his lips.

The reader looked up, startled, and the newspaper slid from his hands and fluttered to his feet. His mouth hung open as he stared up at his unexpected visitor.

As Dante watched, Ciro's man took the other by the elbow and led him down the sidewalk and away from the house in the opposite direction from the Buick. Dante could see him speaking into the second man's ear. Dante took a deep breath and got out of the car.

The house was small and seedy, its tiny front yard a tangle of weeds. The shades were drawn, and Dante could see no movement anywhere. Keeping one hand on the Beretta, he turned the doorknob slowly, and eased himself into the house. Once inside, he stood stock-still, waiting for his eyes to adjust to the semi-darkness. He was in a small living room, he observed. The room was filthy, littered with crumpled paper bags and stained cardboard coffee cups and the moldering remains of delicatessen sandwiches. A coffee table was covered with empty beer cans.

There was a muffled sound coming from somewhere in the back of the house. Dante listened carefully, and realized that it was a girl crying softly. He stepped into the darkened hallway and made his way slowly toward the sound.

A door was ajar, and Dante heard that the sound was coming from the room within. He approached the door, taking one careful step at a time, and peered through the opening into the room.

Sarah Winchester was sitting on a straight-backed chair, her arms tied behind her back. She was naked, and Dante could see ugly red welts on her breasts and her belly and her thighs. They were cigarette burns, he realized. A man was standing beside the chair, his back to the door, clothed only in a t-shirt. The man was chunky and muscular, his heavy buttocks and thighs covered with curly black hairs. His shoulders were wide and massive, his hair long and sleekly black. It suddenly struck Dante as ludicrous that the man was wearing dark glasses, large black ones with horn rims. Corelli had never seen Frank DiNero, but there was no mistaking him now.

As Dante watched, DiNero seized the girl's hair and pulled her head back. Her eyes were swollen from crying, her face dirty and tear-streaked. "Come on, baby," he growled. "Eat."

Sarah shook her head, her shoulders convulsing with sobs. "No, I can't. No more."

DiNero swung his free hand against her face, the open palm striking her cheek with a loud smack. He held his penis in his hand and began to force it into the struggling girl's mouth.

Dante quickly took in the contents of the small room. A bed, a table with a lamp on it, and another chair on which a pile of clothes lay. Atop the clothes was an automatic pistol. Dante estimated that DiNero was about six feet away from the gun. He drew the Beretta and stepped inside the door. At the sound, DiNero spun around, shock registering on his swarthy face. He recovered in a fraction of a second, and dove at Corelli.

Dante fired at DiNero's head, but the shot was high. DiNero slammed into his chest, the impact sending him backward into the wall and knocking the Beretta from his hand. Corelli chopped downward with a fist as DiNero drove a short hard blow into his belly. Pain swept over Corelli, nauseating him, and the gambler sent another punch into his throat, then grappled for his eyes.

Choking, twisting to avoid the fingers digging into his eye sockets, Corelli slid downward, until his head was under DiNero's chin. He encircled the thick body with his arms and locked his fingers behind DiNero's back. Then he applied pressure with all his strength, upward against his adversary's jaw, inward against the man's back.

DiNero pounded Corelli's head with his fists. He tried to ram his knee into Corelli's crotch, but Dante blocked it with his thigh.

DiNero roared in rage and pain, his cry diminishing to a strangled hiss as Corelli relentlessly increased the pressure.

Now. Corelli marshaled all the remaining strength in his powerful body and heaved. A single loud crack sounded, as the gambler's vertebra snapped. DiNero's body instantly went limp in Corelli's arms, muscles twitching reflexively. Dante released his grip, and DiNero slid to the floor.

Corelli stood over the lifeless body for a moment, struggling for breath, holding one hand against the wall to support himself. He looked down at DiNero's face, the skin mottled, the thick lips still contorted in a grimace of rage and pain, the black lenses staring back at him, sightless now and ghoulish on the dead face.

Dante glanced at the girl. She was breathing heavily through her open mouth, her features twisted in terror. He stepped over to her, his head spinning, and untied the cords that bound her wrists. "Come on," he said, still gasping for breath. "Get dressed. We've got to get you out of here."

The muscles across Walters's back felt as if they were on fire. His legs were heavy and clumsy, and their trembling had increased. He looked up at the scoreboard in pain and revulsion. The Frenchman had won the first two sets with ease, 6-2, 6-1, and was leading two games to none in the third. Walters wiped sweat from his eyes with the terrycloth band on his wrist and listened to the crowd. They were on him, as usual, but this time there was a new note—one he had never heard before. Mixed with the catcalls and the banter were jeers of contempt. Sick with humiliation and self-loathing, he also felt an increasing fear for Sarah's safety. What guarantee did he have that DiNero would let her go, even if he did lose? Christ, what a hole he was in—and there was no way out. He blinked into the brilliant glare of sunlight and peered across the court. The meaning of the faint smile on Dumas's face was all too obvious. Now, the frog was saying, at long last I've got you by the balls, and I am going to squeeze until I leave you for dead. Walters took a deep breath and hunched his shoulders, trying to fight back the burning pain.

From his seat near the camera platform, Stan Lockridge looked down on the court. The head of UBS-TV Sports was perplexed. "I don't understand it," he said to the man sitting next to him, a vice president of the network.

"What's to understand?" the other man answered gleefully. "Dumas is kicking the shit out of him, and it couldn't happen to a nicer guy."

"No," Lockridge said. "It's not right."

"Not right? Hell, how could it be righter? I love it."

"Yeah, but that's not what I meant. Excuse me. I want to check the truck." Lockridge got up and made his way down the steps and under the stadium to where the UBS mobile unit was parked.

Inside the tiny control room, Fred Berg, the show's producer, was crouched behind the technical director, staring fixedly at a monitor. Lockridge moved close to him. "Hey, Fred," Lockridge said. "How do you make this?"

"Damned if I know," Berg said, without diverting his eyes from the picture.

"You think Walters is sick?"

Berg shrugged. "Could be. He sure as hell acts like it."

"Then why's he playing? Why didn't he pack it in before this mess ever started?" Lockridge expressed the question musingly, more to himself than to the producer. "I never saw him play like this. It's like he was made of lead."

Down on the court, Walters looked at the grayish Har-Tru surface under his feet and bit his lower lip. Somehow, some goddamn way, he had to hang in. He gripped the ball in one hand and in the other held his racket straight down, shaking his arm to loosen the deltoid and the biceps and triceps muscles, a reflexive move that he was not conscious of, a preparatory action born of years of play, the conditioning of thousands of matches against countless opponents. He lifted his head, and as he did his gaze involuntarily traveled up to where he knew Darla was sitting. He looked, and squinted, and the sight was like a kick in the chest. He saw Sarah Winchester moving into the row of seats, Darla beckoning to her. A tall man was with her, a man Ted had never seen before. The man was holding Sarah by the arm, guiding her. Even from this distance, Walters could see that Sarah's face looked red and blotchy, and that her eyes were swollen. Walters stared, and the racket fell from his hand. He strained to see, to be sure of what his eyes were telling him. It was Sarah, and she was alive. A shout started from deep within him and came welling up out of his mouth. He clenched both fists and the shout became the agonized howl of an animal set loose from a trap. "Oh God," Walters cried. "Thank you."

In her seat in the stands, Darla pulled Sarah down beside her. She looked at the girl, feeling her tremble, hearing her barely controlled weeping, and then looked across at Dante Corelli. He was pale and tense, and there were bruises and small raw wounds under his eyes. But he smiled at her and nodded reassurance. Darla leaned close to Sarah. "Are you all right?"

Sarah shuddered. "Y-yes. I'm all right. But I don't

want to be here. I'm hurt. I want to be away from here. I—I need a doctor."

Darla gripped her hand. "You're okay? You're not badly hurt?"

"N-no," Sarah choked. "But I don't want to be here."

Darla squeezed the girl's fingers in her own. "You're safe now, Sarah. Don't be afraid. Wave to him. To Ted."

"What?" The girl sniffled.

Darla increased the pressure of her hand. "Wave," she commanded. "Lift up your arm and wave. *Do it.*"

Walters saw Sarah's hand go up and tears filled his eyes. He shook his fists again and the crowd roared down at him, engulfing him in sound. Sarah was free. Somehow, Sarah was free, and she was safe and she was here. And that meant that he was free, too.

Inside the UBS truck Fred Berg stared at the monitor. "Jesus Christ," he said out of the corner of his mouth. "What the hell is this?"

"Don't ask me," Lockridge replied. "With Walters I never know."

The volume of the crowd's noise increased, and the sound buffeted Walters. He reached down and picked up the racket. There were hoots and more jeers now, cries of derision. "Hey, showboat," a man called, "cut the act and play tennis."

Walters no longer heard. He looked at his racket as if he had never seen it before, and his fist closed around it. He stared across the net to where Dumas waited, and emotion swept over him. He crouched, and then rose, coming up onto his toes, the hand holding the ball stretching upward, the yellow sphere poised for a moment as if atop a statue, and then the racket came around with a whoosh of air, the braided muscles of his arm whipping it in an arc, the impact sounding a sharp clean crack that mixed with the grunt emitting from his chest.

Ace.

And the crowd gasped and shouted and applauded, and Walters again crouched low, his teeth bared in an exultant, savage grin. "Now, shithead," he growled. "Now."

He was too strong at first, too high, the strength pouring into him from a wellspring of emotion, lifting him, carrying him, and he had to fight to control it, had to force himself to go cold and hard, and if it was not the most controlled tennis he had ever played, it was certainly the best, and he played it all the way as he knew how to play it better than any player in the game, playing it all for power, every stroke as hard as he could hit the ball, a devastating ground game with a fury of topspin, his shots arcing into the corners like cannonfire, then thundering crosscourt, then blasting down the line, every one of them exploding out of his hands and his back and his shoulders and his legs and his arms, the grunt from his gut mingling with each crack of the racket like a ricochet loud and clear above the crowd noise. *Whack!* "Hunhh!" And *whack!* "Hunhh!"

"Holy Jesus," Fred Berg said inside the mobile unit. "I don't believe this. Even from him I don't believe this."

Walters won the third set, and the fourth. And by the beginning of the fifth, the match was in no doubt whatever. Dumas played hard, tough tennis, game and gritty, never backing down, never flagging for an instant, all courage and superb technique.

But Walters played with a reckless fire that could not be checked. He thrilled the crowd, and then he mesmerized them, forcing them to go with him, wringing cries of admiration out of them, making them stand and cheer and respond to Walters the tennis player, and though they did not know it, to Walters the man.

When it was over, Ted put his arms around Jack Mansfield and both of them were crying. He tried to free himself to climb up into the stands to where Sarah was, but it was impossible. He was surrounded by a tumultuous mob. He listened to the announcement, humbly for once in his life, and then he was swept along toward the clubhouse in a sea of reporters and fans, a handheld television camera poking into his face.

Inside his mobile unit, Fred Berg mopped his face

with a handkerchief. "What hoke," he said. "I never in all my life saw such hoke."

"Neither did I," Lockridge replied. "And I never in all my life will forget it."

Chapter 51

Bob Murphy sat stiffly on the edge of his chair and read aloud from the teletype, his lumpy face expressionless. "Subject is in rented house approximately eighty-five miles northeast of Los Angeles in mountain country vicinity of Big Bear Lake. Address is Traprock Road." He looked up.

Darla pulled the terrycloth robe tight about her. They were in the small sitting-dressing room off her bedroom in the Plaza. She nodded. "Go on."

Murphy resumed reading. "Accompanying subject was one female, name Andrea Derringer. Derringer left, has not returned. Subject has remained at house alone through six succeeding days. No movement observed during daytime, but subject was seen moving about house in early morning hours during time of surveillance." Murphy looked up again. "That's it."

"All right," Darla said. "Thank you. You'll leave that with me?"

"Yes, of course." Murphy handed her the teletype and stood up. "Is there anything else I can do, Miss Dawson?"

"No," Darla said, rising. "But I appreciate your help very much." The detective had been brisk and businesslike, and Darla was grateful to him for making this as impersonal as possible.

"Sure," Murphy said. "I'll be outside." He left the room.

Darla went into the bedroom and dialed a number. When Molly answered, Darla said, "I have to get back to Los Angeles. Something personal. I'll be leaving here as soon as possible and I'd like you to come with me. Okay?"

Molly sounded delighted. "Hey, great. After this dump the smog will seem like Chanel."

"Will you call and arrange the tickets?"

"Consider it done."

"I'll see you in the car in twenty minutes." Darla hung up and pulled a bag out of the closet, calling out to Sally Dane. She was stuffing random pieces of clothing into the bag when her secretary entered the bedroom.

Sally looked fresh and bouncy, attired in tight black velvet pants and a light shirt, her hair tied back in a pony tail. Her face registered surprise when she saw what Darla was doing. "You going somewhere?"

"That's right. I'm going to L.A."

Sally's expression turned quickly to one of disappointment. "But we're supposed to be here another three days. Derek said—"

"I said *I'm* going," Darla snapped. "You can stay right to the end. I'll be taking just this one bag, so you see to it that all my other things are packed and that they get home okay."

Sally was wide-eyed now. "You're going alone?"

"Molly will be going with me."

Sally watched Darla for a moment. "Okay, if that's what you want. You know, it's been a great trip."

"I'm glad you think so."

"And I've really kind of learned a lot," Sally said. "About people, and who your friends are."

Darla looked up at her. "Oh?"

The secretary nodded. "I know this isn't really any of my business, but I feel a terrific loyalty to you, and so I kind of think it's my duty, sort of, to tell you."

Darla dropped a toothbrush and other light toilet articles into a small zippered case. "To tell me what?"

"Well, about Betty. She isn't really all that much of a friend of yours, if you want to know the truth."

"She isn't?" Darla went on packing.

"No, she isn't. In fact, this might shock you, but she's been trying to sign up another girl on Superfresh."

"Uh-huh."

Sally sounded perplexed. "Doesn't that surprise you?"

"No. Ben Thompkins told me about it."

The secretary's mouth fell open. "Why did he do that?"

"Because he's an old friend," Darla said. "And as he put it, he owed me one."

"Oh. Well, anyway, the one who's looking out for your best interests is Derek Wasserman. He really cares a lot about you."

"Does he?" Darla pressed the locks of the suitcase shut. She pulled off the terrycloth robe and tossed it aside. "That's nice." She opened a dresser drawer and pulled out a pair of bikini pants. "You can tell the others I'm leaving for L.A. just as soon as I get dressed." She stepped into the pants.

Sally frowned, hesitating for a moment, then left the room.

When Darla had finished dressing, she picked up her bag and walked into the living room. Betty and Derek were sitting there, with consternation showing on both their faces.

Betty spoke first. "Darla, I wish you had consulted me before suddenly deciding to just jump up and run out of here. There are a lot of loose ends that need to be tied together. You know, deals I'm working on."

"I'm sure they can wait," Darla replied.

"I'm sure they can too," Derek said. "But the things I have can't. There's my doll deal, for example."

"*Your* doll deal?" Betty shrieked. "Why you momser son of a bitch!"

"Don't you call me names, you fat hag," Wasserman shouted.

The agent and the manager began screaming at each

other at the same time, Wasserman pounding the arms of his chair, Betty waving her fists.

"Hold it," Darla said. "Damn it, I said *hold it!*"

The room was suddenly quiet.

"I am leaving for Los Angeles," Darla said firmly. "And you two can postpone your fight until I walk out that door." She took a raincoat out of the foyer closet.

"I think," Betty said through clenched teeth, "that the time has come for you to make a decision as to how you want your business to be run. Either with the sound advice and loyalty I've always unselfishly provided, or with that schlunk trying to rip you off."

"Now, goddamn it!" Wasserman grated, rising from his chair.

"I told you to hold it," Darla said, picking up her bag.

"I think she's right about one thing," Wasserman said. "It's time you made a choice."

Darla looked at one, and then at the other. "My decision," she said, "is that what I need is new management. *All* new. When I get back to L.A. I'll appoint a lawyer to help me get my business in order."

"Now wait," Derek said, suddenly flustered. "Let's not do something impetuous that we'll all be sorry for." He glanced at Betty. "Maybe we ought to see if we can't work things out."

"You're right," Betty said. "We ought to see if we can't find a way to work together."

"I'm sure you could work together beautifully," Darla said. She looked at her secretary. "That is, if Sally wouldn't mind. But you're going to do it without me." She walked out the door.

Darla drove the Porsche hard, wheeling the turbocharged white coupe up the twisting road that wound through the San Bernardino Mountains. She turned north off the main highway toward Big Bear, and after covering three more miles came to the address on the teletype Bob Murphy had given her. At first she thought the house was empty. There was no answer to her knock, and the place was totally quiet. But she tried the door and found it open.

As much as Darla had tried to prepare herself, the sight of Mike was a shock. He was asleep, sprawled in a chair in the living room, his unshaven jaw resting on his chest. His hair was long and matted and the flannel shirt and corduroy pants he was wearing looked filthy. On the lamp table beside the chair was a half-filled bottle of red-and-yellow capsules.

Darla glanced around. The blinds were drawn and the room was stifling. The stale air stank of sweat. She raised a blind and opened a window. Fresh, pine-scented air rushed into the room.

"Hello, Darla."

She turned to see Mike staring at her. His eyes were red and swollen in his gaunt, bewhiskered face. Darla had to clench her fists to keep from bursting into tears. She forced herself to sit down calmly in a chair opposite her husband. "Hello, Mike."

He did not answer, but continued to hold her in his strange, unblinking gaze.

"I've come home, Mike."

"So I see."

"I think," Darla said gently, "that both of us have been fools. But I love you, and I know we can work things out."

His face sagged. "That's hard for me to believe."

"I mean it, Mike," Darla said. "For all the agony, you mean more to me than anything. You always have. It just took a lot of experience and a lot of pain for me to come to know that."

He nodded. "Yeah. And I guess I had to go through the same thing. I tried to call you, while you were in New York."

"I wish you had."

"I wish so too. Trouble is, it may already be too late."

"Why?"

"Because I did quite a job on myself. And by the time I had the guts to face it, the damage was done."

Darla shook her head. "It's not too late."

"That's what you think. My career is in pieces, and so am I. The only way I can operate is with a goddamn pill."

"No, Mike. You're still you. And if we've got each other, we can do anything."

"I'm not so sure."

"I am."

He looked at her. "It's terrible, you know that? To think you're one thing, and then to find out you're something else. To find out the truth. To find out that what you really are is rotten."

"Don't say that, Mike. I believe in you, and I always will." She stepped over to him and knelt beside his chair, taking him into her arms.

He slumped against her. "Christ, I've been so stupid. And most of all about you. How could I have treated you the way I did? And how could you forgive me now?"

"All that was yesterday, Mike. Come on." She rose and pulled him to his feet. "What you need is some sleep and some food and a bath."

After Darla got Mike into bed, she went back into the living room for the bottle of capsules. She took it into the bathroom and flushed its contents down the toilet.

Outside it was growing dark, and a cold breeze had come up. Darla got a heavy sweater out of the Porsche and put it on. She sat down on the steps of the cabin, and her emotions fell in on her like a collapsing building. She cried and cried—deep, wracking sobs that shook her body. Then she got up and pulled a Kleenex out of her jeans and blew her nose into it. Somehow she felt stronger and more confident and more at peace with herself than she ever had in her life.

She went back into the house and into the bedroom and pulled her clothes off and slipped into the bed beside her sleeping husband.

Chapter 52

The Emmy Awards Show was held in the Pasadena Auditorium. The telecast pulled a twenty rating and a thirty-five-share of audience, reaching a total of fifteen million homes and a little more than thirty-two million people. John Rawlson watched the show in the study of his duplex on Park Avenue. Peter Fried watched it in his office. Dante Corelli watched it in his Waldorf Towers suite. Ted Walters watched it in the living room of Sarah Winchester's parents' home in Detroit, Michigan. Ben Thompkins watched it in his room in the Beverly Hills Hotel. Betty Frolich watched it in a bar on Sunset Boulevard. Derek Wasserman and Sally Dane watched it in Derek's bedroom in his Brentwood apartment.

The show proceeded at the usual desultory pace of such productions, until it came time for the presentation of the industry's most coveted acting award, Best Female Lead in a Series.

In her seat in the auditorium, Darla looked at Mike, who sat beside her. He was still a bit thin, but the sun and the fresh air of the weeks they had spent together in the mountains had done their work. His skin was firm and deeply tanned. His eyes were clear, and very blue in his dark face. He had never, she reflected, looked more handsome. Darla squeezed his hand.

The auditorium was jammed. Darla glanced around, excitement rising in her as she thought about the upcoming award. She saw Cathy Drake sitting a few rows away, looking stunning, as usual. Cathy glanced over, and returned Darla's gaze coolly.

A little farther back, Darla spotted Andrea Derringer. The actress's deep gray eyes were riveted to the stage, and there were high spots of color in her cheeks.

The presenter was a character actor who had been in television for years. He was a tall man with silver hair. He opened the envelope on the podium before him and smiled.

Darla suddenly realized that her teeth were clenched, and that her nails were digging into Mike's hand. She forced herself to relax.

The presenter read, "For best actress in a series." He looked up and smiled at the audience. "Darla Dawson!"

A roar went up, and Darla felt a wave of emotion sweep over her. She got to her feet, the applause buffeting her, and walked to the steps that led up to the stage. She held her shoulders back and kept her head very high.

The small metal statue felt cool to her touch. Darla cradled it in her arms and looked out at the audience, waiting for their applause to die down. When she spoke, her voice echoed over the PA system in the huge hall. "This award means a great deal to me. It's the culmination of a long, hard struggle. I know it's customary to thank all the people in the crew for making this possible, and I do thank them. But I also know that only one person was really responsible for my winning this Emmy." She paused and looked straight into the UBS camera. "And that person is me."

A gasp went up from the audience, followed by applause. Darla raised a hand, and waited for the noise to diminish.

"Television has taught me a lot," she went on. "But mostly it's taught me that its values are worthless. The only thing that really matters is to be true to yourself, and to someone you love." She held out her hand. "Mike?"

The applause started again as soon as he stood up.

Mike moved quickly to the steps and bounded up them. His eyes glistened as he approached her, and Darla realized that she was crying too, the tears running down her face. She dropped the Emmy onto the podium and put her arms around Mike's neck and kissed him. The applause swelled to a roar, but Darla did not hear it.

THIS YEAR'S MOST EXTRAORDINARY BESTSELLER!

THE WOMEN'S ROOM

BY MARILYN FRENCH

FOR EVERY MAN WHO EVER THOUGHT HE KNEW A WOMAN.

FOR EVERY WOMAN WHO EVER THOUGHT SHE KNEW HERSELF.

FOR EVERYONE WHO EVER GREW UP, GOT MARRIED AND WONDERED WHAT HAPPENED.

jove

$2.50 12047882

Available wherever paperbacks are sold.   NT-31